W9-CAE-798

PANDA BEAR IS CRITICAL

Fern Michaels

LEWIS EGERTON SMOOT MEM'L. LIB
KING GEORGE, VA. 22485

MACMILLAN PUBLISHING CO., INC.

New York

For all our children,
who, in themselves,
are Davey Taylor's prototypes.

Copyright © 1982 by Roberta Anderson and Mary Kuczkir

All rights reserved. No part of this book may be reproduced or transmit-
ted in any form or by any means, electronic or mechanical, including
photocopying, recording or by any information storage and retrieval system, without permission in writing from the Publisher.

Macmillan Publishing Co., Inc.
866 Third Avenue, New York, N.Y. 10022
Collier Macmillan Canada, Inc.

Library of Congress Cataloging in Publication Data

Michaels, Fern.
     Panda Bear is critical.

     I. Title.
PS3563.I27P3   813'.54   81–20940
ISBN 0-02-584550-0   AACR2

10   9   8   7   6   5   4   3   2   1

Printed in the United States of America

Panda Bear Is Critical

I

D AVEY TAYLOR didn't like the shine of the streetlamp that cut through the darkness and played against the filmy curtain of his bedroom. The lamp created shadows that danced on the wall, menacing his toy chest and his favorite stuffed animals on the shelf above. Each night Davey would move his ragged, beloved Panda Bear from the shelf and place it where the shadows couldn't touch it.

Right now the lights in his room were all lit, and the shadows were held at bay. If Davey moved back the curtain, he could even see his own reflection in the glass. But later, after Mom turned off the lights, those dark invaders would enter his room. His mother said he was too old for night lights.

Straightening his room before he went to bed as he had been taught, Davey pursed his mouth as he looked at the Snoopy calendar. "Today is Sunday; yesterday was Saturday," he told the dog sitting quietly near his feet. "I have to change my pajamas on Saturdays, Tuesdays, and Fridays." His brow knit into worried lines. "I didn't change my pajamas last night, Duffy. Do you think I forgot?" he asked.

The Yorkshire terrier squirmed, uncertain of the tone of Davey's voice. "See, I make an X on the days I change my pj's. There's no X for yesterday." Davey looked down at his dog who tipped her head to one side, seemingly listening attentively. Shaking his head over his forgetfulness, Davey walked over to an apple-red bean-bag chair and flopped down.

"Changing my pajamas," he said with five-and-a-half-year-old authority, "is one of those 'almost' things. You know, Duff, like I can almost tie my shoes. I can almost tell time. I almost can walk to the kindergarten bus by myself. Everything is 'almost.' I can't wait to grow up so I can be *'most.'* "

The tan-and-black dog woofed in agreement.

Davey's bright blue eyes swiveled suddenly to the wooden giraffe which served him as a clothes tree. There were no colorful pajamas hanging from the peg. A cherry-red windbreaker and a yellow slicker with matching hood were the only garments hanging there. Davey ran his stubby, little-boy fingers through his thick, flaxen hair, a sign that he was relieved. His breath exploded in a loud whoosh. He must have changed his pj's the night before after all. They must be under his pillow, otherwise they'd be hanging from the peg. Sensing her master's relief, Duffy yipped happily.

"See these sneakers, Duff? My first pair!" his master said proudly, his mind leapfrogging to another subject. "And I almost got them dirty today. I'm wearing them tomorrow with my new red jacket when we leave with Aunt Lorrie and Uncle Tom to go camping. Mom said you can't go camping with dirty sneakers, Duff." His mind searched for the word Mom used. "It would be . . . tacky!" he said enthusiastically. Duffy rolled over on the meadow of green carpet, taking Davey's excitement as a sign that it was time to play. Instead, her friend leaned over to pull up his pants leg. Duffy watched as first one strap and then another was loosened. She growled deep in her throat when the brace fell against the side of the desk. She crawled on her belly, stretching herself to her entire two feet in length to show her disapproval.

Davey stood erect. He could walk without the brace; he just wasn't supposed to be ram–rambunctious. He liked that word even though he wasn't exactly certain he had ever been rambunctious.

Finding the pj's under his pillow, he stripped down and pulled the top over his head, then completed the job with the long-legged bottoms. Jumping onto the bed, he settled himself down with a picture book. The white-gloved finger on his Mickey Mouse watch told him it was almost five minutes until his parents came in to turn off the light. The new watch, a gift from Uncle Tom, was special. The only time he took it off was when he took his bath.

"Jeepers, I forgot to brush my teeth!" If he only had five minutes, he didn't want to waste them brushing his teeth. Davey threw back the covers and marched to the bathroom. He turned on the water, putting his toothbrush under the flow, wetting it thoroughly. His eyes danced merrily as he splashed a little water onto the vanity top. A giggle erupted as he gave the toothpaste tube a quick squeeze in the middle. He then scurried back to bed where Duffy watched her master's antics with a sleepy eye.

"Aunt Lorrie said she used to do that when she was little and forgot to brush her teeth," he told Duffy. Picture book in hand, Davey flipped through the pages. He wasn't interested in Jeremiah the Ant. Not tonight. If only he could talk to his friend Digger on the CB radio. But "if only" was like "almost."

"Time for lights out, little fella."

"I know, Dad. See, the finger is almost on the six. Do I call it six-eight or eight-six?" Davey asked.

There was a slight trace of annoyance in Sara Taylor's voice when she answered for her husband. "No, Davey. It's eight-thirty or half-past eight. The little hand tells you the hour and the big hand tells you the minutes." She refused to call the hands fingers, as her sister Lorrie had suggested. The boy would learn to tell time properly. "We went over all this on Saturday afternoon. I can see where we'll have to practice extensively when you get back from your camping trip."

"I don't think I can fall asleep tonight. I can't wait for tomorrow. Gee, this is almost better than Christmas." Almost. It was going to be better than Christmas, he just knew it. His voice held a bubble of excitement.

Andy Taylor grinned as he bent to kiss his son good-night. "I think you're absolutely correct. Do you have all your gear ready?"

Davey nodded. "I've had it ready for a whole week. Are you going to miss me, Dad?"

"Of course we're going to miss you," Sara replied. "By the time you get back from your trip, we'll be back from ours. We'll all be together again in just a few days. Did you brush your teeth, Davey?"

Her son squirmed. "Go see the toothbrush," he answered, avoiding the lie.

Davey looked from his mother to his father, noticing once again how close they were one to another. They were always like that, he thought. And Mom always knew what Dad was thinking or was going to say. He had heard the phrase "matched set" and that was how he thought of

[3]

his parents. A set was two. Salt and pepper. Two shoes. Two hands. A set was two, not three. Wanting to be part of a set, Davey drew Duffy closer to him. Wordlessly, Sara Taylor pushed the terrier down to the foot of the bed.

"I think I will check that toothbrush," his mother told him. But there was a smile on her face when she leaned over to kiss him good-night. "Did you find your pj's under the pillow or are those clean from your drawer?"

"You bet. See?" He lifted the pillow, "No pj's."

"Davey, we do not say 'you bet.' It's a slang term and I don't want you to use it." Her voice was firm and Davey made a note to try and remember. Her voice was *always* firm. He liked Dad's voice better because there was usually a smile in it. He liked Uncle Tom's voice because there was usually a secret waiting to be told. But he liked Aunt Lorrie's voice best of all. Hers was a tickly, fun kind of voice. You couldn't fool Aunt Lorrie. She would have known about the toothbrush right away.

Davey felt immediately guilty and it made him feel funny inside. He wanted to like his mother's voice best of all. Impulsively, he reached out, hugging Sara around the neck. The stretching pulled back his pajama sleeves from his arms.

Sara Taylor's cinnamon-brown eyes saddened as she saw the needle marks dotting her son's arms. But her movements, when she extricated herself from the small boy, were icily controlled. There was no hugging pressure on her part, no smile in her eyes, when she firmly pushed him back onto his nest of pillows. "Good-night, Davey. Sleep well."

"G'night, Mom. G'night, Dad," the boy said quietly. He still felt funny, as if he had done something wrong. He lay very still until the door closed behind them.

Seconds later, Davey scooted to the bottom of the bed. Duffy lay stretched out on a small carpet bearing her name. "C'mon. You can get up here now." The little dog was on the bed in one leap, her tail wagging furiously. "I've got that funny feeling again, Duff. As if we did something wrong."

Chubby hands cupped the terrier's face in a firm grip. Bright blue eyes stared unblinkingly into Duffy's melting brown ones. "We didn't do anything wrong today, did we?" Duffy wiggled, trying to get free

[4]

and snuggle in the warmth of the blankets. "It's not 'cause you're on the bed, either. It's something else."

Davey stared into the dim corners of the room, trying not to look at the light that filtered through his curtains. Why did his stomach feel so funny after Mom and Dad said good-night? All those times in the hospital his stomach had felt bad too. The tubes going into his veins, the sore, puffy knee joints making him want to cry. But he hadn't cried. Instead he had gripped the pillows and clenched his teeth so hard he'd been afraid they'd crack into pieces. "Don't cry, David. Only babies cry," his mother had cautioned. "You must be brave and not upset Daddy." He had felt sick whenever Mom said that to him, her eyes willing him not to cry.

And the day the tall doctor told him his treatment was going to be different. That the transfusion was done through the jugular vein. He stealed himself not to cry because Dad had looked upset even before the doctor started the transfusion. So instead, Davey had grinned and waved to Dad on his way to the special room for hemophiliacs.

Pills and shots, shots and pills, for days afterward, and David Taylor had taken it all, like the man he must be, for his father, Sara said. Shots, pills, and pain that never left him and still he hadn't cried. And the pain in his middle grew. Davey's eyes searched Andrew's each time his father visited. Always the child saw acceptance in his father's eyes, an acceptance that was totally ignorant of the price his son was paying for Andrew's peace of mind.

Sara should have been proud, Davey thought, disappointed by her coldness toward him. He couldn't understand. After all, he had done as he was told. Wasn't he brave, behaving like a grown-up, so Daddy could laugh and smile when he came to visit? Even when the pain was so bad that he couldn't swallow, Davey Taylor put on a brave front. With a child's sure instinct, he recognized that he was a trial to his parents, less than perfect, a disappointment. More important than his own pain and trauma, he had been carefully instructed from infancy, Daddy's wants and needs came first. In many ways, Sara Taylor had become the mother to Andrew that little Davey needed himself.

Walking after the transfusions can be sheer agony for hemophiliacs, but mobility, while the enemy, is also the cure. Davey never complained of his pain. He was brave. All the doctors and nurses said so,

[5]

glad to be relieved of their ever-present guilt at inflicting pain on children. It was easier for them to believe there was no pain for Davey Taylor.

But the pain in his middle grew, forcing up his meals, doubling him over with misery.

When Lorrie Ryan visited her nephew in the hospital, she'd been appalled by the tight white line around his mouth and the shadows in his eyes. Davey's suffering was obvious to anyone who looked at him carefully. She couldn't understand why he was pretending to feel no pain—until she was in the room when Andrew and Sara came. Then it was all too clear.

That night, after visiting hours, Lorrie returned to Davey's room. Wordlessly, she lowered the bars of the youth bed and sat on the edge. There in the dark, she took the boy in her arms, holding back her own tears of sympathy and compassion as she felt the tension in his little body.

"It's okay to feel tired and sore, Davey," she told him, her voice as soft and sweet as the darkness. "It's all right. You can cry, if you want to. No one will hear. It hurts, doesn't it," she crooned, reaching out to share the weight of his misery, acknowledging Davey's pain, accepting it.

Silently, the child clung to her, taking from her the courage to continue with his charade and face the ordeal. At last he slept, his body wet with exhaustion, the dampness seeping through the thin cotton of his pajamas. But he hadn't cried. Not then nor the last time either. But knowing that it would be okay to cry lightened his burden.

Now the worst was behind him; he was home, and there were just the daily shots of antigen. He had done what his mother wanted; he had been brave. He hadn't upset his dad. He hadn't cried.

Now, sitting with Duffy in the darkness of his room, trying to avoid the light coming through the lacy curtains in his bedroom, Davey was again feeling that tightness in his middle, the alarm that said he had done something wrong. That his mother somehow didn't approve.

In a flash he was off the bed and across the room, dodging the hateful light. A windmill of motion was created as toys sailed from the chest. "See, Duff. Here it is," he whispered triumphantly.

On the bed with Duffy crouched between his legs, Davey held the

[6]

stuffed giraffe up for inspection. "You see, Duff, how shiny Jethroe's eyes are?" Bright, shoe-button eyes on the shabby giraffe stared at Davey.

"Look, Duff," the little boy commanded. "Jethroe's eyes never change, no matter how I move him. I don't like this giraffe!" he cried suddenly. Duffy's head turned as the stuffed toy whizzed across the room. She whimpered, low in her throat.

"I don't like that giraffe," Davey cried belligerently. His lower lip trembled as he stared at the soft lump of matted fur on the far side of the room.

"You know why I don't like that old thing, Duff? I'll tell you. It's . . . it's 'cause I feel like Jethroe sometimes. All wobbly and tired. Aunt Lorrie says it's okay to feel that way sometimes. But not Mom." Five-year-old wisdom rose to the fore. "If I cry and act like Jethroe, Dad will get upset. Mom doesn't want to see Dad upset."

Duffy snuggled deeper into the covers. "Aunt Lorrie knows it hurts sometimes, and she knows I feel like Jethroe. She says it's okay to feel like that because those trips to the hospital for blood tests take all the starch out of me. It's the starch, Duff. They take it all out and I have to get more. Boy, doesn't she smell good, Duff?" Davey sniffed experimentally, willing Aunt Lorrie's perfume to invade the room. When he failed, his bright blue eyes swiveled to the far side of the room, and his shoulders stiffened imperceptibly.

"You settled, Duff?" Davey turned over, nearly toppling the picture of his parents that rested on his night stand. "Whew, that was close," he sighed as he grappled with the slippery frame. Even in the near-dark it seemed he could see the photograph of a smiling Andrew and Sara. Holding it carefully by the edges, he turned the picture to the light coming through the curtains. His gaze intent, he brought the faces closer and then held them at arm's length. Gingerly, he replaced the picture on the night stand.

His whisper was almost fierce, nearly savage, as he pulled up the covers. "I like Aunt Lorrie best! Mom and Dad really only like each other. And when I'm with Aunt Lorrie and Uncle Tom, the pain in my middle goes away."

A soft whine and much wiggling and the little dog was safely tucked against the pillow. "You know, Duff, when I get all my starch, I'm

[7]

going to . . ." He was asleep before he could complete his thought.

In the corridor leading to their room, Sara linked her arm through her husband's and squeezed. "I want to talk to you about something, Andrew."

Andy smiled around the pipe clenched in his teeth. "I'm all yours as soon as the door closes." He turned and leered suggestively at his wife.

Sara laughed, tossing her blonde head. "That too."

"Why don't we go down into the den and have a nightcap? It's early and we're both packed."

Sara always had a better idea, or so it seemed to him, as she returned her husband's intimate grin. "Stuart's downstairs, and I hardly think an FBI agent, even one as nice as Stuart, is conducive to a relaxed drink and lovemaking. Why don't you," she said, dropping her voice to a whisper, "light the fire in our room, shower, and wait for me? I'll go down and lock up and bring our wine up here. I showered an hour ago, darling, and there's nothing beneath this robe but skin. We haven't made love in front of the fire for ages. It's time," she purred.

"Hurry," was all Andrew could say. God, how he loved her. He would never cease to be amazed that she returned his ardor. A man could search his life through for the right woman and never find her, but Sara was perfect. She fulfilled his every need. There seemed no amount of energy and caring that Sara would not put forth for his happiness. She had even interrupted her career as an English literature professor to bear him a son. At the time she had been thirty-nine years old, and he knew it had been no small concession on her part to make their union even more perfect.

Desire, hot and potent, coursed through Andrew as he laid the fire with meticulous care. Satisfied that the kindling would soon burst into flame, he went to shower. Sara would return in exactly the amount of time it would take him to dry off and put on the bathrobe she had bought him for his birthday.

Sara descended the long, circular staircase. Halfway down, she called softly, "It's all right, Mr. Sanders. I'm just coming down to lock up and get a drink for my husband."

Stuart Sanders waited at the bottom of the steps. His appraising, businesslike gaze took in the woman's cool blonde beauty and her regal bearing. He could appreciate her neutral tone of voice. He wasn't a servant, or even a family friend. He was a neutral acquaintance, and Mrs. Taylor addressed him in a neutral tone. It was acceptable.

"I'll stay with you, Mrs. Taylor, until you go back upstairs."

Sara recognized the order behind the words.

"Of course, Mr. Sanders."

Stuart followed her from one end of the house to the other as she checked the locks and turned off the lights. Even though he had locked up himself, she had once explained that the nightly ritual helped her to sleep better. He waited outside the den while she arranged an ice bucket, wine glasses, and a decanter on a silver tray. They weren't just glasses, he told himself, they were lead crystal. He could tell by the buffed sheen of the tray that it was old silver, more than likely sterling.

There was nothing personal in his gaze as he stared about the room and finally at Sara Taylor. He liked a little more flesh on his women. He had never cared much for blondes, and her smooth, delicate complexion lacked the vibrant flush he preferred.

He felt no envy as he surveyed the over-large room with its carefully appointed furnishings. The whole house reflected Sara Taylor's conservative, exacting taste. It was quite unlike his own place, where furnishings, bought one at a time, piece by piece, never seemed to match. The clink of the crystal echoed through the room as Mrs. Taylor prepared the tray, even remembering the tiny cocktail napkins.

When he first came on this job, Sanders couldn't believe that three people and one cook could live in a twenty-room house. That was the problem, he decided, it was a house, not a home. He thought longingly of his own seven-room house crowded with four kids.

"Would you get the lights for me, Mr. Sanders?"

"Sure. Can I help you with that tray?" Stuart offered.

"It's quite all right, I can manage. I like doing things for my husband. It's all part of being a wife." She smiled at him, her widening lips and soft tone belied by her expressionless eyes.

Stuart Sanders returned to his position in front of the television screen. He didn't know why, but he didn't like Sara Taylor.

"You're something, honey," Andrew said, taking the tray from her. "Right on schedule. I just this minute stepped from the shower."

Sara laughed, a warm, rich sound that sent tingles up Andrew's spine.

[9]

He loved to watch her when she laughed. The mirth began around her mouth and ended in her eyes, and he knew it was for him alone. Wanting to savor the moment, he poured the wine slowly while Sara settled herself against a mound of cushions in front of the fire. He handed her a glass and sat down beside her. "A toast. How about to . . ."

"Our happiness," Sara said, extending her glass. Her eyes were glowing, full of desire as she met Andrew's gaze.

It was Andrew who looked away first. "Tell me, what did you want to talk about?"

She placed her goblet on the raised hearth. "I've been thinking that Lorrie and Tom are spending too much time with David. What do you think?"

Andrew's mind raced back in time. He frowned. "You may be right. I understand Lorrie's decision not to have children, but we can't allow her and Tom to intrude themselves into our lives and Davey's affections. I wish you had mentioned it sooner, Sara. How long has this been troubling you?"

"I wasn't certain, Andrew. Not until I saw the way Davey looked at that ridiculous Mickey Mouse watch and the way he's beginning to use slang words. Lorrie and Tom are responsible for that. I think, Andrew, after this camping trip, that we should have a talk with both of them. And," she held up a warning hand, "we have to be prepared for some hysterics from Lorrie."

Sara brushed the hair back from Andrew's forehead. Her touch was cool, confident and soothing. Beneath her fingers, his brow wrinkled in a frown at the thought of the inevitable confrontation with his sister-in-law. He knew that she and her husband loved Davey almost to a fault. That was the problem. Sara found fault with that love. How like Sara to put Davey's welfare above her love for her sister—her only living relative. His only consolation would be that Sara would handle the unpleasantness herself, just the way she handled every situation he found disturbing. He trusted her judgment—she always did the right thing at the right time. Still, Andrew really liked Lorrie and Tom, and he knew Davey loved them. An unsettling sensation grew in the pit of his stomach. "We must think of Davey first . . ." he began, half-developed contradictions forming in his mind. He was never any good at personal relationships, he knew. Andrew was really only comfortable with the undeniable truths of the laws of physics and higher calculus that he taught at Montclair College. And, of course, in his relationship with his wife.

"Yes," Sara smiled warmly, "Davey must come first."

"The little guy is really excited. I think this will be a good experience for him. Since Lorrie is a doctor, we can leave for Florida without worrying about Davey. I meant to go up to his room this afternoon and set up his train tracks for him, but I got involved with something else and I never got around to it. I'll have some free time when all this trial business is over; and I'll be able to do it then." Reaching for Sara's hand, he asked, "Want to sit in with the grand old master of locomotives when he does his thing?"

"I'd love to," Sara assured him, pleased that Andrew always included her in his plans. "I was thinking of taking some time off myself, a day or so at least, and taking Davey to the apple orchard. We could watch them bake pies and buy some to take home. Davey does love apple pie."

Andrew frowned. "I thought you were going to take him a couple of weeks ago. Didn't you?"

Sara laughed ruefully. "Unfortunately, no. Something came up and I couldn't make it."

"Was he disappointed?"

"No, not that I could see." Sara sipped at her drink, eyeing her husband over the rim of the glass.

"Okay. Next thing we have to talk about is our trip tomorrow. Nervous?"

"No," she answered flatly.

"I wish we didn't have to go through with this. I hate the whole thing. And I never liked the FBI's decision to place Sanders and his partner in this house. You know, Sara, I've been thinking. You don't really have to go with me. I'm the one who has to testify, and I don't want you to be upset."

"I'm going and that's final. I wouldn't dream of letting you go off without me. We belong together. That's the way it's always been. Where you go, I go. Final."

Andrew ran his fingers through his thatch of dark hair, salted with gray, in much the same fashion as his son. Sara smiled, knowing the

[11]

gesture signified relief. "I don't like the fact that our names are being splashed all over the papers. And calling me a hostile witness . . ."

"Andrew, I don't pay any attention to nonsense like that. The media is the media. Period. You know how they like to latch onto what they think is a story. Everything is going to work out, and I don't want you losing any sleep over this. Promise me. After tomorrow, or the next day at most, this whole ordeal will be over."

Andrew drank his wine. "I never thought they'd link me with this business, Sara. Not after we took the precaution of leaving the University of Miami and coming here to New Jersey."

"I know all that, darling. I thought we would escape this dreadful mess, too, but it hasn't worked out that way. Don't blame yourself, Andrew. You were simply an innocent witness to a nasty scene between one of your students and a mobster who traffics in drugs. How could you have known that the student would be murdered or that he would have told a friend that you had witnessed the confrontation in the university library? Mr. Sanders says that the only reason you're called a hostile witness is that you didn't come forward voluntarily, but had to be subpoenaed. Once you testify, the state will have its case wrapped up, and we can go back to our normal lives. And Mr. Sanders and his partner can go home and leave us alone."

"I should have stepped forward, Sara. I should have reported the threats I'd overheard as soon as the body was discovered."

"Hush, darling, you'll only upset yourself," Sara said, cradling Andrew's head against her soft bosom. "You were only trying to protect Davey and me, and we love you for it. Even the FBI recognizes that our lives are endangered, otherwise they wouldn't have put us under twenty-four-hour guard. I love you, Andrew Taylor, with all my heart for all my life."

Andrew's pulses pounded as Sara's face swam before his eyes. It never failed to happen when Sara prompted their love-making with those words. God, how he loved her. He knew his life would be meaningless without her. They shared their lives, careers, and interests; theirs was a coming-together, a blending, a loving. His hand slipped beneath the soft velour of her robe, touching her breast. And through the years he had learned the special phrases and words that heightened her response and brought her to life beneath his touch. He told her how

[12]

he loved her; how they fit one another like hand and glove. How perfect she made his life; how perfect she was, her beauty, her womanliness. How complete they were, one with the other, inseparable. And Sara responded, listening, prompting his words with touches, kisses, and murmurs.

Her eyes became liquid, her mouth ripe and open for him, accepting his kiss, his tongue. He loved her like this, soft and yielding, but his pulses quickened, his senses sharpened as he waited, knowing she would slip out from under him and turn, leaning over him, assuming her usual dominant position.

Her thighs were lean and hard-muscled as they closed around his body, the heated, warm center of her pressed against his belly, rubbing, pleasuring.

He submitted himself to her mastery, without inclination to assert a masculine role, trusting her implicitly . . . always trusting himself to Sara.

The wine glass in hand, she watched his reaction as she tipped the rim, allowing the sweet liquid to trickle down his chest, pooling on his belly. The cold wine, her hot tongue. She felt his hands stroking and pressing her head, heard him groaning with pleasure, "Your mouth, Sara, your beautiful mouth . . ."

Contact between their bodies was wet, slick, so warm. Artfully, she lowered herself onto him, feeling him fill her body; an experience that she was dissolving, melting, making him a part of herself. The muscles in her pelvis became rigid; she could feel her womb contract: it was as though she were birthing him.

At the moment of climax she brought her hard-tipped breast to his lips, encouraging him to suckle. And while she held his head, feeling the life spurt into her, she crooned, "Sara's baby, Sara's sweet, perfect baby!"

Blue, radiant light glaring from the television washed the faded colors of the furnished room. Hands gripping the arms of the chair, he sat with his booted feet planted solidly on the floor, his bulky torso leaning slightly forward, poised as though he were about to spring up. The images on the screen flickered, and he seemed to be watching them, staring, unblinking. But the action went unnoticed; the blaring sound unheard.

Chill, wet patches on his back betrayed his anxiety. Perspiration broke out over his sullen mouth and on his scalp beneath his dark, military-short hair. Cudge Balog was waiting, listening for the dull thud of hooves deep inside his head. Cutting hooves, digging at brain matter, tearing it. It would come softly at first, only a hint of the weight and power to come.

He had been watching the tv, his thoughts on Lenny Lombardi who, Cudge knew, would soon be pounding on the door, demanding payment of the borrowed fifty dollars. There was a crap game in the neighborhood tonight, and Lenny would want to sit in well heeled. Little Wop bastard. He didn't need the fifty. Lombardi had more than he could spend from his drug-dealing racket. It was only pot, none of the big stuff, because he didn't want trouble with the syndicate. Still, Lombardi made more in a week than Balog would see in a month of breaking his ass on construction jobs.

His short, thick fingers dug into the threadbare fabric covering the chair. Pressure crowded the back of his brain, driving his squarish head into his neck as his powerful shoulders hunched to bear the weight. Soon, he knew, the hooves would pound through his skull, an unleashed power, irrevocable and ruthless. A dark, hulking shape would break loose from that area of his mind where he kept it penned, under control. Thinking about Lombardi had opened the gate. As far back as he could remember, it had been in the back of his head. As a kid he used to think it was a huge prehistoric monster, with a long, arching neck and rows of jagged, fiercesome teeth. But then he had gone to a summer camp for underprivileged city children, and he had seen his first bull. And he knew; he recognized it—the thick, hulking body, the menacing drift of weight. Black, with dagger-sharp horns and fiery snorts of breath. He feared it, but in doing so, he feared a part of himself. And when he was provoked and lost control of the gate, it would be there lurking, skulking, ready to burst forth from the recesses of his brain and become a pounding, all-powerful force, hooves striking, horns slashing, searching for escape. And finding none, it would stampede wildly, smashing his reserve, pulverizing his restraint, compelling and dominating him until he became *it!*

Some said it was temper. He knew better—it was the bull.

Brenda Kopec, or Elva St. John as she preferred to be called, sat on

[14]

the lumpy daybed, her back against the wall. Her attention was riveted on the man in front of the television. She watched his profile with feral alertness, knowing he was a firecracker about to go off.

The instant Cudge had turned on the tv, she immediately lowered the volume of her small cassette player. Without wasted motion, she jammed the earphones on her head. Elva knew the words to Elvis Presley's "Blue Suede Shoes" by heart, but she wanted to hear the song from beginning to end. Her foot tapped to the rhythm; the scowl on Balog's face deepened.

She knew he wasn't really watching the tv. She'd known that from the minute he had turned the set on. He was sitting there thinking about that little rat-faced Lenny Lombardi and the fifty dollars he owed him. Cudge was mad and getting madder by the minute.

As though feeling her eyes on him, Balog turned and glared at the girl. His square, snub-nosed face registered contempt. Prophetic veins swelled in his short, thick neck. With a speed that contradicted his bulk, he tore the earphones from her head. When she grappled for them, he struck her. Hard. Elva brought her arms up defensively. "Why'd you do that?" she whined. If she cried, Cudge would hit her again.

" 'Cause you're breathin'. Shut that damn thing off and sit still. I'm trying to watch tv."

"No, you're not. Anyway, you've seen that one before. This is the one that . . ." Instantly, she was sorry she'd opened her mouth. Cudge sent her another look, making her cower and slip off the end of the daybed.

He stood looming over her. "How many times have you heard that dumb song, Brenda? Oh, 'scuse me," he sneered at her, "you wanna be called Elva now. In honor of Elvis Presley. You're nothing but a dummy. Say it, Elva, you ain't nothin' but a dummy."

She swallowed hard. The side of her head smarted from the blow. She knew better than to argue with Cudge. "So, okay, I'm a dummy."

"You get hit because you never know when to shut up," his words were an accusation, placing the blame for his actions on her. "Now shut up, if you know what's good for you. Already I missed the first part of the show."

Righting herself, cautious to stay out of his reach, she put the

[15]

cassette player in the paper shopping bag on the floor beside her where she kept all her meager possessions. If Cudge decided they were moving on, he wouldn't give her five minutes to get her gear together.

Wishing she were invisible, she settled herself again on the frayed cushions. She wanted to cry. She wanted to run. But she never would. Cudge scared her sometimes, but the outside world scared her more, and Cudge at least took care of her.

Sometimes he wasn't so bad, she told herself. Once he had bought her a purple scarf, and he took her to the movies regularly. Every cassette in her library of Elvis tapes was from Cudge. So, why then did she take pleasure in goading him the way she did? Even when he was raging at her, even if he was hitting her, she knew there was a small part of herself that took abject pleasure in it. Not that she was a pervert or an s&m freak or anything like that. No, it was more that she was little and helpless, and sometimes it felt good to be able to get a rise out of a hulk like Cudge. It gave her a kind of power, knowing she could set him off any time she wanted. If Cudge was powerful, then she was even more so, in some strange way. Cudge was right, she was a dummy. Someone smarter would know how to get a rise out of Cudge and aim it at somebody else. Whenever she set him off, she was bound to get the brunt of it.

Elva was contrite with tenderness for Cudge. He had his own problems to deal with. And he wasn't so bad, not really. So this dumpy room wasn't the Ritz. People like her and Cudge would never make the Ritz. They'd be lucky if they ever saw the inside of a Holiday Inn.

She risked a quick, sidelong glance at Cudge to see if he was really watching tv. If he was, she could lean back and relax. She stared at the television, fearful that any movement would alert Cudge that she was restless or scared. She wanted to massage her shoulder where it had smacked the wall. Her tooth started to ache.

"Some day I'm gonna get cablevision so's I can see some really good sexy shows," Cudge said during a commercial.

Elva shrugged.

"Why ain't you sayin' something?" he demanded irritably.

"You told me to shut up, that's why. I'm a dummy, remember?"

"That's your trouble, you never know when to shut your mouth. Here," he said, fishing in his pocket for money. "Go get us a pizza and I want the change. And listen . . ."

"I know, I know, I should tell that dumb Wop to put on extra cheese and not charge me for it."

Cudge laughed. "You really think that stupid Guinea has the hots for you, don't you? Well, he don't. And if he did, he knows better than to mess with you. Twenty minutes, Elva, and you better be back here handing me my first slice. And don't lose the change!" He laughed again, his flat blue eyes narrowing.

Feeling like a trapped rat, she scuttled away. If she ran, she might make it there and back again in time. Tony might be nice and give her somebody else's pizza when she told him it was for Cudge. Tony would do it for her, maybe.

Her skinny body bent into the wind as she hurried along the deserted streets of Newark's Ironbound section. The tap of her high heels echoed hollowly off sleeping brickfront tenements. She was wary, jumping at imagined shadows and at the prowlings of a conspiracy of cats lurking in an alley. Her worn navy parka was warm but it hung loosely on her slight frame. She pulled it higher, burrowing her chin against the late October cold.

Just ahead, less than a block away, she saw the dim red halo outlining the storefront of Tony's Pizzeria. She broke into a run, eager to be near the warmth of Tony's ovens and out of the menacing darkness. For an instant she panicked. Pushing her hand deep into the pockets of her parka, she searched for the five one-dollar bills to pay for the pizza. Her shaking fingers recognized only four bills. She dug through all her pockets. Torn tissues and gum wrappers tumbled out, were caught in the wind, and fell along the sidewalk. Biting her lower lip, she prayed silently that five bills would magically appear. The last time Cudge had sent her out to buy something, she had stupidly lost the money and had had to face the rage of his pounding fists.

Her sigh of relief was audible when she inspected her skinny, twitching fingers and found the fifth bill. Holding tightly to the money as though fearful some unseen force might pluck away the bills, she dashed for the glass-paned door.

The glass-paned door was steamy and dripping moisture from the heat of the ovens meeting the cold outside. Throwing her weight against it, she entered into the light and warmth of the restaurant. The jukebox was playing a popular song, and Tony, behind the counter, was singing along in his broken English.

"Hey, Elva! Whatcha doin' out so late? Don't y'know li'l girls should be in bed by now? I'm just closin' up. Business, she's bad tonight. Every Monday, it's the same." His once white apron was stained with tomato sauce and the bright, overhead lights accentuated the stubble on his jowly face.

"I ain't so little," she protested shyly. "I told you I was eighteen last month."

"Elva, you always gonna be a li'l girl. Make no difference how old you gonna get." He smiled at her, showing a space between his front teeth.

Elva liked Tony. He was always friendly and he seemed to know instinctively how scared she was of everything and everyone. "Cudge wants a pizza."

"So? He wants a pizza. I'm just closing up." Tony saw the dread in her dark eyes. "Why you wait so long? It's late. I've got a family waitin' for me," he complained, leaning over the counter. "Hey. How's your eye? It's not so nice what he does to you, that guy. Why you wanna stay with him?" His finger touched her cheek just below her left eye where only last week she had been black and blue from another of Cudge's beatings. Poor little thing, Tony commiserated. Too stupid and too scared to leave that son-of-a-bitch to the dogs where he belonged. Pity overrode his aching feet. "Sure, Elva, for you, anything. What kinda pizza you want?"

Cudge watched the door slam behind Elva. He really had to hand it to her; when she wanted, she could really get that skinny ass of hers moving.

He wished he had a beer. The dull thudding in his head was getting louder; a beer might help. It was a piss-poor world when a man couldn't have a beer. Elva always had her Kool Aid in the fridge. His sullen mouth turned down. He was starting to hate Elva almost as much as he hated that sticky-sweet, artificial drink. It was getting to be time to rip the rug out from under old Elva. Time to move on and he liked to travel light.

Cudge let his eyes go back to the blurry picture on the tv. It was an old rerun. Hutch was saying something to Starsky. Now, that Starsky was a real man, even if he was a Polack.

Starsky, if you hoot with the owls all night, you won't be able to soar with the eagles in the morning.

Cudge rolled Hutch's words around in his head and repeated them aloud. He liked the sound and the meaning. He said it over four times till he was sure he'd remember. It was just the kind of thing a guy would say to his best buddy.

A knock sounded and then the door opened. "Cudge, you in here?"

Lenny! Thudding in his brain matched his pulses. He knew it! He knew it. As soon as he'd heard about that floating crap game, it was a sure bet Lenny would come looking for that fifty. Some best buddy Lenny was. Lenny Lombardi, who would pick the gold from a dead man's teeth, didn't deserve the words Cudge had just heard on the tv. Lenny was a jerk. Christ, didn't he know anybody but jerks? Elva was a jerk. Lenny was a jerk. The whole fuckin' world was full of jerks.

The muscles in Cudge's neck went into a spasm. He feigned a smile, showing his teeth. "C'mon in, Len. Wanna drink? Elva's got some Kool Aid in the fridge." He liked the stupid look on Lenny's face.

"Nah. I didn't come for Kool Aid. I saw that Olive Oyl old lady of yours runnin' down the street. What did you do? Beat the shit out of her again?" He loved to torment Cudge about his uncontrollable temper.

"What's it to you?" Cudge drawled menacingly.

"Nothin'. I come for the bread you owe me. There's a hot crap game and I want to sit in." Lenny sauntered around the room, hands jammed into his pockets. "Cough it up, I'm in a hurry."

Cudge's fist tightened. The lone ten spot in his pants pocket seemed to be burning his leg. He didn't need this cocky little dude with his pointed shoes giving him grief. "I ain't got it."

Lenny's pinched face flattened. He worked his tongue between the space in his front teeth, making a hissing noise that set Cudge's nerves on edge. "You told me that three weeks ago. Your time ran out, now get it up."

Cudge laughed, an obscene sound. "I told you I ain't got it. Gimme another week. Christ, Lenny, we been friends for a long time. You gonna blow it all for a lousy fifty bucks?" He watched Lenny keenly.

Lenny looked nervously over his shoulder before turning back to Cudge. It was a habit that Cudge found irritating. Always looking away and then back again, diverting his attention, making him look over Lenny's shoulder himself, making him half expect to see someone there. "Looks like I'm gonna have to take it in trade, old buddy."

Cudge's mouth tightened. Both hands balled into fists. "How?"

"By taking that camper sittin' down at the curb, that's how. And your truck goes with it. Give me the keys. When you come up with the bread, you get it all back. Simple."

"You ain't taking my rig, so get that idea right out of your head. You want collateral, take Elva's cassette and tapes."

"Hey, man, I don't want your junk. Just give me the keys to your wheels. I gotta get going if I wanna sit in on the game."

Cudge's mind raced. Hooves pounded in his brain. Without his truck, he'd be sunk, unable to get to the construction sites where he could pick up some money, even though he had to work his balls off just to keep body and soul together. He had to think of something. Think fast. Before the thundering hooves blotted out all reason. Lenny was a sneak, a real bastard, when it came to money. He had to get rid of him somehow.

"Don't even think about pulling a fast one, Balog. I know you got money. You think I'm stupid or somethin'? Where did your old lady get the money for eats? That's where she's going, right? Out for beer and somethin' to eat. You can eat, you can pay your debts."

Cudge got up, Elva's tape player in hand. He had no plan as he stared at Lenny Lombardi. He could almost hear the creak of the gate that kept his rage penned in the back of his head. His shoulders hunched from the weight pressing against the top of his spinal column. "I ain't got it. If you don't take my word for it, you ain't my friend."

"My friends don't welch on a loan," Lenny told him. He was bluffing, but he had to stand his ground. The look in Balog's eyes was making him nervous, and he edged back. Maybe he should let it go, forget it as a bad debt. He didn't really need the money; he had more than enough to pay into the game.

Cudge was laughing—an unpleasant sound. Lenny backed up another step, lurching into the kitchen table. His eyes measured the distance to the door. "Okay, okay. Forget the wheels. I'll give you another week to come up with the scratch. Look, I gotta go now," he bleated as he put the table between himself and Cudge.

PANDA BEAR IS CRITICAL

It was loose! Taking off at a gallop, snorting fire. Pressure moved from the back of his head to a point at the center of his skull. Instinct told him that if he frightened Lenny enough the fifty bucks would be called even, and he could forget about ever paying it back. He took a deliberate step in Lenny's direction, hefting the cassette player in his beefy hand.

It was the sheer terror on Lenny's face more than his words that provoked Balog.

"You're crazy, man! Crazy!"

Havoc was loosed in Cudge's brain. He was the beast sensing his prey, moving in for the kill. Blood surged into his face; his skull throbbed and pounded. Fiery breaths scorched his thoughts; dagger horns gouged and ripped.

It was the color of Cudge's face that made Lenny wet his pants. Animal fear choked him as he gave up trying to run for the door. Balog was too fast, too big. He seemed to fill the room with his bulk, growing right before Lenny's eyes. Cudge snorted, saliva glistening on his chin. Frozen, dumbstruck, Lenny watched the cassette player rising over him. He felt it crash into his skull.

Lenny was dead, and still Cudge struck at the bloody mass that had been his head. "Take my wheels, will you? You ain't my friend; now get your ass out of here before I throw you down four flights of stairs."

Lenny was lying with his battered face pressed against the linoleum. Cudge stood over him, seeing only the undamaged back of Lenny's head. "Get up! Move, you little turd!" Square boot-tips prodded the still form, and Balog was surprised when there was no movement. He squeezed his eyes shut against the sudden stab of pain in his temples. Then he noticed the widening pool of blood.

Cautiously Cudge bent over, the cassette player still clutched in his hand. He turned Lenny face up, thinking how light he felt, his still form offering little resistance to his own strength. The wide, staring eyes panicked him, and the cassette player fell from his hand. Jesus. He didn't need anyone to tell him that Lenny was dead. The jerk was dead! Jesus. Oh, Jesus. He had killed his best friend!

As Tony punched down the yeasty dough and stretched it over the shiny pan, he watched her. As always, his heart went out to her. She

[21]

was still a kid. Other girls, by the time they were eighteen, were more woman than child. But not Elva. She would always remain a child, a frightened, winsome, confused child. Too bad she had to meet up with that animal, Cudge Balog. A nice guy could be the salvation of a timid kid like Elva, but in the hands of that hulk she was damned. Pity. She wasn't a bad-looking girl. Too skinny, of course, and a little pinched-looking, and her eyes were always on the edge of panic, but she was pretty in a shy sort of way. With a little fixing she could be really pretty. A haircut and a little meat on her bones would make a world of difference. And something, Tony thought, or someone, to take that haunted look from her eyes.

As he scattered mozzarella cheese on the pizza, Tony found a chunk and handed it to Elva, noticing her severely bitten fingernails. She took the cheese from him with a shy smile and nibbled at it. He pushed the prepared pizza into the oven and went back to cleaning the counter. "Elva—what kind of name is that? Ol' Tony never hear it before you come here."

"It's a name I just like," she answered between nibbles.

"So, it's not your name?"

"It is now. My name used to be Brenda Kopec," she said, putting the last morsel into her mouth.

"Brenda! That's a nice name. Soft, like you. So, how come you change it? My own two daughters, they want names like Brandy and Tiffany. What's wrong with Maria and Theresa anyhow? I'm never gonna understand them. So, tell Tony, how come you changed your name?"

"I call myself Elva St. John after Elvis Presley and John Lennon. I heard somewhere that Elva was the girl's name for Elvis."

"Oh, I see! An' you like Elvis, yeah?"

"I love him!" she said with rare emotion. Tony glanced up, struck by the sadness in her voice. It held the same note he had heard in his wife's voice whenever she mentioned their own dead son.

"You knew this Presley fella?"

"Just from records and tv and stuff. But I loved him, Tony. He was so nice and gentle." She pulled at her dull, brown hair, her fingers working in agitation.

"You like your fellas gentle? So what are you doing with that son-of-a-bitch Cudge?"

"I love him too. He ain't so bad. Sometimes I think he's scared inside, just like me. Only he don't show it like I do."

Tony shrugged. There was no accounting for these American girls. He only prayed that his two daughters wouldn't want anybody like Cudge Balog. If Elva was right about Cudge being scared of something, Tony couldn't imagine what it might be. He'd seen guys that Cudge had worked over, and he knew what Cudge's fists could do to a face. It was only a matter of time before he killed someone, and Tony hoped that it wouldn't be Elva. She was a good kid, even if she was a little stupid. Maybe if she weren't so scared all the time she wouldn't be so dumb.

Elva hurried back to the furnished three-room apartment she shared with Cudge Balog, balancing the hot pizza carefully so the gooey cheese wouldn't run all to one side. She wondered how long she'd been gone. It seemed like a long time, and Cudge would get mad if he was kept waiting. Suddenly, she couldn't remember if she'd picked up the five cents change from Tony's counter. Cudge could be a real stickler about things like that.

Elva stopped in front of a tenement and propped her leg on the stoop, balancing the pizza on her knee. She could feel the heat penetrate the cardboard box and sting her leg while she frantically dug through her pockets looking for the nickel change. Panic bordered on hysteria when she couldn't find it, and she thought of returning to Tony's to see if she'd left it on the counter.

She glanced back up the street. The red fluorescent lights over Tony's door were dark. What should she do? Maybe she could catch up with him at his car . . . her fingers touched the metallic disc. Relief flooded through her. She had found it. She hadn't been stupid after all. For safekeeping, Elva popped the coin into her mouth and gripped the sides of the pizza box as she hurried back to Cudge Balog.

She smiled in the darkness. Everything had gone right for a change. Cudge wouldn't have anything to yell about.

When Elva turned down Courtland Street, she recognized the familiar outline of Cudge's Chevy pickup truck with the flat, square outline of his pop-up camper hitched to the rear. They rarely went camping, but just a few days ago Cudge had talked about taking a weekend in the country. Like so many things Cudge talked about, Elva never expected to see it come to anything.

She loped up the front stoop of their building into the dimly lit hallway. Urine and stale cooking odors came to her nostrils. Just as her foot was on the first step leading upstairs, the door to the landlady's apartment swung open.

"Oh, it's you. I thought maybe it was you he was knocking around up there." Mrs. Fortunati's thin gray hair fell over her eyes, and she brushed it away with an impatient gesture of her work-worn hands. "You'd better get your ass up there and see what's going on. I was thinking about calling the cops."

Elva gulped at the sinking feeling in the pit of her stomach. The night was ruined; Cudge had done it again. Now it wouldn't matter that she had bought the pizza and brought home the right change and had done everything just exactly right. Cudge was going to be nasty and find something, anything, to be mad about any way.

"Well, what are you waiting for? Get up there! From the sound of it he was tearing the place apart." She moved to the banister and watched Elva go up the stairs as she issued her last warnings. "I'm telling you now, there better not be any trouble or out you go! The both of you! Him in particular!"

Elva waited outside the door, dreading to go in. For all Mrs. Fortunati's ravings, it was quiet now. Only the baby from up in 4B broke the silence.

She fumbled with the doorknob, balancing the pizza box on her knee. The door opened a mere three inches. Cudge had latched the chain hook. Puzzled, Elva opened her mouth to call him when the nickel in her mouth clicked against her front tooth, making her wince. The temperamental tooth with its rice grain of decay was going to ache all night.

"Cudge," she whimpered, "open the door, will you?"

"Elva?" It was a hoarse whisper from the other side of the door.

Something was wrong—Cudge never whispered. He yelled and put his fists through walls, but he never whispered. "Yeah, it's me. What's the matter? Why are you whispering?"

The door was forced shut, jamming against a corner of the pizza box, and she heard him fumbling with the chain latch. Then it swung open again, and he grabbed hold of her arm and pulled her into the apartment. The bare lightbulb over the kitchen table swung

[24]

back and forth, creating wild shadows and rhythmic patterns of light.

"Get in here, dummy. Where the hell were you?" He was angry, and he was still whispering. But the annoyance on his face was mingled with something else. Something dreadful she had never seen there before. Now it wouldn't matter that she had done everything exactly right. Nothing would matter except that Cudge was mad, and one way or another she would pay for it.

"I . . . I went for the pizza like you told me. I even got the change."

"Shut up. I gotta think!"

Elva shrank back, still clutching the pizza box. Something was wrong, awfully wrong. What? She'd never seen Cudge like this, so quiet and scared. He moved away from her and sank down on the edge of the daybed, his head in his hands. The tv was still on, but the sound had been turned off. She watched him, not daring to take her eyes away.

Then suddenly, like an uncoiled spring, he jumped to his feet and punched the wall, his lips drawn back over his teeth in a frightening grimace.

"Stupid dumb fuck! He never should've tried to bust my hump. He should've known I didn't have fifty bucks to pay him back." His fist pounded the wall again, punctuating his words. "Thought he'd take my truck and rig. Thought I was stupid or something. He should've known!"

Elva pressed against the wall, eyes wide with terror. In all the time she had lived with Cudge she'd never seen him like this. Cudge was scared. Scared shitless.

"Don't look at me that way!" he turned on her, slamming his fist into the cardboard pizza box, knocking it to the floor.

"You ruined it." Automatically she bent down to pick up the box, but she was hoisted to her feet.

"What the hell are you messing with that for?"

"I . . . I just wanted to clean it up."

He shook her, almost making her teeth chatter. "Oh, yeah? Well, see what you can do about cleaning *that* up!" His knee found its mark on the small of her back and she pitched forward, her slight weight yielding to the force of the blow. Elva fell forward, her hands reaching out to break her fall. She crawled to the far side of the kitchen table,

[25]

and came face to face with Lenny Lombardi. He was lying on the floor, his face barely recognizable. If it hadn't been for his familiar trenchcoat and slick dark hair, she wouldn't have known him.

Elva pulled herself to her knees, her hands extended in a gesture of helplessness. Lenny wasn't *breathing!*

Her mouth opened to scream, but before any sound ripped from her throat, Cudge had his beefy hand clasped over her lips, covering her nose, cutting off her air. Waiting for her to be quiet, he hissed a warning not to scream.

She stared up at him over his hand, her eyes wild and panicky, then shook her head violently, fighting for breath.

"Will you shut up?" Cudge growled. " 'Cause if you don't, you'll get some of the same."

The cords in her neck threatened to burst; she was feeling light-headed and sparks were shooting off inside her head. Frantically, she nodded her head.

Cudge waited a long moment before removing his hand. For an instant, she believed he never would, that he would hold her there forever and ever. Her feet kicked out, touching the soft, unyielding body wedged against the wall. Sickened, she ceased her struggles.

"Now shut up, one sound out of you and you'll look just like him!" Cudge warned in that creepy whisper, a scared look narrowing his eyes.

Revulsed, Elva crawled to the daybed, away from Lenny—from what used to be Lenny. She clamped her hands over her mouth to stay the questions. Unable to control herself any longer, she began to tremble as the words tumbled out.

"Why? Why did you kill him? He was your friend? My God! You killed him!"

Cudge's hand slammed into her head. "I told you to shut up! I don't wanna hear your mouth! Shut up!"

Elva was beyond the point of hysteria, she bordered on dementia. "God! You killed him! You killed Lenny! Your best friend! God!"

"If you don't shut up so I can think, you're gonna get what he got!" Again he slammed the side of her head, knocking her over onto the floor. "One more word, Elva, one more word and you're gonna get it! You stupid broad! I gotta think!"

"But the police! What are you gonna do? They'll find out!"

"You stupid bitch! What did I tell you!" He lunged at her and picked her up by the shoulders, shaking her violently.

Instantly Elva was silent, terrorized.

"Quit your babbling, I gotta think!"

She sank to the floor, shuddering with horror. Cudge had killed Lenny Lombardi, and he would do the same to her if she didn't keep quiet. Everyone always said Cudge would kill somebody some day, and Elva had silently agreed with them, never realizing how his potential for violence fascinated her. But Lenny was his friend.

Cudge paced the floor, his hands constantly kneading his skull in exasperation. While he paced, he kept up a constant monologue, muttering curses at Lenny and whining complaints and praying to God for a solution.

Bit by bit the quarrel between Lenny and Cudge became clear to Elva as she stole quick looks at the body that lay stuffed between the table and the wall.

"We have to get out of here," Cudge decided, intensity sharpening his blunt features. "And we have to get him out of here, too, before anybody starts wondering where Lenny got to."

Elva looked up, puzzled.

"You're an accessory, you know," he informed her. "If I hang, you're gonna hang too!"

"Me? I didn't do anything! I just came in here and found . . . him."

"It don't matter, baby," Cudge told her, his voice showing concern. He knew how easy Elva was to handle—stupid, dumb broad. All he had to do was make her think he cared for her, and she came crawling, willing to do anything he demanded. "Look, baby. According to the law, you should have run out of here and gone straight to the cops. You didn't, so that means you're aiding and abetting. That makes you an accessory and what I get, you get too! Understand?"

Elva really didn't understand, but she knew that Cudge was smart when it came to the law, and he sounded as though he really knew what he was talking about. If he said she was an accessory, then she must be one. He'd been busted by the cops enough times to know what he was saying. "But what can we do? Where can we go?"

Cudge smiled to himself. Poor, stupid, dumb Elva. "Look, baby, we've got to get out of here, and we have to take him with us. I figure we can stuff him into the camper and take off somewhere and bury him."

A tear trickled down her cheek. "Poor Lenny."

"What about 'poor Cudge'? What about me? That stupid fuck tried to rip me off, and he got what was coming to him! And now I ain't got no best friend." He knew that would bring Elva around. There was nothing that could swing Elva around like cheering for the underdog. Just make her feel sorry for you, and you could lead her around by the nose.

"Cudge, I didn't mean anything like that," she went over to put her arms around him. "Sure I know how hard this must be on you and all. Lenny was your friend, and I know you didn't mean to—to hurt him."

"That's right, honey. I never mean to hurt nobody. I just don't know what comes over me sometimes. Hey, I'm sorry I hit you before. Real sorry. Sometimes I don't know my own strength. But don't back out on me, baby. I need you. More now than ever."

Elva's heart went out to him. Poor Cudge, he just couldn't help himself. Any more than her father had been able to control his temper. Hadn't Mama always forgiven him? Hadn't Mama known that she was Daddy's very own salvation here on earth? Daddy had known it too. He always called Mama his own angel. Deciding she couldn't do any less for Cudge, Elva squeezed him hard. "Just tell me what you want me to do. I'll do anything to help you, Cudge, you know that."

"Good girl," he answered her hug with a kiss on the cheek. "Only don't go getting the idea you're doing it for me. It's for you too, baby. Christ, what would I do if they ever took you away from me because you're an accessory?"

"Don't worry, Cudge," she said soothingly. "Nobody will ever take me away from you."

Cudge Balog smiled and began formulating his plans for moving the remains of Lenny Lombardi into the camper.

$$2$$

LISTENING to Sara's slow, regular breathing, Andrew knew she had
fallen asleep. She had climbed into bed beside him after their lovemaking in front of the fire, placed her head on his shoulder and settled
down into his warm, familiar embrace. Now, as he lay here beside her,
he thought about their trip to Florida the next morning.

No need to worry about packing, Sara had seen to it days ago, and
much better than he could have done himself. They would be escorted
by federal agents to the airport, and there was no concern about tickets
or reservations; the government had seen to everything. They would
simply board the plane, and once in Miami go right to the courthouse.
Their hotel accommodations were being kept secret even from them
so there was no possibility of a leak.

No matter how often Sara tried to reassure him, Andrew still felt
uneasy for not coming forward to testify of his own volition. Nothing
should have kept him from going to the authorities as soon as he'd
learned that Jason Forbes's body had been discovered behind an all-
night supermarket.

Forbes had been only twenty, a promising student in Andrew's
second-year physics class. While Andrew had never known Forbes
outside class, he had found him to be an affable young man whose
aptitude for higher mathematics was above average.

Tomorrow Andrew would be asked to review his acquaintance with
Forbes on the witness stand, and there was little he could say beyond
an impersonal recital of Forbes's class attendance and scholastic record.
The prosecuting attorney wouldn't be looking for a personal history,

[29]

LEWIS EGERTON SMOOT MEM'L. LIB.
KING GEORGE, VA. 22485

Andrew reminded himself. He would want to know the details of the last time Andrew had seen Forbes alive.

Andrew and Sara had shared a brown-bag lunch in the faculty room in Farring Building on the Miami University campus that early May afternoon. Between her morning classes, Sara had run home to give Davey his daily injection, and had prepared their lunch of cold chicken sandwiches and iced tea. Afterward they had parted, she to teach her one-thirty class, and Andrew to the university library.

He almost hadn't gone to the library that afternoon. The idea of going home to spend some of the lovely spring afternoon with Davey had occurred to him. If only he had.

The library had been dim and cool, especially in the stacks where he was doing research in preparation for next week's classes. It had been quiet, so quiet one could almost hear the proverbial pin drop. With a scholar's contentment in the musty, hushed atmosphere, Andrew gathered up the heavy physics texts. This was a little-used area, and he had expected to spend the entire time alone at a table in the far alcove. Andrew had been so immersed in his work that he hadn't even been aware of any noise until a voice cried out in alarm.

Curious, Andrew stopped to listen.

Two voices, one with unmistakable tenor of youth, the other harsher, older, more authoritative. They were arguing in hushed tones, but their words were clear and distinct. The older voice was accusing the other of "holding out . . . starting your own business."

"No!" the young man protested. "That was all I picked up. Honest!"

The younger man continued to protest the accusation, his tone becoming more nervous, fearful, and wheedling. Impelled by curiosity and a vague recognition of the younger voice, Andrew quietly closed his book and moved to the archway of the alcove.

He recognized Forbes immediately and overheard him beseeching the older man to believe he was telling the truth. Forbes's accuser was a man in his late forties, heavy of build, wearing a Hawaiian-print shirt. He'd never seen this man before, but there was something menacing about him and the way he was leaning toward Forbes. He was a dangerous man, Andrew thought, and one he wouldn't want to deal with himself. He wondered if he would have Forbes's courage in standing up to him.

[30]

"We know you're lying, kid. I've been told to tell you that you'd better get the rest of the stuff to us by ten o'clock tonight . . . or else." The man jabbed his index finger into Forbes's shoulder for emphasis. "We don't like kids who hold out on us. We know you picked up ten kilos, so how come you only delivered eight? At street prices that would make you a nice little bundle, wouldn't it, kid? Think about it, you've been playing around with the big boys and you'd better come across." Forbes's complexion had turned pasty white beneath his Florida tan, and he was having difficulty choking out his words. "I don't have it, I tell you. You've got this all wrong."

"You've got it all right, kid. We know you do. Word got back to us about that little sale you made yesterday. Ten o'clock, kid, the usual place. Be there with the stuff. Oh, and don't try running home to mama. We've got our connections in St. Louis, too." With the speed of lightning, the man slapped Forbes across the face, the blow so forceful and unexpected that the young man crumpled to his knees.

The man turned and left, walking unhurriedly, his heels clicking through the aisles of books. Andrew hurried over to Forbes to see if he was hurt. As he stepped forward, Forbes rose to his feet, his hand rubbing the side of his face. A low whistle escaped him, and Andrew thought he heard him mutter a curse.

"Are you all right, Forbes?"

The young man stood frozen, staring at Andrew, as he realized that his professor had seen and heard everything.

Andrew took a step toward the student, but the forbidding expression on Forbes's face stopped him. Then, jamming his hands in his jeans pockets, Forbes walked out.

For the rest of the day the scene he had witnessed was replayed in Andrew's mind. That Forbes was involved with drugs was obvious. Florida was the U. S. entry point used by many drug smugglers; from there the drugs were distributed to major cities. There was also no doubt that Forbes had gotten hold of two kilos of whatever—cocaine, heroin, or marijuana—and had kept it. The only uncertainty was whether or not Forbes would return it. But if he had made a sale the day before, did that mean he didn't have it any longer? Then what would happen?

That question occupied Andrew throughout dinner, until Sara complained that he was distracted and secretive, so he finally confided in her.

The next day Forbes's body was found behind the supermarket. Was that the "usual place" the man had spoken of?

The campus was in turmoil at the news of the murder, and an investigation was launched. Detectives and policemen scoured the campus for information. No one approached Andrew to question him; yet he was becoming increasingly uneasy. Two weeks had passed and he was still wrestling with the question of whether or not to come forward with his information.

Then more information came to light. Forbes was found to be involved in drug trafficking, along with his roommate Franklin Pell. Still, nothing in the papers indicated that the police were any closer to finding Forbes's killer. Andrew knew that the police did not reveal all information to the press, yet every day he scanned the papers, learning more about Forbes after his death than he had ever known about him in life. It was becoming an obsession.

In the midst of this quandary, Andrew and Sara had to respond to job offers made to both of them earlier that year by Montclair College in New Jersey. They had talked it over and had agreed they would be fools to leave the "Sunshine State" for the long, cold Jersey winters. But now the opportunity to leave Florida and escape even the remotest involvement in the Forbes case appealed to them. They would leave as soon as classes ended in order to set up housekeeping and prepare for the fall semester.

By the middle of July the Taylors had moved into an old Victorian house on the outskirts of Montclair. Andrew seemed to be returning to his normal self, and Sara was occupied with setting up housekeeping and redecorating. Even Davey seemed to adjust to the move with little difficulty. In fact, the child was thriving on the additional attention provided by Sara's sister Lorrie and her husband Tom Ryan who lived nearby.

September came, and with it a structured schedule, martialed by Sara, of classes, study, chores, and kindergarten for Davey. Then the murder in Florida caught up with them. Andrew and Sara were picked up during their classes by federal agents. Their first thoughts were of Davey who, they were told, was waiting for them at home. Franklin

Pell had told the police about the circumstances leading to his room-mate's death. He also revealed that Forbes had told him that Professor Taylor had witnessed the confrontation in the library. His testimony had leaked to the newspapers, but before the news could be picked up by the wire services, the government hastily arranged for the Taylors to be questioned.

The drug ring that Forbes had been involved with was one of the biggest in the country, and certainly in Florida. Andrew's testimony was vital in linking the syndicate to Forbes's death and hence to other crimes. The government had been waiting for such a link. It would be instrumental in breaking up a wide circle of corruption that the law was determined to destroy. Without Andrew's testimony, the connection between Forbes and the syndicate would be weak, and if the government knew this, so did the killers. Even Franklin Pell had no direct contact with the syndicate. His only contact was Forbes himself.

With awesome speed and thoroughness, the government put the entire Taylor family under twenty-four-hour guard. The syndicate's main objective would be to prevent Andrew from appearing in court, and that end would most likely be accomplished the same way they had dealt with Forbes

Sara had been wonderful, dealing with the government interlopers with the same efficiency she ran the house and prepared for her classes. Davey seemed to like the men assigned to their family who followed him to school and stood outside his kindergarten classroom. If he didn't understand why the men had been assigned for their protection, Sara deemed it unnecessary to tell him. It was more important, she said, that David saw his parents coping with the unusual happenings in their household and going about their lives as normally as possible.

Andrew hated the news media most of all. They referred to his "caution" in coming forward with the information that could "crack the most infamous drug ring operating in the United States," unquote. While he had never had any delusions about being a hero, Andrew despised their use of the word "caution." He knew it was a nonlibelous euphemism for "coward."

Sara turned over onto her side, sleeping deeply now, her blonde hair scattered over the pillow. The sweet, round shape of her haunches pressed against Andrew, and he smoothed his hand over her hip, following the line to the slim valley of her waist. He envied Sara her peace, wanted it for himself, wished he could find sleep instead of laying here thinking.

A soft cough from David's room across the hall drew his attention. He smiled as he thought of his son. Andrew didn't share Sara's reservations about Davey's growing dependence on Lorrie and Tom, but he didn't disagree either. Sara, as his mother, was much closer to Davey and his needs than he was, and he would rely on her instincts.

Andrew and Sara had been married nearly fifteen years before Davey was born. They had resigned themselves to never having a child when the miracle was announced. Methodical thinkers both, they spent the time prior to Davey's birth discussing and rediscussing their ideas of child-rearing. Happily, they found they agreed on almost every point.

At the time the Taylors were teaching in a small college in upstate New York and their professional lives neatly blended with their home life. It was an idyllic time, filled with scholastic achievements and music and love. And even though both were just past forty, their long-awaited child could only enhance their lives.

Shortly after Davey's birth they learned he was a hemophiliac. He was nine months old, and Sara had discovered a swelling near the base of his spine. When the doctor entered the examination room, the first thing he asked was, "How long has he been this color?" Andrew remembered how upset Sara had been, feeling she had been remiss, but neither one of them had noticed a change.

Thinking about what happened next could still cause Andrew to break out in a sweat. After a preliminary blood test the doctor rushed back and said, "This baby is dying. Get him to the hospital, *fast!* Your son is a hemophiliac and his condition is critical."

That immediate crisis passed, but it launched a whole new lifestyle for the Taylors, one predicated on preventing even the slightest injury from occurring. Simple things would send them rushing to the hospital emergency room: bumps, bruises, cutting baby teeth, a tongue bitten when Davey fell while taking his first steps.

Those had been bitter days, and Sara, in particular, agonized over the situation. Hemophilia is a blood disorder usually passed from mother to son. Having no brothers or uncles on her mother's side, Sara was completely ignorant of the fact that she carried the gene. She was burdened with a guilt that could never be overcome. It was *her* fault

[34]

that Davey was imperfect. Sara planned a campaign to protect her son in every way possible. The baby's crib and play areas were padded. Expensive special shoes with rubber soles were purchased so Davey wouldn't slip. Occasionally braces were necessary to assure that his limbs grew straight.

Each little episode bordered on catastrophe. In addition to dealing with the harrowing medical problems of hemophilia, the Taylors had to live with anxiety and uncertainty every day. And still accidents would occur. Because of Davey's young age, his tiny veins would sometimes not accommodate transfusion equipment, and he would have to be strapped to a bed for hours.

Sara's strength of will kept the family on as even a keel as was possible. She could ease Andrew's mind and offer hope when there was none, holding out for the day when Davey could be put on an antigen program.

Before researchers isolated the two antihemophilia factors—Factor VIII and Factor IX—patients had to lie in a bed as bottles of plasma trickled into their veins. Then pharmaceutical companies developed a way to freeze-dry the concentrate and produce it for home use, to be administered in daily shots. Andrew and Sara rejoiced when Davey's condition was stabilized, allowing him to enter the antigen program.

None of the treatments was inexpensive. Even with major medical insurance coverage they were not protected against the heavy financial drain. Year after year they transferred to different colleges, seeking the best-paying positions available. They had even taken on the moonlighting task of reviewing and editing textbooks: Andrew in the field of mathematics and Sara in English and French literature.

As long as Davey received an uninterrupted daily dose of antigen, he could live a normal life. Uninterrupted, Andrew thought uneasily. In this life of uncertainties was that really possible? It had to be. At this point Davey's hemophilia was controlled. But by the very nature of the antigen, it was possible that Davey's own body defenses would reject the drug. Then the drug would be useless to him, and the only treatment that would be effective would entail endless hours strapped to transfusion devices.

Sara and Andrew had been instructed how vitally important it was that Davey receive the antigen at the same time every single day. Even one day without the injection could set up a chemical reaction in his

PANDA BEAR IS CRITICAL

body, whereby the drug would be rejected and rendered useless. *Forever!* There would be no turning back if that ever occurred. Once a week Davey's antigen level had to be checked; it was imperative that it be kept at levels that coincided with his growth.

Sara's sister Lorrie, a doctor, realized the problem. So well in fact that she made a decision not to have children, knowing the odds were against them because she too carried the hemophiliac gene. Lorrie was fourteen years younger than Sara and had been at the height of her child-bearing years when Davey's condition was discovered. Married to Tom Ryan, a promising young attorney, she had happily anticipated having a family. Davey changed all that. So she had continued with her studies and achieved her degree in medicine and devoted herself to her pediatric practice.

Sara threw her arm over her husband's chest. Andrew nuzzled against her, aware of the fresh scent of her shampoo which lingered in her light hair. Firmly setting his reflections aside, he settled into an uneasy sleep.

Cudge sat beside Elva on the daybed. He was certain he had used the right words to settle her down and make her help him. She'd come up with an idea for disposing of Lenny's body, and though he'd never admit it, it was more than he could do.

"Question is, how do we get him downstairs to the camper?" Cudge touched Elva's cheek, brushing back a strand of hair. "We can't just drag him down the stairs and pretend he's drunk. Not with his face all . . ." He didn't complete his statement.

Elva's eyes were scanning the room and rested on the three paper bags that held the laundry. A small bottle of fabric softener and a box of detergent were beside the bags. Frowning, she saw the rusty ironing board with its scorched, dirty gray cover leaning against the wall. She forced her eyes to go to Lenny's body and then back to the ironing board. "I got an idea, Cudge."

"Yeah? What?" He knew it was going to be something stupid, but he'd better hear her out and make her feel important. This was not the time to fight with her and get her screaming loud enough to wake the dead.

"Like you said, we can't just take him down the stairs and pretend he's drunk or sick or something. That nosey old Mrs. Fortunati is

[36]

awake, and she already told me she was thinking of calling the cops because of the noise coming from our apartment. That must have been when you were hitting Lenny and . . ."

Cudge's hair almost stood on end, and the black look in his eyes stopped her flow of words. He clenched his hands to keep them from shaking. "What did that old snoop say she heard, Elva?" It was a monumental effort to keep his voice steady.

"Nothing, she just said it sounded like you were tearing the place apart." She saw him relax. That wasn't anything new with the landlady. She was always saying she was going to call the cops, and she even did once because the baby in 4B was sick and cried all night long. "Anyway, I was thinking we could put Lenny on the ironing board, pile dirty clothes on top of him and pretend we're going to the laundromat. You can put him in the camper and drive him away somewhere."

Cudge's eyes widened. "Sometimes you ain't so stupid after all. It just might work. Hey, you look like you're gonna be sick. If you gotta puke, do it in the toilet."

"I'm not gonna puke. I just don't like seeing dead people. It reminds me of—they look like chalk, and they don't move any more. Not ever." The regret in her voice was lost on Cudge who was busy putting the ironing board next to the body to measure it.

"He'll fit. Come on, don't just sit there, give me a hand."

"Cudge, I . . . I can't touch him," Elva cried.

"If you don't, you'll get what he did. Move it!"

Elva shuffled over to the body and bent down to grasp Lenny's legs while Cudge took hold of him under the armpits. Lenny landed with a thump on the rickety board and Elva backed away, her hands going to her mouth to stifle a retch.

"We'll tie him on it. I don't want him rolling off in front of Mrs. Fortunati's apartment door."

"I don't like that Mrs. Fortunati. She's got little beady eyes that see everything. Tony, the pizza man, is Italian and he doesn't have eyes like that."

Cudge ignored Elva as he began to heap dirty clothes over Lenny's body. Beads of perspiration dotted his upper lip as he leaned back against the table. "Okay, that was the first step. Now we have to clean out this place and make tracks. Get your junk together."

"I got it all in a paper bag. The rest is on top of your friend. Now what?" Elva asked, moving as far away as possible from the ironing board.

"Get everything together. We ain't coming back here, ever again. Take all the food and then clean up this mess," he gestured to the pool of blood under the table. Make damn sure you do a good job. First thing I'll take down to the camper is the tv."

"Cudge, I hate blood. It makes me sick; I can't do it!"

"You're going do it, and you'll do it now before I punch holes in that thing you call a head. Move it!"

"I always get the shitty jobs," Elva protested as she kicked a filthy dishtowel. With the toe of her shoe she picked up the rag and dropped it into a supermarket grocery bag. The towel was so threadbare it barely soaked up any of the blood. Not wanting to be alone with Lenny in the kitchen, she raced to the bathroom and waited till Cudge came back into the apartment. A roll of toilet paper in her hand, she walked back to the dingy kitchen. She unrolled the sheets and wiped with her foot. Satisfied that the blood had been wiped up, she poured a glass of water on the floor and repeated her actions. A whole roll of toilet paper was all it took to wipe up a man's life.

"You got everything?" Cudge asked belligerently.

Elva was tossing food from the refrigerator into a paper bag. "Should I take the eggs?"

He rolled his eyes. "Yes, you should take the eggs," he mimicked. "Take everything. Come on, we ain't got all night. We'll take him down first, but I want to make sure the coast is clear. I left the back of the camper open, all we have to do is stuff him in."

Elva gritted her teeth before picking up her end of the ironing board. "Wait! We have to put the detergent and softener on top to make it look real."

"Christ, Elva, we ain't really going to the laundry. Leave the damn stuff."

Elva was not to be deterred. The detergent and fabric softener were plopped on top of Lenny's stomach. Halting abruptly in mid-stride, Elva's voice was a high-pitched stuttering squeak. "You can't, you just can't—we have to spray him with something."

Cudge's fists were tight, white-knuckled. "Why?" Desperation made him ask, "With what?"

Elva gulped. "Be—because he'll smell. Dead bodies smell. They start to, to rot or something. I'm telling you what to do; I didn't say I knew what to use," she blurted. Her toothache was pounding away like a trip-hammer.

Cudge stared at Elva. His voice was almost patient. "I ain't exactly planning on carrying Lenny around for very long. I don't think he'll have a chance to smell."

"Soon as he gets stiff, he'll smell." Cudge hated the certainty in Elva's voice.

"We don't have anything around to spray him with. Come on, grab your end."

"What about . . . about the mothballs in the bottom of the sink? That's enough to kill any kind of smell. You could stick some in Lenny's coat pockets."

It was evident to Elva that Cudge was going to go along with her idea by the way his gaze shifted to the bottom of the sink.

Elva darted between the table and the body. Her skinny arm was trembling so badly Cudge jerked the container of mothballs from her hand. "This better work, you dizball."

Elva backed away till she was standing in the dingy living room. Cudge sneezed four times in rapid succession as he stuffed the white pellets in Lenny's pockets. "Okay, he's preserved now. You got any more crazy ideas, now is the time to spit 'em out. I'm not planning on touching him again. Let's go—get back over here. You think I can do this myself?"

Elva advanced a step and then backed up two steps. "I can't, Cudge, I just can't do it," she whined.

"Listen, you're the one who came up with this whole idea. Now grab hold of the damn thing and let's get him down to the camper."

She stared at Cudge. As usual he was right. The ironing board and the mothballs had been her idea. It never occurred to her that if Cudge hadn't lost his temper and killed Lenny she wouldn't be standing here now ready to cart a dead body down to the street.

"Grab hold, and God help you if you let him slip," Cudge snarled.

Elva shivered as she picked up the narrow end of the board. Her hold secure, she stopped again, the wide end of the board jamming Cudge in the small of his back.

[39]

"What now?"

"The detergent and bottle of softener," she explained. With a mighty effort, she reached to the top of the sink.

Out of the apartment to the top of the stairs, Lenny's body jounced with each step they took. Elva tried to look anywhere but at the ironing board as she muttered quietly. "All-temp-a-Cheer, whites in hot, colors in cold, all-temp-a-Cheer." Over and over she repeated the words to the commercial. Once, halfway down the stairs, she looked just in time to see the trail of feathery soap powder spilling on the steps. Maybe if she didn't say anything, Cudge wouldn't notice. She repeated the words over and over again, thinking about the trailing powder, remembering the fairy tale about the children who left a trail of breadcrumbs in the forest so they could find their way back home. Elva St. John had a home once, but something told her she never would again.

A sound like rain pelting a roof made Cudge stop at the fourth step from the bottom. Elva's eyes popped open as she toppled over the ironing board. Cudge lost his hold and it plopped and then slid down the remaining steps.

Bile rose to Elva's throat and soured her mouth. "Oh, my God, quick, pick him up! Somebody might hear! Pick him up!"

Cudge moved swiftly to right the board and rearrange the laundry on top of its burden. "I guess you know that funny noise was those fucking mothballs falling out of his pockets. Run around here and get that front door open."

Elva obeyed, never letting her eyes see the bundled board. Cudge grimaced with the effort as he dragged the board forward, holding the door open with his shoulder. "Get around and grab the other end. You and your bright ideas."

Huffing at her end of the board, Elva whispered, "I ain't even sure they'll work in his pockets anyway. Maybe you should've stuffed them in his ears." She watched the back of Cudge's neck and could almost see the stubbles of hair stand on end.

"Either you shut up, Elva, or you're gonna be in the back with Lenny, and it's you who's gonna get mothballs in the ears. Dumb shit!"

His voice was tight and choked and Elva smiled to herself. She could risk being smug. With her own eyes she'd seen Cudge almost gag when he was stuffing the pellets into Lenny's pockets. It was nice to know that Cudge was afraid. "I'm just trying to help," she whined. "I keep tellin' you, I ain't smart. I just know things."

"Right the first time," Balog grunted, bearing almost the full weight of the board and Lenny down the front steps and out to the curb. "Okay, now when I say 'shove' you push your end in. You got that?"

Elva let her breath out in a sob the minute the camper was closed and the top half lowered. She could imagine poor Lenny being squashed in there, in the darkness. "Cudge?" she said hesitantly.

"Jeez, what do I have to do to make you shut up? What?" His tone was hushed, little more than a whisper instead of his usual yelling. Elva liked that; it was the one good thing that had happened all night.

"Should we go back and pick up the mothballs?"

"I'm going back in to make sure you didn't leave anything. You wait right here and don't go getting any ideas about taking off. You go when I say you go. Got that, Elva? And quit your worrying about the mothballs."

It was spooky sometimes the way Cudge could read her mind. No matter what he said, she wasn't getting into the cab of the pickup until he was right there beside her. She didn't know what hurt her more, her shoulders from carrying Lenny down two flights of stairs or her tooth.

The streetlight seemed friendly as Elva leaned against the pole. Her thoughts, however, were gray. She'd been this close to death before, only now it was easier. She didn't really care about Lenny Lombardi, not the way she had about little BJ. She couldn't cry for Lenny—she had spent all her tears on her little brother. And she didn't feel guilty either. She wasn't even there when it happened. Not like with BJ when, if she hadn't been so scared for herself, she might have been able to do something to save him.

The worst behind him, Cudge looked around the apartment and felt nothing except relief. There were no visible signs that anything had happened in the kitchen. He walked through the apartment, taking his time to see that nothing had been left behind. If, and it was a big if, they had to come back for any reason, they could just walk in the door. The rent had been paid for the next month; there was no reason why anyone should come nosing around.

[41]

Cudge made his way down the dim stairway. The mothballs littered the filthy stair treads, and unconsciously, he counted them. When he hit the fourth step from the bottom, he stopped and inched his way closer to the greasy wall. It hit him then. He was a murderer. He felt like a land mine ready to explode. A grin spread across his face, easing the tension between his shoulders. He was the only one who knew he was a murderer, and Elva. Nine mothballs. Wise-ass Elva would have to go. It would be his secret; no one would ever know. Maybe he should pick up the mothballs and jam them down Elva's throat. One balled fist smacked into the other. He wished it were Elva's bony face he was punching out. The crack of bone would be like music to his ears.

He was still grinning when he loped down the steps to the sidewalk. The camper looked just fine, and Elva was leaning against the telephone pole. "Get in, Elva, and if you so much as blubber, even once, I'll knock you right through the damn door."

Elva's toothache was getting worse. If only she could fall asleep and wake up when the pain was gone. If there was someone who could promise her that, she might give up one of her Elvis tapes.

"I'm gonna drive around for a while till I decide what to do with Lenny. You keep your eye peeled for cops or anything that might get us into trouble."

"Like what?" Elva whispered. "I want to know so I don't get us into trouble."

"Like some goddamn jerk trying to mug us as we drive around. I have to think, so watch with both your eyes. I know that trick you use sometimes, when you close one eye and stare with the other. Maybe you think it's sexy, but you look like a ghoul. Now, start looking."

Cudge drove carefully, his eyes alert. While he had searched the apartment, he had toyed with the idea of burying Lenny in the Watchung Mountains. It was as good a place as any. There wouldn't be too many people on the steep mountain roads. The trees were thick and dark around Bernardsville, and he had more than enough gas to get him there and back. Back to what? He couldn't think that far ahead.

As he drove along, his thoughts were confused. It seemed like he was always in trouble of some kind. When he was a kid, he had been in one scrape after another, but he always managed to save his hide at the last moment. So far, the cops had nothing on him except a few drunken driving charges. He had been deprived. He was being deprived now. Pity was drowning out all reason. Pity for himself, pity for the circumstances that controlled his life. When he was a kid, he never had anything except the clothes on his back and what he could steal. Now he was a man, but he still had nothing.

3

E XCITED, HON?" Tom Ryan asked his wife as he maneuvered the long motor-home around a bend. His tanned hands gripped the steering wheel with authority, and it wasn't till he straightened the wheel that he stole a look at the slim, blonde woman beside him.

"Hmm. I've been looking forward to these few days with Davey for weeks now. I'm glad that I could get Dr. Petti to cover for me. He's a good pediatrician and my patients like him, to say nothing of their mothers."

"Tall, dark, and handsome, Douglas Petti."

"Jealous!" Lorrie Ryan accused.

"Sometimes. What man wouldn't be jealous of a wife who looks like you? Small, slim, and gorgeous Lorraine Ryan."

"Stop teasing, Tom. You'll make me ashamed that I've broken my diet three days in a row."

"And three more days ahead. I caught a peek at all those cupcakes you packed in the food locker. Poor diet," he sighed dramatically, making her laugh.

"Davey loves them and I intend to serve them for breakfast, lunch, and dinner, to say nothing of a snack before bedtime. Davey has a sweet tooth, just like me."

"Don't let Sara hear you say that. You know what a strict regimen she follows in the kitchen. I swear, your sister even chews her food twenty times before swallowing. Exactly twenty, no more, no less."

"Oh, stop it, Tom. Sara's okay. She's just overorganized. Even as a little girl I can remember her saying, 'A place for everything; everything in its place.' "

"And does that include Andrew?"

"Yes, I suppose it does. It certainly includes Davey. She's his mother, of course she wants what's best for her son. Lucky Sara, she's got the best material to work with. Davey is the most remarkable, resilient child I've ever known."

Tom looked ahead through the windshield, anticipating a left-hand turn several blocks ahead. "Andrew is the one who surprises me," Tom admitted. "I'd always thought of him as the absent-minded professor, oblivious to everything except mathematical theories—you know, a little sloppy, disorganized, forgetful. I would think he'd balk at Sara's 'organization,' as you call it."

"Oh, Andrew's all right. He's really a dear. It's just that he's *too* comfortable, *too* secure, and Sara is responsible for that. I don't think it would occur to him to rock the boat and make a fuss. After all, if he's happy, he thinks everyone is."

"Unfortunately, that doesn't hold for his son. Davey's a damn sweet kid, Lorrie, but he's been overprotected, overorganized, and raised strictly by the book. I remember when Sara couldn't keep a nursemaid while she taught at the college, because no one could adhere to her stringent schedules. Time to get the baby up, time to feed him, time for a bath—Christ! A living automaton."

"That's just because you came from a family of four children, and every time your poor mother even tried to set a time for dinner she had a mutiny on her hands."

Tom smiled, thinking of his three brothers and their noisy, happy home. "And Dad was a hell-raiser too. I'll tell you, if Mom ever tried some of Sara's tactics, he would have straightened her right out."

"And how would he do that?"

"By getting her pregnant again, of course."

"Chauvinist!" Lorrie laughed.

"Seriously, hon. I've got a feeling we should go easy with Davey. I'm as crazy about the kid as you are, but something tells me Sara doesn't totally approve of our influence over her son. Andrew's a great guy, but he wouldn't stand in Sara's way if she suddenly decided to put an end to our relationship with David."

Lorrie tossed her light blonde head and slid her five-foot height down on the soft vinyl seat. "I should argue with you, but even if she is my sister, I know you're right about her. I don't know Sara as well as I should. She was nearly fifteen years old when I was born. That's quite a gap for sisters to bridge. We've only become close during these last few years since Davey's been born. Even then, Andrew and Sara kept changing posts at colleges all over the country, and I was busy with medical school."

Carefully executing a left-hand turn, Tom glanced at his side-view mirror. "All this business with the drug racket in Florida has put a crimp in Sara's style. Especially since it was plastered all over the news. It's difficult to picture Andrew as the lead witness, isn't it? Actually, he's a hostile witness since he had to be subpoenaed to come forward. It's going to be a rough few days for him, I can assure you. He's not going to like being crossexamined on the witness stand. Lester Weinberg is representing the syndicate, and he's not exactly your typical pussy-cat lawyer. When he faces Andrew on the stand, he's going to do whatever he can to rip apart his testimony."

"Are you speaking as a lawyer now?"

"Damn straight, I am. There's a lot at stake here, Lor. More than just a penny-ante thug threatening a kid entangled in the rackets. That thug is a known connection with the syndicate, and if the government can pin this murder on him it will lead to other important convictions."

"Poor Andrew. Sara has certainly been stalwart, especially since I know she doesn't even like live-in help. Having those FBI agents under foot all the time must be very trying."

"Did I tell you that Andrew told me Sara had one of those agents removed from the case? She refused to allow him in the house. Seems the man took off his jacket and Davey saw him with his shoulder holster and gun."

"Can you blame her? Did Andrew say whether or not Davey commented on the gun? He doesn't know anything about the trial or Andrew's part in it, you know."

"I know. Andrew didn't say if Davey noticed the gun. But you can bet if he had, that little tiger would have been full of questions, and we would have heard about it. The point that I'm trying to make is that Sara is so unforgiving. She could have spoken to the agent and told him to keep his jacket on. But no, first thing she has to do is make a mountain out of a molehill and get the man reassigned. I can imagine she cut him to ribbons first before she called his superiors. Must have made him feel terrible."

"Tom, you don't know that. It's your imagination working overtime. Sara only wants what's best for Davey and you know it."

"Yes, I know, and that's what bothers me. Sara demands perfection, and she sits as both judge and jury. Honey, your sister would turn on anyone who didn't live up to her standards, and she'd do it ruthlessly, without conscience, all in the name of what's best for her son. Or her husband, for that matter."

"And you think Sara finds us short of her standards, is that it?" Lorrie's voice held a slight tremor.

Tom reached out and took her hand, picking it up and pressing it against his lips. "Sometimes I do, honey. And then sometimes I just get the feeling that she's jealous of anyone having a place in Davey's or Andrew's life besides herself. Be careful, honey, don't let yourself get hurt. No matter how much Davey means to you."

There were tears in Lorrie's blue eyes. "I know, I know. It's just that sometimes I feel as though Davey is my own child. Don't lecture me, Tom. I've heard your arguments for adopting a child. It's just that I don't feel I'm ready."

Damning himself for upsetting her, Tom made an attempt at cheerfulness. "We're here, wife o'mine. And if there's one thing you *should* be ready for, it's facing that sister of yours so early in the morning."

Davey Taylor kept vigil at the front windows, waiting for the first sight of the long motor-home coming down the street. The vehicle turned the corner, a white and green RV with a wide expanse of tinted windows and gold decals that proclaimed it was "King of the Road." "They're here! They're here!" he shouted excitedly, hurrying into the dining room with Duffy chasing at his heels.

Andrew and Sara Taylor sat at the table with their morning coffee. "Well, get over to the door and help Mr. Sanders let them in," Andrew smiled as he put down his mug. "Mr. Sanders knows they're coming."

Davey raced to the front door and almost ran headlong into Stuart Sanders at his usual post in the foyer.

"Hey, little buddy, what's your hurry?" Sanders asked, well aware of Davey's excitement over his first camping trip.

"Aunt Lorrie and Uncle Tom are here to take me camping and to the zoo! I'm going to sleep in the RV and cook outside and everything!" His bright blue eyes shone, and a heightening flush colored his baby-round cheeks.

"So I hear," Sanders said jovially, keeping a professionally watchful eye on the RV as it pulled into the Taylors' wide driveway.

"Let them in, Mr. Sanders, they're taking me camping!" Davey pleaded.

"Now, just a minute, Davey. Wait till your uncle gets around to the door, and I'll let them in together." Sanders had his keys ready to insert into the double locks. As a matter of routine, he had already unsnapped the flap on his shoulder holster although, as per his instructions, it was done in such a way that Davey didn't notice.

Tom Ryan joined his wife on the front steps and waited for the door to open. He was uneasy at his in-laws' home ever since the FBI agents had come. Christ, what a way to live! Monitored and watched. Unable even to open the door without a security check.

"Hurry up, Mr. Sanders," Davey urged.

At last the barrier between himself and his aunt and uncle was down and he threw himself at his aunt's legs, hugging her tightly. "Are you going to take me? Huh? Did you come for me?"

Lorrie laughed as she knelt to hug her nephew. "You bet! Are you all packed and ready to go?"

"Boy, am I ever ready, Aunt Lorrie. I've been ready since before it got light out. Duffy was ready before that too. We're both ready. Look, Aunt Lorrie, I got new sneakers, my first pair," he said holding out his foot. "Hug me again, you smell good."

Lorrie laughed as she glanced over her shoulder at her husband. "You see, it was worth all the money you spent for the perfume. The little guy here says I smell good."

"Then it was worth every cent I paid for it," Tom replied. "How's it going, sport, you all set for our big trip?" He ruffled Davey's hair. Uncle Tom smelled good too, but it was a different smell, an outside smell. Smells were important; they could tell you things. Duffy smelled everything and could find her way if she got lost.

"Where are your mom and dad, Davey?" Aunt Lorrie asked, looking around.

[48]

"In the dining room. Here they come now," Davey said quietly as he moved slightly to remove himself from his Aunt Lorrie's embrace. Duffy scampered between his legs, knocking him slightly off balance. Tom caught him with one hand by the shoulder and held firm till the little boy was steady on his feet.

Sara Taylor's eyes wore a guarded look as she stared at her sister and brother-in-law. "You're right on schedule," she smiled. She offered her cheek for Lorrie's kiss and stepped aside so her husband could shake hands with Tom.

Davey watched the family scene closely. Some day he would be tall like Uncle Tom and Daddy, and he would shake hands. But he wouldn't wait till no one was looking and then wipe them on his pants leg like his father did. Maybe his dad didn't like Uncle Tom's big hands that looked like his cinnamon toast in the morning with all the splotch-es. Freckles. He liked freckles almost as much as he liked good smells.

Joining the Taylors at the table while Davey went to his room for his bag, Lorrie stirred her coffee. "He's really excited, isn't he?"

"That he is!" Sara agreed. "I only hope he's this happy at bedtime. He's never spent the night away from us before, except for hospital stays."

"Now, Sis, don't go worrying. Tom and I will take good care of him, and if he has any problem tonight, he can just crawl in the bunk with us. Can't he, Tom?" she turned to her husband.

"There you go, setting up obstacles again. I'm going to get you alone in the wilderness, woman, if it's the last thing I do." Andrew laughed, appreciating Tom's licentious humor.

"What's the matter, Sis?" Lorrie asked, noticing Sara's frown.

"I don't want you taking David into bed with you," she said flatly. "Andrew and I have never done that, and frankly, we find it unacceptable."

"Hey, okay," Tom agreed, smoothing over the rough spot. "Your wish is my command, madame," he said gallantly.

"It might be rough on him, being away from home for the first time, Sara. What harm . . ."

"No, Andrew. I won't hear of it. David is our son and we must do what we think best."

"I understand, Sis. If you say no, then it's no. I don't anticipate any problem, anyway. He'll probably be so worn out, he'll go to sleep right after supper."

Tom Ryan watched his wife smooth Sara's ruffled feathers. He didn't like it when she had to ingratiate herself with her sister this way, but he knew she only did it to prevent Sara's acting to come between her and Davey. Lorrie loved the boy. A familiar sadness crept up on Tom when he thought of Lorrie and Davey and the love they shared. It was a love Lorrie should be sharing with her own children. As if reading his thoughts, Sara stood up and moved from the table, returning with a small box and set it before her sister. "Here's Davey's medication. Keep it refrigerated. His usual time is at noon. That makes it easy to remember." A hint of a frown drew her brows together.

"Understood. Don't worry, will you? I promise not to forget. As a matter of fact, Tom has already set the alarm on his watch for noon."

"I know I shouldn't worry, but I do. Davey's been doing so well, and the doctors say it's mainly due to the strict regimen we adhere to. Last month he had another test for antibodies, and he's still within the two point range. As far as we're concerned, that's great. He could possibly go on using the antigen for a long time to come. Perhaps by then, please God, they'll have come up with something better to help people like Davey."

"I don't get it. What's all this about antibodies?" Tom asked Andrew, always interested in the most recent finding on hemophilia. The single sorrow of his life was that he and Lorrie had agreed never to have children because she also carried the gene. Even if they were to have a girl, the child would be a carrier.

"It all has to do with the body's natural rejection of a foreign substance," Andrew explained. "In approximately eight percent of all hemophiliacs, an antibody will develop with specificity against Factor VIII. That means for the rest of their lives the antigen is useless. On the best authority, by using only the freshest globulin and adhering to a strict time schedule, the antibody build-up could almost be avoided. Not always, but almost."

"You see, Tom," Lorrie interjected, "AHG is more or less a replacement for the factor in Davey's blood that his body doesn't manufacture on its own. In itself, the AHG is an antigen and elicits an antibody response. With careful regulation the odds can be switched to Davey's favor."

Tom nodded. He knew that Davey was a Class Two hemophiliac, and with AHG Davey could almost live a normal life. He would be free of the spontaneous bleeding beneath the skin and into the joints that would result from a minor trauma such as a spill from his tricycle or a skinned knee. It also lessened the danger of any necessary surgery or something as normal as the loss of a baby tooth. Class One hemophiliacs really had a rough time of it with the possibility of spontaneous intramuscular bleeding, bleeding into the subcutaneous tissues, involvement with the gastrointestinal tract and even intracranial bleeding into the brain. A Class Three hemophiliac, the mildest form, was someone whose bleeding became uncontrolled during major surgery or dental operations. While their clotting time might be prolonged, it wasn't usually critical. In all cases, the antigen, AHG, could produce a miracle, but not if antibodies existed to cancel out the refined Factor VIII. "So this two-point range of Davey's is good, right?"

"It would be better if he hadn't any antibody development at all," Andrew explained. "But everyone's tolerance is different. The doctors feel that the lower it is the better. But he needs regular checkups. Prolonged discontinuance of AHG could shoot that level up, especially if there's a disproportionate amount of stress present. That's when all systems are go, as far as the body is concerned. Adrenalin flow is greater, the heart pumps faster—it's very involved. There are so many variables."

"Well, don't worry about Davey this weekend. We'll take care of him, won't we, honey," Tom smiled at his wife, warming to the loving smile she returned. "And we've got some really great plans for the next two days. Has Lorrie told you about them?"

"I haven't had the chance," Lorrie said. "Listen, Sis, I want to clear it with you before we tell Davey. We're going to the Philadelphia zoo today and plan to spend the best part of the day there. Then we come back into Jersey and spend the night at a camping ground that Tom's heard about. It has all the modern conveniences, etc. Then tomorrow morning, we take him to New York City. I've got tickets to the lazar show at the planetarium. How's that sound to you? Then back into Jersey where we'll spend tomorrow night, and home Wednesday afternoon."

"Sounds great!" Andrew interjected before Sara could find fault with the plans. He knew she would worry about Davey becoming overtired and overexcited.

"I suppose that will be all right."

"Of course it is, honey. Davey will love it. Only one word of warning, Tom, don't tell him about the planetarium until *after* he's slept the night through. It sounds so good I feel like playing hookey and coming along with you."

"Oh, no you don't," Lorrie scolded her brother-in-law playfully. "This is our chance to get Davey all to ourselves and you're not invited. We intend to treat that kid as though he were our own. Better."

"That's just the point, he's our child, not yours," Sara said, careful to avoid Andrew's warning glance. She knew he didn't think this was the right time to tell the Ryans they intended to reduce the amount of time they spent with Davey.

At a sound from the doorway they turned and saw Davey, Duffy clutched in his arms, his face crestfallen.

"What's the matter, son? Not having second thoughts, are you?" Andrew teased.

Davey sniffed. "It's Duffy. She doesn't want me to go. Look at her eyes, she's been crying."

"Duffy will be fine in the kennel," Sara told her son.

"Yeah! But I won't be all right without Duff." A tear slipped down the boy's cheek and his lower lip trembled. "If I can't have you and Dad with me, why can't I have Duffy?" He glanced shyly at his uncle, feeling like a crybaby yet unable to help himself.

"Come over here, Davey," Tom said gently. Slowly Davey obeyed, Duffy still held tightly in his arms. Head down, shoulders slumped, he stood before his uncle.

"That's one sorry-looking dog you've got there. Doesn't look to me as though she'd last a day without you. What do you say? Shall we bring her with us?"

Andrew began to protest, but he was quieted by a warning glance from Tom.

Immediately Davey brightened. "Really? Can I? Dad said she'd be too much trouble. Did you hear that, Duff? Uncle Tom said you can come with us! I'll go get her dog food. C'mon, Duff. We need your leash and your dish, too." Davey scampered off to the kitchen leaving his uncle to bear the weight of his parents' remonstrances.

"You're taking on a handful, Tom," Andrew warned.

"Where will Duffy stay while you're at the planetarium and the zoo?" Sara questioned, not liking a last-minute change in the plans she had carefully made.

"She'll stay right in the RV. It'll be just like being at home, and will only be a matter of hours at the most. She's been alone longer than that," Andrew said, his voice dropping as he remembered the long days when Davey required hospitalization, and the dog was without her young master.

Davey ran through the dining room carrying Duffy's red plastic dish and metal-link leash and a bag of dry dog food. He headed for the front door with Duffy scrambling after him, yipping fervor at the sight of her leash. "I'm going to tell Mr. Sanders that Duff's going with me!"

The bag of dog food tumbled out of Davey's little arms and fell with a clatter with the rest of Duffy's possessions. "Duff's coming too!" he told Stuart Sanders.

"That right? Good for Duffy! Hey, Davey, come over here. I've got something for you." Sanders withdrew something from his pocket. "It's a penlight, just like the Boy Scouts use." He flipped the switch and displayed the light against the palm of his hand.

"Gee! Thanks, Mr. Sanders."

"And see, it has a lariat attached so you can hook it through your belt loop like this." Sanders attached the penlight to the narrow belt loop and dropped it into Davey's pocket. "For your very first camping trip."

Davey's smile was the agent's reward. Shyly the youngster held out his hand just the way Sara had taught him. Then he was off to show his parents his surprise.

Over a second cup of coffee, Tom held Davey on his lap, a map of New Jersey spread on the table in front of him, pointing out the campground where they would be spending the night.

"Mom, you said I could call Digger on the CB to say goodbye. Can I tell him about my camping trip, Mom, can I? I'm going to tell him that we're staying at a campground right near Wild Adventure Park, and Uncle Tom says that at night you can hear the lions roar."

When Davey had left the room, Andrew turned to Tom. "That CB was a godsend. Best thing you could have given him."

"Well, Lorrie and I knew that Davey would be cooped up in the house for a while because of the trial in Florida and those guardian angels of yours, the FBI. When Lorrie mentioned the Junior CB Club for kids who are shut in for medical reasons, I thought of Davey. He really enjoys it, does he?" Tom smiled, gratified at having brought Davey some pleasure in what he thought of as Sara's sterile atmosphere.

"Enjoys it! He's crazy about it, and you should hear the way he's picked up the lingo! Sara and I explained that operating a citizen's band radio is a responsibility, and I'm proud to say that Davey doesn't abuse it. One half-hour each afternoon, that's all. Of course, Sara promised him he could call this friend he's made through the club. After all this is over we'll make arrangements for him to meet this 'Digger' in person."

"Digger? That's a funny handle. I've heard some of them are outrageous. What's Davey's?" Lorrie asked.

"Panda Bear," Sara answered, long white tapered fingers shredding the paper napkin near her cup. "It's the only one he came up with that Andrew and I would agree to. You should have heard some of the others."

"Then you approve of Davey belonging to this Junior CB Club?"

Sara faced her sister. "Generally. However, I don't approve of some of the 'lingo' as Andrew calls it. It goes against my grain. Whatever happened to the king's English?"

Elva and Cudge sat stiffly on the front seat of the Chevy pickup truck, fully aware of Lenny Lombardi's body behind them on the floor of the pop-up camper.

Cudge kept a careful eye for traffic signals and speed limits. This was definitely not the time to attract the attention of some cop who might demand an inspection of the camper. Cudge damned himself for painting the truck with wild colors and applying decals that just barely came within the limits of the law. Cops were always stopping vans and pickups, looking for drugs, and the wild decorations on the old Chevy just begged for police to get nosy, if only on principle.

The CB on the dashboard emitted its usual static, picking up a trucker here and there. He intended to keep the CB going all the while they were on the road, regardless of Elva's whining protests that she wanted to listen to her Elvis cassettes. If there were speed traps or any cops in the vicinity, he wanted to know while he could still do something about it.

They headed west out of Newark, traveling city streets. Elva had never seen Cudge drive so carefully. She knew better than to complain about the static coming from the CB that was giving her a roaring headache. This was no time for Cudge to lose his cool.

About nine o'clock they were going through the town of Montclair, two miles away from the Taylors house. As they entered the town, the transmission on the CB became clearer.

". . . that sounds great, Panda Bear. When will you get back? Over." A click.

"We'll be back Wednesday, Digger. How long will you stay in the hospital to get your legs fixed? Over." A click.

"Don't know, Panda Bear. Where are you camping? Over." A click. The second young voice sounded louder, clearer, coming through the speaker.

"Down at a campground near the Wild Adventure Amusement Park. Uncle Tom says you can hear the lions roar at night. Over."

"Too bad the park isn't open yet," the second voice said. "I know you'd like the ferris wheel they have there. Over." Click.

"That's what Uncle Tom says is so great. When the park is open, it's so crowded you can never get in; this time of year there won't be hardly anybody there. It'll be like being out all alone in the woods. Over."

"Have a great time, Panda Bear. Wish I could go with you rather than to the hospital. Over." The older, yet youthful, voice sounded mournful.

"Digger? I hope they fix your legs this time. Over."

"Yeah, me too. Gotta go now, Panda Bear. Have a great time for me. Out."

"I will, Digger. I know I will! Out."

The transmission ended and the static sounded again.

"Get that map out of the glove compartment, Elva." Cudge instructed, keeping his eye on the road. "Find out where that Wild Adventure place is."

Federal Bureau of Investigation Special Agent Stuart Sanders, stood outside Davey's door. He could hear the excited voices on Davey's CB. He still had some time. He would wait till the conversation was over before he said goodbye.

The agent looked into Davey's immaculate room, so different from his children's bedrooms. Where were the personal touches in this carefully planned room? Everything was expensive, from the porcelain clowns on the shelf to the leather-bound editions of Dickens. An interior decorator might find it in perfect taste, but to Sanders it seemed like a model room in a department store. Where were the bits and pieces of games that were standard in a kid's room? Where were the stubby crayons in coffee cans? Or the slipper without a mate that was a standard fixture in most children's bedrooms? Where were the comics and storybooks that took a kid on trips to fantasy land? He knew if he looked under the bed he would find nothing but a clean. vacuumed carpet. There would be no forgotten toys, no dirty pajamas, no pennies. Just a clean floor. As he watched the Yorkshire terrier nip at Davey's pant leg he thought, at least Duffy was real. Davey was real.

It was impossible, but the bed was already made. It annoyed him. His own kids never made their beds till five minutes before their mother came in from the office, and then all they did was throw the comforter up over the pillow. There was no life in this room. Sanders had a sudden urge to scoop up dog and boy and run to his own house with the noise and disorder that four kids made. He wanted to take the boy and the dog to Nancy, his wife. She would take one look at Davey and cradle him in her arms and croon some indistinguishable words that only kids understood. Nancy called it "mother magic." Disgust washed through him. This room, this kid, could use a double dose of Nancy.

The minute Davey broke his connection Duffy barked to let Stuart know it was all right to enter the room. Walking in, he held out his hand. "I came to say goodbye, Davey."

Manfully, Davey extended his hand. "It was nice of you to come up to see me and Duffy, sir."

Stuart Sanders squatted down till he was eye level with the little boy. "Listen, tiger, I hope you have a whale of a good time on your camping trip. Take good care of this bundle of dynamite," he said motioning to the dog.

"I will, sir. And, sir, thanks again for the flashlight. I have it in my jacket pocket so I can use it whenever I want."

Stuart stared into Davey's bright eyes. Despite the room, the kid would be all right. Stuart felt it in his guts. His eyes dropped to the needle marks on Davey's arms.

Davey grinned when he noticed Stuart staring at his arms. Playfully, he punched the agent on the arm. "I almost don't need them any more."

Suddenly, Stuart didn't want to leave. He had never in his life believed in premonitions or anything supernatural, but he was experiencing something now. And the dog, the dog was staring up at him with what Stuart would later describe as questioning eyes. "Davey, I'm going to give you a card that has my telephone number on it. If you ever want to talk to me or if you think I might able to help you sometime—you know, if you ever join the Scouts or something like that —you call me. It doesn't make any difference what time it is, day or night. If I'm not there, you tell my wife or kids who you are, and they'll get in touch with me."

"Sure, Mr. Sanders," David said taking the card and sticking it in his hip pocket. "Maybe you should give me two cards. I'll take this one with me, and I'll leave this one home in my desk."

Stuart got to his feet. He didn't know why but it was important for him to make the kid promise. "Promise me, Davey." Purposely he made his tone light.

Duffy barked sharply and Davey's tone was solemn. "I promise, Mr. Sanders. It should be really, really important for me to disturb you. Two really's, right, Mr. Sanders?"

One really, two really's, what the hell was this? Again, he forced a lightness to his voice he didn't feel. "I think you'll know when the time comes. I just don't want you to think that you're disturbing me. You call me whenever you think it's necessary. Listen, tiger, you got any money on you?"

Davey shook his head. "Mom and Dad said I don't need any money."

Sanders winced slightly. "I'm sure they're right, but when I was a kid, my dad always gave me a nickel to carry around. I think you should have some change. My dad always called it kid money. Here, take these three quarters."

Dutifully, Davey accepted the three quarters and put them down into his jeans pocket. The jangle sounded nice. "What should I use them for?"

Sanders shrugged. He grinned. "A licorice stick, a Popsicle, an all-day sucker." His face sobered. "Or you could make a phone call. When I was your age, a nickel could buy all those things. Today, with inflation, it costs a lot more. It's a going-away kind of present, Davey."

Duffy barked excitedly as Davey jangled the three coins in his pocket.

"It's a grand present, Mr. Sanders. I'll be careful when I spend it. I might not even spend it at all. I like the way it sounds in my pocket. I feel," he sought the right word, "rich."

Sanders laughed. "As long as you have money in your pocket, you'll never be poor. I have to go, tiger. You take good care of this pup, hear?" He choked a little as he tousled Davey's hair. "Don't you go chasing any squirrels when you get out in the woods, Duffy," he called over his shoulder.

Davey fell back on the bed, laughing as Duffy rolled on top of him. "We're rich, Duffy. I bet I could buy you the biggest bone in the whole world and still have some money left for a Popsicle."

"Got everything, sport? Ready to go? Your mom and dad have a plane to catch to Florida and we can't hold them up." Although Davey was aware that his parents were flying to Florida, Tom knew he wasn't aware of the reason. He had been told it was on school business.

"Yes, sir! Everything's ready. Right, Mom?"

"That's right, David." The emphasis was on the boy's Christian name. Tom knew he had committed another faux pas. Sara disliked nicknames like "sport" or "tiger," and she only allowed "Davey" out of deference to Andrew.

"You'd better be on your way, son," Andrew said, then turned to his brother-in-law. "His gear is on the front porch. Sanders took it out a while ago."

Sara, issuing last-minute instructions, was still talking when she pecked Davey on the cheek. Her hand lingered a moment on his shoulder before she stepped back.

Andrew Taylor clapped Davey gently on the back and patted his head. "I want you to be a good boy for your aunt and uncle, and don't give them a bit of trouble."

"And keep Duffy out of trouble," Sara instructed. "We'll see you in a few days. All of you, have a good time," she added quietly.

Lorrie looked at Tom. They had been dismissed. It was Sara's inimitable style. She didn't just say hello or goodbye like other people. Not Sara. She welcomed you for the moment and then when some invisible clock in her head reached the appropriate time, she dismissed you. Lorrie wondered as she ushered Davey out the door if Sara ever dismissed Andrew that way, and what he thought of it. Or even if he was aware of it. Sara was her sister and she loved her dearly. Still, she *was* different.

At the bottom of the porch steps, Davey turned. The front door was closing and he could see Mr. Sanders waving to him. Quickly, he brought up his arm and waved back. The nylon windbreaker whispered with the motion. Duffy woofed.

Bright, blue eyes searched the long panes beside the front door and then scanned the living-room windows for a last look at his parents. There was no shadow behind the lace curtains.

"Don't help me up, Uncle Tom. I can do it myself."

"Wasn't going to help you, sport. I did give some thought to giving Duffy a boost, but you're on your own, fella." Tom's eyes met his wife's amused gaze and he grinned.

"Us guys are good at reading each other's minds, right, Uncle Tom? Duff's waiting for you to boost her."

"In you go, Duffy. Say, you've never seen the inside of the RV before, have you? Well, sport, what do you think?"

Davey looked around, eyes widening in awe. "It's a house! A real house! On wheels!" Tom smiled. He was proud of the recreation vehicle and had selected each accessory with great deliberation. The thick, grass-green carpeting added softness to the hard-surfaced, utilitarian appliances. The bench seats, which also served as a dining booth when the table was extended, were upholstered in soft brown vinyl, and the kitchen stove and refrigerator were avocado green. The first place Davey asked to see was the bunk where he would sleep. Laughing, Tom showed him how the bench seats flipped over to form a foam-rubber bed.

"Where are you and Aunt Lorrie going to sleep?" Davey questioned, looking around for a big, king-sized bed like his parents used.

"Back here, sport," Tom continued the tour, showing Davey a couch at the far end that served as a double bed.

"That's nice," the boy told him. "It's so small you and Aunt Lorrie get to hug each other all night long."

"Hear that, Lor? Remember, we can't disappoint the tiger."

"I heard. You sure you two don't have some kind of conspiracy going?"

"What's a conspiracy? Where's the bathroom?"

"Over here," Lorrie showed him the tiny space alloted for the toilet, sink, and a narrow shower stall. "Of course, if you have to use it, you'll have to tell us. Then Uncle Tom will pull over to the side of the road. You mustn't use it while the RV is moving, understand?"

"Right, sport. If I have to swerve or we go over a bump or something, you'll bounce right off the john and we'll catch you with your pants down."

Davey giggled at the picture his uncle created in his mind. "I know, you told me that the other day. And I'm not to move around or anything while we're moving. Right?"

"Right. Okay, Lorrie, get out your check-list. I'll get the tiger here buckled into his seat." As Tom secured the safety belt across Davey, who was in the swivel seat behind the driver's, he told him, "I want you to know this expedition is in no way a Mickey Mouse production. This is a first-class, grade-A, super-colossal expedition to the Philadelphia zoo and other points of interest. Any comments?"

"No, sir," Davey responded with mock solemnity.

"First things first. All present and accounted for."

"Right," Lorrie giggled as she made a check on her paper.

"Davey's medicine. What time do you get your shot, fella?"

"You know I get it every day at noon. That makes it easy to remember."

"Right. We've all got that straight. I've got the alarm on my watch set for twelve noon. Can you handle the responsibility of reminding us when you hear the alarm go off, Dave?"

"Yes, sir. If you don't believe me, ask Duffy."

"I believe you, Dave. I know that you don't lie. You do know what a lie is, don't you?"

Davey thought for a moment. He squinted for a second before he replied. He really liked it when Uncle Tom called him Dave. It almost made him a grown-up. Another almost. "It's when you don't say something all the way." He waited, hardly daring to breathe. Was that the right answer? It must be, Aunt Lorrie was smiling. Aunt Lorrie smiled a lot, especially when she looked at him.

"You've got it, Dave. That's close enough. Always tell the truth and you have nothing to fear. Okay, now, I'm going to start up this engine and we're going to be on our way. Dog food! Did you remember to bring dog food?"

"A whole box. It has as many packages as I have fingers, plus two more. Duffy eats two a day."

"Who's for gumdrops?" Lorrie asked as she fished in her purse for a cellophane package.

"A bit early for candy, isn't it?" Tom asked grinning at the hopeful look he saw on Davey's face in the rear-view mirror.

"No sir, Uncle Tom. I brushed all my sweet teeth before I left. Duffy can't have any or she'll get spoiled. I'll eat hers."

"This is a special treat for the first day of vacation, so gumdrops are the first order of the day. We'll divvy up evenly with Davey getting Duffy's portion," Lorrie giggled.

"Sounds fair to me," Tom said as he expertly guided the RV through traffic and out to the New Jersey Turnpike.

Davey chattered excitedly as the RV ate up the miles on the crowded highway. He was having such a good time just sitting here in the RV with Uncle Tom and Aunt Lorrie. Once he thought of his mother and father as he popped a gumdrop into his mouth. Were they on the airplane yet? Were they thinking about him the way he was thinking about them? He chewed methodically, savoring each morsel of the gooey candy. He listened with half an ear to Tom telling Lorrie about the Philadelphia zoo. He had never been to a zoo before. His CB buddy, Digger, told him it was "humungus," whatever that meant. It must be good, he reasoned, because his buddy got all excited just telling him about it. He said it was almost as good as being there just telling Davey so he would know what to expect. A giggle erupted in his throat. Panda Bear going to a zoo.

A large white dome with red lettering caught his eye as the RV slowed to move with the traffic. "What's that, Aunt Lorrie?"

"The dome? It says, Cherry Hill. That's the name of a town next to Philadelphia. That's just a kind of welcome for travelers. It lets them know Cherry Hill is the next turnoff. Did you know Mohammed Ali, the prizefighter, is said to have a house in Cherry Hill?"

Davey shrugged. Fighting didn't make sense to him. Sometimes adults were strange. He cuddled Duffy closer. They were always saying don't fight, and then the man who lived in Cherry Hill went on television and fought with another man for money. His attention was diverted when a battered truck painted with bright designs neared the RV. Pressing his face to the glass, he stared at the pickup and saw it was pulling a big square box on wheels. The glare on the windshield made it impossible to see who was sitting in the front. It didn't really matter who it was. He would never see them again once Uncle Tom turned off the road for the zoo. Gradually, the pickup moved up till it was almost side by side with the RV. On closer inspection he saw that the pickup truck was pulling a pop-up trailer. Davey watched the truck as it moved still closer to the RV. A man and a woman were sitting in the front. Pressing his face so close to the glass that it steamed, he stared at the woman; she looked scared. His eyes widened when he saw the man reach out and slap her across the face. He swallowed hard as he clutched Duffy.

"Another five minutes and we'll be getting off the turnpike. Are you excited, Dave?" Tom asked heartily.

"Uh-huh," Davey mumbled as he slid another gumdrop into his mouth. The woman in the pickup wasn't like Aunt Lorrie or his mother. She was more like Millicent, the babysitter who used to watch him when his parents went out. Only she wasn't pretty like Millicent. And Millicent would never look scared like that. And Millicent would never cry like the woman in the truck. Millicent said only babies cried. Millicent was tough; she said you had to be tough to survive. When he told his mother about Millicent's ideas, he had gotten a new babysitter named Mrs. Goodeve.

Davey's golden eyebrows drew together as he stared pointedly at the girl in the truck. She stared across at him through the glass before she wiped at her eyes with the back of her hand.

"Get ready, everyone, here we go, exit four. Time to get off and make tracks for the zoo."

"Yah," Lorrie chortled happily. "Monkey cage first. What about you, Davey, what do you want to see first?"

Davey turned, trying to get still another look at the pickup and the girl with the white face. He was too late. The pickup didn't turn off behind Uncle Tom but kept moving with the traffic, gradually easing into the spot Uncle Tom had vacated with his turnoff. "Elephants," he said. Why did the man hit the girl? What could she have done? She had just been sitting, looking out the window. "She should have hit him back," he whispered in Duffy's ear. "She was just looking out the window. I saw her, she didn't do anything."

As the Ryans' RV kept abreast of him, Balog caught a look at it. Out of the wide, scenic window he saw a blonde kid holding up his pooch. There were wet nose-prints on the glass. He was driving carefully. There was no way he wanted a trooper pulling him over. Damn, he wasn't even going to sneeze for fear his foot would jam down on the accelerator. Slow and easy was the way to do it. No wise-ass trooper with polished sunglasses was going to chew him out for anything, real or imagined.

He didn't know what made him remember: he hadn't thought of it in such a long time now. Maybe it was that dog he'd just seen the kid holding up to the window. He didn't like dogs, never had. At least not since old Peggy, anyway.

He'd only been a kid himself, little Edmund Balog then. Just a little kid not even seven years old yet, trying to find justice for the violence he'd been forced to commit. Justice had finally arrived, years later, when his brother Norman was killed in the jungles of 'Nam. But it was too late for Edmund Balog.

It had been a hot day in the middle of August. He remembered he'd been playing in the shade of a tree, pushing a wheelless truck through the dust.

Mom was in the house, bending over the scrub board, doing laundry. "It doesn't matter much if you're poor," she always told them, "but it does matter if you're dirty." Looking back, he could never picture her without a scrub rag or a mop in her hands. If hard work and strong brown soap were money, they would have been millionaires.

"Norman! Norman!" their mother called as Edmund's fifteen-year-old brother strolled into the yard from his paper route. "Grandma wants you to go over there right away." The back-door screen slammed shut. "You know what she wants." Her tone was grim, making Edmund lift his head in puzzlement.

"C'mon. You come with me," Norman said, stirring the dust with his torn sneaker, making a cloud of grit that blew right into Edmund's face.

"Whatcha do that for?" he choked, spitting out grit.

" 'Cause. You coming or not?"

"Do I have to? I was just playing deliveryman."

"Yeah, sure. You can play later. We're going to have more fun than that. Come on."

Edmund dropped the battered truck and stood up. He'd go with Norman whether he wanted to or not. It wasn't that he was afraid not to go; Mom was right there in the kitchen, and Norm wouldn't dare be a bully now. And maybe Grandma had some cold lemonade and cookies. Old Peggy would be there, and she would let him pet her.

"Jeez!" Norm whistled. "Does Mom know what you look like? I'll bet she don't." Norman's eyes traveled the short distance from the top of Edmund's head to the ground. Little, skinny legs stuck out from dust-stained short pants coated with a fine layer of gray. And down one leg ran a dry rivulet of white into the top of a grimy sock. "Crissakes, how many times do you have to be told to shake that thing off after you take a pee. You always have to have a few drops left to run down your leg or you ain't happy, huh? Let's get out of here before Mom sees you. She'd never let you out on the street looking like that."

Edmund followed Norman down the driveway. Grandma's house was only a block away. The heat from the pavement burned through his worn sneakers, making him take short, skipping steps. Norman pretended not to notice but walked ahead, never allowing his little brother to catch up to him. With the vanity of a teenager, Norman believed the whole world was watching him, and he didn't want to be associated with a scrawny brat with stains running down his legs. He never would have taken Edmund with him if it weren't for some perverse wish to have a witness. What Grandma wanted him to do wasn't going to be easy, but what the hell, why not show off for his kid brother?

Grandma was sitting on the porch waiting for them, her clean, starched housedress moving stiffly against her legs as she rocked in her chair. On the table near her elbow, Edmund was disappointed to see there was no frosty pitcher of lemonade or plate of cookies. But he noticed the way Grandma's hand drooped over the arm of her chair, petting old Peggy. Her crooked fingers hardly lifted from old Peg's head before she brought them down again.

Old Peggy leaned against the side of the rocking chair, her eyes glazed with contentment as the old woman's hand stroked and rubbed. The dog was old, a muttish mixture of Boston bull and "parts unknown," Grandma always said. Her black-and-white-blotched body had grown fat over the years, and even moving made old Peg breathe hard.

"You know what I want you to do, Norman?" Grandma asked. "You ain't going to take Edmund along, are you?"

"Nah, I'll take him home first, Gram. You sure you want to do this?"

"It's gotta be done, son. She's too old and crippled to take care of herself any more. Can't hardly get up the back steps when I let her out, and I'm too old and crippled to carry her. Grandpa's twenty-two is inside on the kitchen table and there's a box of bullets. So is the shovel."

Edmund's head perked up when she mentioned the gun. Then his eyes went to old Peggy and back to Grandma, whose watery blue eyes seemed brighter than usual.

When Norman bounded out of the house, he was carrying a dull, black rifle, and the box of ammo was rattling in his hand. "You think she'll follow us, Gram? Or should I get a wagon or something?" He thrust the garden spade at Edmund, forcing him to carry it.

"She'll follow. Once you carry her off the porch." Grandma's voice was hard-edged and brittle. "You take her out in the fields and do what you have to do. Just make a good job of it, you hear? Peggy's been a good dog and I want her to go out easy." The old woman fixed a stare on Norman, making the youth tremble. "When you bring the rifle back, there'll be a dollar waiting for you."

Norman carried Peg off the porch, and just as Grandma predicted, the old dog followed them down the street. Once, when Edmund looked back, Grandma was gone, and the chair was rocking wildly back and forth as though she'd just left it.

Denville was a small farming community and it was not unusual to see a boy walking down the street with a rifle over his shoulder. The fields where they were heading were only a few blocks away, where the town broke off into swampy meadow before butting up against the new highway. Less than five minutes' walk was dragged into half an hour because of Peggy's slow and painful gait. Obedient by nature and knowing the boys since they were born, Peggy followed, a vague light of anticipation in her clouded eyes, as though she remembered days long past when she had raced into these same fields to romp and play and even, perhaps, pursue a romance that would lead to one of the seven litters she had borne in unswerving dedication to the propagation of her kind.

"Right here's okay," Norman told an unusually silent Edmund. The tall grasses had given way to a bare knoll that was just on the perimeter of shade from several scrub oaks. "You can start digging."

"Huh? I don't want to dig, Norm. I don't want to dig a grave for old Peg."

"Stop your sniveling. When the hell are you gonna grow up? When I was your age, I was already a man! Now start digging."

Edmund didn't point out that at fifteen Norman was still not a man. In his little-boy logic, anyone who was older than himself was what he claimed to be.

When the first few attempts at digging were unsuccessful, Norman grabbed the shovel from Edmund and started the hole himself, his greater weight pushing the spade deep into the loamy earth and turning it over. Old Peggy sat nearby watching, her pink mottled tongue lolling from the side of her mouth as she panted in the heat. Instinctively, she painfully lifted herself and sought the deeper shade of the scrub oaks.

"You take it from here," Norm told him, using his forearm to brush the trickling sweat from running into his eyes. It was hot, damn hot! He stooped to pick up the rifle, the bullets making a rattling noise in the half-empty box.

"I don't want to dig a hole for Peggy! I want to go home."

"You ain't going nowhere. Pick up that shovel." Norman's voice held a threat Edmund didn't dare challenge. "Now dig or else you're going in that hole *with* Peggy. Mom'll be glad to have one less mouth to feed, or ain't you thought of that?"

Edmund retrieved the spade. Holding it awkwardly, he tried to imitate Norman's action with the tool. There wasn't a doubt in his mind that Norman would use the rifle on him if he didn't do as he was told. In the past, the difference in their ages or the fact that Edmund was his little brother hadn't stopped Norman from bullying and beating him.

A strong breeze rolled through the tall rye grasses that were scorched yellow beneath the summer sun, making the stalks bend and ripple like the waves at the seashore. The sky was blue and scrubbed, not a cloud in sight. As the little boy worked he choked back his fear of the rifle pointed so casually at his back and his deeper dread of what remained to be done.

Slowly, shovelful by shovelful, the yawning hole grew. It was wider than it was deep and Edmund wondered how much more had to be dug to hold old Peggy's carcass. "Ain't this enough?" he pleaded with Norman.

"I'll tell you when it's enough. Any asshole can see that ain't big enough to hold her. Keep digging."

Eyes tearing, nose running, Edmund wailed as he worked, ever conscious of Norman's heavily voiced threats to put him in the hole with Peggy. It wasn't hard for Edmund to believe he would. They were a poor family, Mom always complained about the rising prices of food.

By the time the hole had grown to Peggy's size, Edmund had convinced himself that Norman wouldn't even get scolded for shooting his little brother and putting him in the hole with Grandma's dog. Norman was the older, the favorite, the one able to work, while he, Edmund, was only a little boy, good for nothing and wanted by no one.

"Quit your crying for crissakes! My trigger finger's getting real itchy! Get the dog over here and put her in the hole."

Edmund turned and faced Norman, disbelief twisting his features. "You're not going to put her in the hole before she's dead, are you, Norm? You wouldn't do that, would you, Norm?"

"It ain't easy lifting a dead body. It's easier to put her in and then shoot her. Do what I say."

[67]

Wails of banshees howled in his head as Edmund looked at Peggy. She was lying under the tree in the shade, her clouded eyes looking up expectantly, waiting for him to come and pet her. "I can't."

"You'll do it, or else in the hole you go with her. Crissakes, am I supposed to do everything?"

"I . . . I can't carry her. She's too heavy."

"Did I say you had to carry her," Norm taunted. "She likes you, she'll come for you. Just call her. When she gets near the hole, just shove her in. Hurry up, I can't wait here all day."

The name formed on his lips, but it refused to sound in his throat. Only the impatient tapping of Norman's foot and the rattle of the ammo box evoked the sound. "Peg, here Peggy. Atta girl."

The old dog lifted her head, perhaps some memory of happier times in these fields spurring her forward. She practically dragged her hind-quarters for a few feet until she gained her legs. Her objective was the little boy who had always been so kind to her, and she anticipated his scratching her head and her belly and she would reward him with slurpy kisses on his cheeks.

"You're being mean, Norm. I don't want to stay here and see this. I don't want old Peggy to be dead!"

"Shut up, I have to do it. Grandma said she's old and needs to be put out of her misery and that's what I'm going to do."

"But Grandma said you were supposed to take me home first."

"You need to learn how to be a man, Edmund, and I'm the guy to teach you. Now get her over there!"

"All you're doing is trying to show off! You just need somebody to see what a big man you are."

Norman's eyes narrowed. The rifle was raised and trained on Edmund. The little boy had come too close to the truth. Norman would never be able to go through with it unless someone was there to see to it. Even if that someone was only his little brother who always had a pee streak running down his dirty leg. "You got your choice. Do what I say or you go with her."

Whimpering, Edmund called to Peggy, encouraging her to come to him. He stood in the hole he had dug, little more than a foot and a half deep. He patted her head, and Peggy gave him a great wet-nosed slurp.

"Take it easy, old Peg. I ain't going to hurt you." He lifted an accusing glance to Norman.

"Pull her in there and hurry up. I got somewhere to go later."

"Where ya going, Norm?" Edmund tried to distract his brother.

"The movies and, no, you can't come. I already got somebody I want to take."

"That what you're gonna do with Grandma's dollar? What movie you gonna see?"

"Shut up, will ya, Edmund. Just get that damned dog in there. And remember what a big favor I would be doing for Mom if I didn't drag you home with me."

Edmund called to Peggy, bringing her close enough to get a grip around her heavy belly. It was true what Norm said about Mom. Hadn't he heard her say time and again that if it wasn't for Edmund she could be living her own life, now that Norman was all grown?

He pulled Peggy across the few feet to the edge of the hole, easing her in. She seemed frightened by this unfamiliar treatment. To Edmund it seemed as though she were accusing him, because she knew what was going to happen to her.

Norman loaded the rifle with the old shot. The gun was over forty years old, and the bullets at least half that age. The yellow cardboard ammo box was dry and literally crumbling in his fingers. "Get out of the way if you don't want to get hit," he warned Edmund.

Norman raised the rifle to his shoulder and then to firing position. He'd learned about guns from his mother's brother who had taken him hunting several times. He looked down the sight, aiming for Peggy's head. The dog watched him, her half-blind eyes trustful. The gun wavered in the boy's trembling hands. He was icy cold in the full heat of the August sun. Slowly, he shifted the barrel, aiming again down the sight.

The shot broke the stillness. Edmund, who had moved behind Norman, covered his head with his arms, eyes squeezed shut, and a dribble of urine rolled down his leg. As the sound of gunfire split the air, he screamed louder than the gunshot, so loud he almost didn't hear the noise that would kill Peggy.

Silence.

"Damn! Goddamn!" he heard Norman curse. He turned and looked into the hole.

There lay Peggy, whining in shock and pain. A thin slit of red marked the top of her head where the bullet had grazed it. Her sides still heaved with life.

"Damn! Damn!" Again came the report of a shot, making Edmund clap his hands over his ears. He screamed again.

"Die, damn you! Die!"

The second shot had nearly pierced Peggy's side, but still she lived, bleeding, in pain.

"It's the bullets!" Norm shouted, arms waving, face red with rage. "The goddamned bullets! They're too old! They're from the Civil War, for crissakes!" He fumbled with the rifle, reloading.

"No! No!" the scream was Edmund's. "Don't do it! Tell Grandma the bullets are too old! Don't do it!" He ran toward Norman. Reaching for the gun barrel he pulled it away and pointed it toward the ground away from Peggy.

"Get out of here! Let go! Let go!" Norman's outrage and frustration were directed at Edmund. Greater weight and strength subdued the little boy, leaving him flat on his back, breathless.

"Don't do it, Norm. Don't do it," he panted, finding breath and voice.

"I have to! I need that dollar!" The gun sounded again and again.

Edmund lay on the ground, his head buried in his arms. His eyes were squeezed shut. Nobody needed Peggy anymore, just like they didn't need him!

"Sonovabitch!" Edmund was aware of something falling on his arm and then onto the ground. It was the ammo box. Empty.

Slowly, full of blood-freezing dread, he sat up and looked.

Peggy lay in the hole he had dug, her head and side bleeding. Her eyes were closed as though in sleep, or death. Still, so still. Then she emitted a high-pitched, whistling whine, and she raised her head.

"Cover her over." Norman's voice was flat—void of emotion and heavy with authority.

Edmund stood there, unable to bear the sight of old Peggy's pain. But she was alive. Alive! And there were no more bullets. Norman couldn't kill her now.

"Didn't you hear me? I said to cover her up!"

Not understanding, Edmund looked at his older brother. Cover her up? With what? Was she cold?

"The dirt, asshole. Fill in the grave!"

"Norman, she ain't dead. She don't have to be covered up. Not like Daddy. She ain't dead."

"No, she only wishes she was! Look at her! Goddamned bullets, older than moldy cheese! Do what I said, I can't stand here all day. I told Grandma I'd bury her proper and that means covering her up! Do it right and I won't tell Mom how you peed in your pants again."

Norman slung the rifle over his shoulder, crushing the yellow ammo box beneath his foot as he turned to leave. Peggy's whine sent a shiver up his back. Damn bullets were so old they couldn't pierce the dog's tough old hide. He decided he'd better get over to Grandma's and get that dollar before old Peggy pulled herself out of the hole and crawled back home.

"Norman! Don't go! Don't leave me here!" He clawed at Norman's back, pulling his shirt. "Look at her, Norm, she's hurt. Real bad!"

"That's your problem. If she had any sense she would have died so she wouldn't have to suffer. Let go!" He shrugged Edmund off violently, leaving the little boy sprawled on the dry, baked ground.

Edmund lay there for a long time. He didn't want to stay here, but he couldn't leave Peggy either. She'd always been a good dog, and Norman said she was suffering. He couldn't leave her alone to wonder why two boys that she'd played with and loved would do this to her.

A whine brought Edmund back to the grave. Peggy lifted her head with monumental effort, eyes glazed, yet seeing him. He wanted to crawl into the hole with her, hold her head, and tell her she was going to get better. The crumbling soil scratched his bare legs as he slid into the hole with Peggy. Her side was bleeding and so was her head. The blood, bright and red, flowed slowly and thickly. Low, barely audible groans sounded in her neck.

Tears streamed down Edmund's face. This shouldn't be; Peggy shouldn't have to suffer. Edmund was a country boy who'd seen how carrion crows could pick a body apart until it was a mass of shriveled skin and bare bones, and he didn't want that to happen to Peggy. Her head lay heavy in his hands. There was no place to pet her any more that wasn't sticky with blood.

Norman. Norman was bad! He'd just turned and walked away, gone to get the dollar from Grandma. And he'd probably tell her he'd made a good job of it and that it was all over. Only Edmund saw her suffering and heard her pained whines. Norman was bad!

His shirt was soaking wet with perspiration and his drawers felt uncomfortably wet. Pressure crowded the back of his brain at the injustice of it all. He must find a way to put Peggy out of her suffering.

Slowly Edmund's small hands closed around Peggy's neck. They were strong little hands, capable of holding Peggy still to keep her from fighting. Strong hands that could provide the relief from pain that the bullets had not.

It was Norman's neck Edmund wished he was holding. It was Norman's face he wanted to see before him, eyes dulled with pain, tongue lolling.

The deeper his anger grew, the greater became the pressure at the back of his skull. His little shoulders hunched to support the weight. The world grew black before his eyes and a pounding began in his brain, imparting to him a portion of power from the restless, ominous tread of hooves that belonged to the shapeless monster within him.

Crying, sobbing, his fingers tightened around Peggy's throat. Crying, squeezing, bellowing with the horror of it, Edmund brought Peggy through her agony into the sweet oblivion beyond.

He was shaking, with the deed he had done. He had killed old Peggy. There was a monster some place inside him; he knew it. It was big, thudding through his brain and giving him its strength and making him a killer.

He hated Norman. He hated Grandma. He even hated Peggy but most of all, he hated himself.

Over the years, little Edmund had become known as Cudge, a name that seemed to fit him. It had a brutal sound—as brutal as the man.

Cudge's hands tightened on the steering wheel. A beading of sweat dotted his upper lip. Unconsciously, his shoulders hunched, straining to support the weight inside his head. He had to get a grip on himself. Now wasn't the time to reflect on the past and remember and feel all over again. There were no rewards in memories.

"Why ain't you saying anything, Elva? It ain't like you to sit so quiet. You up to something or what? If you got any ideas at all about jumping out or taking off, forget it." His voice was mean and low.

"You told me to sit here and keep my mouth shut. Make up your

[72]

mind. Either you want me to talk or you want me to keep quiet." God, now why had she said that? She was so in tune with Cudge's voice that she knew exactly what his next move and statement would be. You did what Cudge said when Cudge said it, and you didn't ask questions. You didn't volunteer anything with Cudge either. What was wrong with her; why was she acting this way. Her stomach churned and she felt bile rise in her throat. She was afraid to stay with him and afraid to leave him. Fear of walking the streets, with no place to go at the end of the day, was worse than living with Cudge. Everyone needed someone, something—a place, that was theirs at the end of the day when darkness fell. She remembered only too well the darkness of the pantry where her father locked her in to punish her. She hated the dark and the creatures that came out in the dark. In a way Cudge was like one of the rats back in the cold water flat. His eyes were just as beady, his lips just as thin, his ears just as pointed.

Cudge ignored her; this was no time to let Elva get under his skin. He had to concentrate. "I want you to keep your eyes peeled for anything suspicious, like a trooper in an unmarked car, that kind of thing. Keep what wits you have sharp. If I get pulled over for any reason, you just sit there deaf, dumb, and blind. Don't open that mouth of yours. You got that, Elva?"

"Yeah, I'm watching. How am I supposed to spot a trooper in an unmarked car. They don't wear their trooper hats in plain cars. I might pick the wrong person and then you'll get mad," she whined.

"You can always tell a trooper because they wear those fancy polished sunglasses. I'm obeying all the traffic rules, so I think we're safe, but that's usually when something goes wrong. There's no way I could make a run for it in this old buggy. If we get caught, it's jail for both of us. You're an accessory and don't you ever forget it."

"I won't," Elva said in a relieved tone. She had to think about what she was going to do when they got to the Wild Adventure campgrounds. She knew she shouldn't stay with Cudge after this. Enough was enough. Even her fear of the dark and the creatures that prowled in the night wouldn't make her wind up as dead as Lenny, but Cudge could. She couldn't let him know what she was planning. The thought was so daring, so alien to her, that she broke into a cold sweat. Fear, it always came down to fear. If Cudge made her help dig the grave for

[73]

Lenny, she would bawl. And if he made the grave wider than Lenny, she would die on the spot; he wouldn't *have* to kill her.

"Damn you, Elva, didn't you see that trooper? What the hell is wrong with you? Look, in the next lane, that's a trooper or my name ain't Cudge Balog. When we get to the campgrounds, I'm going to teach you a lesson you'll never forget. Pay attention. I ain't gonna tell you a second time."

"He don't look like a trooper to me," Elva said defensively. "There's two kids in the back seat. Troopers don't ride with kids. I'm watching the best I can."

"Okay, okay. He could still be a trooper. Just because he had kids doesn't mean a thing. Always go by the sunglasses. They try and trick honest drivers. I saw it on *Starsky and Hutch* and on *Chips*. I'm gonna move up now and get in the right lane. Keep your eyes peeled on the road and don't screw up, Elva."

"If you're moving to the right lane, what should I be looking for? There ain't no traffic to the right of the right lane." Her gaze shifted from Cudge's profile to her window. BJ! The kid in the RV looked just like her little brother BJ. Another bummer. There was really something wrong with her. BJ was dead. She stared at him for a moment before she turned back to Cudge.

Cudge clenched his teeth. One long arm reached out and yanked at Elva's shoulder. Before she knew what was happening, she felt the hard sting of his hand against her face. She blinked as scalding tears burned her eyes. She turned away before Cudge could see the result of his handiwork. The little boy in the RV with the dog clutched to him was staring at her as she wiped the tears with the back of her hand. He looked scared the way BJ used to look scared. He was holding the dog too tight.

"You bawl one more time and you've bought it, Elva. The RV is turning off and I'm going to slide over and we'll coast from there. We'll get off this 'pike and get something to eat. We have to kill time. I don't want to show up at that campground too early."

Elva said nothing, wishing she knew who the little boy with the dog was. Just like BJ. Same color hair, same bright blue eyes, same scared look. Only this kid had a dog to love him. Poor little BJ only had her and what good did it do him? When it counted, she didn't help him at all. The little kid in the RV was alive and BJ was dead. And here she was with Cudge. How soon would it be before she joined BJ wherever he was? Fear of the unknown or fear of Cudge. Six of one and half dozen of the other. Fear.

It was mid-afternoon when Tom, Lorrie, and Davey left the reptile house. Lorrie was taking long gulps of fresh air, to Tom and Davey's amusement. Duffy frolicked at their feet, glad to be outdoors even if she was confined to a leash.

Tom rolled back his sleeve to look at his watch. "I think we've had enough zoo for one day. What do you say we head for the campgrounds and set up camp. You, my love," he said to Lorrie, "can fix a dinner for Dave and me that will be fit for two kings."

"And one queen," Davey quipped as he snuggled closer to Lorrie. "Boy, I didn't like the smell in that snake house, did you?"

"Not too much," Lorrie laughed. "Your Uncle Tom is right, though. We should be starting out for the campgrounds so we can get things ready before it gets dark."

"Are you tired, Dave?" Tom asked as he noticed the little boy trail behind with Duffy.

"A little bit. But I won't be tired when I get into the RV and sit down. We did a whole lot of walking today." His voice was full of awe. "I think Duffy is more tired than I am. What are you cooking for dinner, Aunt Lorrie?"

"Just like your Uncle Tom said, a dinner fit for two kings and one queen. Hamburgers and baked beans. Cupcakes for dessert. Chocolate milk for you and coffee for Uncle Tom and me. How does that sound?" Lorrie asked looking down at the little boy.

"It sounds just super-great. You know I love hamburgers with lots and lots of ketchup."

"Climb in, gang, and let's head for the wilds," Tom said as he unlocked the RV and slid behind the driver's seat. Lorrie waited till Davey and Duffy were secure in the back before she climbed in and then locked her door.

"Next stop, Wild Adventure," Tom said.

Lorrie nudged her husband. "Look in the back seat," she whispered. Tom risked a quick look over his shoulder as he swung onto the highway from the parking lot. Davey was sound asleep with Duffy snuggled in his lap. "Do you think we overdid it? That brace is pretty heavy to lug around. Poor thing, he's exhausted. Maybe we should have left sooner." There was more than concern in Lorrie's voice, there was agitation that she might have harmed the little boy she loved so much.

"Not a chance. That kid had the time of his life. He's not bashful. If he was too tired, he would have called a halt himself. He should be tired; I'm tired and you look exhausted yourself. It was a good day, Lorrie, for all of us. Don't spoil it by acting like a mother hen and fussing. By the time we get to the campgrounds he's going to be full of vinegar and raring to go. You'll see. You can't smother him; you promised to let him go at his own pace. That still holds, doesn't it?"

Lorrie smiled. "Of course. Sometimes I get carried away. I'm just so crazy about him that I want to do everything just right. I would hate to see Sara's wrath if something went wrong. You know what I'm talking about, Tom."

"Yes, I know, Lorrie," Tom said quietly. "But always in the back of your head you have to remember that Sara is Davey's mother, not you. I know that seems cold and hard coming from me, and I also know that you, for the most part, don't need any reminders; but sometimes, like now, I see you getting all misty-eyed and it hurts me. It hurts me because I know that you can get hurt."

Lorrie leaned closer to her husband. "That's why I love you, because you make such good sense. And for a few other reasons," she grinned.

"Oh yeah," Tom growled. "Tell me those few other reasons."

Lorrie laughed. She liked the few moments of close intimacy that they had at the oddest times, like now. "For starters, I like the way you kiss. I like the way you shave your neck and you have great thighs," she said pinching the inside of Tom's right leg.

"Why don't you just say you love my body," Tom laughed. "What's wrong with my mind?"

"Not a thing. You're just absolutely perfect." The easy chatter continued. Tom's quick glances in the rear-view mirror when he thought she wasn't looking did not go unnoticed by Lorrie. Sometimes she thought Tom had been given a small measure of mother instinct, too.

"Next exit is ours. You know something, I am really tired. While you make dinner, I think I'll take a nap. Would you mind?"

"Not at all. I'll cook outside on the grill and set up the table next to the camper. We did bring the colored lanterns and the little sweet pickles Davey likes, didn't we?"

"I brought everything that wasn't nailed down. There's the first sign for the campgrounds. Guess we just follow the arrows and look for the office. It looks pretty deserted here." Lorrie glanced quickly at her husband to see if that bothered him. Deserted meant there wouldn't be a lot of people to get in their way. Deserted also meant Davey wouldn't have any playmates, and she and Tom could have him all to themselves.

"Here we are. You guys wait here and I'll sign in and get our spot. Did you ever see such glorious color?" he asked as he craned his neck to look at the giant trees with their spirals of autumn colors.

Lorrie twisted in her seat to check on Davey. He was sound asleep. Duffy opened one eye and then closed it. It was obvious that the little dog didn't care where she was as long as she was with her master. She wiggled slightly, flicked at her nose with a shaggy paw, and then was still. Davey remained asleep.

Tom climbed back into the RV with a map and a card that was to be hung over the rear-view mirror. "I took a site at the far side of the pond."

"Are we near any other campers?"

Tom raised his eyebrows à la Groucho Marx and leered. "We'll be all alone," he leaned closer, making her giggle, "where no one can hear your screams while I do delicious things to your body."

"Seriously, Tom," she pushed him away with a playful hand, "Can't you ever be serious?"

"Yes, ma'am. Corporal Thomas J. Ryan reporting, ma'am. The management reports an elderly couple on the entrance trail, equipment Air Stream trailer, Massachusetts license. Young couple camped on far side of pond across from our designated location, equipment Traveler Pop-up, New Jersey plates." Standing at mock attention, shoulders back, hand to head in a stiff salute, Tom brought another peal of laughter from his wife. "The manager drove ahead of us so he can hook us up when we back in our 'King of the Road.' Looks like we're all set. Davey's still sleeping, I see."

"He'll wake up as soon as we're hooked up. I'll bet my Twinkie against yours."

"No way," Tom said, slipping the RV into gear. "You always win and I'm dying for a Twinkie."

The RV slid into a deep rut and then bounced out. Davey was struggling to sit upright and hang onto Duffy at the same time. "Are we here? Is it time to get out? How much more to go, Uncle Tom? I have to go to the bathroom. What time are we going to eat?"

Tom grinned. "Yes. Almost. Two minutes away. You can go to the bathroom as soon as the RV is hooked up. Your last question has to be directed to your aunt."

"I'll start dinner as soon as we're hooked up. Your Uncle Tom is going to take a nap and you and Duffy can explore if you'd like, but you can't go too far."

Davey's blue eyes were round. "I can't wait. I have to go to the bathroom, but I can wait for that. I can't wait to get out and see everything. Right, Duffy?" Exactly on cue, the terrier woofed.

"Guess that's the young couple the manager was talking about," Tom pointed to a garishly decorated pickup truck with a pop-up trailer parked in a grove of trees. "Our site is just around the bend and to the right. We'll be out of their way and they'll be out of ours."

Davey turned around to look out the long scenic side window. He rubbed at his eyes and stared at the pickup. It looked like the one where the man hit the girl who reminded him of Millicent. His thoughts were diverted when Tom deftly maneuvered the RV into the assigned slot. Within minutes, the manager had them hooked up to water and electricity and was bouncing down the road in his jeep, back to his office.

Climbing from the RV, Lorrie stretched luxuriously. "Okay, guys, here's the plan. Davey, scoot back there and go to the bathroom. Tom, you can take your nap while I prepare dinner. Davey and Duffy can explore for a little while."

Davey was back in seconds, zipping his jeans, as he trotted over to his aunt. "Is it okay if Duffy and I take a walk now?" Tousling his blonde head, Lorrie was once again taken with her nephew's grammar. Sara's influence, no doubt. Most of the kids who came into Lorrie's office would have said, "Duffy and me." "Sure, but first let's set down the rules. Look at your watch. What time is it?"

"The big hand is on the nine and the little hand is almost on the five. What time is that?"

"A quarter to five. It's another way of saying fifteen minutes before five o'clock. Now, when the big hand is on the three, I want you back here. And you must stay within earshot. Do you know what that means?"

"Sure! That means you have to hear me if I call or I have to hear you. Right?" he asked, proud and certain he was correct.

"Right. Now, Davey, what time do you have to be back here?"

"When Mickey's white glove is on the three. What time is that?"

"A quarter after five or fifteen minutes after five. Don't let Duffy wander off, and if she does, call her, don't chase after her or you could lose your bearings."

"Aw, you shouldn't worry, Aunt Lorrie. Mr. Sanders gave me a real Cub Scout flashlight and money for a phone call. See!" He rummaged in his jeans pocket for his two gifts. "I'm prepared."

"And I'm impressed." Not for the world would she tell Davey there were no phones attached to the trees. And as far as the little penlight went, he'd be lucky if he could see his hand in the dark with it. "I think you can make it. Big hand on the three, remember. What's the matter, Davey?" Lorrie asked, concern drawing her finely arched brows together when she noticed the pained expression on the little boy's face.

"It's nothing . . . yes, it is. It's my brace. I must have it strapped too tight or something. Dad knows how to fix it." A shadow slipped over his face, and Lorrie knew he was suddenly anxious about being separated from his parents for the first time.

"Let's have a look, sport. Maybe I can help."

Chuckling, Davey lifted his pants leg. "It's funny when you call me 'sport.' That's Uncle Tom's name for me."

"Yes. Well, since your uncle is sawing wood like a buzz saw in the back, I'll have to do for the present. Let's see." Hunkering down to inspect the brace, Lorrie winced when she saw how the leather straps were cutting into the fragile flesh of his calf. "No wonder. Your sock slipped down. How long has this been irritating you this way, Davey?" From the abrasion on his leg and the look on his face, Lorrie knew it must have been bothering him at the zoo. "Oh, honey, this was hurting you at the zoo, wasn't it? And you didn't say anything. Why?"

"Mom and Dad said I wasn't to be any trouble."

"Davey, you're the best kind of trouble your Uncle Tom and Aunt Lorrie could ever have. We love you, don't you know? How could you be trouble? Now, come on and sit up here where I can fix that brace. I'll pull up your sock and loosen the strap a notch." As she worked, Lorrie noticed the new sneakers that had never had an opportunity to get dirty. It wasn't fair, she told herself. Davey was too overprotected, too housebound. And instinct told her it wasn't because of the hemophilia that Andrew and Sara restricted the child to the house. A child who played in his room all day was a lot less trouble than a boy who could explore the regions of his own backyard and bring in dirt on Sara's perfectly clean carpet. "How's that?"

Davey tested the brace and smiled. "Lots better. Really. I like my new sneakers. But Mom says I can't wear them all the time. Is it because sneakers are special?"

"In a way they are. They're for playing and running. I think it's nice that you can have sneakers. Some children who wear a brace must wear heavy, high-top shoes. But your brace is only to give strength to your leg. See how it's made? This strap slips under your sneaker and you can wear it with any shoe."

Davey shook his head. "I saw a boy in the doctor's office and his braces went over his knees. He had to push these clamps so he could sit down with his knees bent. But I don't know why he had to wear those braces. And I don't know why I have to wear mine."

"Didn't the doctor tell you that it's only for a short time? When you were a very little boy, before you started the daily shots of antigen, you had injured yourself somehow and your knee was bleeding. Because of your shots, you don't have that any more. Now everyone wants to be certain that your knee has every opportunity to grow straight and strong. The brace keeps your shinbone," she ran her fingers down the length of Davey's leg, "in line with your knee joint."

"Oh," the boy murmured, deliberating on this explanation. "But I can walk real good and I can run." Suddenly he wrapped his arms around Lorrie's neck, giving her a tight hug. "I love you, Aunt Lorrie. You're a foxy lady."

"And just where did you hear that term, young man?"

"In the Junior CB Club. Shhh!" he put his fingers to his lips. "Don't tell Mom. She doesn't like it when I learn new words."

"I promise. It's our secret. I'm your secret foxy lady."

"Hey, Aunt Lorrie, that could be your handle on the CB. I'm Panda

Bear and you're Foxy Lady!" Delighted with himself, Davey trotted off, Duffy at his heels.

Lorrie watched them through the panoramic window. There was a slight unevenness to Davey's step because of the brace, and his red nylon windbreaker blended with the autumn colors in the woods. Her eyes focused on the blonde head and she wanted to reach out and touch him again. Duffy's short legs stirred the thick layer of leaves on the ground as she followed her master. With the same sense of loss that she always felt whenever she parted from the little boy, Lorrie turned to the icebox to begin dinner.

Davey and Duffy kicked their way through fallen leaves until they reached the pond. The water was still and a deep, mossy green, and the red gold of the sunset broke through the surrounding trees to create a golden path on the pond's surface.

"I saw this on Sesame Street, Duff. Now watch. You pick up a stone and skip it across the water." Duffy sat patiently on her haunches, watching pebble after pebble hit the water with a splash and sink.

"Guess it's another of my 'almosts,' Duff. I can almost do it, can't I?" Losing interest, Davey picked up a twig and poked at the dry pine needles and soft leaves. He was surprised to see the snowy shoelaces on his new sneakers were now a dirty brown. He laughed delightedly; now they looked used, like Uncle Tom's sneakers that had the hole in the toe.

Pushing back the sleeve of the windbreaker, Davey took note of Mickey's index finger. It was on the one. He had two more numbers to go. "C'mon, Duff, let's see what's over on this side of the pond."

John and Sophie Koval stood outside their silver trailer watching the Ryan's RV bump down the road. Sophie wiped her hands on her apron, relieved that there were other campers besides themselves and those— those hippies!

Camping certainly wasn't turning out to be the lark that John and the brochures promised. "Meet new friends, see the country, get back to nature." The "new friends" for the most part had turned out to be families with many children who couldn't afford to get away from home any other way. Instead of the nice, sociable bridge games to liven the evenings that Sophie had envisioned, she had had to endure the sounds of children's squabbling, parents chasing after them, and the endless lines of laundry hanging between the trees. And there was always the smell of that disinfectant they used. It was everywhere, even in the dirt. In every camp there was the same smell; it got into everything, and now the shiny inside of their trailer even smelled of it. At night it seemed to fill her nose and parch her throat. Whoever said there was no place like home must have gone camping.

Now that summer was over and the northeastern states were well into fall, John and Sophie felt lonely and apart from everyone and everything. The campgrounds were desolate, like this one, stopping-places only, where in the dew-heavy mornings they would break camp and ride on and on for hours at a time, pushing the speedometer and the clock to arrive at their next destination before dark. As the days grew shorter, camping was becoming an ordeal, a rat race, the very thing that John had promised they were leaving behind.

Sophie Koval longed for the ease and comfort of her home back in Massachusetts where she could spend the afternoons watching her soap operas on tv instead of growing stiff from long hours in the car, watching for obscure turnoffs to their next stop. John's retirement was becoming a trial and a punishment.

"Why couldn't we have gotten one of those nice buses, John? Then I could stay right in the back and prepare lunch or dinner and still be able to talk to you."

"Watch your soap operas, you mean. I've already told you, Sophie, those things guzzle gas. We've got to watch our pennies now. Social Security doesn't bring much and you know it." He watched her from behind his wire-rimmed glasses. The annoyance that he felt whenever she complained about their new lifestyle made him chomp down on his pipe. For over thirty years he'd made a nice home for her, giving her an easy life, while he went to work every day at the mill and dreamed of the day he could retire. He'd given up most of his dreams and all of his energies to Sophie's comfort, and he wasn't going to let her make him feel guilty now.

"They looked like nice people, didn't you think?" she asked, changing the subject, almost able to read his mind after all those years. "Maybe we could go over and meet them later."

John's eyes narrowed. "No, don't think so. Be getting dark soon and you've got supper to fix. Imagine they do too, what with setting up camp and all."

Sophie frowned. She didn't like this new John and for certain she didn't like their new lifestyle. She didn't know who or what she could trust any more. Gone were all the comfortable, familiar things from over the years. Instead, in their place, everything was stiff and new. She comforted herself with the knowledge that she had at least refused to allow John to sell their home. She'd just wait for John to tire of this vagabond existence, and then she could go back to her nice electric range and a refrigerator that could hold a week's supply of food. She couldn't get used to shopping every other day at strange supermarkets where she couldn't seem to find the simplest item. And the propane cook stove in the trailer—how could any self-respecting cook prepare a meal with two burners and no oven? She kept her mouth shut, careful not to complain about the absence of an oven. John would start speculating whether they could afford a microwave oven. Everybody knew that you could poison yourself with radioactive food!

Worst of all were the doubts she had about John. It had been fine back in Massachusetts when he drove her to the neighborhood supermarket and even to the shopping mall. But out here, on the open road, John had become a man she didn't know, a stranger. A . . . a Seattle cowboy! His driving had become aggressive instead of defensive. And hadn't she always heard warnings to drive defensively? Now, John was constantly cursing under his breath about this one cutting him off or that one driving with his brights on. Whatever made John think he knew how to handle a twenty-two-foot trailer being pulled by their treasured Grand Prix?

Looking at her husband, she saw him staring off in the direction of the camp where those hippies were parked. She knew they were hippies because of the way their pickup truck was painted in psychedelic colors with obscene slogans scrawled in every available place. "You're just as glad as I am that we're not alone here with them, aren't you?" More than a question, her words were a challenge.

"Sophie, this isn't the old neighborhood. We're bound to meet people from other walks of life. You've got to learn to live and let live." He'd never admit it, but he was glad there were other campers besides themselves. Old people were easy prey for some types. "Go on in and

[83]

get dinner, Sophie. We've got a long drive ahead of us in the morning, and I want to get started early." He refolded a road map and traced the lines with his fingers. "The manager of this camp told me about a real nice place down near Virginia Beach."

Cudge watched Elva set up the barbeque grill. "Why are you using that? Why don't you use the stove?"

Elva continued to pour briquettes into the grill. "Cause we don't have any more cooking gas, that's why." She lifted her head and glared at him.

Ignoring her unspoken accusation, Cudge leaned against the camper. "What's for supper?"

"Eggs, corned beef hash, and Kool Aid."

"Shit."

"Well, if you'd stopped at the store the way I wanted we could be having hamburgers or something. Eggs is all we got. And beans. You want beans?"

"Shit. That's what it is. Shit. I could go for a steak, rare and juicy, and maybe a baked potato."

"Yeah, well couldn't we all," she sniped.

"Don't we have anything but Kool Aid? Don't we have any beer around here?"

"If we did you'd have drunk it before now. All we have is Kool Aid."

"Hey, I don't like your tone of voice. Don't get smart with me." His voice was suddenly menacing. Elva hung her head a little lower and went on trying to start the fire.

"Be careful with that charcoal lighter. I don't need you setting fire to yourself and needing to go to the hospital. We still got some work to do," he gestured to the closed pop-up with his head.

When they had first arrived, Cudge had gone about setting up camp. Elva had been afraid to open the pop-up, afraid that Lenny was going to jump out at her. "He's dead, as dead as you'll be if you don't give me a hand here," Cudge had growled.

After cranking up the top section that served as the roof, Cudge had opened the front and back canvas wings that expanded into bunks. "We have to do this right or else somebody might start asking questions. Just keep the door closed so nobody can see inside," he warned.

"I need the eggs and stuff," Elva was saying, bringing him back to the present. "And I don't want to go in there so you'll have to get them."

"What's the matter? Little Elva afraid that Lenny'll jump up and bite her ass?" Cudge mocked.

"So what if I'm afraid? I don't like dead people. You killed him, so you go in there and get the food."

"Don't get fresh, Elva. I'm warning you. I've had more than a man can take today, and I've been real patient with you."

"It's not my fault that we were stopped by the state trooper. You're the one who had the truck painted that way."

"Shut up, or you're going to get it."

Elva looked at Cudge, saw the way his lips were curled in a snarl, saw his eyes boring into her and the way his neck seemed to disappear into his shoulders. Prickles of apprehension rose on her arms and she could feel them through the scratchy woolen poncho she had crocheted for herself. "You gonna get me the stuff?" she squeaked.

"Yeah, I'll get it. But you better not turn chicken on me tonight when we haul his ass out of here. I took a walk around before and I found the ideal spot. It's down there in that shallow gully." He pointed to a spot near the pond on the far side of the campground.

"How are we going to get him there? I can't carry him that far."

"Well, you're going to. Just make up your mind. What do you think I feed you for? Just remember, you're an accessory, Elva, and I don't want to hear any of your shit. You just do what I tell you, understand?" His fingers closed over her arm like a vise and Elva wriggled away.

"Lemme go! I understand. Just lemme go!"

"I don't want you fuckin' up the way you did with that trooper."

"That wasn't my fault! He was on your side and you should've seen him in the side-view mirror. It wasn't like he was in an unmarked car or anything like that."

"So you say. And I say you should've been watching! That was a close call, too close."

They had been on the turnpike after riding the back roads around Brick Township. It was too early in the day to appear at the campgrounds without provoking questions. Elva had her nose buried in the map, looking for the exit, and Cudge was tuned to the CB, listening to the truckers' conversation over the airwaves. Usually he could count on truckers to report a "Smokey" in the area, but not this time. The next thing Cudge knew the bright blue light of a trooper's car was flashing, and he was instructed to pull over.

"One word out of your mouth, Elva, and I'm going to make sure you ain't got no teeth left," had been his last words before climbing down out of the pick-up, his hand reaching for his back pocket for his license and registration.

"Take it out of your wallet, please," the trooper said, the afternoon sun reflected off his mirrored sunglasses. Like most troopers he was tall, taller than Cudge, but he didn't have his bulk. Sizing him up, Cudge decided he wouldn't have the least bit of trouble in pounding the man to the ground. Then he saw the trooper's side holster and the blue-black grip of his pistol.

"Where are you heading?"

Cudge was so preoccupied with half-formed plans of escape he hardly heard the question. "Huh? Oh, we're camping. Heading north."

"Sir, your license says you're from Newark. That is north."

"Uh, we have been camping, in Maryland. We're heading home."

The trooper leaned forward to peer through the dirty window at Elva. She was young, at least ten years younger than the man. "Would you open the door, sir," he asked Cudge.

"What for? There ain't nothing in there that shouldn't be." Cudge bristled. He didn't want the trooper talking to Elva, and he didn't like his condescending attitude. The trooper called him "sir" but it could have been "shit" from the way he said it.

"Open the door, sir."

"Okay, okay." Cudge pulled the door open. The trooper looked in at Elva, sitting on her legs on the seat. His trained eye observed her long, dull brown hair, her painfully thin body, and the worn clothes. He also noticed the panic in her eyes.

"Everything all right, miss?" He spoke from over Cudge's shoulder, some instinct telling him he didn't want this man behind him where he couldn't see him.

Elva nodded.

"Are you Mrs.—" he glanced at Cudge's license, "—Balog?"

Elva shook her head.

[86]

"How long have you known Mr. Balog?" He deliberately asked a question that would require a verbal answer. Something was wrong here —he could almost smell it. His mind clicked back to his last radio transmission, calculating how long it would take for assistance to arrive.

Elva remained silent, her eyes searching Cudge's.

"Miss, how long have you known Mr. Balog?" the uniformed trooper persisted.

A long pause ensued. Elva's eyes were locked with Cudge's. The scent of trouble grew stronger in the trooper's nostrils.

"Jesus Christ! Will you tell him, Elva? What's wrong with you anyway?" He was shouting, knowing that he was alarming the trooper, yet unable to control himself. The beast in his brain pawed, the hooves biting into tissue, alerting him. Struggling for control, Cudge lowered his voice. "Elva, for crissake!" He thought of Lenny hidden in the pop-up, saw the blue flash of the dome light on the trooper's car, and felt the threat of the trooper's pistol.

"Miss, would you like to get down out of the truck, please?"

Elva shook her head, her face whitening.

"Elva, for crissake, do what he tells you."

"Would you please assist the lady from the cab, Mr. Balog?" Something was amiss here. The girl's silence, the panic in her eyes, the man's agitation. Even the pickup truck looked like trouble—electric colors, slogans, and decals that were just short of obscene. Only the pop-up trailing behind was still a light beige, devoid of decorations except for a few four-letter words fingered in the grime. In fact, the pop-up was in pretty good condition compared to the old Chevy pickup pulling it. "I'd like to see your registration for the trailer."

Cudge's eyes widened, his hand shook as he pulled Elva from the truck. What in the hell did the cop want to see the registration to the trailer for? His glance darted from the trooper to the trailer and back again. "Damn you, Elva, this is all your fault. Whyn't you answer him like he wanted?"

"You told me to shut my mouth and not to say a word," she whined.

"Shut up," he hissed. "If he wants a look inside, you better be in this truck when I take off or else I'll leave you on the side of the road."

"Cudge, I didn't . . ."

"Shut up!"

"Any problem over there?" the trooper inquired.

"No, no, nothing's wrong. Right, Elva?"

Elva nodded.

"Crissake! Tell him, will ya? Tell him!" Cudge saw the trooper's mouth tighten and he could sense his eyes narrow behind those glasses.

"Your registration, please."

Digging in his wallet again, Cudge presented his identification.

"What have you got in the back?" the face behind the glasses asked, checking the information on the card Cudge had handed him.

"Whatever goes into a camper, a toilet, sink, beds." The trooper was starting to piss him off. He'd like to punch his fist right into those glasses and push them through the back of his head. The silent pawing in his head became the restless shifting of weight, leaning against the gate, wanting to be let out.

"Let's take a look."

"Christ, you know how much trouble it is to open one of those things? To say nothing of putting it together again. I've been thinking of getting a regular trailer, one of those Airstreams or something. This kind is a real pain in the ass."

"Let's take a look, buddy. Now!"

Gone was the "Mr. Balog." No more "sir." Now it was "buddy." His spine stiffening and a light spray of sweat breaking out on his brow, Cudge moved to the rear of the trailer. His mind raced but no solution was found. And it was all Elva's fault.

"Mind telling me what I did wrong? I wasn't speeding or nothing. I was just cruising along. This is harassment."

"Police brutality!" Elva prompted. "Tell him, Cudge, you want to talk to your lawyer!"

Balog's eyes rolled back in his head. If she said one more word, he was going to let her have it.

"Finally found your tongue, miss? What's this about police brutality?"

"You have no right to bother us. We weren't doing anything. You can't just sneak up on people like that. Cudge told me to watch out for cops, and I was, but you came up on the wrong side."

"Shut up, Elva, for crissakes, shut up!"

"While you're cranking open your camper, I'll call in your license," the trooper told him in a somber tone that made Cudge wonder whether or not he'd heard what Elva had said about watching out for the law. "Get going!" There it was, the authority, the suspicions that made Cudge's skin prickle.

The trooper moved toward his patrol car, senses alert for danger. It wasn't unheard of for a trooper to be shot down just asking a guy for his registration. Damn those politicians for cutting back on two-man teams. If he ever needed a partner, it was now. There was something fishy going on here, and he didn't like this Balog. And when that mouse he was traveling with decided finally to open her mouth, it was to tell him that she'd been on the lookout for the law. Was she trying to tell him she was being kidnapped? What was in the camper? Drugs, contraband cigarettes? What? Not only was he going to call in Balog's license, he was going to ask for assistance.

Turning his back on the couple, he took the few steps to the patrol car. He could feel Balog's eyes on him, piercing and angry. For a second back there, when the guy was telling him what was in the camper, Balog's anger had become almost tangible, thick and viscous. For that one second he had felt as though all his air had been cut off and he was trying to breathe through a vacuum.

Christ! He was getting paranoid, jumping at shadows. Still, that feeling had been real—a warning. Fleetingly, he thought of how many times his wife had begged him to change jobs. His brother-in-law had even offered him a job managing one of his used car lots. Maybe it was time to consider it. Scared troopers didn't do their jobs; and the ones who did often ended up with half their heads blown away.

He wondered again how far away the nearest assistance was.

The patrol car was still flashing its blue lights when a loud squawk sounded through the open window. "Car 169, Car 169, proceed to mile 43 southbound. Emergency vehicle needed. Car 169, collision at mile 43, New Jersey Turnpike. Assistance en route, do you read?"

The trooper looked at Cudge and Elva and then back at the patrol car. He hadn't realized how damp his shirt had become or how eager he was to get away before he found out what Balog was hiding in the camper. Thrusting the registration and license back into Cudge's hand, he hurried to his car and took off, lights flashing, siren blaring.

"Get in the truck, Elva. Move!"

"Cudge," she whined. "Cudge."

Balog blinked, she was still whining. . . . "Are you going to get me the eggs? This fire's ready. And don't forget the black iron frypan."

For a long moment Cudge looked at Elva; the menace and power in his gaze was so tangible that she backed away.

"Cudge, what's the matter? Cudge, don't look at me that way, I don't like it."

Wordlessly, Balog stepped inside. If he'd had to look at her for one more minute, he would have killed her.

Duffy scampered ahead of Davey, intent on a gray squirrel. Davey shook his head with exasperation. The squirrel would run up a tree, and Duffy would have led him on a merry chase for nothing.

Nearby a cook fire was burning; he could identify the smell from watching Dad barbecue steaks in the backyard. As expected, the squirrel ran up a tree, leaving Duffy barking near the base. "C'mon, Duffy, you can't climb trees and that squirrel won't come down until we're gone. C'mon, Duff!"

Reluctantly, Duffy obeyed, coming to heel near her master. Davey looked at his watch. Mickey's finger was on the two. That gave him one more number to get back to Aunt Lorrie. He frowned. Running through the woods with Duffy was so much fun, maybe Aunt Lorrie wouldn't be too upset if he got back when the finger was almost off the three. That would make it almost one more number. No, he promised to be back on time and he would be.

The trail led away from the pond to the road, and if he turned to the right and followed it around, he would come back to their campsite. Breaking through the growth at the side of the gravel road, Davey took another glance at his watch. He wasn't certain how far it was back to the site, and he thought he would have to hurry. Anyway, his legs were tired and even though Aunt Lorrie had fixed his sock and adjusted the strap, it was still sore.

"C'mon, Duffy! I'll race you back to the RV!"

Duffy woofed, stubby tail wagging and ears lifted, watching Davey for his next move. When she saw that Davey wanted to run, she obliged happily, scooting ahead to lead the way.

Just around the road's bend, Elva and Cudge were eating when their attention was caught by Duffy's yips and Davey's calling to her. They watched the little dog and the boy run headlong into their campsite. Elva recognized Davey immediately. He was the little boy who looked so much like BJ, the one that she had seen in the RV on the turnpike.

"That's a cute puppy you've got there," Elva called to Davey, bringing him up short. Davey's pride in Duffy was evident in his shy smile. He liked hearing that Duffy was smart and cute.

"Her name's Duffy," he told Elva, realizing that she was the woman from the pickup who looked like Millicent, his babysitter. Remembering the man who had hit her, Davey turned to see Cudge sitting on a camping stool, his elbows on his knees, and an empty dish in his hands. Davey didn't like this man who had such a mean face and eyes that could eat you up.

"Where's your campsite, kid," Cudge asked. It was a piece of information worth having. If their campsite was too close to where he intended to bury Lenny's body, then he'd have to make other plans while it was still light out.

"Over there, on the other side of the pond," Davey told him, fidgeting beneath Balog's appraising stare. Duffy's exploring nose was put to the ground and she followed it to the tip of the man's boots. For an instant Davey thought the man was reaching down to pet Duffy and for a reason he couldn't explain he didn't want the man to touch his dog.

"Duffy, come here," Davey ordered. His nose wrinkled. Something smelled different over here near the man's camper. Like the way his snow jacket smelled before his mother hung it on the line to get fresh air. It was the little white balls in the pocket that made it smell that way. Mothballs, Mom called them. Curiously, his eyes dropped to the ground, expecting to see some sign of the candylike circles. He decided he liked the smell on the other side of the pond better.

"Hey, kid, how many brothers and sisters you got camping with you? Not too many, I hope. I don't like all kinds of noise at night when I'm trying to sleep."

"I'm the only—I don't have any brothers or sisters. I'm camping with my Aunt Lorrie and Uncle Tom."

"I don't want to scare you or anything, but you shouldn't go walking through the woods after dark. I hear there's bears and wild cats that'll eat that dog of yours for supper." A satisfied smirk lifted the side of Balog's mouth as he saw Davey gulp.

"Aw, why d'ya have to scare the kid that way? There ain't no bears in these woods!" Elva raised her voice, moving forward, her half-eaten eggs sliding around on her dish.

"Shut up, will you? That's right, kid; there's no bears, only tigers, and there's nothing they like better for supper than a nice juicy little dog like that one." Balog glanced around looking for Duffy, then his eyes darted to the open door of the pop-up. In the shadows he could just make out Duffy nosing around the blanket-wrapped corpse. In two long steps he was inside the camper and a second later Duffy came flying out.

Duffy grappled for her footing, barking in pain. Before Davey's wide-eyed horror, Cudge leapt down and grabbed the dog by the scruff of the neck, shaking her helpless body. "Fuckin' little bitch! I'll teach you to go snoopin' around where you don't belong!"

"Cudge! Stop it! Cudge!" Elva screamed.

With his free hand Balog smacked Duffy, and the dog growled threateningly, struggling to sink her teeth into Balog's hand.

Davey was confused and frightened.

"Cudge, for crissakes, leave the dog alone! Put her down, Cudge! Cudge!" Elva screamed. She was hanging on Balog's arms, preventing him from hitting the dog again. With a mutter of disgust, Balog threw the dog to the ground, ready to plant a boot in her side if she came after him.

"Get your puppy, little boy, get away from here!" Elva was telling him. "Get your puppy!"

Sparked to action by Elva's commands, Davey moved forward and scooped Duffy into his arms.

"Get out of here!" Cudge thundered. "Don't come snooping around here no more, hear? And if I see that dog again, I'll kill her! Understand?"

The boy didn't move. His mouth dropped open, wide eyes staring at the man. He couldn't think, couldn't breathe.

"You brazen little son-of-a-bitch!" He made a motion toward the boy who was clutching his panting dog.

"No, Cudge, don't. You can't!" Elva knew Davey wasn't being

stubborn and brazen, he was just scared stiff. Just like BJ. Just like herself. "Don't hurt the kid, okay?" she pleaded with Cudge. "He's scared, that's all. Just scared."

Cudge shook Elva off his arm, tossing her backward onto the ground. The behemoth in his brain was charging the gate. He had to get control and force it back. His heart pounded with the effort, his knees became rubbery, incapable of holding his weight. Warning signals were going off inside his ears, telling him that if he wasn't careful, he'd have trouble with the kid's family.

Jaw jutting forward, fists clenched, Balog leaned over, placing himself at eye level with Davey. "Get out of here," he growled, "and if you want that dog, keep her away from me!"

Suddenly, charged with an energy that enabled him to move his feet, Davey turned and ran. And ran. The brace on his leg hampered free movement; Duffy's weight was heavy in his arms, and still he found the strength to run. Little red sneakers pounded the dirt road, sending up spirals of dust. Laces snapped and twisted together in agitation, socks slipped downward, wrinkling at the ankles. The nylon windbreaker whispered, louder and louder, urging him to run. Faster! Faster!

Down the road, through the trees, the Ryan's RV stood sentinel waiting for Davey's return. He could see it now, all lit from within, radiating a welcome refuge. He put Duffy down, watching her, checking her for injuries. He walked, Duffy followed, her movements normal. Duffy seemed to be all right. Davey bent down and gathered Duffy close to him. Her cold wet nose brushed against his flushed cheek. One thought and only one raced through Davey's head. *He must never let Duffy go near that bad man again!*

4

LORRIE'S CONCERN was evident to Tom. They both sat quietly as Davey ate his hamburger. Lorrie imagined she could hear the child's red sneakers rubbing against each other restlessly beneath the picnic table. When kids did that, something was wrong. She restrained herself from lifting the colorful picnic cloth and peeking to see if she was right. She sipped at her coffee, never taking her eyes from Davey.

Davey reached for his glass of chocolate milk and swigged it down. He didn't hear Tom's sigh of relief or Lorrie's indrawn breath, nor did he see his uncle's gaze which clearly stated, "You see, any kid that can eat and guzzle chocolate milk like that is okay."

"I'm finished, Aunt Lorrie. That really was good. I even liked the hard stuff on the hamburgers."

Tom threw back his head and laughed. "Tell it like it is, Davey. Your aunt flubbed up. That hard stuff is a deep, chewy crust as in burned or overdone, but they were good. I have to agree with you on that score. The cupcakes are going to taste even better."

Davey grimaced slightly. "Can I save mine till later?" He wanted to go inside the camper and lie down and think about the woman who looked like Millicent. He waited dutifully to be excused from the table. The moment his aunt nodded, he went inside the RV, climbed up on his bunk, and motioned for Duffy to join him. If he thought about her, he would have to think about the bad man. "He's not mean, Duff," he whispered to the little dog. "He's bad. We have a lot of things to think about, Duff, so you be quiet or Aunt Lorrie will come in and take my temperature." Duffy settled herself in the crook of Davey's right arm.

All manner of jumbled thoughts raced through the little boy's mind as he absently reached for his new Dr. Seuss book. His voice, when he spoke next, was controlled yet squeaky. "You weren't around, Duff, when Puffy got put in the ground. She was killed by a bad person who was going too fast in his car. Then they gave me you. You were supposed to be a boy dog, but Aunt Lorrie got all mixed up and gave you a name before she figured out that you were a girl dog. I don't want that bad man to get you, Duff. I don't want you to get killed. That's why we aren't going back there again. Now, you have to listen to me when we wake up in the morning. You have to stay with me," he wagged a pudgy finger under Duffy's nose, "we're going to stay on this side of the pond so we don't see *him!*"

For answer, Duffy snuggled closer to the little boy. "I know that you're supposed to protect your master; that's what Aunt Lorrie and Uncle Tom said, but I know and you know that I have to be the one to protect you. That man is bad. I didn't know you didn't like him, Duff, till you made that awful noise. You have a lot of teeth too. I was scared, but you were mad, I could tell. The woman liked us, but she's scared of him too!"

Idly, he flipped a page of the book and then played with the sharp corner until it was limp. When he saw the curled edge of the paper, he spit on his finger and tried to smooth it out. He pursed his mouth and then quickly turned three pages before he risked a look at the door. Aunt Lorrie wouldn't really care if he curled the pages. Books were supposed to be fun, and she had even given him some of her own that had crayon marks and spilled jam on the pages. She said they were hers when she was a little girl.

"Now I forgot what I was thinking about." Davey swallowed hard when the spectre of Cudge's face appeared before him. He didn't want to think about him or the woman who looked like Millicent any more.

"C'mon, Duff, let's go get our cupcakes, and maybe Uncle Tom will let me talk on the CB."

"Aunt Lorrie, can I have the cupcake now, and can Duffy have one too?"

"You bet," Lorrie smiled happily as she untied her red-checkered apron. What a relief. Tom was right as usual. The boy was just tired from his long tramp through the woods. Maybe it wouldn't hurt to take his temperature just to be on the safe side. Immediately she squelched the idea; she wasn't going to risk another disapproving look from Tom.

"So tell me, big guy, where did you and Duffy go and what did you see?" Lorrie said, peeling back the cupcake wrapper.

Davey settled himself on the picnic bench. It was okay to pretend, and he really had looked at the pictures in his new book. But he couldn't lie, especially to Aunt Lorrie. Duffy woofed begging for her dessert. Absently, Lorrie peeled a third cupcake and fed it to the dog.

"We walked around the pond. We visited the people in the camper. You can't see their truck from here, but it's there. I guess that's all we did. Duffy doesn't like it over there."

"I see," Lorrie said as she watched Duffy devour her treat.

Davey wiped his hands on his blue jeans. "Aunt Lorrie, do you think Uncle Tom will let me listen to the CB before I go to bed?"

"I'm sure he will, Davey. Tell you what, why don't you get ready for bed, and when you're clean, you can talk for a while. You scoot along now, and your uncle and I will wait for you."

As soon as the little boy was inside the RV, Lorrie turned to Tom. "I know you're going to say I'm crazy, but I know something is wrong. Something is bothering Davey."

"Okay, okay. I grant you he looks like he has something on his mind. I think I can guess what it is. Will you go with a little homesickness? He probably misses Sara and Andrew. After all, this is his first time away from them. He's doing remarkably well, all things considered. And, Lorrie, the kid is tired; he's had a busy day. You have to stop with the 'mother magic' bit, otherwise we're going to have a problem. I'm going to let him listen to the CB and then put him to bed. You can go in later and tuck him in and kiss him good-night. Deal, Lorrie?"

Lorrie grinned. "Deal."

The lanterns made an oasis of light in the darkness surrounding the campsite. Davey sat between his aunt and uncle at the picnic table, listening. The autumn night was crisp, almost cold, and only the gentle winds disturbed the tree tops, rustling them in hushed whispers. Duffy placed herself near Davey, resting her fuzzy head on his sneaker. She too was listening, waiting to hear the screaming of the lions prowling in the wildlife refuge less than a mile away. Spirits of the night imbued the animals with a power and restlessness born of some instinctive race memory of wide and endless prairies. Lifted by the wind, their roars shattered the night.

Davey listened, spellbound, imagining the golden beasts with bright amber eyes seeing into the darkness, crying for a home that was no longer theirs.

Cudge Balog's voice was hardly more than a whisper. "It's almost ten o'clock, Elva. Time to take Lenny out. I've been watching that RV on the other side of the pond, and their lights have been out for more than an hour. Get that shovel out from under the bunk. I can't wait to get rid of old Lenny and split."

Elva, who was snuggled down in a blanket near the campfire, sat up. "Are we leaving here tonight?"

"Nah! I told you before. We can't make any false moves. Everything has to look natural. C'mon, give me a hand."

This was the moment she had been dreading—the moment when she would have to go near Lenny. "How are you gonna get him to that place you picked out this afternoon?" Her dun-colored eyes drifted away from Cudge to the fire, the light. She didn't want to be near Lenny again, in the dark with him. She didn't want to hear Cudge say she had to help carry him. If he told her she would have to touch Lenny, she'd be sick right here and now.

"Same way we got him out of the apartment, on the ironing board. He's still tied on it, ain't he?"

"Cudge, I don't want to do it! It's dark and I don't like dead people," her whine grated on Cudge's already tightly strung nerves.

"I don't give a shit what you like or don't like. You'll do what I tell you. Now, get your ass over here and grab your end of the board." He cursed viciously as he dragged the narrow end of the board over the aluminum step so Elva could grasp it. "Now, pull it out and I'll grab the other end." He checked his pocket for the flashlight.

Balog led the way through the light underbrush near the road and into the darkness under the trees. "Just keep up and make sure you hold up your end."

"It's too heavy."

"You made it down the stairs at the apartment all right. You've got the light end, so shut up and quit your crying."

"Maybe people get heavier when they're dead. Maybe that's what they mean when they say a 'dead weight.' I don't think . . ."

"That's right, don't think! I've had enough of your bright ideas. Christ! The smell of those mothballs is making me sick."

The harvest moon shone through the trees and once their eyes adjusted to the night they were able to see surprisingly well. "See, it ain't so dark. What's to be scared of? We'll be through before you know it."

Elva trudged along behind Cudge, struggling with her end of the ironing board, wishing she could put it down even for a minute. The aluminum frame was biting into her fingers. If only she could stop and change her grip.

"Okay, here it is," Cudge whispered, huffing with the exertion. "Drop your end and I'll slide him the rest of the way down. Take this flashlight and turn it on so I can see what I'm doing. And for crissakes, keep it pointed at the ground."

Elva took the flashlight and turned it on, pointing it at the ground in front of Cudge. She trembled violently making the light skitter in all directions.

After sliding down the embankment to the shallow gully, Balog asked for the shovel that had traveled along on Lenny's stomach. Careful not to touch the blanket or to think about the body beneath it, Elva gingerly lifted the shovel and handed it to Cudge.

Balog felt better now that he was at Lenny's last resting place. It wasn't bad, he told himself. Lots of trees, quiet, shade in the summer —Lenny could have done worse.

"Are we gonna bury him with my ironing board?" Elva's voice squeaked.

"Dumb broad. No! How'd you like to spend the rest of eternity strapped to an ironing board. Point that light over this way." Clearing away the underbrush, Cudge put the spade into the loamy earth and forced it deep with his foot. Shovelful by shovelful, the rich, black dirt piled up beside him as he dug deeper, calculating the size of the hole into which Lenny would fit.

"Your turn, Elva. And I don't want to hear any complaints. Just dig while I take a breather."

Balog's venomous growl left no room for argument. It wasn't long

[98]

before perspiration dripped down Elva's face and between her shoulders. She didn't want to be a gravedigger. How deep was deep enough?

Her arms ached from the unfamiliar exertion. Now she had to stand in the hole to excavate the heavy earth. The woods surrounding them seemed unnaturally quiet. "Quiet as a grave," her mother used to say, and now Elva understood it.

"Move over, Elva. I want this done and over with. You operate somewhere between slow and stop, and we ain't got all night." The grave was almost four feet deep and Cudge decided that was deep enough. "Get over there and untie him from that board. Then you can help me roll him into the hole."

"I—I can't," she gulped. "Don't make me, I can't touch him!"

"When I tell you to do something, I mean for you to do it. He'll roll easy; don't think about it. If you don't want to share this hole with him, you better do what I say!"

His no-nonsense tone propelled Elva toward the body. Cudge meant what he said; she could tell by the sound of his voice. He would put her in the hole with Lenny; she knew it as sure as she knew she was breathing. Shakily, she untied the knot that held Lenny to the board, trying not to touch the body or feel the yield of flesh beneath the blanket. One good thing, she thought. If she was the one who rolled Lenny into the hole, that meant she'd be outside, not inside. Cudge was right about Lenny rolling easy. The incline of the gully aided her efforts as she prodded and pushed toward the grave. She nearly gagged from each dull thud the body made as it rolled over. "Watch out, Cudge, here he comes," she said in a quivering voice. The loud thwack of Lenny's body falling into the grave made Elva squeal with fright. An awful sound. The last sound poor Lenny would ever make.

"Right. He's down. Now we shovel the dirt back on top of him."

"No! Wait! He's . . . he's laying on his face." The flashlight beam revealed Elva to be right.

"So what, he'll be facing the way he's going."

"No, we can't, you have to turn him over. He was your best friend, you can't leave him like that."

Revulsion filled Balog at the thought of touching Lenny. What if the blanket slipped and Lenny was looking up at him? Christ! No man should be expected to see his best friend before he threw the dirt over him. Yet Elva was right. Besides, if he left Lenny face down, Elva would never stop whining or let him forget it. He was tempted to tell Elva to turn Lenny over, but the grave was shallow and narrow; it would take a fair amount of strength to position the body within the confines of the grave. He shuddered. "Here, hold the light and get ready with the shovel. And whatever you do, don't shine it on his face. I don't want to look at him."

Taking the flashlight, Elva trained it into the grave. Cudge slid in near Lenny's feet and reach over to grasp the body near the shoulders and turn it over. Some demon of perversity made Elva flash the light on Lenny's face just as Cudge turned him over.

What remained of the face stared sightlessly upward. Glazed eyes reflected the light; the mouth was agape in a soundless cry. The blood had congealed; it was sticky and black with traces of freshly turned earth.

"God!" Scrambling as though his life depended on it, Balog climbed out of the hole, his stomach heaving, his lower intestines loosening. The underbrush holding his legs seemed to be Lenny's hands pulling him back into the grave. He pulled himself forward into the darkness where he retched and felt himself almost foul his pants.

"Cudge, Cudge, you all right? I didn't mean for the light . . ."

"So help me, Elva, I'm gonna kill you one of these days. What the hell's wrong with you anyway?" He spit, clearing his mouth and knowing the sour taste of his own bile. "Get that shovel and start covering him over, and if you stop, even for a minute, you're going in there with him. You got me?"

Elva grabbed the shovel, pushing the dirt into the hole to cover Lenny as fast as she could. She'd seen Lenny's face, and it was something she never wanted to see again. It was worse than what had happened to BJ, but then he'd only been a little boy.

Twenty minutes later, they were finished. Cudge played the flashlight around the area, scanning the gully till he was satisfied everything looked normal. At the last minute he added a fallen branch, heavy with red-gold leaves, to the new grave.

"Can we go now, Cudge? I hate this place, I really hate it." In the chill night air Elva shivered, all the way back to the campsite.

"There's no point in hanging around here," Cudge told her in the light of their campfire as he brushed the dirt from his jeans. I'm going to take a ride and find a bar. I need a few beers. You're staying here so nothing looks suspicious."

"You want me to stay in that pop-up after . . . Cudge, a dead body was in there and it stinks."

"The stink is your own fault. Just where do you think you can sleep tonight? It's cold out here and we only have thin blankets. What's the matter, Elva, 'fraid of spooks coming back to haunt you?" he taunted.

"I'm not as scared as you," she shot back. "I ain't the one who almost shit his pants." She wished she could take back her words. Cudge's hand came down with the force of a wrecking ball. She crumpled to her knees, holding the back of her head and whimpering.

"Now who's scared, Elva?" he sneered, his booted foot kicking her thigh with staccato blows. "I should've put you in that hole with Lenny, but I didn't. You remember that."

As if she could ever forget. Those moments at the gully would never be forgotten as long as she lived. Cudge jumped into the pickup and drove down the road, the tail lights becoming fainter and fainter until they were tiny red eyes staring at her through the darkness.

She was all alone in the darkness, with Lenny's body only yards away in the gully. It was like being left in a graveyard. Death was all around; she could feel it and smell it. It was cold, so cold. If only she wasn't afraid to go into the camper, but Lenny's body had been there for all those hours.

A gust of wind swayed the trees, knocking a dead branch to the ground near her feet. Elva screamed and covered her face with her bony hands. Then she crawled up the step into the pop-up.

Davey Taylor rolled over in his sleep and then sat bolt upright in his bunk. He listened, straining. Someone had screamed. He lay down again, his hands cupped beneath his head. Duffy stirred restlessly at the foot of the bed and wriggled her way up into Davey's arms. "I think the bad man hit the lady again, Duffy."

Sophie Koval rolled over on the hard-mattressed bed, reassured by John's warm body beside her. Sometimes it occurred to Sophie that John gave up the comfort of their twin beds back home in Massachusetts just to get her under the same covers with him. She tossed restlessly, "For all the good it did him!"

Then she lay very still, listening. She could swear that was a scream she'd heard—a woman's scream.

She came to the only possible conclusion: A drug-induced orgy was taking place in that hippie camper!

Sophie would keep this to herself; She wouldn't tell John. Because the first rule of a good camper was "Join in!"

5

ORNING ARRIVED, fresh and clear. The sunlight streaming through the hardwood trees, sent a kaleidoscope of color through the windows of the Ryans' RV. Davey tumbled from bed, looking around for Duffy.

"She went fishing with Uncle Tom. You are a sleepyhead this morning, aren't you?" Lorrie said hugging the sleepy boy. "Uncle Tom says you're to get dressed and go down to the pond. He took your fishing pole with him, so you better get a move on." She brushed his light, silky hair back from his forehead. It would need cutting soon.

"I'll be ready in no time. Could I have a cupcake to take with me? And one for Uncle Tom?"

"You bet, and a banana for good measure. Hurry up, sleepyhead. If I know your Uncle Tom, he'll get lonely down there and head back soon. You won't get a chance to fish if he does."

"Uncle Tom whistles when he fishes, that's why he doesn't catch too many. That's what someone said when Uncle Tom took me fishing in Florida," Davey told her as he peeled the golden skin from his banana.

"Is that why?" Lorrie pretended amazement. "And he told me it was because they just weren't biting. Run along and get dressed, and don't forget to brush your teeth. I'm going to make up the bunks and clean around here, and then I'll be down to see how you fishermen are doing."

Dressed, with his sneakers tied and leg brace adjusted, Davey put on his windbreaker, careful not to mash his half-eaten banana. He was ready.

Davey walked down the road to the pond. He could hear Uncle Tom whistling a song they had heard on the radio yesterday.

"They aren't biting," Tom told him morosely as Davey came to the clearing near the edge of the pond. "You were smart to have that cupcake and the banana. All I had was an apple."

"I brought a cupcake for you, Uncle Tom. Aunt Lorrie said it was okay. How do you know there are any fish in the pond?"

"I don't, but it looks like a good place for fish, doesn't it? Besides, Davey my boy, there's more to fishing than meets the eye. It's not always important to bring home the dinner, if you know what I mean."

Davey looked up at his uncle, his head tilted to one side, trying to understand.

"Look, sport, it's this way. Fishing is getting out into the fresh air and sunshine. You sit around, watch the water, listen to the birds, and commune with nature. Understand?"

"Yes, I do," Davey told him seriously. "Fishermen don't have to stay at camp and clean up and do dishes."

"Dave, you have the instincts of a true sportsman!"

It was nice when Uncle Tom smiled at him the way he was now. His eyes got crinkly and it made Davey feel warm inside.

"Tell you what. If you want to take a walk with Duffy, go ahead. No sense both of us staying here catching nothing. I'll prop your pole up and whistle if there's a tug on your line. Then you can come back and reel him in. How's that?"

"Uncle Tom, maybe if you didn't whistle, the fish would bite."

"Dave! I have to whistle to let them know where to find the bait." He watched with amusement as Davey pondered his answer. When the boy shook his head from side to side, Tom burst into laughter. It was clear Davey had his own views on fishing.

Elva watched Cudge sleep. Even though she had pretended to be asleep when he returned to the camper in the early morning hours, she could not relax. He had come back drunk, and within seconds had fallen across the bunk, his loud snores bouncing off the canvas walls of the pop-up. She had been even more afraid with him than she had been alone. She'd seen him like this before, many times. When Cudge got drunk, he got meaner.

Inside the pop-up everything smelled of mold and mildew, sour liquor, and mothballs. Bright sunlight shone through the nylon mesh windows which were backed by clear plastic to keep out the wind. The plastic warped the sun's rays, making lacy patterns on the filthy floor. Elva scraped at the floor with the toe of her shoe. The grime was imbedded so deeply that her rubber sole left no mark. That annoyed her still more. Her mother had always said that "being poor doesn't mean we have to be dirty."

Elva needed to use the bathroom. There was a pot stashed in the camper but she didn't want to use that. There were showers and bathrooms at the end of the road, but she didn't want to have to walk that far. She decided to wait.

Cudge mumbled in his sleep and thrashed about on the narrow bunk. Elva held her breath. Was he going to wake up or would he sleep some more? His long arm hung disjointedly, and from where she sat she could read the numerals on his watch. Ten minutes past eight.

Most people were up by eight o'clock. The family in the RV across the pond were probably up and eating their breakfast. Maybe they were finished with breakfast by now. They were probably arranging their day, the kitchen all cleaned and everyone dressed. They would be clean and neat. They must have money, Elva decided. You had to have money to drive an RV that only got six or eight miles to the gallon and dress your kid in new clothes to go camping!

Slowly Elva stretched one cramped leg from beneath her. She rubbed her aching calf before she brought her other leg out straight in front of her, careful not to make a sound. She took turns massaging each leg, and when she was certain she could stand, she slowly inched to her knees, holding onto the handle of the small refrigerator door for support.

A hand gripped her from behind as she heard Cudge's voice. "Wherever you thought you were going, Elva, forget it. We have something we have to do this morning, and then we'll get out of here."

"I wasn't going nowhere. And what do we have to do this morning?" She was surprised to see him so lucid and alert. Something told her that he had been awake all this time, thinking. And when Cudge Balog started thinking, it didn't bode well for her.

Balog swung his legs over the side of the bunk. His watchful eyes never left Elva's face. "We have to dig Lenny up again."

Elva gasped, the wind knocked from her. The thought of going down into that gully, even in bright daylight, started her shaking. "Why?"

" 'Cause we don't have any money, that's why. Lenny was on his way to a crap game, wasn't he? Well, he wouldn't go unless he was well heeled. I blew what money I had last night in the tavern or else I was rolled in the can. Don't open your yap, Elva; I'm in no mood for you."

Oh, God, not again! She couldn't look into that hole again and see Lenny's eyes staring up at her. It was a sin to open a grave, wasn't it? She couldn't do it, but one look at Cudge's face told her she would.

Standing, he loomed over her. "You're the one with the bright ideas, so how come you never thought about taking the money out of Lenny's pockets? Why do I have to think of everything? Every cent we've got is buried in that hole with what's left of Lenny Lombardi."

Cudge was looking at her strangely. And his voice, while hardly pleasant, was different somehow. He wasn't yelling. Normally, he'd be yelling at her. Something about him was making Elva's flesh crawl.

"Go outside and take a look around. Where's that Kool Aid you made last night. Christ, I feel as though my mouth's lined with cotton."

Elva handed him the plastic pitcher of grape Kool Aid. "We can't go down there in the daytime. Somebody might see."

"So what if they see. All they'll see is us taking a little walk. What's wrong with that? One of us will stand guard while the other digs Lenny up. We need that money."

All Elva heard was the word "we." "We" meant both of them. They both needed the money. He wasn't going to shove her into the hole with Lenny. Thank God.

"Go outside and see if anybody's moving around out there. We don't want anybody to come up on us when we have Lenny laid bare to the daylight." He laughed, a horrible sound, that made the bile rise in Elva's throat. She nodded and closed the door behind her.

Shading her eyes as she peered off into the distance, she couldn't see anyone or anything. The campground was thick with trees and undergrowth, making it impossible to see too far in any direction. The campsites were all set away from the road, with a modicum of privacy. Off in the direction of the pond and the gully there was nothing to be seen. With only two other camping parties besides themselves, Elva really hadn't expected to see anyone.

Stepping out beyond the perimeter of their campsite into the bushes, she dropped her jeans to her ankles. She'd better go now, otherwise she'd probably pee in her pants when Cudge opened Lenny's grave. Cudge's bellow made her hurry, pulling her jeans up quickly.

"Took you long enough," he grumbled as she stepped back into the clearing. "Get over here and give me a hand with the camper. I'm going to close up the sides so's all we have to do when we're finished is throw the shovels in and crank the top down."

Obedient, Elva helped him fold in the canvas eaves and put away the barbecue grill and utensils they had used the day before. She knew they should have been put in before the canvas eaves were folded, but she was afraid to argue with Cudge this morning. In went the ice chest, the nearly empty bag of briquettes, and the dirty frying pan. Used paper plates and plastic cups littered the campsite and she began to clear the area.

"Leave it! We paid enough to stay here; let them clean it up. I ain't no garbage picker. Grab the shovel and let's go."

Following him through the woods, Elva's steps dragged. The thought of what they were about to do revolted her. It was a sin, she knew it.

At the edge of the pond Cudge stopped, coming up short, waving her back with his hand. Across the pond sat a man fishing. "Dumb jerk, he's not going to catch anything there," Balog whispered. "I don't like it."

"Me neither. Cudge, let's forget it. Huh? It's a sin to dig up a body, I know it is."

"Shut up. It don't look like that guy is going to walk this way, and even if he did, it would take him a while to go around the pond to the gully. By that time we'll have old Lenny dug up and planted again. This time, permanently."

Elva swallowed hard as she followed Cudge.

Davey tossed a stick high in the air, watching to see where it would land. "Go get it, Duff. Bring it back." The little dog scampered off to do his bidding. Davey followed her into the grove of trees that circled the pond.

Again and again he threw the stick and followed Duffy. Once or twice he turned around and looked back; his Uncle Tom was growing smaller and smaller as he walked away. Now he couldn't see his uncle. Looking at Mickey Mouse he realized he'd walked for three numbers, and his eyes widened as he looked around him. He was on the other side of the pond now, the side where the mean man was camping!

His first thought was of Duffy. He could see her, carrying the stick back. There was a funny smell in the air. The smell like his snow jacket. "Good girl, Duffy. Here, give me the stick. Time to go back and see what Uncle Tom caught in the pond. I don't like it over here; I don't like the way it smells."

Duffy cocked her head to one side, growling deep in her throat. Someone was there. Davey looked around, trying to detect the direction the sound came from. He thought he heard a voice. He held his arms out to Duffy who needed no second urging. "Shhh," Davey whispered close to the dog's ear. "It's that mean man who hit the lady. The one who screamed last night and woke us up. Be real quiet, Duff."

The little boy moved away from where he thought the sounds were coming; crouching low, afraid for his dog, he went deeper into the woods, hiding in the low growth of scrubby pines.

He heard the sounds again, and he knew he had chosen the wrong direction. They were there, right in front of him, and he could look between the green branches and see them. "Quiet, Duff. Quiet. That man said he'd kill you if he saw you again. We have to be still and hide and wait till they go away." Davey wished they'd never walked so far, never left the side of the pond.

Duffy wriggling in his arms, Davey moved to the edge of a gully and caught his breath sharply. They were there. The mean man and the girl who looked like Millicent were down in the gully. The girl kept wiping at her eyes, and she looked scared. The man was digging with a short-handled shovel, and it crossed Davey's mind that he was digging for buried treasure. Davey wanted to know what was in the ditch; he wanted to see what buried treasure looked like. Unnoticed, his grasp of Duffy loosened.

"I hit something," the man told the girl. "God, he's buried deeper than I thought."

Elva forced herself to look down into the open grave. It was deeper than she had thought too, almost deep enough for two. Her tongue stuck to the roof of her mouth.

Davey looked at the open hole. A man's shoe. A man's leg. A blanket. What was the man doing in the hole, and why did the mean man have to dig out the dirt?

The truth dawned on Davey. When Puffy the cat was killed by a car, Daddy had dug a hole in the backyard and put him there. He had wrapped the kitten in a clean towel, not like the dirty blanket the man was wrapped in. When you were dead and didn't breathe any more, they put you in a hole and planted flowers. But there weren't any flowers here. He had cried the day Dad had buried Puffy, and he understood why the girl kept crying. She felt the way he had when Puffy stopped breathing. His simple deduction pleased him; he must be growing up to know all this without having to ask an adult. He felt a vague disappointment that he wasn't going to see a buried treasure of gold coins and jewels. Just a dead man.

"Reach down there and go through Lenny's pockets, Elva." Cudge's voice was cool and controlled. He had purposely kept a thick layer of soil over Lenny's face, knowing he didn't have the stomach to see it in broad daylight. Besides, something was eating at him. Elva kept saying it was a sin to open a grave. What if for once in her dumb life she was right? He couldn't think about that now; he still had work to do. And Elva wouldn't be around to help him.

"What? I can't . . . no, Cudge, I won't do that. I'll puke." Elva's face was a sickly green.

"Do what I tell you and quit your yapping. Reach down and go through his pockets. We need that money, Elva. I did all the digging."

His last remark stopped her. Illogically, she saw the justice in what he wanted her to do. He had done all the digging. Hesitantly she reached down, knowing she'd have to get on her hands and knees to reach inside the grave. She'd have to get close, real close to Lenny—actually touch him!

Cudge saw her get down on her knees and stretch out to the body. "C'mon, Elva, we ain't got all day. Just get the wallet. Try the back right-hand pocket first."

Elva's hand made contact with the blanket, but it might have been the slime of a giant slug, making her recoil. "Do it, damn it! Get it and hand it up!"

Lenny was heavy and cold. She could feel how cold he was right through the blanket, even through his clothes. She managed to lift him slightly and get her hand underneath him, feeling for the square bulge that would be his wallet. Closing her eyes, she found it and pulled it free. Cudge reached down and grabbed it away from her.

"Good girl, now try the other pockets. He must have had a good-sized roll." While Elva struggled with her revulsion and Lenny's stiff body, Cudge opened the wallet and pulled out two twenties and a single. "Find it, Elva. This can't be all he had. Lenny liked to go into a game well heeled." Putting the bills into his own pockets, he dropped the wallet onto Lenny's chest.

"I think I got it, Cudge," Elva told him, spirits lifting because he had called her a good girl. "It's a wad, all right."

"Hand it over." Must be a couple of hundred dollars, he told himself, satisfied. Ol' Lenny was worth a lot more dead than alive. "Try those other pockets."

"I already did and there was nothing. Cudge, I don't want to touch him anymore. And jeez, this blanket stinks. I think we used too many mothballs."

"Search him, Elva, do like I tell you." His hands closed over the shovel handle, eyes intent, watching. He wouldn't like hitting Elva and rolling her into Lenny's grave, but he had to do it. She was stupid, too stupid, and stupid was dangerous.

Elva looked up to plead with him, to tell him that it made her sick to touch Lenny. She had to convince him that there was nothing else in the earth-damp pockets. Her mouth opened but no sound came out. Cudge was staring down at her, shovel held high over his head. Doom crowded her and she knew she was going to be lying next to Lenny. "Cudge! No, don't!"

A sharp yipping followed by an angry bark broke the stillness.

"What the hell?" Balog shouted, leaping back from the open grave, as the shovel clattered to the ground. "I thought I told you to have a look around! Now you blew it!" He stepped forward, backhanding her across the face.

She tasted the coppery salt of blood and knew her nose would swell. Confusion roared in her head. What had happened? What was that sound? The puppy. The little boy's puppy.

"Get that damn kid, Elva. Get him now! Where the hell did that mutt go?"

"I don't know! I don't know!" she wailed.

"Get him! Find him! I'll fill in the hole!" Cudge's words were cut off by a streak of black fur, charging from the bushes.

Davey was stunned. He stood transfixed by the sight of Duffy running toward the mean man and the crying girl. Growls and snarls burst from Duffy as she tried unsuccessfully to chew at the man's leg. Davey wanted to run to get his dog, but the girl was running toward him. For one instant he looked directly into her eyes. "I saw him hit you. He hurt you! I heard you scream last night. I told Duffy he hit you again and that's why you screamed. You shouldn't let him hit you!" The words tumbled out—faster than firecrackers.

It was all too much for Elva. She sank to her knees. BJ would have said the same thing to her. BJ, little as he was, always knew when someone else was hurt, even if you didn't cry. "Run, kid! Run as fast as you can," she whispered. "If he gets his hands on you, he'll kill you and you'll end up like Lenny. Run, damn you! Run!" That's what she had said to BJ, but BJ couldn't run. BJ had just stared at her, willing her with his great saucer eyes to help him. But she hadn't. Couldn't. This kid wasn't moving either. Panicking, she reached for him, pushing, shoving. "Now, damn it! Run! Get away from here!"

Davey backed away—who was Lenny? His eyes went from the girl to the man. He had to get Duffy and take her away. The man would kill Duffy too. Then she would have to be buried like the kitten, and she wouldn't run and play any more, just like Puffy. Davey charged past the girl who wanted him to run away. He would. But not without Duffy.

He called Duffy's name and ordered her to come to him. Something brushed by him, he couldn't see. He couldn't take his eyes from Duffy who was performing a macabre dance with the mean man who was trying to catch her. The girl was there now too, pushing the man.

Quicker than mercury, Davey reached down and grabbed Duffy, holding her fast. She was still growling, erupting into agitated barks as Davey climbed the ridge of the gully, heading for freedom. For safety.

Encumbered by his brace and confused by his panic, Davey ran. Duffy fell from his arms, tumbling into the leaves. Half dragging his leg behind him, he scooted beneath low overhanging branches, in and out of the brush, Duffy loping behind him. In the distance he could hear something tearing through the woods, breaking branches, snapping twigs, pounding the soft earth. He thought he could hear someone panting, and remembered the distant roar of the lions he had heard last night and knew he was being pursued by a wild animal—a big one, with horns and evil red eyes. It would bellow with rage and cover the ground in great, long strides.

Davey had to hide; he had to keep Duffy safe. The dog ran ahead of him, ears erect, tail held high. She thought it was a game. The man was forgotten; her master's terror unrealized. Davey followed her through the brush into the bright sunshine, as they reached the winding road. They had to hide. If they didn't, the man would put him in the hole like Puffy. It wasn't clear to him. He was still breathing and so was Duffy. You didn't go in the hole till you stopped breathing. "He'll kill you," the girl had said. How? He knew that cars could kill and so could sickness. How did people kill? Instinct told Davey that the man would make sure he wasn't breathing when he went into the hole. It was this certainty that spurred him forward, following Duffy, ignoring the weakness in his leg.

On and on the red sneakers raced, covering the ground, laces snapping in their frenzy to reach safety. Aunt Lorrie, Uncle Tom.

The truck and pop-up sprang into Davey's line of vision. The beast behind him was getting closer. The camper was half-closed; the sides were folded in, but the door stood open.

Duffy picked up speed, heading away from the pop-up, toward Uncle Tom's RV. Davey was breathless, nearly exhausted. He knew the man was nearby, knew that the man would already have him if it hadn't been for the trees with low hanging branches that he had been able to scoot under but which slowed the man down. Davey heard the timber crashing behind him. The decision was made. He ran up the aluminum step into the camper and slammed the door shut behind him. He had to hide where the man couldn't see him. There was no time for Duffy. Duffy was smart; she would lead the man away from the camper; Davey was sure of it. Then he would be able to get back to Aunt Lorrie and Uncle Tom.

Covering his mouth with his hand to quiet his ragged breathing, he crawled to the back of the camper, down between empty boxes and the bunk. He waited, listening. There was no sound, no scratching from outside to tell him that Duffy was out there. Just silence.

A loud bellow ripped close to Davey, making him jump. "That

goddamn kid got away and it's your fault, Elva. You dumb, fucking broad! Once that kid tells his folks what he's seen, it's curtains for you. The manager has our license number and knows who we are. That means jail, Elva. You'll be locked up for the rest of your life!"

Davey held his breath, expecting the man to walk into the camper any minute. Instead a rusty creaking filled the pop-up, making it vibrate. The scraping of metal against metal pierced his ears, making his teeth hurt. Daring a glance upward, he saw the camper's roof lowering, coming down to squash him like a bug under Daddy's shoe.

6

Elva climbed into the truck, her face white with terror. She had every reason to be terrified of Cudge, but being left behind was somehow more frightening. "You were going to kill me back there!" she hissed as she lifted herself onto the seat beside him.

His face was set in lines of panic and it gave her a small satisfaction to see him this way. Big, bad Cudge Balog, scared of what a little kid could do to him! "Don't try and lie to me, I seen it in your face." She wanted to hear him say she was wrong, that she was crazy and imagined things. Elva couldn't come to grips with reality. She needed to believe that she was safe with Cudge Balog.

He turned the ignition key, foot pressing on the gas pedal. The engine cranked and almost caught before winding down. Again, he pressed the gas, twisting the ignition key viciously as he pumped the pedal, willing the engine to turn over and dreading the thought that he might have flooded it. He was sweating. Elva looked at him, desperately wanting him to defend his actions back at Lenny's grave. "I ain't going with you!"

Before she could think twice she was out of the truck and running across the dusty road, heading for the cover of the trees. Bullet swift, Cudge was out of the cab and racing after her.

Resolution died in Elva even before she felt his hands on her shoulders. "This is all your fault, you stupid jerk-off! You're not running out on me now. Get it through your head, Elva; you blew it. Get in the truck and don't open your mouth unless I tell you. In a couple of hours we're gonna be wanted for murder because of that fucking kid. Murder, Elva! And it's all your fault."

Cudge wasn't sure which way to go—north or south? Maybe he'd stand a better chance if he ditched the camper. No, he'd worked too hard to get it, and he wasn't going to part with it. Why did that mangy mutt have to chow up? Of all the fucking bad luck! And that kid—what in damn hell had happened to him? If only he could have gotten his hands on him. "By now that kid is spilling his guts to his old man. Hear me, Elva? That kid is blabbing and his old man is going to the cops. We got another hour of freedom and then . . . *pow!*" His arm shot out, knocking Elva against the door.

Elva huddled against the door, unable to move. And if she did move, Cudge would hit her again. If the cops got her, she would be locked up. If she made a move, Cudge would kill her. Why couldn't she win, just once? At least the kid had gotten away. If it hadn't been for her, he would be dead and his parents would be crying over his body, trying to figure out what had happened. She was a heroine of sorts. She had saved the kid and got the good looking guy. Only Cudge wasn't a good-looking guy and she didn't want him. The kid got away, thanks to her, and she felt good about it. She wished she could bless herself and maybe go to confession. She could do it in her mind. Cudge wouldn't have to know she was praying and confessing. In the name of the Father and the Son and the Holy Ghost, amen. Bless me, father, for I have sinned. It has been many years since my last confession, I haven't been to confession since my . . . since B.J. Father help me, somebody help me.

There was no father with his clerical collar behind the screen in the small confessional. She was in a dirty pickup with a murderer. What good was pretending to go to confession? She needed a real priest to give her penance. The kid was safe; that was what was important. If there was a God up there somewhere, then He would know she had saved the little boy.

"Get the map out, Elva, and make it snappy. You know where we are; find some back roads and give me directions. We'll head south and maybe our chances will be better once we hit Delaware and Maryland. We'll ditch the pop-up as soon as we can. I'll smear the license plates with mud and maybe we can hole up in some other campground. For now, it's the only thing I can think of. Don't even say you're sorry because I don't want to hear your sniveling. I'm dumping you, Elva, first chance I get. You ain't nothin' but trouble."

Elva clenched her teeth and then bit her tongue. Dump me, my ass, she thought bitterly. Kill me is more like it. Well, I'm glad I did it, and I'd do it again. She felt suddenly defiant as she flipped the map over. Maybe she was stupid like Cudge said and then again, maybe she wasn't. "If you take Route 535 south for a while, you can either pick up 33, or at that point look for some other back roads. There ain't too much on this map, or if there is, I can't see it, the print is too small. This map must be twenty years old. The amusement park ain't even on it."

"Do you see any campgrounds listed?" Cudge asked.

"No."

"Then get out the camp guide and find one. Do I have to think for you too?"

Elva dug under the seat and pulled out a tattered looseleaf book. With nimble fingers she found the page she wanted. "There's two KOA camps open and the others are closed for the year. This is October."

"Shit!"

Davey was wedged in between the bunks on either side of the pop-up. It hurt when he took a deep breath and something was pounding inside his chest. If only Duffy were here to hug.

He sniffled, wishing for a tissue to blow his nose. The dark didn't scare him, only the smell of mothballs was making him sick. The floor smelled just like his snow jacket after Mom put it away for the summer in that really dark corner of the attic. Davey didn't like that corner of the attic, and he didn't like where he was now.

Motion, rocking—the camper was moving! The tires were bouncing over the road; the bad man was taking him away. Davey realized that the man didn't know he was trapped inside the camper. If he just stayed very quiet and waited, he would have his chance to get away. Wait, instinct told him. Wait.

The rocking wasn't so bad now. It didn't seem as though the wheels of the camper were bounding over holes and ruts. No, it seemed almost smooth, like when he rode his tricycle off the back lawn and onto the paved drive. It was a road—a highway, Davey thought, making the connection.

His legs hurt. The leather strap from the brace was cutting into his good knee, making it throb like a drum. He wanted to cry but instead bit his lip and tried to work the strap free of his good leg. If he could just catch the metal brace against the side of the refrigerator, he might be able to push with both hands and roll free. Time and again he tried and failed. A sob caught in his throat. If only Duffy were here. Again he tried hooking the side of the brace that curved around his sneaker against the greasy refrigerator, and he was successful. The metal brace clanked against the refrigerator with a loud bang. Would the man and woman hear? What would they do to him? Would she help him get away again? Somehow he knew the man wouldn't let that happen.

It was cold in the pop-up; a draft was coming up from the crack where the sides and floor of the camper met.

How long was he going to have to hide in here? Aunt Lorrie and Uncle Tom must be looking for him. He wished he could see Mickey's hands so he would know if he missed breakfast. When he didn't get back for breakfast, Aunt Lorrie would start to call him and Uncle Tom would go looking. Aunt Lorrie would cry and Uncle Tom would put his finger on her lip and say, "Shhh." Davey smiled in the dark. He liked it when Uncle Tom did that.

He had to get out of here and back to Aunt Lorrie and Uncle Tom. He would hate it if she had to cry over him. He sighed deeply. How nice it would be if she would appear and take him in her arms and hold him close. He would sniff and sniff until he couldn't sniff anymore. Then he would hug her as tight as she hugged him. He would even hug Uncle Tom.

Maneuvering a little, he tried to stretch his cramped legs. A look of horror crossed his face as a warm trickle coursed down his leg. Tears stung his eyes as the wetness seeped into his sock and sneaker. Small fists banged against the filthy floor as the tears continued to flow.

Lorrie clapped her hands in satisfaction. The campsite was tidy, and everything was back in place. She looked around, appreciating the crisp, bright day. Either she could walk down to the lake or settle in a camp chair and read a book. A quick glance at her watch told her it was after ten. Tom should be back by now, looking for something more substantial than a cupcake and an apple. Davey should be tiring about now. Sighing deeply, she rummaged inside the small compartment that

[117]

stored the pots and pans. With a loud clanking, she withdrew a heavy frying pan. They must have caught a lot of fish for them to be gone so long.

She would just see with her own eyes the catch of the day before she made any rash preparations. Giggling to herself, she skirted trees and scrub and scuffed through the dry, crackling leaves till she reached the pond. Hands on hips, she threw back her head and laughed. Tom was propped against an old, decayed tree, both poles almost bent double with fish biting at the lines. He was sound asleep and snoring with his usual gusto. There was no sign of Davey. Duffy was snoozing next to Tom.

"Now look what you've gone and done," Tom grumbled. "You've scared away all the fish. I would expect that from Davey but not from you. I guess that means we have tuna for lunch, right?"

Lorrie shielded her eyes from the bright sun. "Just where is Davey, Tom?"

"He was here a while ago and then he trotted off with Duffy. The dog's here so he can't be far off. Davey!" he shouted loudly.

Lorrie looked at the dog chasing Tom's pants legs as he moved about shouting to Davey. "The dog is always with Davey, Tom. Why is she here?" Her voice rose a decibel and then another as she scolded, "How could you have fallen asleep? I thought you were taking care of him."

Tom backed off a step. "Whoa there. I might have closed my eyes, but I wasn't sleeping. The dog has been here for some time chewing on my pants leg, just like she's doing now. The boy is around here somewhere. Easy does it, Lorrie." The reassuring words came out easily, but Tom was apprehensive; just how long had the dog been chewing on his pants leg? He felt his stomach muscles knot as he looked around at the quiet woods. The kid should be making some kind of noise. He couldn't have been asleep more than forty-five minutes. Cupping his hands around his mouth, he bellowed Davey's name so loudly that Duffy stopped chewing.

"Something's wrong, Tom, I can feel it. Oh, God, we have to find him. What if something happened to him?"

"Stop it, Lorrie," Tom said grabbing her by both shoulders. "Look, you go around the far side of the lake and I'll take this side. Call out if you spot him."

Lorrie needed no second urging. She raced through the leaves shouting Davey's name over and over. Only once did she notice that the little dog was right on her heels. "Some hell of a watch dog you are. Where is he, Duffy? Find Davey," she pleaded. "Go on, girl, find Davey."

Duffy raced ahead, her short legs spewing the dry leaves in her wake like spindrift. Faster and faster the little dog raced, Lorrie right behind her. Gasping for breath, she skidded to a stop when Duffy pulled up short, wildly barking. What was that smell? Mothballs, here in the middle of the woods?

Lorrie walked around peering into the brush and underneath low-spreading evergreens. Nothing. Over and over she called Davey, her voice becoming hoarser with each agitated call. There was nothing to be seen and only silence around them. It must be the odd smell that was exciting the jittery dog. "There's nothing here," she said scooping up the excited Duffy. "Come on, we'll find Tom and see if he's had better luck." But she knew there would be no little boy in a bright red windbreaker to greet her. Something was wrong; she could feel it in every fiber of her body. Oh, God, she groaned as she raced back to the other side of the lake. What was she going to tell Sara? Tom and I lost your son. Where was Davey?

Tom held out his arms and Lorrie fell into them sobbing. "Oh, Tom, I couldn't find him. Duffy couldn't find him. Did you see or find anything?"

Unwillingly, Tom's eyes wandered to the still water of the pond. Looking back at his wife's face, he banished the fear from his voice. "Nothing," Tom said, holding her close. "Now, listen to me, Lorrie. We're going to go back to the RV and you're going to make lunch. Davey knows it's lunchtime when both Mickey's hands are on the twelve. He knows that's when he gets his shot of antigen. The little guy is sharp, so let's not sell him short. We'll wait till 12:15, and if he isn't back by then, we'll call the police. It's my theory that he just went a little too far exploring." He knew it was all a lie and knew that Lorrie knew it was a lie, but it was the best he could do at the moment. The muscles in his stomach and chest were ripcord tight, making breathing difficult. There wasn't much he could do about that either.

"Lorrie, we're going to behave in a normal, rational way. For now, until 12:15, we have to assume that Davey just went a little too far and the brace is slowing down his return."

"Tom, I can't. I'm so worried. Sara . . ."

"You will do it; you have no other choice. Forget about Sara for now. Make lunch and bring it out here. That's an order, Lorrie," Tom said firmly. The moment the RV door closed behind his wife, Tom slumped down in the canvas chair. Jesus, where was the boy? He looked at Duffy who was sniffing around the steps of the motor home. Why didn't we get Davey a big, protective dog instead of this ball of fluff?

Tom let his mind race to what he was going to do the minute the watch on his wrist read 12:15. He'd go to the nearest town and get in touch with the local police. Then he would head back immediately and have the managers of the campground initiate a search of the wooded area. Once it got dark, he would call Sara and Andrew. Or should he wait till morning? No, they had a right to know as soon as possible. After all, Davey was their son. Their son, not his and Lorrie's. Never his and Lorrie's after today. Christ, he'd be lucky if Sara ever let them set eyes on the kid again. Maybe on his eighteenth birthday Sara would take pity on Lorrie and let her see her nephew come of age. Goddamn it, where could the kid be? Why had Duffy come back to the lake by herself? Did Davey send her back for help or did the little dog just tire of the walk and wander back on her own.

Lorrie maneuvered her way through the RV door and down the steps, a tray clutched in her hands.

Lunch consisted of tuna fish sandwiches, potato chips, a small jar of pickles, milk, Coke, and fear. Lorrie said nothing as she sat on the picnic bench. A muscle twitched in her eyelid as she stared at the hands of her watch.

They waited.

At precisely 12:15 they both rose. Tom scooped Duffy up in his arms and climbed into the RV. Lorrie lifted the aluminum steps and slid them in the back and then climbed in beside Tom. Neither said a word as Tom drove the RV to the office. "Wait here, Lorrie, this will only take a minute. They can start the search while we're in town."

When Tom returned minutes later, Lorrie demanded, "Well, what did they say?"

"They said they would start looking right away. You might as well know that no one but us is going to be unduly alarmed. Kids wander off every day and eventually find their way back home. I expect we'll get a lukewarm reception from the police, too."

"I know, I thought of all that. Other kids aren't Davey and don't have Davey's problem. Oh, Tom, what if he comes back while we're gone?"

Tom didn't want to tell her how unlikely that was. "Well, he'll be so busy gobbling up the potato chips and Coke, he'll just assume we went to the office or for gas. The kid's a whip, Lorrie. He isn't going to stand there and cry. Davey is not a crybaby; we both know that."

"That's what worries me, that he doesn't cry. He's just a baby, Tom, he can't cope with all of this." What "this" was she didn't elaborate.

"We're doing the best we can. You have to relax, Lorrie. If you cave in on me, I'll wipe out and you know it. We both have to keep our wits about us. Deal?"

"But what about Sara?" Lorrie said, a sob catching in her throat.

"Fuck Sara. Even if that wizard of a sister of yours were here, she couldn't do anymore than we're doing. Now, is it a deal or not?"

"Deal," Lorrie said with a weak, watery smile.

Davey Taylor sneezed. Immediately he clapped his hands over his mouth. He sneezed again as dry, gritty dust blew up at him through the crack between the floor and sides of the pop-up. Angrily, he pounded small fists against the side of the refrigerator and tried to kick out at the cardboard boxes near the tips of his sneakers. He couldn't even see his bright red sneakers with their white shoelaces, but he knew they were dirty. It would have been all right to get the laces and the rubber-soled shoes dirty tramping through the woods with Uncle Tom, but this was different. Now the canvas sneakers were ruined. As soon as he found Uncle Tom he would throw them away. Would three quarters buy new sneakers? Three quarters for two shoes sounded right to him. He sneezed again. And then again. He was hungry and he wanted a drink. He wanted out of this dark, scary place. He lashed out with his foot at the carton filled with Cudge Balog's bar bells. His foot shot back as quick as a rattler. Gently, he nursed his aching foot by holding it in both hands. "I want out of here!" he shouted. "Let me out of here!" The only response was a jolting thump as the pop-up hit a bump, and a spiral of dust came in from the crack. Wearily, he let his head fall to his propped-up knees. Suddenly, his head jerked up and he strained to hear. Was the camper slowing down? His tongue worked frantically in his mouth as he tried to wet his lips. He needed more spit if he was going to shout so someone could hear him. The woman would let him out when she heard him call. But how was he going to know where the bad man was? What would he do if it was the man who raised the top? She would try to help him, he was sure of it. It was slowing down. He would be quiet and wait.

Cudge Balog eased up on the throttle. "Keep your eye peeled for a gas station, Elva. This ain't the time to run out of gas. You listening to me?"

"Yeah, I hear you. I don't see anything but grass and trees. I'm hungry," she whined.

"Ain't we all. My advice to you is to suck in your gut because it might be a long time before we eat."

"Can't we stop, and I can get something from the pop-up? How long would it take?" Elva persisted. "I can't remember the last time I had something to eat. I'm really hungry, Cudge. If I don't eat, I'm gonna be sick. I can feel it in my stomach."

"Jesus Christ! You don't hear good, do you? After that dumb stunt you pulled this morning, you don't deserve to eat. You had the kid, Elva. You actually had him in your hands, and what do you do, you let him get away. That kid is spilling his goddamn guts to the police right now, and all you can think of is your fucking stomach. Shut up and I mean it."

Elva slouched back against the seat. Cudge was probably right. Scared as he was, he was right. Maybe when they stopped for gas she could crank open the top and get something. How long could it take? A minute, two or three at the most. It took that long for the tank to be filled. She decided she would risk it. She needed her strength to run if she found the opportunity. Her stomach seemed to settle down with her decision.

She wondered where the little boy was right now. Was he talking to the police like Cudge said? She had tried to help. Cudge would never understand; he was too concerned with not being blamed for Lenny's murder. Her stomach heaved as she remembered the body in the open grave. Poor Lenny, he didn't even have a coffin. The worms and bugs would eat through the blanket real quick. Her stomach heaved and then quieted down as she swallowed hard.

Elva risked a quick glance at Cudge. She really wasn't hungry. She might not be the smartest person in the world, but right now, this minute, if somebody offered her a Big Mac, she wouldn't be able to swallow past the fear in her throat. Cudge had tried to kill her once, and he would try again. She must never forget that, never pretend to herself she hadn't seen that look on his face when he wanted to put her in that hole with Lenny. It was okay to pretend sometimes, when reality hurt too much, but this time pretending could get her killed.

"Asshole!" Cudge spat. "I can't depend on you to do anything. See that gas station, Elva. That's where you get gas. I thought I told you to keep your eyes open." Elva shrugged. When you were going to die, what did it matter if you saw a gas station or not. Cudge's foot moved from the gas pedal, and he swung it to the right and then brought it down with all his force on Elva's ankle bone. She yelped in pain as she jerked her foot away. "Next time you do what I tell you," Cudge laughed at the expression on Elva's face. "Now shut up and try and act normal."

The pickup truck bounced over and around deep ruts as Cudge maneuvered around the entrance ramp to the gas station. A homemade sign with big red letters said shocks were a specialty of the station. "Rip-offs," Cudge muttered, "they probably dug the damn holes themselves."

The truck pulled alongside the pump. "You get out and watch those dials, Elva. I gotta take a leak. This joint looks like a rip-off place to me."

Elva climbed from the truck. She looked around for some sign of an attendant. The place looked empty. Limping, Elva walked to the opposite side of the pumps. Maybe she should pump the gas herself to save time. She was just about to lift the nozzle from the rack when two things happened. A needle-thin youth called, "What'll it be?" and a muffled voice called, "Let me out of here." Elva's brain felt like cold, wet spaghetti as her eyes went to the door marked Gents.

"Fill it up with unleaded." She backed off and tried to appear nonchalant as she leaned against the pop-up. Thank God for the transistor radio blaring from the kid's breast pocket. She slouched lower. "Is that you, little boy?" She waited, hardly daring to breathe as the kid danced around on one foot, watching the nozzle with unseeing eyes. This time her voice was louder, "Little boy, is that you?"

Davey's eyes closed in relief. She heard him. Where was the man? *Fill it up with unleaded*, was gas. That's what Uncle Tom always said when he stopped to fill up. "Please let me out," he yelled excitedly.

"You say something to me?" the boy asked, turning down the volume on the transistor. "You want the water and oil checked? Hey, are you all right? You look sick."

Elva's eyes remained glued to the restroom door. "Sick? No, I'm not sick. The water and oil is okay." As if he cared if she were sick. He was just being polite. She felt sorry for him with his acne that he kept scratching. For want of anything better to say, she blurted, "You got a problem or what? How come you bounce around like that on one foot and then the other?"

The boy pointed to his pocket and then to the ear plug in his ear. "I got music in my soul. I even sleep with this in my ear. My boss, he don't understand. He likes Lawrence Welk and all those bubbles. You sure you're okay?"

"Yeah, I'm okay. I like Elvis Presley myself. I have every single one of his tapes. I got earphones too," Elva confided.

"There was a time when I was an Elvis fan myself, but I'm into Bruce Springsteen now. Whatcha doin' way out here?"

Elva clamped her mouth shut. What business was it of his what she was doing out here—wherever here was. She better play it cool. It would be just like that dumb Cudge to get jealous. And the little boy. God, what was she going to do?

"Let me out, please let me out!" came the muffled plea to Elva's left.

"Little boy, please be quiet. I have to think. I'll try but you have to be quiet. If Cudge hears . . ."

"What did you say?" the acne-scarred youth asked as he slammed the gas pump back onto the rack.

"I didn't say nothing," Elva replied as her eyes flew to the digital numbers on the gas pump. $24.90. Cudge would have a fit. Let him. Right now she had enough problems. Where was he anyway?

"I heard you say something and I saw your lips move. My old lady used to talk to herself before they took her away. You better watch it. She said she didn't talk to herself either."

Elva's heart fluttered. What if this kid said something when Cudge got back? What if he said she was talking to herself. Cudge wasn't dumb. "Yeah, you're right, I wasn't actually talking, I was kind of singing. I miss playing my tapes. I was just saying the words to a song to myself. That's what you saw me doing. I ain't like your mother, believe me, I ain't."

The boy looked skeptical as he held out his hand for the money.

"You have to wait a few minutes till my, till Cudge—here he comes." She didn't know if she was sorry or relieved. "Hey, why don't you turn your set up a little so I can hear it. I haven't heard anything but the CB for two days." Anything to drown out the feeble, muffled pleas of the little boy.

"You got it!" Never taking his eyes from Elva, the boy put his hand in his pocket and turned the volume up on the transistor. "And now for all you cats who have a fix on Bruce Springsteen, here he is with 'Born to Run,' " the disc jockey bellowed so loud Elva clamped her hands over her ears.

"Shut that goddamned thing off," Cudge shouted.

The gas station attendant's eyes widened. His head jerked around as he backed off a step. It was suddenly hot and airless around the pumps, like the night a pump had exploded when someone tossed a smoldering cigarette into a puddle of gasoline. It wasn't hot by any means. In fact, it was cool and a brisk wind was blowing. Where was it? What happened? His eyes locked with Elva's. He wanted to run home to his mother, but she was in her own sound studio, cutting her nonstop records. In the stillness around him he thought he could hear breathing, thick and heavy. He must be as nuts as his old lady. Defiantly, he reached into his shirt pocket. Blaring music ricocheted around the pumps. He didn't have to listen to this creep. It was his radio and he could damn well please do anything he wanted for $2.00 an hour.

"I thought I told you to shut that thing off," Cudge bellowed.

"That's what you told me all right, but this is my turf, buddy, and I don't give a damn what you say. Pay up and get that lousy rig out of here."

Cudge balled his hands into hard fists. Damn nigger, who the hell did he think he was with all those ugly pimples on his face. Niggers didn't have any right to get stuff white people got, even if it was pimples. He was just about to raise his fist when he saw the boy looking at the license plate. Everyone knew niggers couldn't read, so why was he worried. Because, he told himself, if this cocky little bastard could get white folks' pimples, he could probably read too. "Okay, okay, play your damn radio. I got a headache and that's why I didn't—never mind. Here, keep the change."

"Big spender, a whole dime," the kid smirked.

"And it's nine cents more than you're worth."

Elva stared at the boy and knew that he would have helped her if she had asked. Maybe it was the pity in his eyes or his defiance when he raised the volume on Cudge. Whatever, it was too late now. She nodded slightly as she climbed into the truck.

Cudge's tone was menacing. "You're a loser, Elva. I saw the way you was sucking up to that nigger. You really thought you could get him to help you, didn't you. Well, let me tell you something. I saw that bastard look at our license plates. He's going to remember us. You in particular."

"No, he isn't," Elva said defensively. God, what was she going to do about the little boy. She had to get him out before he suffocated. Reason, crystal clear, seemed to come back to her. He couldn't suffocate with the cracks in the outer shell of the pop-up. She knew there had to be hundreds because of the way road dust filtered inside and stuck to everything. The boy might be stiff and sore but he wouldn't die, like B. J. Not if she could help it anyway. The black kid would have helped her. Between the two of them they could have killed Cudge and freed the little boy. Her teeth clamped together as she visualized stuffing Cudge's body into the camper. Divine retribution. She had heard those words in church one time. Then she and the black kid could take off; he could listen to his transistor and she could play her tapes. They would take the little boy back and receive a reward and everyone would live happily ever after. Everybody but Cudge. She *must* be nuts! If anyone got killed, it was going to be her. She was cold, almost as cold as Lenny. Cudge was perspiring. Serves him right, she thought viciously, as she rolled up her window.

The boy lowered the volume on his radio as he saw his employer approach from the bay area of the station. The pickup came to life beneath Cudge's hands. Slowly, it moved until the pop-up was almost next to his legs. "Let me out of here. Open the door, let me out!" The boy's eyes popped. What the hell! Did he hear right? He laughed. The dude in the pickup was a ventriloquist. He was probably laughing his fool head off right this second, thinking he was going to call the cops and then the dude would have the last laugh. Not likely. Crazy honky.

"Anything wrong?" the gray-haired owner asked.

"Nah, Mr. Connors. The guy in the truck was a comedian. He wanted me to think he had a kid locked in the back. He must be one of those ventriloquists. It really did sound like a little kid."

"How do you know it wasn't?" Jake Connors asked as he stared after the pickup.

"Because there ain't no room once those things get folded up. How could a kid fit in there?" he blustered. His dark eyes narrowed when he remembered how the girl had denied talking to herself. Quickly, he looked at Jake Connors to see if by some chance his thoughts betrayed him. Jake was walking back to the grease pit. The license plate number was UML-432. Before he could forget, he scribbled the number on the back of a charge slip and he put it on the bottom of the pile.

Davey felt the pop-up start to move. "Let me out of here. Open the door! Let me out!" he shouted. Why didn't she open the door? Did the man hear her talking to him? Was she waiting till a better time? Why didn't she open the door so he could get back to his aunt and uncle? Davey thought for a moment; she had sounded as scared as he felt, her voice all shaky and bumpy. It was hard to hear with the radio on so loud. The man didn't know he was here, that was for sure, because if he did know . . . He scrunched himself even tighter into the space between the refrigerator and the hard, wooden bunk. It was dark and scary, but it was better than having the man catch him. The girl would let him out as soon as she could. She might even take him to his aunt and uncle. His eyes drooped wearily—he was so tired, and he didn't feel well.

7

STUART SANDERS watched the people in the anteroom with clinical detachment. It was a hell of a job, all things considered. When you came all the way from New Jersey to Florida you expected to get a little sun and fun, not to sit inside a courthouse waiting for the prize witness to be recalled to the stand.

The waiting was hard on the Taylors too. Annoyance was clearly written over both their faces, yet Sanders would have staked a week's salary that he was the only one aware of it. There they sat, chatting in companionable comfort, occasionally puffing on a cigarette.

As he watched them he realized it was difficult to imagine Sara Taylor without her husband, just as it was difficult to picture Andrew without Sara at his side. He tried, unsuccessfully, to complete the family picture by imagining Davey between them. He wouldn't fit. His eyes narrowed as he watched a nylon-clad leg move just a fraction closer to the polyester trouser leg. No, there was no room between them for a little boy. Sanders saw an intimate smile play around Andrew's mouth as he looked up from his magazine, acknowledging the pressure of Sara's leg. There was no trace of a smile on her face as she lowered her gaze to her own magazine.

Sanders had seen their silent communication when Andrew Taylor had been questioned on the stand by the prosecutor, Roman DeLuca. The preliminary questions had focused on Andrew's university position and were designed to show the jury that he was a solid, upstanding citizen, testifying at personal cost and possible jeopardy to himself and his family.

Then the prosecuting attorney's questions shifted to Andrew's relationship with Jason Forbes.

It had been clear to Sanders that whenever a question was put to Taylor, his eyes would seek out his wife sitting in the first row, just behind the table where Roman DeLuca's assistants were taking notes. Once or twice DeLuca would turn his back on Andrew, and Sanders saw the man's eyes on Mrs. Taylor. DeLuca was sharp. He hadn't known the Taylors for more than a few hours and yet he was able to read their silent signals as well as Sanders did himself after living with them for months.

Andrew Taylor's poise and confidence were unshakable, even under the hostile stare of the accused killer, and his confidence was reinforced by small, almost imperceptible nods of Sara's head. Her eyes never left her husband, and from the proud set of her shoulders and the slight smile around her lips, Sanders realized that she looked a lot like his own Nancy when one of their girls was in a dance recital.

Only once, did DeLuca look at Sara. But in that glance DeLuca seemed to acknowledge that Andrew was getting his strength from Sara's approval. She was his rock—his mainstay. Almost reading the attorney's mind, Sanders wondered how unshakable Andrew would be in his testimony if Sara were not present.

Sanders wondered how long the trial would continue. While he had always considered himself patient, Sanders decided he liked his company a little more jovial. He disliked hushed whispers and dusty rooms, the smell of furniture polish and dry, cracked leather. Most of all he disliked the stale air and the austerity of the countless courthouses in which he had spent half of his life. And to be honest, he disliked the Taylors with a passion unusual for so conservative a man. The thought surprised him. He hadn't thought himself capable of hating. Everyone had faults, he supposed, and God knew, he was far from perfect himself. That was it. The Taylors were just too perfect to suit his tastes. At that precise moment he would have sold his soul to be at home with Nancy and his kids. Hell, he'd even be happy to rake the lawn, a job he loathed, if it meant he could leave this place.

Sanders wished he had a cigarette, but he had emptied his pack of Chesterfields a half hour ago. He'd have to go out into the hall and find a cigarette machine.

"Mrs. Taylor, I'm going outside for a smoke. If you need me, I'll be right outside the door." That was another thing that angered him— why did he always defer to her? Why hadn't he spoken to Andrew

Taylor instead? Sara nodded, not bothering to glance up from her magazine.

Sanders spotted a cigarette machine just outside the courtroom. One hand inside his pocket feeling for change, he headed for it, already tasting the acrid, hot smoke on his tongue. Eighty cents in the slot and a soft pack of Chesterfields fell into the tray. Expert fingers tore away the cello wrapper as he watched the activity around him. Andrew Taylor should have been called to the stand by now, he told himself.

Automatically, Sanders slid a slim cylinder from the cigarette pack and put it in his mouth. A fifty-nine-cent Bic lighter flashed and he drew deeply, the spiraling smoke making his eyes narrow. Christ, there went the assistant D. A.

"Mr. Sanders, there's a call for the Taylors. Would you care to tell them or should I?"

Sanders scanned the sheriff's department uniform, hardly seeing the man behind the badge. "You stand outside the anteroom and don't allow anyone to enter. That means anyone!" he ordered, a grim expression on his face.

"The party is holding, Mr. Sanders. One of your people is on his way from the courtroom," the man offered the information as he took his position outside the anteroom door.

Sanders nodded as he glanced at his watch. It was 3:50. Another five minutes and court would adjourn for the day. Phone calls to courthouses at this time of day were trouble. He knew it.

Jake Matthews raced down the hall. Sanders signaled him and continued down the corridor toward the clerk's office. His hand was steady as he picked up the receiver. He hadn't known what to expect, but it wasn't Tom Ryan's voice. "Sanders here."

"Sanders. Tom Ryan. Listen. We've got a problem. I'm not certain how serious it is, but Sara and Andrew should be told. Davey's gone."

"When?"

"The last time we saw him was about 8:30 this morning. He took the dog and walked around the pond. The dog came back and Davey, well, Davey didn't."

"Who knows about this?" Sanders voice was clipped, offering no hint of concern for the boy himself.

"I notified the police, of course. And the management of the campground. Lorrie and I haven't come up with anything."

"Dumb move, Ryan. You should have called me first. Why didn't you?"

"Why don't they serve ice water in hell?" Tom said bitterly. "How do I know? We were only thinking about Davey, that's why. Look, neither my wife nor I are into this cloak and dagger stuff. Most people in trouble call the police and that's what we did. I'm calling now because it's nearly dark, and Davey's parents have a right to know their son is missing."

Sanders's sharp gray eyes traveled the length of the corridor, coming to rest on the nattily dressed young lawyer who was assistant to the defense. In the old days he would have been called a "mouthpiece." Not for the first time Sanders wondered why a promising young attorney would align himself with known syndicate bosses. He had to face the fact that Davey might have been kidnapped by a branch of the syndicate and was being used as a pawn to discourage Andrew Taylor from testifying.

"I'll handle it, Ryan. You stay put until you hear from me. Give me a number where I can reach you."

Tom quietly gave Sanders their location and the name of the camp-ground. "Sanders, this couldn't be . . . what I mean is, you don't think Davey's disappearance has anything to do with Andrew's testifying in this case, do you?"

"Ryan, I didn't know a thing about this until you called. Anything is possible, and that thought has occurred to me." He was instantly sorry he'd admitted his suspicions. "I want you and your wife to sit tight. We'll take over now. I like that little boy about as much as you do. You'll hear from me. Now get back to that RV and stay put." Before Tom could reply, Sanders replaced the phone.

This was exactly what the FBI had been guarding against; it was the reason why he had practically moved into the Taylor house. What kind of scum would snatch a kid? The kind of scum Andrew Taylor was testifying against, he answered himself.

His steps were heavy as he made his way down the hall. In a husky whisper he repeated the phone conversation to Jake Matthews, giving him orders to report to headquarters. "I'll be waiting here, so make it snappy. I don't want to tell the Taylors until I get an okay from upstairs. There's a good possibility the boy is just lost."

Matthews nodded and took off on a run. He was back ten minutes later. "We wait. Not a word to the Taylors; this case is too important. Something is brewing around here, Sanders," the younger man told him. "I get the feeling that everybody is watching and waiting. What's your hunch? Do you think that friends of the syndicate snatched the Taylor kid?"

Before he replied, Stuart Sanders took a last drag on his cigarette as he watched the conversations outside the courtroom door between Louis Weintraub, counsel for the defense, and his young assistant. "Matthews, it's enough to know that the bad guys already know the kid is gone. I'm not sure how they know—maybe they have him, or there may have been a leak through the Jersey police or from any of a thousand sources. But they know. Our aim, right now, is to keep the Taylors from knowing until we get the go-ahead. You better get word to Roman DeLuca. As state prosecutor, he's got to know that his case might fly out the window if Taylor refuses to jeopardize his son by testifying."

Lorrie Ryan's white-knuckled fingers were digging into Tom's upper arm. He would carry the bruises for days to come. All the words had been said, and neither of them could find the comfort they so desperately needed. Now it was time to wait. Tom kept going over his phone conversation with Sanders down in Florida. Was it possible that Davey had been kidnapped by someone affiliated with the syndicate? Is that what he hoped? He didn't know exactly. On the one hand, if Davey had been kidnapped, then it was reasonably sure that he was safe somewhere. But if he'd just wandered off—what had happened to him? Where was he? Tom once again scanned the still surface of the pond. Since talking to Sanders, he'd been tempted to tell Lorrie of the possibility of a kidnapping, but each time the words came to his mouth, he restrained them. Kidnapping victims didn't always make it home alive. It was easier to think that Davey was lost, and before too long he'd come wandering out of the woods, safe and sound.

Lorrie watched the police prowl the woods, dogs sniffing as they strained at their leashes. The local police had called in state troopers and were grateful for the extra manpower. It was late in the day, and the Ryans had been told that if the boy wasn't found by morning, the police would drag the pond. Lorrie remembered the blood rushing from her head when she heard her worst fears spoken aloud by a stranger.

Where was Davey? What could have happened to him? Terrible things. Unmentionable things that only happened in the dark of night and then only to other people.

Davey Taylor was as close to a flesh-and-blood son as she was ever going to get. He was part of her, no matter what Sara or Andrew said to the contrary. She loved him as much as Sara did—maybe more. A sob rose in her throat and her grip on Tom's arm tightened.

"Hey, easy does it, honey." Gently, Tom pried her fingers loose. "C'mon. Let's walk down to the pond. We can see better from there and be within earshot when the police report in." He drew her to him. "Davey isn't your ordinary, garden variety five-year-old, Lorrie. He's got savvy and logic. Wherever he is, it's just temporary. Hold on to that."

Lorrie looked up at him, trust flashing behind her tear-smudged eyes. How beautiful she is, Tom thought for the millionth time since marrying her. He wiped her tears and smiled. Damned genes, hormones, chromosones . . . whatever. Lorrie should have had a flock of kids all her own to fuss over and tuck in at night. His hold on her was almost savage as he steered her down toward the pond.

Leaning against Tom, Lorrie thought that he was always right when it came to Davey. She had to trust him and wait. Wait for Sara. Wait for Davey. Wait for the police. She stopped in midstride. She didn't like the order of her waiting list. Why had she put Sara first? Why Davey second and the police third? Her eyes widened. Sara first because she was afraid of her; Davey second because she believed in her heart what Tom had said, he did have savvy and he would make it back; she just knew it. The police last because they weren't going to be any help at all. Davey was on his own; she could feel it. She accepted it.

Tom sensed the resolute stiffening of his wife's shoulders. A soft sigh escaped his tight lips. Lorrie would be all right.

It was late afternoon when Tom and Lorrie saw a tall, lanky police officer come into the clearing to make his hourly report. Suddenly uniformed figures were everywhere. "They found something! Quick, Tom, find out if it's Davey."

The lanky officer backed off a step as he watched the Ryans running toward him. He made up his mind never to get married. He never wanted to have that look on his face or have to see his feelings mirrored on his wife's face. If he ever got lonely for kids or a wife, he'd stifle the impulse. This was never going to happen to him. Christ, what would they look like if they were the kid's actual parents. "Stay here, Mr. and Mrs. Ryan. This isn't for you to see. No," he answered their unasked questions, "we didn't find the boy. This is something else. Stay here," he repeated firmly.

"No," Lorrie said just as firmly. "I want to see what it is. Whatever it is, will it help you find Davey?"

"I don't know," the officer replied honestly. Women! Why did they always have to come right to the heart of the matter. He couldn't let her see what was in the shallow grave. Women fell apart when they saw things like that. They might be the fairer sex, but they were also the weaker. He should know; he had five sisters who couldn't even tie a knot. "That's an order," he said briskly.

"Put some back into it, Delaney; if there was a six-pack in that hole you'd have it out by now!" a local policeman with a noticeable beer paunch bellowed.

The lanky cop, Delaney, was shoveling at his own speed. "Whatever's down here isn't going to come up any faster with your yelling. And who the hell appointed you my superior? You want speed, grab a shovel and do it yourself. If not, shut up and let me do it my way."

Delaney hefted his shovel and gently prodded into the soft dirt. It was a body, no doubt about it. The dirt was barely covering it. He was in no hurry. Christ, what if it was the little kid they were looking for? He didn't want to see the little boy's body, and worse, he didn't want to be with the Ryans when they found out. What else could it be? The grave was fresh, a few hours old at the most. Overnight, at the most. It had to be the kid. He didn't like digging up bodies, and he was in no hurry. Let Jackowsky call him anything he wanted. Delaney gritted his teeth and went back to work. For sure he wasn't getting married. Imagine having to go home and tell your wife you dug up a kid's grave. Jesus! Cold sweat broke out on his forehead.

"You playing around or something?" Jackowsky yelled. "Simpson, get in there with Delaney and be careful! We don't want any marks on the body made by our department."

Delaney nudged Simpson. "How does he know for sure there's a body in here?"

Simpson sneezed. "Jesus! What's that smell?"

"Mothballs! It's a body, all right. Jackowsky!"

"A white male, Caucasian. Twenty-five, twenty-eight years." Delaney gagged, carefully brushing earth away from the soft mound. "His eyes are open. Something's wrong; there's dirt in his eyes."

"Cover his face," Jackowsky offered a wrinkled handkerchief. "This ain't no funeral parlor, you know," Jackowsky grumbled. "Lift him out while I call this in. You sure it's not the kid and you guys are squeamish?"

"It ain't the kid, Jackowsky. I know a kid when I see one. This is a man, full grown. I closed his eyes—the least I could do. He smells like mothballs."

As Delaney covered Lenny's face with Jackowsky's handkerchief, he grimaced. If he were married, how in the hell would he be able to go home and tell his wife he closed some stiff's eyes and that the body smelled like mothballs? She'd divorce him in a minute. None of that "till death do us part" stuff for her; whoever "her" was. The stiff's eyes felt like round, hard marbles.

"What is it with you, Delaney? You writing a book or somethin'?" Jackowsky yelled. "Why you staring at your fingers? You got something we don't know about?"

"Why don't you shut up, Jackowsky? What's the order? Do we haul him in or do we leave him here?"

"Leave him. The chief is on the way with the coroner, and if you're one of those guys that's gonna puke, do it somewhere else. What's that you got, Simpson?"

"Looks like the guy's wallet. Hell, I picked it up and now my prints are on it."

"Then throw it back in." Jackowsky sighed. A veteran of twenty years on the force and he was forced to deal with rookies like Simpson and Delaney.

Lorrie broke free of Tom's arm and ran to the side of the grave. She held her breath as she stared down at the inert form. Thank you, God, she whispered silently. She looked up and Tom's relieved gaze met hers.

"Now, ma'am, what did you want to do that for? I told you to stay behind and make coffee. Now you won't be able to sleep tonight," Delaney mumbled.

"Officer, I'm a doctor. I've seen more dead bodies than you ever will in your lifetime. I did not make the coffee because I don't want to make the coffee. I wanted to see what you were trying to hide from me. I'm satisfied. I didn't want it to be . . . I prayed it wasn't. . . . You're right, I won't be able to sleep tonight or any night until you find Davey. Do you know who that is?" she asked, pointing to the grave.

"Not yet, but we'll find out. Ma'am, why don't you go back to the camp and we'll get back to you as soon as we clear this up."

Lorrie looked around. "There are seven of you here. Why do you need seven people to dig up a dead person? Why aren't six of you out looking for my nephew? I'm sorry that the man is dead, but nothing can be done for him. Davey is just a little boy, and he needs all the help he can get, and you aren't doing anything. Make them do something, Tom!"

Tom took Lorrie by the arm and led her away from the yawning grave. He said nothing as they walked back to the campsite. Delaney cursed, using words he wasn't aware he knew until that moment. The others were silent, each intent on his own thoughts.

A large cloud drifted across the afternoon sun. Lorrie shivered. She needed the sun, needed to feel the warmth on her bare arms. Things didn't look so evil, so forbidding, when the sun was shining. Today was a day she never wanted to live through again. Tomorrow had to be better. But how could tomorrow be better when it meant Sara would be here. Even tonight was a possibility. When Sara found out, she would take the next plane from Miami. Lorrie shivered again but not with cold, with fear of Sara and how she would retaliate. She felt guilty even thinking that of Sara. It would be Sara against Lorrie and Tom and the police. Somehow Sara would manage to stay on the sidelines and yet control things—alone. There would be no closeness, no weeping together, no hoping together. Sara would never share her emotions with anyone but Andrew. Sara would be the judge and the jury, and she, Lorrie, would never get an acquittal. Sara would find her guilty and judge her accordingly. Her punishment would be the loss of Davey from her life.

"Lorrie, stop thinking. Shift into neutral and work from there. Let's take a walk to the office. You've got comfortable shoes on? Good," he said, looking down at her frayed sneakers that had gone through four years of college and eight years of medical school. A treasure, Lorrie called them, they didn't make sneakers like that any more. "We could take the RV, but I think we could both use the walk."

"Good idea, Tom. Hey, I'm okay I can handle this. Truly I can. I may have a bad moment here or there, but not to worry. I may not come from hearty, peasant stock, but I can hold my own."

"I know, hon. Look, sometimes I've got the tact of a buzz saw, but I'm concerned about how your sister is going to react to all this. If she wasn't such a bitch, maybe I could hack it better."

Lorrie plodded alongside Tom, knowing she should defend Sara but having neither the energy nor the impulse to do so. Sara was a bitch.

"Looks like something's doing," Tom motioned to the three patrol cars lined up outside the camp office. "Let's take a look and see if we can learn something."

"Ma'am, we stopped by your RV for coffee, but you weren't there, so we came on down here," Officer Delaney said in a brisk tone. "We still have men combing the woods."

"Sorry about that outburst," Lorrie mumbled.

"Delaney, isn't it? Have you heard anything?" Tom asked, covering Lorrie's embarrassment.

"About your nephew, no. Sorry, Mr. Ryan. But you know we found a body out near the pond. We also found a wallet and from the driver's license, it's safe to assume it belongs to the dead man. The description fits. According to the identification, the deceased is Leonard Lombardi, and the address is Newark, New Jersey. How he came to be buried out here, we don't know. Right now, there's an all-points bulletin out for the two other campers who were here last night. According to the manager here, one was an older, retired couple and the other was younger. Seems the young couple camped in the vicinity of the grave. Both campers left early this morning. We're checking it all out."

"What about Davey?" Lorrie asked anxiously. It seemed to her that the excitement of finding the body was superseding the search for her nephew.

Reading her thoughts, Delaney became defensive. "We're working on that, Mrs. Ryan. There's always the possibility that your nephew's disappearance is linked with the dead man. I'm not saying that's the case, ma'am, only that it's a possibility."

Tom's voice was low and controlled when he questioned the young officer. "Did the manager say if he knew where the other couples were heading? Campers, as a rule, usually make inquiries about where their next stop is going to be."

"The older couple, Koval is their name, said they were going to Virginia Beach and expected to set up camp around about now. We have a call in to the local police and are waiting for them to get back to us. The young couple is another story. They paid in advance and didn't stop on their way out. The guy didn't even have a hook-up, so we don't know when he left or where he was heading. Hold it, looks like something just came in. Stay here and I'll be right back. Ma'am?"

"I'll wait officer," Lorrie said quietly. "We won't get in your way."

Tom Ryan watched as his wife dug a trail in the powdery dirt at her feet. He wondered what color the sneakers were originally. Possibly white and then again they could have been blue for all he could tell. They looked like they still had the original laces. Knots actually. He counted six knots in one lace as he fought to keep his emotions in check. He wished he knew exactly what time it was, but he didn't dare look at his watch. Lorrie would pick up on that immediately and start counting.

"What did you find out?" Lorrie asked. Delaney wondered why she looked so lopsided all of a sudden. He watched her shift from one foot to the other and then noticed the hole she had dug with the toe of her sneaker. "The young couple I was telling you about. Well, it seems their rig is registered to an Edmund Balog of Newark. Yesterday he was stopped on the turnpike by a state police officer. Seems there was some uneasiness on the part of the trooper, and he had his license checked and then a call came in. There was an accident further down on the pike and he had to cover it. We have a call in to him now. He'll be going off duty soon and will call in. That's it, folks."

"Did you get an address for the couple in Newark?" Tom asked.

Officer Delaney looked pained. Such novices. The public always seemed to think cops did nothing productive. "Yes, sir, and right now there's a team of officers on the way to the apartment. I don't know if you know anything about Newark, but the guy's pad is in the Iron-bound section. Tough neighborhood, if you know what I mean. We'll hear soon. Why don't you go back to your camper? I give you my word that as soon as I hear something, I'll come by and report to you. The other teams will be checking in, and the new crew will be coming on duty. Make yourself some dinner and try to eat. We may need you later. What do you say?" he asked hopefully. Christ, he couldn't stand looking into Mrs. Ryan's eyes another minute.

"Sounds fair to me," Tom said. "Come on, Lorrie, he's right; it's time to eat. We'll make that coffee for you this time."

"Yes, we will, officer. I am sorry about not making it before, but I don't think I could have gotten the measurements right. I was upset," she said simply.

Delaney nodded. "Make it hot and strong. This lady in here," he said, motioning toward the manager's office, "thinks coffee is colored water." He gave Lorrie a conspiratorial wink and strode back to the office to wait for the latest news. He felt uneasy. There should have been some news by now on the kid. Someone should have seen him somewhere. Too many hours had gone by for him to have simply wandered off. Responsible adults usually noticed a lost kid, especially one that young.

Especially if the kid acted sick. While he hadn't understood everything she said, it was clear that the boy had hemophilia and was supposed to have his medication around noontime. Delaney looked at his watch. Five-thirty. Nearly six hours. He'd heard Jackowsky ask Mrs. Ryan if the kid would bleed to death without the drug. And that was when she'd explained that the drug, antigen, she called it, only controlled the disease, and it had to be administered at regular intervals, otherwise the kid could actually become allergic to it, and it would never do him any good again. Ever. While Delaney hadn't completely understood, Lorrie had communicated the urgency of the situation.

"Hey, Delaney! Get over here and give us a hand!" Jackowsky again. Christ! When would he be relieved from duty so he could go back to his apartment and take a hot shower? He felt contaminated from touching that body.

"I guess autumn is really here," Tom Ryan said. He watched the crimson and gold leaves sailing through the air. The soft rustle of the brilliant leaves overhead did nothing for his nerves. Out of the corner of his eye he saw his wife pleat the hem of her cotton shirt over and over. Her long, tapered fingers creased the material and then smoothed it out, only to pleat it again.

"I used to love this time of year. Now I hate it," Lorrie said quietly. "It's starting to get chilly. It was downright cold last night. Davey had only that windbreaker on; it just has a thin flannel lining. I wonder if he's hungry."

"About as hungry as you are," Tom said quietly. "I know I must sound like a broken record, but I know he's okay. I can't explain it, but I know it here," he said thumping his chest. "Here comes Delaney." Seeing his wife about to jump up, Tom cleared his throat. "Sit down, Lorrie." It was the voice of her old math teacher when he had had enough of her rowdiness in his orderly classroom. Lorrie sat, her heart in her eyes.

"See, I told you I'd be back. Did you have something to eat, Mrs. Ryan?" Delaney questioned.

"Yes," Lorrie lied.

Delaney directed his conversation to Tom. He felt more at ease with the man. "Okay, this is what we got." Delaney took a deep breath and went into his spiel. "The state trooper that stopped Edmund Balog called in as soon as he got off duty. He said there was something about Balog that made him nervous, something that didn't ring right. I don't know if it has anything to do with your nephew or not. The trooper called Balog's license plates in and was about to have him open the pop-up for his inspection when a call came in for help. An accident further down the pike. There was a young woman with him who seemed scared to death. That's it, folks. Nothing definite, a cop's gut feelings. That's what police work is all about in a lot of ways."

"Then you still have no clues, no leads on Davey." It wasn't so much a question as it was an accusation on Lorrie's part.

"Yes, ma'am, that's about it." Christ, she wasn't going to cry, was she? He hated it when women cried. Ryan was staring at his wife with a peculiar kind of intensity, perhaps willing her not to cry. They looked like they belonged together.

"What about the old couple that was going to Virginia Beach?" Tom asked.

"A dud. Nothing. Zero. They didn't see your nephew. They had some thoughts, but that's all they were, about the young couple. Mrs. Koval says she heard a scream. Mr. Koval said he was sleeping, and his wife always hears screams, blames it on all the soap operas she watches and something about a fish tank. Sometimes this happens. People don't want to get involved and they mind their own business. The Kovals are a mind-your-own-business couple—and those are the words of Detective First-grade Harry Thatcher. They checked out fine. Sorry."

"Thanks for coming out to talk to us, Officer Delaney. You'll let us know about any further developments, right?"

"I'm going off duty shortly. One of the other men will check in with you. We've set up temporary offices next to the manager's quarters. If you need us, or if the boy comes back on his own, you'll know where to find us. Try not to worry."

"I knew they wouldn't find anything. All they can think about is that dead body. Davey's disappearance is lost in the shuffle now! It's not fair."

Stuart Sanders's ulcer was beginning to act up, and he had the two-and-a-half-hour plane ride back to New Jersey to look forward to. And an airline dinner. He popped two Rolaids into his mouth, hoping to ward off what he knew would be an acute case of indigestion. The thought of sitting beside Sara Taylor for the entire trip played hell with his whole body chemistry. Perhaps she would sleep, or he would. Out of the question. He'd have to remain awake to play bodyguard. Ridiculous. It was like playing nursemaid to a barracuda in open water.

He wanted this case to be over and done with. He wanted Davey back home, safe and sound. He yearned to feel Nancy's arms around him as they snuggled in bed while she recounted the children's antics. It wasn't too much to ask. Hell, yes it was. That would be the reward for a job well done, and so far he hadn't earned it. He should have anticipated something like this.

His footsteps were silent in the thickly carpeted hallway leading to the Taylors' hotel suite. Could it have been only half an hour ago that he'd presented them with the facts about Davey, carefully omitting any mention of the possibility of foul play. He intentionally reinforced their suppositions that Davey was lost or had wandered off. Whatever it was that he'd expected, it hadn't happened. Sanders knew that he had wanted to be the one to tell them because he wanted to see Sara Taylor go to pieces. He should have known better, he told himself, and wondered when he'd become so vicious in his thinking. If it had been any other woman, he would have dreaded telling her that her son was missing. But not Sara Taylor. For once he wanted to see her rattled, confused, and desperate. Out of control.

Andrew Taylor was the one Sanders pitied. The man kept running a frantic hand through his hair, his features drawn and pained. Sara had been the strong one, comforting her husband, telling him that she was certain Davey had wandered off and would find his way back soon.

Sara's eyes held Sanders's attention. Was he wrong, or was there an accusation in their depths, even while her hand tenderly stroked Andrew's arm? That was it, Sanders decided. Andrew Taylor's witnessing that scene in the university library had upset the order of Sara's household. Things were beyond her control and she blamed Andrew.

Matthews stood outside the Taylor suite, arms crossed over his chest. "They wanted to be alone," he explained.

Sanders nodded and rapped on the door. Andrew opened it, the anguished lines of half an hour ago gone from his face. Sara had worked her magic with him once again. But how, Sanders wondered, did you get a man to forget that his son might be in grave danger?

"Mrs. Taylor, our plane leaves at six-ten. A car will pick us up. The airport is only a few minutes from here. Can you be ready?"

Sara's eyebrows shot up. "Mr. Sanders, I won't be leaving with you after all. My husband and I talked it over, and I'm going to remain here with him."

Sanders was incredulous. Wild horses couldn't keep Nancy away if one of their kids was in trouble.

"And Mr. Sanders," Sara continued in her cool voice, "tell my sister I want to talk to her as soon as possible." The words held a threat, and Sanders pitied Lorrie Ryan, and Davey too. Every child needed a loving, tender, mother figure in his life. Somehow he just knew that if Sara had anything to say about it, and she would, Lorrie Ryan might as well forget she ever knew and loved little Davey Taylor.

"Now, Mr. Sanders, I don't want you to waste your time trying to persuade me to go back with you. My mind is made up. I must be here with Andrew. We started this together, and we'll finish it together.

What kind of wife would I be if I deserted my husband now when he needs me? You'd better hurry; you don't have much time and there's bound to be traffic at this hour. We wouldn't want to be responsible for your missing your plane. After all, it is your job."

Sanders turned to Andrew. "Mr. Taylor, do you agree with your wife's decision to remain here?" Make her go, dammit! Make her be a mother to that kid for once in her life. But Sanders did not give voice to his thoughts. He'd been warned that the Taylors weren't to be unnecessarily alarmed—at least Andrew Taylor wasn't. He was the key witness in the trial, and his testimony was all-important in the case against the multimillion-dollar drug ring. State needed to prove a connection between the murdered man and the syndicate, and Andrew would provide the connection.

"My wife has assured me that she believes Davey wandered off from the campsite. What would her presence accomplish? The Ryans will do all they can; we know that. Right now, as I see it, the imminent danger to Davey is his missing his daily antigen shot. Unfortunately, nothing can be done about that until he returns."

Could he believe his ears? Taylor was talking as though Davey were a naughty child who had wandered away, and he was able to return when he was good and ready! Sanders wanted to take Andrew and shake him and hear his stiff neck crack. Still, he couldn't go against departmental orders. Even a hint that Davey might be held by friends of the Miami syndicate could discourage Andrew's testimony.

As time went on Sanders was becoming more and more skeptical of that possibility. Surely, if Davey had been kidnapped, the Taylors would have been apprised of that fact, word would have been gotten to them, either directly or through the bureau itself.

"As my husband has told you, Mr. Sanders, we'll be staying here until Andrew takes the stand. Tomorrow afternoon, at the latest, and then we'll be back in New Jersey. By that time, Davey will have returned."

Sanders stiffened. What kind of mother was she? That poor little kid. Christ, he felt like smashing something. Something was on fire in his stomach—damn ulcer was acting up. At least he could sleep on the plane and hope for the best. Just because she gave birth to Davey didn't make her a mother. Schooling his face to impassivity, he said good-bye and walked away. He hoped he would never have to see either one of them again. Back in New Jersey he would be in the field, his contact with the Taylors over. From this moment on he would be with the Ryans, and that meant Davey. Hang in there, little buddy, I'll find you somehow. He dismissed the lump in his throat. Must have something to do with his ulcer he told himself.

Andrew Taylor watched his wife through narrowed lids. Another day and they would be back home, safe in New Jersey. Now why had he used the word safe? Here they were, locked in a hotel room with an armed guard outside the door. How much safer could he be than he was at this moment?

He still wasn't certain of Sara's decision to stay with him. Was it a mistake for Sanders to go back alone? Sara had made the decision to stay at his side; he knew she would. Her argument that two heads were better than one convinced him. Sara was always right. Everything that could possibly be done for Davey was being done. Sanders would take charge. Davey. Alone, lost in the woods. Sanders would find him and take him home safely. Sanders was a man to depend on, a family man, and he knew how important children were to a family.

Andrew's shoulders slumped when he remembered the agent's look when Sara told him she wasn't leaving with him. Her duty, she had said, was to stay with her husband. Sanders should understand that, but Andrew knew he didn't. At first the look had been disbelief, but that had given way to sour acceptance. His good-bye had been barely audible. Sara was right; she was always right. Davey had just lost his bearings and would turn up before dark.

Sara walked around the edge of the bed and lightly touched Andrew's shoulder. "Would you like roast beef or chicken for dinner?"

"What do you suggest?"

"I think a broiled spring chicken sounds fine. With a garden salad and some fresh peas—it's much too hot for a heavy dinner. Andrew, you aren't upset with me because I decided to stay on with you, are you?"

"Of course not, Sara. Why would you even think such a thing? I know everything is being done to find Davey. The truth of the matter is we would probably be in the way. Besides, he'll turn up before dark,

[144]

most kids do. I used to get lost at least once a week and always managed to find my way back."

"And Davey is his father's son," Sara said briskly. "After dinner I'm going to place a call to Lorrie through the campground manager's office. I want to know how this happened. She always was a feather-brain, but I expected more from Tom. I'm so disappointed in both of them. It just bears out, Andrew, what I told you before we left home. We must curtail their involvement with Davey."

Any doubts Andrew might have had concerning Tom and Lorrie's attentions toward his son were wiped away with Sara's words. It was uncanny how she was always right. "I quite agree, Sara."

"Police!" Sara made the term sound obscene. "It isn't bad enough we're surrounded with guards and police twenty-four hours a day, but now we have to be subjected to more police. What would you like to drink, Andrew? Why don't we order wine and we can have it for the rest of the evening. It will help us to unwind and relax."

All Andrew heard was the word relax. He had been looking forward to a double scotch, straight up. A couple of liters of wine while he went over his testimony would certainly help. Sara was one step ahead of him all the time. Scotch wasn't really a drink to sip in a hotel room. He hoped the wine glasses had long stems.

"I think I have it all now. You don't want dessert, do you?" Sara said, putting the hotel pen back in the desk drawer.

If he ordered dessert, he would still be eating after Sara was finished. "No."

"I didn't think so," Sara's eyes twinkled down at him. Fondly, she stroked his hair. "I'll give this to the guard and you can watch the news while we wait."

Just as Sara was about to open the door a sharp knock sounded. She glanced at Andrew who was already engrossed in the early evening news. It was probably the guard wondering why she was taking so long with the dinner menu. She smiled when she opened the door, the menu extended. She backed off a step and let her eyes flash to the bellboy and then to the guard. "A message came in for you a few minutes ago, ma'am."

Sara looked at Jake Matthews. "It's all right. We checked, it just came in. Is that your menu? Good, the boy can take it down when he leaves. I'll tip him, Mrs. Taylor. You go back inside now and lock the door."

Sara made a face the minute she turned her back. As if she needed to be told to lock the door. The message was probably from Lorrie and full of all kinds of apologies, or else it was to say Davey had returned to the campsite. She sighed as she sat down next to Andrew and withdrew a slip of paper from the envelope. She read it once, then read it again. The message was brief:

It's urgent that you call 943-0773 as soon as possible. There was no signature, just the time the message was logged in. Sara read it again. Was it a local number? Certainly a Florida number or the operator would have included an area code. What could it mean? Should she show it to Andrew? He would worry. Roman DeLuca. Of course. It didn't matter that she detested the suave district attorney; he looked like Cesar Romero. She would wait till a commercial came on before telling Andrew. The anchorman's voice droned on as he reported on the unrest in Ireland. A sleek Datsun 280Z flashed on the screen as a pitch came on for a local car dealer. "Darling, look at me. It seems we have a message. A bellboy gave it to me when I opened the door to give our dinner menu to the guard. Read it and tell me what you think."

Andrew read the curt message. He shrugged. "Did you show it to the guard?"

"Of course not, Andrew. After all, we are entitled to some privacy. Perhaps it's something personal, although I can't think what it could be. It appears to be a local number or at least a Florida number. At first I thought it might be a message from Tom or Lorrie, even Sanders, but I don't think that's the case."

"Well, there's only one way to find out; call the number and see what it is," Andrew suggested.

"I don't know if that's such a good idea, Andrew. Perhaps we should wait for Roman DeLuca to get here and show it to him. I really don't want to get involved in anything else right now. It could be some pervert or a weird person who watches the news and does things like this. You know how some people get a thrill out of tormenting others. It could even be a threat against us."

[146]

"I don't want anyone threatening you, ever," Andrew said adamantly. "We'll wait for Roman to get here and let him handle it."

Sara smiled. "How gallant of you, Andrew. I think it's wise to wait too."

Andrew let out a long sigh. She agreed with him. He smiled at her in an intimate way and she responded in kind. Gently, she blew him a kiss. He smiled again as the caravan of Datsuns left the screen to be replaced with a silver-haired, somber-faced news commentator.

Stuart Sanders settled himself in his aisle seat aboard the Pan Am 727. He wanted a cigarette but knew he had to wait until the silver-tipped jet was airborn. It was something most people thought he did well—wait. He knew he didn't—his insides always felt as though they were on fire. He detested inactivity almost as much as he hated certain people. Once he hated someone, God Almighty couldn't get him to revise his opinion. And by the same token, when someone got close to his heart, that person stayed close forever. Nancy said he loved with a vengeance. Maybe he did, he thought sheepishly. He withdrew a cigarette from his shirt pocket and held it in readiness. It was a nail in his coffin. When he went down for the count, he thought it would be with the big C. He already was coughing and hacking in the morning. The thought of his own death didn't bother him. It was the death of other people that made him want to lash out.

Davey Taylor. Was the kid suffering wherever he was? As soon as this plane got off the ground and he got his cigarette lit, he was going to open his briefcase and take a look at the Polaroid shot he had taken of Davey in his red windbreaker. It was something he wanted to share with Nancy. He knew what she would say the minute she saw the little towhead. Her eyes would mist, and she'd hug his arm. She would know why he took the picture. To share with her, the way they shared everything. He felt good knowing he was going home to her soon.

Sanders leaned back and grasped the cross he always wore around his neck. He didn't like take-offs any more than he liked landings. As long as he could smoke and sleep in between, he didn't care. The silver bird climbed and climbed and then leveled off. The "No Smoking" sign went off. Sanders lit his cigarette and inhaled deeply. If he had a bourbon and branchwater, he would be just fine for the next two and a half hours. Now he wanted to see the picture of Davey Taylor. A deep, paternal feeling swelled in him for the little boy. There was something about this kid, something that bothered him. Nancy would spot it in a minute, know exactly what it was and what to do about it. It was something he just couldn't put his finger on. He would have to chalk it up to a gut feeling, and twenty-three years with the bureau.

Back in Miami he had felt that someone or some force was at work against the kid. It was a feeling Nancy would listen to with respect. His chief would listen, nod, and ask for concrete evidence or substantiated facts. It was possible the little boy was a pawn of some sort. But he felt that was more improbable than probable. So then what was it? He was starting to feel ornery. He had been away from Nancy too long. She had probably raked the leaves today. She had done his job; he was sure of it. And she had no doubt car-pooled the guys on the football team, another one of his jobs. Jim was playing football and Nancy loved it. She loved it because the kid and his old man loved it. That was Nancy.

Now why in the hell did Sara Taylor's face have to appear before him? She was the direct opposite of Nancy. She had a cool, patrician kind of beauty, he had to give her that. But that was all he would give her. Her place was with her husband? How could she ignore her son? Was it possible she knew something he didn't know? Did she really think the kid just wandered off? Who knew what she thought behind that frozen mask she wore. He might not know what made Sara Taylor tick, but there was one man who did know—Roman DeLuca. He had watched the suave district attorney at his first meeting with the Taylors. DeLuca had sized Sara up in five minutes flat and had immediately discounted her—to Sara's chagrin.

Sanders stared at the snapshot of Davey Taylor for a while longer. What was he looking for? What did he hope to see in the colored picture of the little kid? Some answer? Some clue? There was nothing. He laid the picture back on top of a yellow legal pad. He groped for a paper clip and attached it to several thicknesses of the pad. He didn't want to lose it. It was important not to lose the kid. Satisfied that the picture was secure, he fished and fumbled, looking for his favorite treat —salted peanuts. He found two bags and laid them on the seat next to him.

8

CUDGE BALOG wished he had three eyes—one for watching the road, one for the back of his head, and one for Elva. He didn't like the way she was acting, nor did he care for the creepy way she kept looking at him. And, he thought grimly, she hadn't bawled at all when he stepped on her ankle. That wasn't at all like Elva. Crying and whining were the things she did best, besides making Kool Aid. Time to give her another jolt.

"You ever see a guy get the electric chair, Elva?" That should do it, he thought, satisfied with his cleverness.

Her answer was a flat, disappointing, "No." No wincing, no sudden catch of breath.

"Not even in a movie?"

"I always close my eyes. You know I hate that kind of stuff. I only like television. All the raunch and violence is edited out. Stuff like what you just said."

"What did I just say?" he asked innocently, knowing he was getting to her.

"About electric chairs. You're only trying to scare me, Cudge. Besides, they don't have electric chairs anymore. I heard it on the news; there's no more capital punishment."

"Only in some states. When they send a broad to the chair, they shave her head. Bald, Elva. Not a hair left. Like Kojak's." He took his eye from the road for an instant and sneaked a look at her. She was nervous, of that he was certain, but it was annoying him that she was in control of it. Meanly, he pressed the subject. "They don't let you wear no underwear under the dress they give you. You gotta wear paper slippers on your feet. But you get to eat whatever you want for your last meal. What would you order, Elva? This is good a time as any to decide because you been belly-aching how hungry you are. What would you order?"

Elva listened to him and knew exactly what Cudge was trying to do. Unnerve her. Make her fall apart, and when she was hysterical, he would kill her. She couldn't let that happen. She had to help the little boy get out of the camper and get away. She couldn't let Cudge do anything to her until the boy was safe.

Cautiously, she turned in her seat and stared at Cudge for a long time. It was Cudge who was becoming unnerved as he kept taking his eyes from the road to look at her and then quickly looked back at the road. Her voice was light, almost airy, and seemed to come from far away. "I think I'd order veal cutlets, because they cost about eight dollars a pound. And shrimp. Big juicy ones with a real spicy sauce to start with. Baked potatoes, with lots of sour cream. And rolls. Hot ones with butter. And that dessert I always hear about, Cherries Jubilee; whatever it is, it sounds good. And beer. A really icy cold beer. Coffee, with rich cream, none of that fake stuff, to top it off. Maybe a pepper-mint Lifesaver to settle my stomach as I walk to the chair. What are you gonna order, Cudge?"

He glared at Elva. She'd turned the tables on him. She made her question sound as though it was definite he'd have to order his last meal because he was really going to the chair. "You're dumb, Elva. You'd be so piss-ass scared you wouldn't be able to eat a thing. And if you did, you'd puke your guts out."

"Maybe you're gonna be too scared to eat, but I wouldn't." That should settle him down for the time being, she thought. She had to think about the little boy and how to get him out of the pop-up. She wouldn't mess up this time, not again. Poor little thing, he must be miserable, cooped up in there. I won't let anything happen to you *this* time, B.J., she crooned to herself. *This* time I'll make sure you're safe! Bald, like Kojak. No underwear. It wasn't decent. Especially if they took pictures. Don't worry, B.J., I'm gonna take care of you. Somehow, I'll make him let you go.

Cudge didn't like Elva's wise-ass answers. By now, she should have been a glob of Silly Putty, jabbering away at him to stop tormenting her. Stupid broad. Sitting there in a dream world, smiling to herself.

[150]

It was her smile that started to awaken his anger. Maybe she was thinking about Elvis Presley again. No, that wasn't like her usual dumb smile when she dreamed about Elvis. This was more ominous. Maybe she was plotting his death, just the way he was planning hers—this very minute. Old Elva might be skinny as a pencil, but she was wiry and strong, like a bull terrier. Just like old Peggy, he found himself thinking, knowing that Elva would be as tough to kill as that old dog had been, fighting to the last, refusing to give up the ghost.

He hated dogs. He hated Elva and everyone and everything. But mostly, he hated that little bastard who was finking on him to the cops. If I had a gun, I would have killed the two of them on the spot. People like Elva and that brat kid could ruin a person's life. He'd get out of this mess yet, and without Elva.

Hours passed as Cudge concentrated on his driving. For Elva it was impossible to think clearly with Cudge being so controlled at the wheel. The road map in her lap was nothing more than a blur. Her neck and shoulders were stiff with the effort she made to sit straight in the jouncing truck seat. Her ankle throbbed painfully and her tooth was aching. She was sure of just one thing: She had to find a way to open the pop-up and set B.J. free. Even if she died doing it. Once in a while God and the fates allowed you a second chance, and this was hers. She couldn't flub up, not now. Maybe she should pray for a miracle. Or just pray. Could she remember how? Maybe there wasn't a god after all. If there was a god, what was he thinking of, to allow B.J. to be penned in the camper and her to be stuck with Cudge Balog. God was as make-believe as Ali Baba and the Forty Thieves.

At that moment Cudge would have bet the remainder of Lenny's bankroll that Elva was up to something. He didn't like the ramrod stiffness of her back nor the way she stared staight ahead. Her silence now was different from the times when she had her damned earphones on, listening to that gyrating prick Elvis Presley. "There's a rest stop ahead at the next exit. I think we can get some eats. Elva, are you listening to me?"

"I ain't hungry."

"What do you mean, you ain't hungry? You been busting me to stop and eat, and now you ain't hungry. Why ain't you hungry, Elva?" he asked suspiciously.

'Because I ain't."

"Well, I am, and we're going to stop. We can get a carry-out order. You go in and get it, and I'll wait for you. We need to fill up the water bottles anyway. Make up your mind we're stopping."

Elva hoped her relief wasn't evident. If she had learned anything at Cudge Balog's knee, it was that to disagree would make him more determined. Just a little more play-acting and maybe she could free B.J. "I can't do it, Cudge. My foot hurts too bad, and I'll be limping. Someone will remember that I limped. You have to be careful and use your head now."

"I got a bad feeling about you, Elva, like you're planning something."

"Yeah, like what I'm gonna buy you for Christmas. What I said is the truth. If you want to be stupid, go ahead, but don't say I didn't warn you. I didn't ask you to kick me."

Cudge eased up on the gas pedal as he turned off at the exit sign. It was a Howard Johnson's.

"Where you gonna park this thing?" Elva asked quietly. "Maybe it would be best if you park right in front and that way no one will think it's at all suspicious. It's just a suggestion." Now, if she was half as smart as she knew she was, Cudge would park at the end of the parking lot, away from all the families with their little kids. The last slot would be perfect. She could open the pop-up, scoop up B.J. and run like hell.

"Maybe that's what you would do, but it ain't what I'm gonna do. I'm parking at the end of the lot. There ain't enough cars around to lose ourselves in the crowd. We don't need to be noticed. You keep your yap shut, and do what I tell you when I tell you. You got that?"

"Does that mean you're going in for the food? I told you I can't walk. Look at how swollen my ankle is. I think you broke a bone or something."

"You're walking, Elva, and I'm gonna be right behind you. If you fall, you're gonna get my knee in the small of your back. And I don't want to hear anymore of your crap about someone noticing you either. Ain't nobody gonna pay any attention to you."

"Oh, yeah, what about those two guys?" Elva said, pointing toward the entrance.

Cudge's eyes followed her finger. Two troopers in tight gray pants and the inevitable polished sunglasses were just getting out of an unmarked car. His features tightened. One hand curled into a fist. The two men slowly walked through the entrance. Booths were next to the long row of windows. Did troopers sit at counters or did they take booths? Either way he had to make some kind of move. If they sat down in one of the window booths, they had a clear view of the entire parking lot. Should he go in alone, as Elva had suggested, and take out the food, or should he drag Elva with him? Christ, what should he do? It was the smirk on Elva's face that forced his decision. She wouldn't dare try anything. "You're coming with me. We'll eat inside. Act like we didn't do nothin' and everything will be all right."

Elva squared her shoulders. "*We* didn't do anything; *you* did it." She felt more powerful at that moment than she had ever felt in her life. "Ain't you afraid I'll spill my guts to those cops? I could, you know. Just remember that, Cudge. You should have killed me back at the campground. I seen it in your eyes. You were gonna kill me. You leave me out here, I got just as good a chance as I do if I go inside with you. I want to stay out here. I told you, I ain't hungry."

Cudge's pent-up rage swelled till his eyes seemed to roll back. Elva watched him, neither afraid nor relieved. Nothing mattered to her anymore, except freeing the little boy who looked like B.J.

"Okay, okay. You stay here and watch the rig. Make sure no one comes nosing around." Each word was slow and distinct, spoken with great effort. He had to close the gate, *now,* before it was too late. A loud sigh escaped from Cudge's lips. Now all he had to do was convince Elva that he was going to take care of her. "I been thinking, Elva, about what you just said, that I was gonna kill you. Now, wait a minute. I was just thinking. I wouldn't have done it. Lenny was something else. You ain't never done anything bad to me like Lenny did. Jesus, Elva, you're all I live for. Look what you've done for me so far. Without you, my ass would be in jail. I ain't never gonna forget that. I mean it, and as soon as we get out of this mess, I'm gonna bankroll this wad and take you to the Poconos to that lodge where they have heart-shaped bathtubs. I was even thinking of marrying you. I don't expect you to believe me, but it's what I want and I think it'll work. What do you say, honey?"

"You really think I'm dumb, don't you? I know wives can't testify against their husbands. I ain't ready to get married, and if I never see a heart-shaped bathtub, I'll live. You can't snow me any more, Cudge, so forget it. If you're gonna get the eats, go ahead. Them troopers must be wondering what you're doing just sitting here. Most people either go to the bathroom or the restaurant when they stop at a place like this. You're gonna look suspicious if you don't get moving."

Cudge knew she was right. If she was telling the truth and she couldn't walk, then he was safe. "Okay, I'm going in. You get out and stretch your legs like everyone else. Hop around on one foot and stay put. Don't you have to go to the bathroom?" he asked as he suddenly remembered that she hadn't gone when they stopped for gas. Maybe she was part camel.

"I don't have to go. I didn't drink any Kool Aid today."

"You better be here when I get back, Elva." She nodded. She would be here but not the kid. There was no point in fooling herself; there was no way she could walk, much less run, with her swollen ankle.

"While you're getting the food, I'll open the pop-up and get out the water bottles to save time."

"Like hell you will. I can just see you cranking it the wrong way and bam, one pop-up shot to hell. You know you can't do nothin' right. I'll do it when I get back. If you even think of trying to open my rig, your neck is gonna look like your foot. Now, you get out and we'll talk a minute and then I'll walk real slow into the restaurant, and you damn well better act like you know what the hell you're doing."

Cudge stretched luxuriously like he had all the time in the world. He worked first one leg and then the other. He hitched up his jeans and threw back his shoulders like a man who was bone tired from traveling all day. Walking to the back of the rig, he thumped on the pop-up. It was his, all his. The one thing in his whole stinking life that was his alone. No one was going to take it away from him, and no skinny bag of bones was going to crank it open and screw it up. "You stay right here, Elva, and don't move. I'm gonna be watching from the restaurant."

Davey woke with a start. He wasn't moving any more. He squirmed around, trying to get comfortable. Why did the man stop? Was it nighttime? Where was the woman? Would she let him out? Frantically, he was about to shout, let me out! Get me out of here! And then he heard *him*. He had to be quiet and not make a sound. He had to act the way he did in the hospital and be brave. Quiet and still. A trickle of warmth coursed down his leg. He bit his lips, tasting the salty flavor of his own blood. No matter how scared he was, he had to be quiet. Very quiet. One, two, three strikes and you're out! Uncle Tom was always saying that. This was his third time. If she didn't get him free, he was out. Uncle Tom never said what happened when you were out. He thought he knew. The trickle was now a stream as it seeped into his socks and down into his shoe. He was tired. He was almost too tired to care. He frowned in the darkness. It was a different kind of almost. He felt so tired.

As soon as Cudge entered the restaurant, Elva made her way to the back of the rig. "Little boy, can you hear me?"

"I hear you. Let me out of here! I can't move. Please let me out."

"I am going to let you out as soon as I can. Can you be quiet for just a little longer. I know you must be hungry, but I can't do anything about it right now. Cudge just went inside to get some food. I think he's going to open the pop-up, and you gotta be ready to run. Do you think you can run? Little boy, can you run?"

Davey's thought were jumbled. He knew he couldn't run. He was too tired and too weak. "Yes," he said loudly.

"Good. There's two cops here, and if you run inside the restaurant, they'll take you back home. But you have to be quick. Real quick. Are you okay? You ain't sick or anything are you, little boy?"

Davey thought a minute. "I'm almost sick. I didn't get my shot today."

"What shot?" Elva asked fearfully.

"My antigen shot. I'm a hemophiliac."

"You mean you bleed?" Elva asked in horror.

"I used to, but now I get shots. Please, can't you let me out before *he* comes back?"

"You have to trust me, little boy. I'm gonna help you." Bleed. Shots. If the kid didn't get his shots, he might die. She would be just as guilty as Cudge this time around. He was just a kid, a little boy like B.J. She had to do something. The hell with what Cudge said. What did she care if the cranks fell apart? Her hand was on the crank ready to turn when Cudge walked through the doorway. Behind him were the two troopers. Elva froze. "Little boy, something's wrong. Don't say anything and be real quiet."

"Here we go, honey. Food at last," Cudge shouted with false gaiety. Elva stared at him. Didn't he see the troopers behind him?

Suddenly, a voice shouted. "Sir, sir, the manager wants to see you." Cudge ignored the voice. Elva gagged and her face drained of all color. As if in slow motion, she watched one of the troopers put a hand on Cudge's shoulder. "Mister, someone is calling you. They want you back inside."

Cudge turned slowly and stared at the two troopers. His brain was swelling, every instinct prepared him to fight, to defend himself. The very sight of a uniform could do this to him but to have the trooper speak to him—*touch* him! A hoof cut into the soft tissue of his brain. A hulking, dark shape shouldered the restraining gate. Superhuman effort quelled the restlessness of the beast. "Me?" he asked stupidly.

"Yes, you. The cashier is calling you. She wants you back inside."

The trooper's partner smirked as Cudge turned and walked into the restaurant. "They're all alike. Two weeks on the road and they're in another world. Kind of airless around here, isn't it." His fingers worked at his collar.

"I thought it was me," the first trooper said quietly. "You ever hear about the Santa Ana winds? They say it's weird." He laughed sheepishly. "Come on, let's get it in gear and hit the road. I got a date tonight that would set your hair on end. She's got the biggest boobs on the entire East Coast."

"Seeing is believing," the second trooper grinned. "I don't take a cop's word for anything. Everyone knows you can't trust a cop."

"Fuck you," the first trooper grinned as he climbed behind the wheel. The car came to life just as Cudge hit the parking lot. "Would you believe they shortchanged me," he said holding out his palm with thirty-seven cents in it for proof.

The trooper stared at the change for a full second. His eyes behind the polished glasses were cold. He nodded curtly and switched from park to reverse. Cudge stood back respectfully and watched till the yellow Plymouth left the parking lot.

"Close your mouth, Elva, and get in the truck."

"What about the water bottles. We ain't even got a drop. We need the water. You crank open the top and I'll get the bottles. You'll have to fill them though."

"Christ, you're stupid. Two cops just left here. We were eyeball to eyeball, and you want to stop for water. We ain't opening that pop up till we make camp. When the shit hits the fan, those guys are gonna remember me. Now get your ass in that truck and let's move!"

Elva started to hobble back to the truck when a noisy family got out of a maroon station wagon. Seven children squealed and shouted as they romped about the parking lot, trying to catch a frisky, fuzzy-looking dog. Cudge and Elva were suddenly surrounded by yelping kids and a barking dog. "C'mere, Bizzy. Good girl. C'mon, we got some popcorn for you."

"Jesus Christ!" Cudge shouted to be heard above the noise. "Get that damn dog out of here and get him out now! All of you get out of here. I want to start this rig up and I'm running late."

"Bizzy is just sniffing your pop-up, mister. You got something in there she likes. She's not hurting anything. See, she's just trying to get in to see what you got," a boy in tattered overalls grinned.

"Well, I ain't got nothin' in here for your dog, so get her out of here."

"We can't catch her," a little girl in pigtails complained. "She's fast, mister. Her mother's name was Flash; that's why we picked her from the litter."

"I don't give a damn what her mother's name was, get her out of here."

"Kids, kids, what's going on here. Where's the dog? Not that I care, but I can't see leaving her behind." Their mother approached, herding her children into a close group, her eyes flicking over them as if taking a habitual headcount. Her work-worn hands pushed back frizzy hair from her perspiring brow. "Hey, Max, you better get your butt out here and settle this. These people want to get on the way and your kids are holding up the works. Max, you hear me?"

"Yeah, yeah, I hear you. I been listening to you all the way from Milwaukee. What's wrong this time?" a bear of a man demanded as he climbed from the dust-streaked station wagon.

"There isn't any problem," Cudge said patiently. "We just want you to get your dog, Flash, out of here so we can be on our way."

"Name's Bizzy. Flash was her mother," the girl with the pigtails chirped.

"What you carrying in that pop-up, mister, that attracts our dog? She usually ain't interested in other people and their belongings. Kind of a mind-your-own-business mutt if you know what I mean," the man said.

"Just get that dog out of here. We're running behind schedule now."

Max LeRoy stared at Cudge. He didn't like what he saw. "Bizzy, up," he commanded in a sharp, clear voice. The little dog leaped in mid-air to land in his arms. He nodded curtly to Cudge, and without so much as a word, the kids backed off, allowing Cudge and Elva to enter the pickup. It was Mrs. LeRoy who memorized the license plate without realizing what she was doing.

Elva sighed heavily. She felt like an old newspaper that had been cut up to paper-train a new pup. How much more could she take? And the kid, how much more could he take? What if he started to bleed back there, all alone, and then died on her? Please, God, don't let anything happen to the little boy. I don't care about me, just don't let anything happen to him. I know that I was thinking before that there wasn't a God, but you must be real or Cudge would have found him by now. I don't need a miracle, just a diversion of some kind. You can't let him die, he's just a little boy, hardly more than a baby! Elva choked back a tear. She knew God *did* let little boys die. Remember B.J.

"What are you doing, Elva? Tell me you ain't talking to yourself, tell me you ain't."

"Okay, I ain't talking to myself. I was praying."

Cudge's eyes widened. His head bobbed up and down. "It figures," was all he said.

"Where we going and how much longer are we going to stay on the road?" Elva demanded.

"Soon as I see a spot that looks like it's off the beaten track. You going somewhere, Elva?" he baited her. She ignored him, her mind racing ahead. The kid had said he could run, so he must be all right. Little kids were always hungry. Whatever it was Cudge had bought, she would save her portion for the little boy to take with him. A heart-shaped bathtub. He tries to kill me and he thinks a heart-shaped bathtub will make everything all right. The thought was too ludicrous even to warrant a smile. She was just beginning to realize how stupid Cudge really was. Now, when it was too late.

"Elva, get that map out and take a look-see. I just seen something that makes me nervous. Take a look over there and tell me what you see. Ain't that the same diner and ain't that the same gas station we seen when we started out. It is!" he bellowed. "There's that mom-and-pop camp store. Of all the friggin' luck." For the first time in his life Cudge felt raw gut fear. Right back at the scene of the burial. The kid. His folks. Cops. Fear swooped up into his throat and he gagged. Now, what was he going to do? Head back to Newark? Turn around and drive all night. Camp? Where?

Elva felt herself go limp. This was her miracle. Think, she had to think. "That's good, ain't it, Cudge? Who would think we would come back here. By now the cops been down the other side of the road and are heading south. We can even stop at the store and get the water and stuff." She held her breath, hardly daring to breathe. "We don't have to camp in the Wild Adventure campground. We don't need no hookups. You could pull deep into the woods. A flashlight is all we need. What do you think, Cudge?" she asked anxiously. "But we better get off the road now, before it gets dark." So the little boy could find his way to the highway before the black night descended. "Take a look at the sky, looks like rain to me. If we're going to stop, we better do it now." Childishly she crossed her fingers, waiting for his answer. Make it the right answer, she pleaded silently. You're almost free, little boy, she said over and over in her mind.

Cudge risked a glance at Elva and then made up his mind. She was probably right, but he wouldn't give her the satisfaction of telling her. Without thinking, he signaled for a right turn and was off the road. He had done what she wanted, now she would let the little boy out. Her teeth clamped together in relief. "You're right, it's gonna rain pretty soon." He frowned. "Elva, you notice anything, feel anything?"

Now what. "No, is something wrong?"

"Feels like the pop-up is dragging or something. Maybe we're getting a flat. I'll have to check it out when we stop."

This couldn't be happening to her. All the tools were in the pop-up in a tool kit under the bunk. Cudge would crank it open and it would be all over for her and the little boy. She tried for a light tone. "You're just uptight, Cudge. I don't think there's anything wrong."

"We'll know soon enough. There's the store. I'll pull around the back and take a look. Here's some money, you go in and get a few things. No gabbin', Elva."

As soon as Cudge braked the pickup, Elva had the door open and was outside in the damp air. She shivered. "Little boy, be quiet. Don't make a sound. Please, listen to me, you have to be real quiet. Looks okay to me, Cudge," she called loudly.

Cudge walked around to the back of the truck. He bent down to inspect the worn tread on the tires. The left rear was almost flat. "I gotta change it, but I think we can hold out till we make camp. No point in giving that old biddy inside any reason to remember us. Look at her sneaking a look out the window, pretending she's bird-watching. Get inside and make it snappy."

"Cudge, I got to go to the bathroom real bad. You go in and get the stuff," she said holding out the money. "I'm still limping. Look," she said holding out her swollen foot. "You're sure you ain't gonna change the tire here?"

"Yeah, I'm sure. What about the water bottles? You said we ain't got a drop."

"Crank open the top and I'll get one bottle. That should do us for the night. I'll do that as soon as I go to the bathroom."

"Nah, I'll get the stuff first, and no, I ain't buying Kool Aid; goes against my grain to buy that crap. We'd have water if you didn't keep making that slop. Besides, it's going to take too long to fill the bottles. I'll get a jug of bottled water. You wait right here by the door, I ain't letting you out of my sight. We're too close to trouble. When I get out, then you go to the bathroom."

Elva swallowed hard. "But I gotta go now."

"Okay, you go now and I'll wait right outside the door, and I better hear tinkle-tinkle, splish-splash." While Cudge waited, his eyes kept going to the pop-up. Once he heard what he thought was a scraping sound, but when he turned, it was Elva pushing the door of the restroom closed.

Elva looked around the tiny parking area. Thank God, he hadn't cranked open the camper. She couldn't do anything now, that was for sure. "I'll wait here, I ain't going anywhere. I need something to lean against." Cudge believed her.

"Little boy, can you hear me? Say something. Are you all right? You ain't bleeding, are you? I been real worried."

"I'm okay. Let me out. When are you going to let me out?" Davey pleaded.

"I was going to do it now, but Cudge is watching me. We're going to stop real soon because it looks like it might rain. You gotta be ready to run real fast. I'm sorry I couldn't let you out before, but he was watching all the time. I couldn't take the chance. You just have to hang tight for a little longer. I'll get you out; I promise."

A promise. That was real. Something true that happened even when you thought it wouldn't. Like when Aunt Lorrie made a promise. "Okay, I can wait. Did he hit you anymore?" Davey asked in a tremulous voice.

Now wasn't that just like little B. J., to be worried about her? "Nah, he give me a kick in my foot, but I'm okay. I ain't gonna be able to run with you, but you can make it by yourself. I got a flashlight you can use. It's the best I can do. Shhh, he's coming now."

"Who the hell you talking to, Elva? I seen your mouth going a mile a minute from inside."

If it worked once, it would work again. "I was singing to myself, making my lips move, like this," she said demonstrating the words to an Elvis favorite. "I miss not hearing my music."

"Get in. I got eggs, bacon, instant coffee, and some cupcakes. They had a special on a sixpack so I got two. Here's a coke for you," he said generously. "The bread was stale," he said as an afterthought. "I got us a little information. A quarter of a mile down the road there's a deserted quarry. What do you think?"

Deserted. Could the kid get lost or hurt with only a flashlight to guide him. "How far in are you planning on going?" Elva questioned. If it was too far, the kid wouldn't be able to make it to the highway.

"Just till we're out of sight. I don't want to bust up this rig. She said there were potholes big as craters. Ain't no way I could fix a busted axle out here. Beats the shit out of me how we ended up back where we started. See those trees over there? That's the back of the wild life preserve of the Wild Adventure Park, and to the right of that is where

[161]

old Lenny is planted. It's your fault, Elva. Somehow you screwed this all up. Everybody said 1980 was a big year for assholes, but you carried over to '81."

There was no point in arguing with Cudge. The more he talked, the less time he had to think. She could listen to his harangue with one ear and still use her brain to figure something out for the little boy. God, where was it all going to end? Imagine returning to the same place they started out from. She knew in her gut that God was punishing her and Cudge. But the little boy shouldn't be punished. He didn't do nothing. Cudge wasn't going to hurt him except over her dead body.

"Here we go, hold on now. The old woman was right, would you look at those holes!" Deftly, he maneuvered the truck around the bushel-basket-sized openings in the dirt road. "Son-of-a-bitch!" Cudge exploded as he swerved to avoid a yawning crater, only to hit another. His head hit the roof of the truck and Elva bounced almost as high. "Goddamn it! I think that tire blew." He shifted into neutral and banged open the door. "Shit!"

"Did it blow?" Elva asked fearfully.

"Damn right it blew. I don't even know if I can get this rig out of here. Slide over, Elva, and gun it. I'll push from here." Elva did what she was told. The rig jockeyed back and forth and then was free.

"Okay, we're stopping right over there. There's room to back the pop-up under the trees. If it rains, it will have some protection. I gotta change it now before it gets too dark."

Elva was out of the pickup like a whirlwind. "Let me help you. Where's the tire, Cudge? And the tool box? Just crank open the top and I'll get it for you."

"How come you're so damn helpful all of a sudden? You want to help me, get me a beer and then shut up."

In her haste to open the can, Elva shook it and bubbles of foam shot up, soaking the front of her shirt. With shaking hands she held it out to Cudge, who grabbed it from her and consumed it in one swallow. "Gimme another and don't shake it."

"Cudge, it's gonna be dark soon. If you can't fix the tire what are we gonna do?"

"Then we walk." He finished the last of the beer and tossed the can into the brush. Before Elva knew what was happening, he had the spare tire off its rack on the rear of the pop-up. "If this ain't one hell of a fucking mess," he said disgustedly. "I didn't get it fixed the last time." Elva felt overwhelming relief. Now he wouldn't open the pop-up. "I'm gonna have to unhitch the rig and go into the nearest town and see if I can get this fixed. What time is it, Elva?" She shrugged and looked at the sky. "Must be after five, at least."

"I suppose they roll up the sidewalks early, so I better get moving. I want to eat when I get back. That greasy hamburger wasn't fit to eat. Help me unhook the camper." Elva's hands were shaking so badly, she was next to useless. "Get out of here; you ain't no help at all. Next thing you'll be pissing your pants and bawling your damn head off. Okay, it's off. Now look, me and you, we gotta have a talk. I don't like the idea of leaving you here while I go into town, but I ain't got no other choice. This is my rig, see, and I gotta take care of it. It's all I got in the whole world—except for you, Elva. I want you to promise that you'll be here cooking supper when I get back. I shouldn't be gone more than an hour, two at the most."

She'd promise anything as long as he left. "Okay, Cudge. I'll be cookin' supper when you get back. Where can I go? Don't worry, just get the tire fixed and get back here. You know I don't like the dark."

"First, I have to get my tool kit in the camper. I'll open it for you." A drowning fear engulfed Elva. She couldn't let him open it. "Cudge, if the garage man sees you with your own tool kit, he ain't gonna do nothin' for you. You know how those guys are. He's gonna think you couldn't do it yourself, and you're only going to him as a last resort because you botched up the job. You don't like people making a fool out of you. You don't need it." An ominous roll of thunder helped Cudge with his decision. He threw the spare tire into the back of the pick-up and then climbed behind the wheel. Another roar of thunder ripped through the sky. "Turn that crank carefully, Elva. You jam those cranks on me, Elva, and you're good as dead."

Elva's tongue was so thick she could only nod. Miracles. They did really happen and at the oddest times. Somehow she just knew that the roll of thunder had something to do with this particular miracle.

She limped down the road, watching till Cudge hit the highway. Hobbling and grasping at low branches, she made her way back to the pop-up. Trembling and shaking, she forced herself to take deep breaths.

"Little boy, I'm going to let you out now. Can you hear me?" Not waiting for a reply, she yanked viciously at the crank and lifted the top, the worn, khaki canvas unfolding like a flower. Her breathing was ragged; her gaze almost unseeing. She forced herself to take deep breaths. "Where are you, it's so dark under the trees I can barely see you. Come on, little boy, I'll help you."

Davey wiggled from his makeshift nest and slid down to the cardboard cartons. Elva quickly shoved them aside and reached for the boy. How wonderful he felt in her arms. He was okay. "You ain't bleeding, are you, little boy?" she demanded as she gathered him in her bony arms.

Davey Taylor let himself be hugged and petted. He liked it. He liked this girl who talked to him and told him not to be afraid. She wasn't Aunt Lorrie; she was different. She was as scared as he was; he could tell by the way her arms were shaking even if she was holding him tight. "No, I'm not bleeding. I told you I get shots so I don't bleed." Maybe she forgot what he had told her. "Can you call my aunt and uncle and tell them to come and get me?" he asked hopefully.

"I can't do that. All I can do is give you a flashlight and something to eat. You have to go by yourself. Cudge is gonna be coming back pretty soon and he can't find you here. I don't know if your folks are still at your campsite or not. You see those trees over there? That's where you were camped. That's where Len—what I mean is, if you can find your way back toward the trees, you stand a better chance of finding your folks than going to the highway. Cudge could find you too easy. I know it's scary in the dark. I hate the dark and don't like to be by myself, but it's best for you. It's all I can do, little boy. I can't go with you, my ankle is too sore. Do you think you can make it?"

She was hugging him so hard, Davey could barely breathe. With all his might, he pushed against her arms and gasped. "Yes, I can make it. Mr. Sanders gave me a flashlight and three quarters. What's your name? Mine is Davey. I have to know your name so I can tell my aunt and uncle you helped me."

"Brenda. Brenda Kopec. We have to get you settled and on your way. Cudge will be back soon. Are you hungry?"

"I sure am," Davey responded, with a weariness in his voice that made Elva clasp him to her, squeezing and crooning softly as B.J.'s little face seemed to be before her eyes.

[164]

Elva recognized the smell that was wafting toward her nostrils. Dry urine. Poor kid. How many times B.J. had wet his pants with no one to change them for him. And the beatings, the constant, everlasting beatings. As if a thrashing could make a little kid stop wetting his pants. Right now she had more important things to do. First, she had to feed B.J. and get him away from the pop-up before Cudge got back. A quick glance at the sky told her rain would pepper the camper shortly. And then what? Could the kid find his way? The rain would be cold, and he would be soaked in minutes. God, what if he started to bleed in the rain? "Rain, rain, go away, come again some other day," she crooned to Davey, who smiled at her with the trust of a five-year-old.

"Here we go, you sit down and eat. You gotta be quick, B.J., and get away from here before *he* comes back." Elva's eyes were glazed and watery as she watched Davey wolf down his food. Starved. B.J. was always starved. He could eat one minute and be looking for something else five minutes later. A bottomless pit was what B.J. was. A bottomless pit who wet his pants when he was scared.

"That was good, Brenda. Thank you. Could I have a drink?" Davey asked at he licked at his fingers.

"I saved my Coke for you. Drink it all, I'm not thirsty. It's kind of watery now because the ice melted and the cardboard is all squishy." Davey gulped and gulped until the soggy container was empty. Carefully Elva pulled at the hem of his shirt and wiped his mouth. "There now, your mouth is clean and no one will know that you were snacking. I won't tell, B.J., it's our secret. I just wish I could find some underwear for you to change into." She looked around, not seeming to notice the dark sky overhead.

Davey sat quietly on the step of the pop-up, trusting Brenda to help him. So what if she called him B.J.? Grown-ups made mistakes sometimes. Not all grown-ups, he corrected the thought. He sucked in his cheeks. His mother never made mistakes. A growl of thunder roared overhead. He flinched. If you think a thing through to the end, you won't make a mistake. That's what his mother always said. Lightning danced across the sky, revealing Elva's face in the eerie yellow light. Davey flinched again. Her eyes looked like Duffy's in the dark, all bright and shiny. He inched his way to the end of the step and waited, eyes on the winding road. From where he sat, he couldn't see the deep ruts made by the countless trucks that had traveled the road over the years.

The woods were dark and gloomy, like on the cartoons at Halloween. He wondered what time it was. In the lightning he noticed that Mickey's finger hadn't moved at all. "Do you know what time it is, Brenda?"

"Time?" Elva replied blankly. She shrugged. "It must be close to six o'clock. Maybe five-thirty. Why do you want to know?"

Davey frowned. "So I can set my watch and wind it. A man always needs to know the time. Is it still yesterday or today?"

Jesus. She didn't remember B. J. being so smart, and where did he get a watch? A stolen watch would only get him another beating. B. J. wouldn't steal. Or would he? She looked around. It was darker now, and she didn't have time to worry about where he got the watch.

"If it's five-thirty, what are the fingers on, Brenda?"

"Fingers?" Elva asked stupidly.

"See," Davey held out his wrist proudly. "What should I put the hands on?"

Comprehension dawned on Elva. "The little hand goes on the five and the big hand goes on the six. The hands are the fingers, right?" Davey nodded. That was good; she wasn't losing it after all. Then again, maybe she was wrong about the time. It was later than five-thirty— maybe six-thirty—maybe later.

Davey held out his hand. "It's raining, Brenda, what should we do?"

"Come on, get inside, and I'll light the lantern. I have to get you ready to go even if it is raining. I don't have an umbrella," she said fretfully. "I don't have a single thing that will keep you dry. I don't want you to get sick, B.J. You know there's no money for doctors."

"Aunt Lorrie is a doctor," Davey said helpfully. "If I can get to her and Uncle Tom, they'll take care of me. How do I get there, Brenda?"

"Sometimes you talk crazy, B.J. We don't have an Aunt Lorrie, just an Aunt Stella and an Aunt Helen. Don't you remember? There, the lamp is going. Isn't this cozy, B.J.? Just me and you. I hate the dark as much as you hate the beatings. I think I'd rather have a beating than be locked in a dark closet with the rats and roaches."

Maybe she was making up a story so he wouldn't think about Aunt Lorrie and Uncle Tom. But he didn't want to be entertained. He wanted to be out of here and back with Uncle Tom and Aunt Lorrie. He looked at his watch. He had to leave Brenda and the security of the pop-up. But first he had to make a checklist. He had set and wound his watch. His flashlight from Mr. Sanders was in his pocket. The three quarters jangled in his pocket. Something to eat. Brenda might have something left in the bag that he could stuff in his pocket. Carefully he twisted his watch to the inside of his wrist. He tugged at the elastic on the cuff of his windbreaker to make sure the colorful little watch was covered. It wasn't waterproof like his dad's. "Brenda, is there anything left in the bag that I can put in my pocket in case I get hungry later on?"

Elva fished in the bag and came up with a box of cupcakes. "I can give you two of them. He'll think I ate them. It's raining hard, B.J. I don't think you should go out. Stay here with me. I hate the dark," Elva said hugging her thin arms against her chest.

Davey felt confused. He didn't understand. "If I stay here with you, the man will catch me. I thought you wanted to help me get away. If he comes back, he'll hit you again."

It was Elva's turn to be confused. "B.J.," she said patiently. "I'm supposed to take care of you and I will. But you have to stay with me. I won't let anything happen to you. Not again. The last time it was all a mistake. I won't let that happen again."

"He might kill us both, Brenda. I want to go back to Uncle Tom and Aunt Lorrie. They're worried about me, I know they are. I don't like the dark either, but I don't care if I'm scared. I want to go home. You can come with me, Brenda. I have a flashlight and three quarters. And," he said importantly, "I have a watch."

It was the word watch that triggered something in Elva's head. Cudge. "What time is it?" she demanded fearfully.

"The big hand is on the three and the little hand is on the six."

Elva screwed her pinched features into a frown. "Quarter after six. God, Cudge will be back here any minute now. You have to get out of here fast."

Davey didn't like the way Brenda's hands were shaking. He sighed. "I know. Tell me how to go, Brenda."

"It's raining so hard. Let me think. The rain will slow Cudge down and he won't be able to see the holes in the road. I don't know which way is best for you to go. Probably through the trees so you don't pass him on the road. Will you be afraid to go through the woods?"

Davey debated his choices. The road and the bad man, or the woods and the rain and dark. "I'll go through the woods. I told you I have a flashlight."

A sob caught in Elva's throat. She couldn't let him go out in the dark and rain. God, she was tired, almost too tired to think. Where was Cudge? Probably in some bar. For a moment the thought pleased her. If he were in a bar, he wouldn't be coming through the door any second now. The kid was safe, for the moment. If he were in a bar, he would start off with beer and switch to boilermakers, and from there anything that came out of a bottle. He would be good for a couple of hours. When he saw the sky and the rain, he probably headed for the nearest bar and was drowning his guilt in alcohol. They were both safe now.

A deep bellow of thunder rolled across the tree tops. Elva shivered. She drew Davey into her arms for comfort. Streak after streak of lightning skittered overhead, lighting the inside of the camper. Elva swallowed hard. She feared thunder and lightning almost as much as she feared the dark.

Davey liked the feel of Elva's arms around him. She might be mixed-up and make mistakes, but she was afraid. When she settled back on the bunk, she drew Davey back with her, never loosening her hold on him. "We're going to sit quietly for a little while so I can think. I have to think about what's best for you. Do you understand that, B.J.?" Davey nodded his head and felt himself relax in the crook of her bony arm. He felt *almost* safe.

9

THE SKY WAS DARKENING, more from the threatening storm than from the on-coming night. The roads were almost completely deserted, even the main road that led back to the garage. An occasional car passed, going in the opposite direction, and the drivers were mostly men intent on getting home for supper after a long day on the job.

Cudge stopped the pickup in the bay area of the garage, relieved to see a dim light shining through the door. Quickly he climbed out of the cab in search of the mechanic on duty.

"Hey, fella," he tried for his most pleasant tone, "I've got a tire needs fixin' in a hurry. I'm camped down the road, and I left my wife there havin' a fit because she's afraid of storms. I'll throw in a buck for you if you do it now."

"Sure, why not? I was about to close up for the night, but a buck's a buck. Cost you five bucks for the tire, though, and it's gonna take me at least half an hour." The tall, slim man wiped his hands on the seat of his coveralls. "Why don't you go next door and have a beer? They got topless dancers in there for the after-work crowd."

Cudge relaxed; the mechanic seemed more interested in the tire than in him. "Sounds good to me, I could use a cold beer." Sensing that the man expected him to make some remark about the dancers, he added, "I haven't seen a good set of tits in a long time."

"Ain't it the truth," the mechanic grinned. "I thought my wife had a good pair when I married her. You should see them now. Two lemons and all nipple. Hell, it don't hurt to look, so I go in every so often and get my fill. Ain't nothin' wrong in lookin', I always say."

Cudge followed the man out to the pickup, where he retrieved the tire. Lowering his voice and looking over his shoulder, the man continued, "There's one little gal in there that's a piece of work. I ain't never seen her do it, but I heard about it. Calls herself Candy Striper, and she's got knockers on her that'll knock your eyes out. She does her number on the bar, and listen to this. She picks out one of the guys and lets him stick an ice cube up her and then she dances over the glasses, dripping all over the place. Never seen it myself, but heard it's quite a trick. You can think about it while you watch her dance and dream a little."

"Sounds like a waste of good beer to me," Cudge grunted. "You said half an hour, right?" Everywhere you looked there were perverts.

"More or less. When I'm done, I'll throw it back in your truck. Pay up now."

Cudge handed over the five dollars and then added one extra as promised. Pervert. He'd probably blow the buck on beer and pray that Candy what's-her-name would dribble in it.

He walked across the gravel-topped parking area surrounding the bar. A weather-worn sign beneath the orange neon proclaimed BEER— SNOOKIE'S. The thrum of disco music blared as someone opened the door to leave. He'd been in bars like this before. Smelling of beer and cigarettes, sawdust littering the floor. There was a crowd at the curving bar, and he spotted an empty stool.

Resting his elbows on the bar and reaching for some change, he ordered a draft. He glanced around at the packed bar and grinned. Strictly no class. The men were sweatstained, and more than half of them were tired-faced blacks.

Tightening his lips against his teeth, Cudge seethed. He didn't like blacks, didn't trust anyone with a different color skin. The dancers better not be black; he wasn't in the mood for dark tits. He wanted to see big white ones with bright pink nipples like on a kid's bottle. Tits that needed two hands to hold them. He grinned, thinking of what the mechanic told him about his wife's breasts. Hell, anything was better than old Elva, whose hard little breasts reminded him of overgrown walnuts, and you had to look to find the nipple.

A blast of tinny music pounded and two scantily costumed girls mounted a step-stool onto the beer-splattered bar. Cudge stared at their jiggling bodies, too preoccupied with his dilemma over Lenny to give them his full attention. He knew he had to think of a plan. Naked bosoms and gyrating pelvises would have to wait for another day. He wondered if the chick with the varicose veins was Candy Striper. It was getting late. Time for another beer and then he had to hit the road.

The music ended just as the bartender slid Cudge's beer down the length of the bar. Cudge took a long swallow and looked around. He hated dumps like this. Someday he was going to get all duded up and strut into a first-class cocktail lounge and drink champagne. He'd have a pearl-gray Lincoln like undertakers drive and a cigar clamped in his mouth. Cigars always added a touch of class, especially if they were Havana cigars. He'd go to Canada to get them if he had to. He shook his head at his fantasy. This bar was his speed, and he'd never move on. If he were lucky enough to move on at all. Lousy cops would be on his tail any time now. No point in fooling anyone, least of all himself. Get rid of Elva before first light and travel light. Even if he had to ditch the pop-up and come back for it later. He was shaken from his thoughts when a sweat-soaked black beside him called out. "C'mon, Candy, do your stuff. Show a poor old nigger how a white girl turns a man on. Jest forgit I'm black, baby, and turn me on."

"And after I turn you on, what am I going to do with you," the second girl from the end shouted over the music.

"The same thing you did last week, baby. I got thirty bucks if you're interested."

The girl laughed as she swayed her hips and cupped her breasts, making them stand erect. Cudge's eyes popped. She went with a nigger! Christ! He nudged the black sitting next to him. He had to know. "You got into her?" he demanded.

The black man stared at Cudge. What the hell, it took all kinds. Yet, he looked like he belonged in a place like this. "She'll take on anything, mister, as long as you got thirty bucks. She locks in on thirty for some reason. Not a penny less. She likes two tens, a five, and five ones. Anything else is a problem for her." Round brown eyes stared at Cudge. "She gives you your money's worth, too. You interested?"

"Not if I have to pay for it," Cudge snorted. The day he'd pay a hooker would be the day he tied his cock in a knot.

"You in the wrong place, buddy. Candy don't hand out no freebies. She's putting her baby brother through medical school."

My ass she's putting her brother through medical school, Cudge thought to himself.

"She likes her money up front too; you can't get around old Candy. She's a businesswoman."

Cudge took a better look at the prancing women on the bar. "Old Candy" was right.

He concentrated on Candy Striper, and for the first time thought of the relationship between her name and that make-believe brother she was putting through medical school. His amusement was signified by a disgusted snort. As for looks, Candy wasn't half bad. Better than scrawny Elva, at any rate. He'd been to bed with a bag of bones for so long, he'd almost forgotten how nice it was to be cushioned between a pair of thighs that had some meat on them. Her belly was slightly rounded and fleshy; it jiggled as she danced. Nice to slap his own belly into, he thought, feeling a sensation of life in his loins.

Thirty bucks. That's what she wanted. A dollar for each year of her age. Still, she did have a nice smile. Friendly. There weren't too many friendly people in his life lately, God knew. And her legs were long. Real long. Long enough to wrap around a man when he was . . . Cudge laughed at himself then, a dry, humorless laugh that made the man beside him turn to look at him. What did he care? He'd learned long ago that it didn't show on his face that he was really a prude when it came to women. He could spout dirty words right along with the best of them, but when it came to using that four-letter word for what it really stood for, he always reverted to phrases like "getting it on, you know, doing it."

Candy's bright smile took in everyone at the bar. Including the blacks. He didn't like that. And it proved that old saying that color didn't rub off. Candy's skin was white, pale white, almost translucent under the blue-tinted lights. Again that stirring below his belt as she gyrated, her breasts bouncing. He'd heard there was a burlesque stripper who wore tassels on her pasties and could make them twirl in different directions at the same time. He bet Candy could do that and he'd love to watch her try.

"You got thirty bucks?" he asked the sweating man next to him.

"Right here," the black said, slapping three tens on the bar.

"You a gambling man?"

"In a manner of speaking," the black mumbled.

"I got thirty bucks that says I can get Candy to leave here with me with no cash up front. A freebie. You want to cover the bet or not?"

"You on, man. I know Candy a long time, and she don't give it away."

"Candy, come over here," Cudge shouted.

Candy Striper stared down the length of the bar. A new dude. Loaded. Been a while since she had been with a white man. What the hell. His thirty bucks was just as good as a black man's. Pig eyes. She distrusted pig eyes and tattoos. Candy weaved her way among the bar glasses till she was standing in front of Cudge. She squatted down and Cudge whispered in her ear.

She laughed delightedly. "You putting me on?"

Cudge shook his head. "Tell this nigger you're coming with me and you're givin' me a freebie."

"You heard the man," Candy told the black man who was watching her with a shocked expression.

Cudge scooped up the three tens and put them in his shirt pocket. Thirty bucks was better than nothing. When you were on the run, thirty bucks could be the means to an end.

"C'mon, let's go."

"Not so fast. I got a job to do here."

"Yeah, well forget it," he answered. "I can't wait around all night."

"Listen, I got a break coming after the next set. Twenty minutes at the most and then I'm all yours. Have another beer and watch me dance while I warm things up for you."

Cudge almost told her to forget it, but some promise in her eyes stopped him. And what was waiting for him back at the pop-up. Elva? Skinny, scared Elva? She would be there when he got back, cowering inside the pop-up, cheeks streaked with tears, body shaking from every clap of the storm.

"Do your thing, baby," he told her, assuming his most debonair manner. "You ain't got nothin' I can't wait for."

Outside in the wind and rain he looked at Candy. "How far do you live from here?"

"Behind the bar. This dump used to be a motel and those little one-room cottages are still out back. Were you serious about Las

Vegas? I never been outside this town, much less to Las Vegas. I mean, do you really know show people there who can get me a job on the stage? When are we leaving?"

"Right after you give me your freebie."

"Man, you can have all the freebies you want if you take me to Las Vegas. On the hour if you want. I gotta be honest with you though. I got this little problem. I don't mind giving if you don't mind getting."

"What the hell?" Then it dawned on him what she had said. He had a condom he'd been carrying around for just such an emergency. He wasn't "getting" anything he didn't bargain for. "No problem."

"Where's your motor home? I like those things; all the comforts of home. You don't look like a rich promoter."

"Now, did you ever see a rich promoter?" Cudge demanded as he hustled her around the side of the bar. "I parked it behind the garage. This looks like the kind of neighborhood that means trouble."

"You scared me there for a minute. I thought that pile of junk over there was yours. I wouldn't be caught dead riding in something like that" —she motioned to his Chevy pickup parked in front of the garage bay.

Cudge's eyes narrowed. "Wouldn't you now? Probably belongs to some hard-working slob who's sitting in that bar watching you gals toss your tits around."

Concentrating on keeping her balance on the gravel despite her incredibly high heels, she led him toward the cottage nearest the road.

A slat-ribbed dog near the cottage growled to show he resented their intrusion. Cudge watched the dog while Candy dug in her purse for the keys, clutching the edges of the sweater she had thrown over her shoulders to hide her nakedness.

"Don't let the dog bother you, honey. Just like the rest of us, he's only looking for a good meal." The door swung open and she reached inside for the light switch. "Course, things are different out in Las Vegas. Nobody, but nobody, goes hungry out there. Say, how long did you say it would take to get out there?"

"I didn't," Cudge answered, his voice harsh. He didn't like answering questions, especially ones that challenged his lies. Besides, if she was dumb enough to think she was good enough for Las Vegas, she deserved anything she got.

"Here it is, home. Should I pack first or do you want to ball? Don't make no never mind to me."

"You got any booze around here?"

"A whole gallon. You want some?"

"Get it out, I feel like getting drunk. How can you fuck a nigger for thirty bucks?"

"I close my eyes. I really need the money. I'm putting my kid brother through medical school," Candy said uncorking the jug of wine.

"You need a better story than that one. No wonder you only get thirty bucks. Niggers! That's disgusting," Cudge said virtuously.

"I'm not putting you on. My kid brother Jackie is going to be an orthopedic surgeon some day. If you get me a job on the line in Las Vegas, I can send him more money. He's having a real tough time. Do you know just one medical book costs seventy-five dollars, sometimes more! Inflation, I guess. Here," she said handing Cudge a full glass of wine. "I think I'll have some myself to get in the mood. How do you like it? Don't be afraid to tell me what you want."

"No problem," Cudge's eyes started to water. This dump was no better than that furnished apartment he'd left in Newark. The iron bed in the corner looked like George Washington could have slept in it, and the sheets hadn't been changed since. Candy had a Panasonic radio-cassette player on the table. Her brightly polished finger pressed the "on" button and Kenny Rogers was singing "Lady." The wine was tart, almost vinegary on his tongue. Candy casually shrugged out of the sweater. She always enjoyed the way men who acted so cool in the bar got so excited when they were alone with her, seeing the same flesh they'd been looking at while she danced.

"You can see it won't take me long to pack my gear. Ten minutes should have it done. So, you want to ball first or you want to bring your motor-home around and we'll throw my stuff in?"

Cudge didn't answer. Holding his empty glass out, he indicated that she should fill it again. "First, we'll drink the wine. Then we'll see what happens."

Candy refilled his glass, her bleached blonde hair falling over her face. She didn't like the way he was looking at her, and she wondered how she'd ever believed that somebody like him could have connections in Las Vegas. Still, a girl had to have hope, and working in a dump like Snookie's made those hopes turn to needs.

"So, you really ball niggers, huh?" he was asking her, his voice on the raw edge of menace. "Is it true what they say about those black dudes? Are they built bigger than white men?"

"Some is and some ain't," she tried to keep her tone light, feeling increasingly uneasy about this stranger and wondering whatever prompted her to invite him to her cottage.

He downed his wine and held his glass out again. "What's that supposed to mean? They're either bigger down there or they ain't."

Candy decided she definitely should have stuck with the men who frequented Snookie's. There wasn't one who would go out of his way to do anything for her, but they wouldn't scare her either. And when she was with them the air didn't seem to go stale.

"You were only teasing me about Las Vegas, weren't you?" she asked, hearing the quaking in her own voice. She had to get out of here, away from this man.

"Why're you jumpy?" Cudge asked. "You always get jumpy when it's time to hit the sack?" His voice was almost genial and Candy decided it must be a trick of the light that made his eyes glitter and emphasized the grim lines around his mouth.

Forcing herself to relax, she leaned over to undo the tiny straps on her shoes.

"No, leave them on. They make your legs look nice and long."

Now this was the kind of talk she was used to hearing from her customers. So what if he was a little kinky and liked women's shoes. She had a steady who liked enemas. And even if he didn't take her to Vegas, there was still the thirty bucks.

Stuart Sanders lost no time once the plane touched down. Nancy could pick his luggage up later. She wouldn't mind the thirty-minute ride to the airport. He ran down the endless concourse. Having no patience for the escalator, he walked down the steps two at a time and elbowed his way through the milling travelers in search of the car that would be waiting for him. Mac Feeley sat behind the wheel, cigar clamped in his mouth. He reached over to open the door for Sanders. "How goes it, big guy?"

"You don't want to know," Sanders replied in way of greeting. "Let's move it. Take the turnpike. Is this one of those souped-up jobs the motor pool hands out to speed demons like you?"

Feeley grinned. "This little number is slick; it starts out at ninety and works up to one-eighty. You think you're flying. Five bucks says I get you there in thirty minutes."

"Is that with or without the siren?" Sanders asked irritably.

"Either or, you name it."

"I'd hate like hell to get pulled over and lose time."

"No way. This car has official government plates with the right code numbers, and I guess you didn't see the state seal on the door. You look done in. You hear anything? How did things go?"

"Nothing on my end. Mrs. Taylor elected to stay behind with her husband. She said she trusts me and the others to find her son. Mr. Taylor is convinced the kid wandered off and will turn up as soon as he gets tired and hungry."

Feeley switched the cigar from one side of his mouth to the other. "There's a lot to be said for devotion." His voice was sour when he spoke.

"What's new here? Any leads? How are the Ryans taking it? What's the latest on the guy with the painted truck? How did the old couple check out?"

"The Ryans are holding on. Mrs. Ryan tends to get upset, but her husband calms her down. A retired couple was camping there last night and we managed to track them down to Virginia and ask a few questions, but it was a dead end. The local police think they have a couple of leads, but they aren't ones for sharing and think this is their baby all the way down. Our guys had to pull badges to remind them who's in charge—what can I tell you? From here on out it's going to be legwork."

"What are your hunches, Feeley?"

"I'd like to know more about the body they found. Coroner's making his report in the morning, but it's pretty certain the poor stiff was beaten to death. Nasty head wounds. Leonard Lombardi, twenty-eight or so, lived in Newark. Putting the pieces together, we believe he was already dead when he was brought to the campground. Best lead we've got is a guy named Edmund Balog, a/k/a Cudge Balog. Everything is pointing in his direction, right down to a report from a trooper who stopped him on the road. Said he was real nervous about opening the pop-up rig he was dragging. Emergency called the trooper away so he never got a look inside. Description fits. Nah, it's a snatch all right. But I don't think the big boys in Florida have him. And it's not for ransom, either. My bet says the kid saw something he wasn't supposed to. From there," Feeley shrugged, "your guess is as good as mine."

Sanders said, "I let this one get under my skin as far back as house duty in Montclair. I feel responsible, somehow. Did the Ryans tell you Davey is a hemophiliac? He has to have a shot every day, regular as clockwork, to keep it under control."

"Yep. I know if he misses his shots there's no telling if the drug will work for him anymore—something about the body's defenses rejecting the drug."

"Right. It's sort of an internal sabotage, his own body rejecting the very drug that would keep him from bleeding to death. How many has he missed so far?"

"According to Lorrie Ryan, one—at twelve noon today. It's been over thirty hours since his last injection. Mrs. Ryan is a doctor, and she's been on the phone with a specialist. No one knows how fast those antibodies in the kid's body will develop. Their best guess is that at forty-eight hours it starts getting critical. By the way, we have a code name for radio contact. Transmissions relating to this case are called in to Panda Bear." Feeley shook his head. "Whoever thought that one up?"

"It's the name Davey uses in the CB club he belongs to," Sanders scowled, sliding down in the seat.

Feeley bit down hard on his cigar. Everyone knew Sanders's feelings about kids, especially his own. He was a family man and didn't care who knew about it. Feeley couldn't say the same for himself. Wives were okay as long as they did what they were told, when they were told. Kids were okay too, in their place. Feeley felt that he contributed to the general welfare; he put his life on the line every day of the week. What more could anyone expect from him? Still, he always envied Sanders when he talked about his wife and family. Hell, maybe he should have worked harder at his own marriage instead of looking at all the chicks that were his downfall.

The men fell into an easy silence that ended with Sanders complaining, "I thought you said you were going to get us there in thirty minutes."

Feeley worked at his watch. One of these days he was going to get a timepiece that didn't require two hands to operate. "So, you want to quibble about one minute and ten seconds, go ahead."

Sanders grunted as he climbed from the car. Why spoil Feeley's day, or what was left of his day? "Who's in charge?"

"You are, now that you're here. You're senior officer. The local police will bow and kiss your hand, if you play your cards right. We have a temporary office in back."

Sanders grunted again as he made his way in the faded yellow light that shone through the camp store's grimy office. The fresh pungent scent of pine was everywhere. The smell reminded him of Christmas and the six-foot tree that filled the living room every year. Autumn leaves heralded a new season that would soon give way to sharp, cold winds and, he hoped, snow. He liked snow, didn't even mind driving in it. Hell, he liked life and everything it had to offer. He felt a chill and stopped in mid-stride. "What do you think the chances are for a frost tonight?"

Feeley worked at the cigar. The kid only had a light windbreaker on. A little kid could freeze, especially a kid in his condition. And the forecasts were predicting rain for tonight, possibly thunderstorms. "Jesus, I'm no goddamn weatherman. Fifty-fifty would be my guess."

Inside the storeroom Feeley lounged against stacked cartons of cereal. He looked around at the assorted merchandise that would eventually fill the camp-store shelves. Beans, Spam, instant coffee—he grimaced. His taste ran to prime ribs, baked potato, garden salad, fresh vegetables. Key lime or pecan pie for dessert. He looked around again to see what the storeroom held in the way of dessert. A meal wasn't a meal without dessert. He snorted as he removed the mangled cigar from his mouth. He should have known—canned fruit cocktail. He trampled the ruined cigar under his foot. Sanders was shaking hands with the local police. A new cigar found its way to his mouth. Without taking his eyes off the assembled men, he dextrously bit off the end of another fifteen-cent cigar. Small, square yellowish teeth bit down firmly. A butane lighter snapped to life, almost singeing his thick eyebrows. He paid it no mind. Black, evil-smelling smoke circled and spiraled around his head. If nothing else, it would curtail the locals expounding all night on their theories which, in his eyes, weren't theories at all, but asshole assumptions that any first-week rookie cop could make.

"You've got a dead body, with positive identification. That's good. I have a missing kid who's a hemophiliac. It seems to me you've been doing a hell of a lot of work on a case that should be cut and dried. It beats the hell out of me how you haven't managed to pick up that psychedelic truck and pop-up. Your all-points bulletin is worthless. We have to get moving. Why haven't extra men been brought in? Good police instinct should have told you that the boy is mixed up in this somehow. How much longer are you going to sit on your asses? Are you aware of the kid's medical history? Now, let's sit down and lay out a plan of action. I'm the chief and you guys are the Indians. You got it? If not, I have a badge saying that's the way it goes."

Feeley blew another cloud of smoke in Sanders's direction. He grinned to himself. Old war-horses could take charge quickly when they wanted to.

"Come here, Feeley," Sanders called over his shoulder as a cloud of smoke circled his head. "See that this picture is in every morning paper in the area. Start with the *Asbury Park Press.* Don't let them give you any crap about it's being a color Polaroid shot either. If they even think about giving you trouble with the deadline, tell them you know the paper isn't put to bed till ten, and then there is a two-hour grace period. Call ahead if you want. Just get it done."

Sanders issued orders grimly. He believed that Davey was somewhere near the park. The moment the others cleared out, he spoke to the young officer across the makeshift table.

"If you're asking me what I think professionally, I have to say that I go along with the department. If you're asking me what I think off the record, I think the kid saw something and was picked up. He could be anywhere and he could be dead. Unless the guy is a real psycho, my personal feeling is the kid is alive. It takes guts to kill a little kid in cold blood.

"No matter what, the kid could be dead anyway. He needs his antigen shots and he missed one. The experts can't predict what will happen," Sanders said harshly. His cigarette butt was burning low.

"What's he like, the kid, I mean?" the young officer asked curiously.

"He's a kid with lots of savvy, if you know what I mean. He's been through a rough time, and he's just now coming into his own. I know some adults who couldn't take the medical treatment this kid has been through. Do you think you could stand being transfused through your jugular vein? No? That kid has, many times. I'll tell you who he looks like. You ever see that airline commercial where the kid gets a pair of wings from the flight captain and then says, "Oooh, thank you, captain"? Well, he looks just like him. I'm sure there are thousands of kids who look like that, but Davey Taylor is special. Very special. I'm going to the Ryans' campsite. Which way is it?" Talking about Davey Taylor made his stomach churn.

"Take the main road and follow it to the fork, bear left, and it's the only RV in sight."

Just as Sanders stepped outside, the RV pulled to a stop at the camp office. Sanders looked at Lorrie Ryan, knowing the same stripped-down naked hurt would have been on Nancy's face if one of their kids was missing. Nobody deserved to endure what she was going through.

"Mr. Sanders, when did you get here? Where's Sara? Do you have word of Davey, is that why you're here? Oh, Tom, something must have happened. Tell us, I have to know," she pleaded.

"Slow down," Sanders grinned. Holding up both hands palm out, he tried to quiet her with his own calmness. "Nothing definite yet. Your sister—well, she elected to stay behind with Mr. Taylor." How bitter the words sounded.

"She what?" Tom barked.

Sanders tried to make his voice sound neutral, feeling that his own judgment would only serve to aggravate the Ryans. Christ, maybe he was getting too old for field work. A desk job, that was what he needed. He wasn't impartial. He wasn't neutral. He repeated his carefully chosen words. "Mrs. Taylor elected to stay behind."

"Just what the hell does that mean? She 'elected' to stay behind?" Tom asked angrily.

Sanders kept control of his voice. "Mr. Taylor took the stand for thirty minutes today."

"What the hell does that have to do with Sara and Davey? She's the kid's mother! You did tell her we called, didn't you?"

Lorrie didn't like Tom's anger. She withdrew her hand from her heavy sweater pocket and laid it gently on her husband's knee. Her voice was soft. "I find it almost impossible to believe that Sara didn't come back with you. She must be worried sick; how could she stay behind? Is there something you aren't telling us, something we should know?"

"Ma'am, I've told you what I know." He searched his mind for the right words. "Mrs. Taylor said she trusted me to handle the matter. Both Mr. and Mrs. Taylor feel that the boy . . . the boy wandered off and will find his way back." Should he volunteer the rest or be quiet? The book said to be quiet, but he hadn't worked by the book in a long time. "Mr. Taylor was a very convincing witness today. It was unfortunate that court adjourned when it did. The whole thing could have been wrapped up today."

"Aha! So, Sara's little boy Andrew made a good showing for himself under Mommy's watchful eye! And she didn't come back to Jersey with you because she knows he'll screw up without her there to protect him! Disgusting!" Tom snorted. "Sara's afraid she'll be disgraced if Andrew screws up. Poor Davey. He always comes last. Sonovabitch!" he thundered smacking a fist into his open palm.

Charitable to the end, Lorrie said, "Tom, it's not like you to be cruel. You don't know what you're saying."

Tom glared at Sanders. "I know what I'm saying, don't I? One look at you and you know it's the truth. You must have seen it for yourself. The way that Andrew constantly looks to Sara for approval. The way she communicates to him with her eyes. What did he do? Keep looking at her every time a question was asked? Don't tell me, I'll get sick!"

Sanders watched Ryan, a baleful expression in his eyes. There was no avoiding the truth. "I wasn't the only one to see it; that cagey prosecutor Roman DeLuca saw it too. I caught him sneaking peeks at Mrs. Taylor."

"And I could just see her as her little boy made a good showing of himself. All pride and possession, preening. Bah! But it's no excuse for not being here where Davey needs her."

Sanders' silence was agreement.

"Why don't you folks go back to your campsite. I'll be in touch if anything breaks. What is it, Feeley?" he looked over his shoulder.

"Phone call for Mrs. Ryan. Miami. You want to take it or what?"

Sanders watched Lorrie Ryan as she seemed to shrink into herself. His voice was protective when he spoke. "Why don't you let me take the call, Mrs. Ryan. I can tell her you've retired for the night."

"Thank you, Mr. Sanders, but that's the easy way. I'll talk to her."

Two pairs of eyes watched Lorrie enter the office. For want of something to say, Sanders blurted. "Does she eat? How much does she weigh? She's too defenseless. I don't mind telling you that her sister is like a barracuda and your wife is a guppy in comparison."

"She eats like a horse. She weighs a hundred and three with her clothes on. You're right about Sara but wrong about Lorrie. Lorrie has guts, street smarts, and she's a survivor. The one thing I learned about my wife right at the beginning is never sell her short. She'll handle the call."

Sanders nodded morosely. She was Ryan's wife; he should know what he was talking about. His Nancy was like that. Christ, she could handle anything. Like the time Ben fell out of the tree. The doctors said he might not walk again, but she had looked them right in the eye and told them her son would not only walk, he would run. To this day Sanders didn't know if she had really believed it or was just praying aloud. What he did know was that Ben was the best first-year quarterback Princeton had seen in many long years.

"This is Lorrie. Is that you, Sara?" Lorrie asked calmly. She would not permit Sara to rattle her. She simply wouldn't. Her free hand held the cold pack with the hypodermic and the vial of antigen firmly.

"Yes, this is Sara, Lorrie. How could you have allowed my son to wander off? I trusted you and Tom. Andrew and I just can't believe you allowed this to happen. It's unforgivable. Well, has he returned yet?"

"No, Sara, he hasn't come back to camp yet. The police are still searching for him. Mr. Sanders arrived a short while ago. I don't think he's going to 'wander' back as you put it. We all think it's more serious than a little boy lost in the woods. I'm not sure if you know it or not, but the police found a dead body near where Davey was playing. We're not sure if Davey saw or overheard something. We're doing everything we can. I am sorry, Sara. I take full responsibility." How firm her voice sounded, in control. Her fingers on the cold pack were numb.

"That's absurd. What could Davey possibly have to do with a dead

body? You're grasping at straws, Lorrie, to cover your own ineffective-
ness. There won't be a next time, Lorraine. Andrew and I both feel
Davey wandered off; Andrew admitted that he used to do the same
thing when he was a child. Like father, like son. I want you to call me
the minute he gets back, no matter what time of the day or night it
is." Her voice was frigid, bordering on open hostility. "I suppose if
there's anything we can be grateful for in this . . . this outing you
insisted on, it's that Davey had his shot."

Lorrie swallowed hard. Evidently, Sara didn't know Davey had been
missing since early morning. "Davey missed his shot. He wandered off
shortly after breakfast. I thought you knew," Lorrie said as she wound
her fingers tighter around the cold pack. "Davey is on minus hours now.
Why aren't you here, Sara? Your place is here so Davey . . ."

"Why aren't I there? Because I'm here seeing to something very
important. I trusted my son to you and your husband. The only reason
you want me there is so I can make everything right for you, the way
I did when we were children. You never did anything right. I was always
the one who had to pull your chestnuts out of the fire and get you out
of one scrape after another. Not this time. You and you alone are
responsible for my son. I don't want to hear another word from you
or Tom until you can call me and tell me my son is safe. Do you
understand me, Lorrie?"

Lorrie felt goosebumps on her arms, not because she was cold, but
from Sara's icy, brittle voice. She should hang up on Sara. Did she think
Lorrie didn't care? Didn't Sara know she loved Davey as though he
were her own son? She'd breathe for him if she could. Hang up, her
mind shrieked. Don't pay attention to what Sara is saying. You know
that Sara began all the scrapes and horrors of childhood, and she,
Lorrie, had paid the piper. Ignore her. She's upset. Don't say another
word. Lorrie couldn't be as stupid as Sara said. Not if she graduated
tenth out of a class of two hundred and sixty in medical school. You
always have to take the responsibility for your own actions, she repeated
the words to herself.

"Lorrie, are you there? Answer me."

"I'm here, Sara. I was thinking about something." It took every
ounce of will power she possessed to square her shoulders. "I always
thought I liked you because you were my sister, but I don't like you,

Sara. I didn't like you when we were children, and I don't like you now that we're adults. I love Davey; you know that. I won't bore you with what I've gone through today. There's no way you could possibly understand. Just because you're Davey's biological parent doesn't mean you love him more, or as much as I do. Because if you did, you'd be here. I don't have anything else to say, so I'm going to hang up. If we hear anything, you'll be the first to know." She couldn't move her hand from the cold pack. She would never remove her hand unless it was to replace it with the other. Damn Sara to hell.

Feeley heaved a sigh of relief when he saw the color seep back into Lorrie Ryan's face. What the hell, there was always a squabble or two in families. He and his brother Sam were always arguing and they were middle-aged. He smiled when he remembered how his mother had said over the weekend that Sam and he were the oldest kids she knew.

10

THE PHONE was still in Sara's hand when Andrew admitted Roman DeLuca into the hotel suite. Her conversation with Lorrie had not been satisfying, and it rankled that Lorrie had hung up on her.

But Sara schooled her face to impassivity before facing the prosecuting attorney. Everything about him annoyed her. He was as bogus as a three-dollar bill, capitalizing on his movie-star good looks, from his meticulously clipped gray hair to the tips of his manicured fingers. A snakeskin briefcase matched his shoes and belt, and his dove-gray suit and sparkling white shirt were custom-tailored to his slim body in an expensive salute to his vanity.

Andrew scoffed when she told him that she thought the impeccable attorney had his eye on the governor's seat.

Sara knew better, and Roman DeLuca seemed to read Sara's thought. It didn't upset him. Somehow his reaction added to Sara's dislike.

"Mrs. Taylor," DeLuca said quietly. Sara nodded her head slightly in return to his greeting. The phone receiver was still clutched in her hand. And was he wrong, or was there a glimmer of self-righteousness in her eyes?

"Were you about to make a phone call, Mrs. Taylor?" he asked.

"Oh, no, as a matter of fact, I've just completed one. To my sister in New Jersey." Damn, now why had she needed to explain?

DeLuca noticed the stiffening of her shoulders; he had been right about the self-righteous glimmer. Sara Taylor must have berated her sister, blaming her for the boy's disappearance. He wished he had arrived just a moment earlier to hear it for himself. He would have liked to see Sara in action.

"Andrew, we must talk," DeLuca sat near the window, careful of the creases in his slacks. "Don't be alarmed. I want to congratulate you on your fine performance on the stand this afternoon. There's only one point that's annoying me," he looked up at Andrew from beneath his dark, bushy brows. "Must you continually glance at Mrs. Taylor before you answer each question?"

Andrew was stunned. He knew he hadn't been a star witness, but he hadn't thought he'd done badly. And Sara had told him how wonderfully he'd behaved on the witness stand.

"If the judge had let the defense attorney begin his cross-examination, you'd be on the scrap heap by now. The judge adjourned as a favor to me when he saw how perturbed I was by your attention to your wife. If the jury had noticed, it may have jeopardized our case. Do you realize that each time I asked you a question about what you witnessed or your acquaintance with Jason Forbes, you looked to your wife before you answered? You almost never took your eyes from her. Perhaps you noticed that I attempted to block your line of vision. And when I did, I saw that you became rattled, unsure of yourself and your statements. Rather than make you appear a fool, I allowed the visual contact between yourself and Mrs. Taylor. Do you understand what I'm saying?"

"Of course he understands, Mr. DeLuca. He's not a child," Sara snapped. "It was your own inept questioning techniques that rattled Andrew."

Roman DeLuca's eyes narrowed to bits of chipped ice. "You should know, my dear, what makes your husband tick. I say he behaved sophomorically and so does the judge. Instead of giving me his undivided attention, he gave it to you. Why don't you ask him why?"

"Andrew doesn't have to tell me anything, Mr. DeLuca. I was there; I saw what went on. You could have put Andrew on the stand earlier but you didn't. Why? You deliberately waited till court was about to adjourn before you made a move. I want to know why, Mr. DeLuca," Sara said coldly. "I want to know now."

DeLuca smiled wryly. He didn't like Sara Taylor—she was sapling thin with ramrod strength. Two traits he himself possessed. In himself he admired them; in Sara Taylor he detested them.

"Strategy, Mrs. Taylor. I don't exactly understand what you're accusing me of, and I don't believe you understand either. Let's just put it down to your desire to protect your husband. I'm merely making the point that a witness who continually directs the jury's attention away from his testimony is of little or no use. I know it's merely a loving habit, Mr. Taylor's looking to you, but it is a habit that could lose this case for the state, and I won't have it." His tone was smooth, and he waited for the Taylors to digest what he had said before continuing. "Tomorrow is another day, Mr. Taylor; oh, you did say I may call you Andrew. Andrew, I'm here tonight to go over your testimony with you. I've studied your written deposition, and I think we'll work directly from that. I hope we'll get it all together, and you'll be unwavering in the face of cross examination." DeLuca smiled.

He has a snake's smile, Sara caught herself thinking, disliking DeLuca intensely, almost hating him. "You're very confident for a man who was so angry a moment ago," Sara told him.

Her voice was urbane now, charming in its suaveness. "Mrs. Taylor, what you mistook for anger was concern for Andrew and yourself. As they would say back in New York, this is my turf and I know every blade of grass. I always win, Mrs. Taylor, remember that."

Sara's eyes narrowed. It sounded like a threat, or was it a warning? How dare the man. How dare he!

Andrew intervened. "Sara, before we go over my testimony, why don't you show Mr. DeLuca the message that was delivered before dinner?"

Sara gathered her indignation close about her. She walked stiffly over to the desk and picked up the square of white paper and held it out, eyes cold and hard.

DeLuca scanned the message. "Well, who was it and what did they want?" he asked, listening closely for her answer.

"We didn't call the number. We waited to show it to you," Sara said. God, how she detested this phony movie-star lawyer.

"Let me understand something, Mrs. Taylor. You say this message was delivered before dinner. Which, I assume, was between six and seven, am I right?" At Andrew's nod he continued. "It's 9:45 now. Did it ever occur to either of you that it might be a message concerning your son who is missing, possibly kidnapped?" He watched her carefully, admiring the way she took in his statement and managed to appear unruffled. Was it possible she didn't make the connection? He opened his mouth to drive it home. "Mrs. Taylor, I like to consider myself a friend of the family, and I feel it my duty to tell you there's a possibility that someone associated with the drug syndicate we're prosecuting may have taken your son."

For one instant Sara was taken aback. The heavy intake of breath belonged to Andrew as he sank down on the chair. DeLuca realized that the Taylors had never considered such a possibility, and now it left them stunned.

"You must believe I care about your son," he added in his most sober tone.

Sara was the first to rally.

"Your concern is most appreciated, Mr. DeLuca. Of course we care, but neither Andrew nor I owe you any explanations concerning our son or our private life. Experts, Mr. DeLuca, are handling matters back in New Jersey," Sara said stiffly, not liking the look in Andrew's eyes. "Andrew is here to do a job, and I'm here because I choose to be here. Do we understand each other? There's nothing in this case to suggest kidnapping. Davey merely wandered off." Sara refused to think about the dead man discovered at the camp.

"But, of course, my dear. I understand everything you've done and said since our first meeting. I was merely thinking of you and your family. If the media got hold of information like this . . . why, I can't be responsible. They always start off by using the term 'unfit mother,' and from there they usually go to a philandering, drinking husband. I'm not saying any of it's true, or that I condone it, I am just pointing a possibility out to you. If my information is correct, Mrs. Taylor, Mr. Sanders urged you to take the next plane home. Andrew is certainly capable of speaking for himself."

Sara Taylor was shaken, but she seemed to recover quickly and moved toward the phone. "This is Sara Taylor. I understand you left a message for me at the desk." No emotion showed on her elegant features as she listened. Carefully she replaced the phone and then turned to face the two men. Her voice, when she spoke, was neutral.

"Some insane person on the other end of the line said he has our son, and if Andrew testifies, we'll never see him again. Obviously, he's demented. Our son has just wandered off and is temporarily lost. If it was anything more serious, my sister would have called me by now. There *are* some people who enjoy trying to make other people miserable. I'm standing by my decision to stay with Andrew. My son's problem is in capable hands."

"Is that what you call it? Your son's problem?" Roman DeLuca questioned unbelievingly.

"For the moment, Mr. DeLuca, I'm not calling it anything. In my opinion the matter is ended. Andrew, what's your feeling?"

Andrew looked from his wife to his attorney. "I quite agree, Sara. Why don't we get down to business, Mr. DeLuca? It's after ten now, and we have an early day in court."

"Can I order something for either of you from room service?" Sara asked. At both men's negative nod, Sara left the sitting room and entered the bedroom. A manicure, a complete manicure, was in order.

It was 12:45 when Andrew tapped on the door. "Mr. DeLuca is leaving now, darling."

"One moment, dear," Sara said tying the sash of her peach-colored dressing gown.

"Andrew, take a shower, a nice hot one. It'll do you a world of good. Stand under the spray for at least ten minutes. I can see how tense you are. Relax, darling, this is almost over. By this time tomorrow all of this will be nothing more than a bad memory. You go along now and I'll see Mr. DeLuca out. I've laid fresh pajamas out for you in the bathroom. I'll even pour us a nightcap."

Sara moved past Andrew, her scent circling above and around her. Andrew sniffed, liking it. Must be new or were his senses exceptionally keen tonight?

"Mr. DeLuca, I'll see you out," Sara said formally.

The attorney dropped all pretense. Lowering his voice, he said curtly, "Mrs. Taylor, I want you on the morning plane back to New Jersey."

"I won't do that. My place is here with my husband," she answered tightly.

"Then let me put it to you another way. If you aren't on that morning plane, certain friends of mine will not be responsible for your son's safety. Now do we understand one another?"

Sara's world was turning upside down. She knew DeLuca would not repeat himself, nor would he ever admit to saying what he had just told her. "Certain friends" he called them, obviously meaning the syndicate against whom Andrew was testifying.

"Why?"

"It's not important for you to know why. Just be on that plane."

Sara needed time to think. Roman DeLuca had hinted that "certain friends" of his had Davey. Yet Mr. Sanders had led her to believe that Davey had just wandered off and was having difficulty finding his way back. Poor Andrew. If anything ever happened to Davey, Andrew would be devastated.

"Can I have my office make your airline reservation, Mrs. Taylor?"

"No, you can't. I'm staying. You wouldn't dare have my son harmed. You're too respectable for that, Mr. DeLuca. And I understand you're thinking of running for governor of Florida."

"It has crossed my mind," DeLuca replied. "I meant what I said about your son. And remember something else, I always win."

A chill washed over Sara. Her tone, however, was just as menacing as his. "So do I, Mr. DeLuca."

"There's a first time for everything. You're out of your depth here. You can't win. I'll have your reservation made just in case you change your mind. I believe your flight leaves at 10:10."

"Why are you doing this?" Sara hissed.

"Because I don't want you in the courtroom supporting your husband, Mrs. Taylor. Without you, his testimony will fall apart. Goodnight, Mrs. Taylor."

Sara Taylor stood for a full five minutes at the door after it closed on the attorney. She had caught a glimpse of Sanders's colleague in the hallway. She was furious and frightened, and she thought of calling in the guard and telling him about DeLuca's threat. But she knew he'd never believe her. Still, perhaps she should tell him about the phone message at the desk and the results of her call. Maybe he could trace it—no one would believe it—the number was more than likely a public phone. Who would believe that the upstanding Roman DeLuca would subvert the very laws he had sworn to uphold. He hadn't achieved his position by being careless. More compelling still was her own feeling that this would be a personal confrontation between the attorney and herself. All she had to do to win was be smarter and faster than he was. And as for going back to New Jersey, she would have to do that too. She was going to have to buckle under to a hoodlum in a six hundred dollar suit!

"Sara? Where are you, darling?"

"Right here, dear. I was just turning off the lights. I'll be in in a moment."

Settled in the bed beside Andrew, Sara searched for the right words. She had to be very careful what she said. "Darling, there's something I want to talk to you about. I've been thinking about going home. There is a 10:10 flight tomorrow morning for home. Davey needs me. I know you need me too, but my place is with our son. I know he's safe, but I want to see with my own eyes. You know how I am," she said affectionately.

"Of course, I understand. Mr. DeLuca assured me I would finish with my testimony by noontime; I'll take the 1:15 flight. I'm pleased you're going, Sara. You're the most perfect mother I've ever known."

"It is hard to be humble when you're perfect," Sara teased lightly. Not for anything in the world would she let Andrew know that she was going back only because of Roman DeLuca's implied threat. No, it wasn't implied. It had been clearly stated, and she had to deal with it. "I'll go with you to the courthouse and see that you're settled in and leave from there. I want to be sure that you're all right before I leave."

"It's not necessary, but I do feel better knowing you're there. Is anything else on your mind, Sara? You haven't been yourself since DeLuca arrived. I know he upset you with all that eye-contact nonsense, but now that you're going home, it's hardly important."

"You always see right through me, don't you, darling? Yes, something has been bothering me. It's about your testimony this afternoon. I can't be certain, but I think there's a small problem we've overlooked. Remember when we were in school and had to learn the answers to a long list of questions? I don't know about you, but I always had the answers down pat as long as the questions were asked in order. Once the questions were out of sequence, I failed miserably. Perhaps that may be a problem for you. I heard Mr. DeLuca going over your testimony with you. Everything was in sequence, and you had all the facts down perfectly. But what would happen if those questions were asked out of sequence?"

"By whom?" Andrew asked.

"Anyone. The attorney for the defense—anyone. It could rattle you, Andrew. It could rattle anyone!" she added, touching his shoulder lightly. "Darling, I have every confidence that you'll be wonderful. But perhaps it wouldn't hurt to have our own rehearsal. I'll go over the questions with you just like Mr. DeLuca, only I'll mix them up so you'll be prepared for any eventuality. Darling, in an hour or so, you'll be letter perfect. Remember that old saying, 'Anything worth doing is worth doing well'? Andrew, you've put too much time and effort and, yes, sacrifice to yourself and our family not to be the best possible witness you can." Sara waited, hardly daring to breathe, for his answer.

"Sara, I think you're right. You've hit the nail on the head. But why didn't Roman DeLuca warn me? Why didn't he think of it?"

Sara shrugged. *Because, dear Andrew, Roman DeLuca is part of the syndicate. He's a hoodlum and a crook, and with the help of "certain friends" he wants to buy himself the governorship. Roman DeLuca knows that without me in the courtroom he can make you appear a fool and your testimony worthless. If the state doesn't win a conviction for this murder, there will be no connection with the syndicate. And it will all seem as though it's your fault—the absent-minded professor. That's why I have to go back to New Jersey and rescue our son. But I'll have both, Andrew darling. David and my pride in you. I'll have won!*

"Sara? You didn't answer me. Why didn't DeLuca think of asking me the questions out of sequence?"

Sara smiled warmly. "Who knows why lawyers do the things they do? Your job is to get on that stand tomorrow and be a creditable witness. If you agree, let's get down to work. I want you to make me proud. I want to pick up the evening paper and see that you've proven yourself to the court. I want no sly innuendoes about my husband being an absent-minded professor. Now, darling, here's the first question."

Sara mercilessly drilled her husband, making him letter perfect, unshakable, no matter what tack her questioning took. Hour after hour she pounded away, refusing to hear Andrew's complaints of weariness.

[193]

At last, his responses were clear, confident and, above all, honest. None of her grilling had removed his spontaneity. Roman DeLuca was going to be in for a big surprise when Andrew took the stand; he would do a creditable job. Her husband wasn't going to be intimidated by the glib speaking attorney. Not if she had anything to do with it. DeLuca's mistake was underestimating her. He had not realized how important Andrew was to her, or to what lengths she would go to be certain he was first-rate in the public eye. Sara smiled in the early morning light. It always paid to know one's adversary. A pity DeLuca hadn't applied that rule to her.

"Enough, darling, you've got it down. There's no possibility of becoming mixed up now. Truth is on your side, and you've shown me a confidence I hadn't realized you possessed. Each day, darling, I love you more. I'm so proud of you."

Andrew returned Sara's smile as he basked in her praise. He did feel confident now, able to handle anything. Sleepily, he reached out to his wife, who said, "Darling, you still have time for a short nap. I'm going to shower and pack for us. I'll lay your suit out so you can sleep till the last minute. I want you bright and relaxed when you enter the court-room in the morning."

"I'll be so relieved when you get back to Jersey, Sara. If anyone can find Davey, it's you. You're so capable; you'll know what to do. All these hours I've been thinking about testifying, and I haven't given Davey much thought. I can't understand why we haven't heard anything. . . ."

"Hush, darling, everything will be fine. You'll see. I don't want you worrying about Davey or anyone. You have your civic duty to perform and you'll make me proud. I know it. Now close your eyes and don't think of anything."

"Hmmm," he answered, closing his eyes obediently and nodding off. Poor *baby,* he looked so tired. A nap would refresh him, and within a few hours he'd rock DeLuca back on his heels, and the attorney would be powerless to do a thing about it. She would have followed his orders by returning to New Jersey, and Andrew would have testified in the service of justice, making himself a hero.

Roman DeLuca was a loser. He had counted on Andrew making a poor showing, something he must have depended upon from the first because Andrew had been a hostile witness, not coming forward immediately with his information about Jason Forbes. When Andrew had made his deposition with the state attorney's office in New Jersey, it had been too late for DeLuca to do anything other than base his case on Andrew's testimony. And it certainly would have looked strange if Andrew refused to testify because either she or Davey was threatened. No, DeLuca had to go along appearing to be on the side of the law. Instead, he had secretly counted on discrediting Andrew's testimony, knowing the weak points and sharing them with the opposition. But he hadn't counted on Sara. That's why he was forcing her to return to New Jersey for Davey's safety.

She could handle Roman DeLuca. He was nothing more than a scab on a sore. Scabs could be pulled off. The proper ointment could prevent a second scab from forming. Roman DeLuca was nothing more than a bloody, crusted scab that was going to be yanked off in a few hours.

Sara leaned back on the pillows, folding her hands primly on her rising bosom. She would sleep.

Precisely twenty minutes later the alarm on her watch beeped softly. Sara woke instantly, ready for the day ahead.

Everything Sara did was controlled. She moved about the hotel suite, putting everything in order. Noticing Andrew huddled beneath the covers, she adjusted the thermostat in the room. She looked around to see if she had missed anything. Satisfied that everything was in order, she stepped out of her nightgown, folded it neatly, and placed it on top of her other clothes. She walked naked into the bathroom and stared at her reflection with clinical interest. For her age she had a firm, supple body. High round breasts, narrow waist, flat belly. Long, slender legs that, when flexed, were like steel springs, or so Andrew said. She smiled. She turned to adjust the shower head and regulate the water. Sara wondered briefly with what kind of women Roman DeLuca associated. Probably fleshy, big-bosomed women who wore heavy makeup. He had strong hands. Would those hands be gentle or savage on a woman? Her tense muscles relaxed as the steam spiraled upward in search of the vent. What kind of words would he whisper into a woman's ear? Her eyes narrowed. She could almost imagine. He would be a demanding lover, uncontrollable when driven by lust. An animal, savage in his intent and even more savage as he pounded against his prey.

Sara shook her thoughts away as she stepped beneath the spray. She didn't want to think about that handsome, leonine head, the profile that could have been minted into an ancient Roman coin. The width of his shoulders, the slimness of his waist, the length of his thighs, the power of the man—the challenge.

The needlesharp spray hit her breasts, erecting their crests. A sudden intake of breath brought with it a mouthful of water. She doused her head, struggling to control her traitorous thoughts.

He was there with her, watching her, his eyes touching her with their glinting desire. He was inches away from her, just outside the shower spray. She could feel the heat from his naked body, hotter than the shower, touching the most intimate parts of her with the flaring licks of a blast furnace. He watched her, face impassive, eyes devouring, as she soaped her breasts, lifting them, displaying them for him, knowing that the drumbeat of his desire was quickening to wildness. Her arms, the pleasure points behind her ears, the base of her throat, his eyes followed her hands, always watching.

She was mad with her own sense of power over this man who had become her enemy. She was returning his gaze brazenly, impudence lifting the corners of her mouth. If she wanted, she could reach out and touch him, sending him beyond the parameters of sanity. She was preening beneath his gaze, perpetuating his madness for her.

A growing ache was voicing an appeal between her strong, supple thighs. Her skin felt pink, shining from an inner glow. Her breasts were heavy, hard, thrust high on her torso in a silent petition to be crushed beneath his hands.

As she was watching him, his hands dropped to his loins, holding himself. Taking her cue from her fantasy, her own fingers slipped between her legs, surprising her with a heat that rivaled the steamy spray. Never taking her eyes from him, she threw back her head, the water pelleting the full length of her nakedness.

As a low, throaty moan came from her throat, she recognized the need building in her. The misty steam was fast obliterating her fantasy image. Spasm after spasm racked her body. Her knees crumpled beneath her as she sank to the bottom of the tub, doubling over in a paroxysm of seemingly endless joy that left her on the far edge of consciousness.

11

IT HAD BEEN A LONG NIGHT. One of the longest Stuart Sanders could remember. "I know you're out there, kid, I know it in my gut." How had he allowed himself to get so caught up in this case? A case was a case. A kid was a kid. Not true. His stomach rumbled ominously. He had taken one look at the peppers and steak on the airline tray and pushed it away; he had no desire to tempt his ulcer. He should call Nancy, but she might be asleep. It was going to be a long night—he had to do something, anything but sit and wait for reports to filter in.

Sanders opened the door and called out. "I'm taking the camp lantern to browse around. Do I go left around the lake or right to find the grave?"

"Go down to the lake; there's a path that sort of veers to the right. It's a couple hundred feet. You can't miss it; there's a deep gully. You're not going to be able to see much, and from the sound of the wind out there, you might get blown away." Officer Ordway's replacement laughed as he stripped a banana. The sight of the yellow fruit made Sanders' stomach growl in protest.

Sanders walked away, the lantern bobbing at his side. For a big man he was light on his feet. He stopped as he neared the pond, sensing a presence. He turned and was about to reach for the gun under his armpit. A grin split his tight features when he looked down into the pool of light from the lantern.

"How goes it, dog? Kind of late for you, isn't it? You're supposed to bark when you see someone. Some watchdog," he said as he dropped to his haunches to fondle the dog's ears. Duffy rolled over and let her paws go straight in the air, her signal that her belly was to be scratched.

Sanders obliged. "What happened, dog? Where's the kid. Where's Davey? Jesus, if only you could talk."

At the sound of Davey's name Duffy woofed softly. She waited expectantly for Sanders to get on with his brisk massage. "You're one of those safe dogs that's meant to be a companion for a little boy. I'm not blaming you, dog. Hey, what's this?" Sanders exclaimed as his fingers probed the dog's groin. Duffy yelped and rolled over. "Let me see what that is." Obediently, the little dog came back to the crouching man. It was apparent that she trusted him as she started to nuzzle his ankle and whine. Sanders could feel the dog tremble as he gently ran his hands over her body. "You've been hurt, haven't you? It's okay. No one is going to hurt you anymore." His picked up the fuzzy bundle. "We're going for a walk, Duffy. We're going to that grave and maybe you can tell me something in your own way."

Sanders unzipped his vest and held Duffy close to his chest, making sure the dog was comfortable. "I can't take any chances on your getting lost. You've been hurt and you deserve a ride." Duffy yipped as she buried her head in Sanders's warm shirt.

The wind whipped through the trees, making them whistle and shriek. A three-quarter moon slid from behind a cloud, lighting the way for Sanders.

Duffy poked her head up and growled low and deep in her throat. "Gotcha, little buddy, we're close, is that it?" Some familiar scent teased at Sanders's nostrils. It wasn't the leaves or the pine needles; it was something more everyday, something commonplace. Something he smelled once in a while. He wrinkled his nose trying to place the faint aroma. Goddamn, it was mothballs. Cautiously, Sanders approached the gully, the lantern held straight in front of him. Duffy cowered against his chest, whimpering and whining. He dropped to his ankles and peered into the gully. Duffy was out of his jacket, wriggling and squirming. At first the little dog's bark was fretful. She approached the yawning gully and then backed away, growling ferociously. Gaining her courage against some unseen or remembered terror, she used her front paws to dig into the soft earth. Sanders lowered the lantern, illuminating the spot where Duffy was digging. Nosing and pawing, she made high-pitched whining noises, finally breaking into a howl, stopping only to stare up at him, waiting.

Sanders pawed through the dirt looking for whatever the dog wanted him to find. The small, round pellet felt rock hard as he fingered it. It was a mothball! No bigger than the gumballs that kids got out of a candy machine. "Good dog, good Duffy. I know this means something, but for the life of me, I can't imagine what it is." When Nancy stored away the winter coats, she always packed them in mothballs. Then in the fall, she would bring the boxes down from the attic and hang everything on the line to air.

Sanders spent another half hour walking around and searching the area near the gully. He found nothing. Aside from the mothball in his pocket, it was a dry run—a bust. What had he hoped to find? Davey, of course. Always Davey.

Duffy backed off a step and barked. She planted her feet firmly on the soft earth. Her ears were straight up when she barked again.

"You got something in mind?" Duffy backed off. "Okay, show me." Duffy was swift as she turned to follow Sanders's order, and he was hard-pressed to keep up with the terrier in the dim light of the lantern. Too much of Nancy's cooking and too many Chesterfields. He was breathless when he stopped next to Duffy. In all the time he had spent guarding the Taylors, he had never seen the dog so agitated. He lifted the lantern higher into the leaves of the low-branched trees. An electrical wire and black box told him they were at a campsite. *The* campsite, if Duffy were any judge.

"Good girl, good girl," Sanders said squatting down. "You've gotten me this far, now what? Where's Davey? What happened here?" He didn't feel foolish at all talking to the dog. Duffy whined and then howled. Sanders swallowed. "I need more than that, Duffy. You must help me now. It's me and you; we have to find Davey." Duffy stared at Sanders as she continued to whimper and whine, setting the agent's nerves on edge. "Look, I get it; we're at a campsite, but what does it mean? Was Davey here? Were you here?" Duffy listened and cocked her head as though she understood every word the man was saying.

Duffy barked once, then twice, a mean, chilling bark. He watched as the dog dropped to her belly, shimmying toward him. When she was within five feet of him, she lay down and then rolled over, belly up. Sanders reached out to touch Duffy, to touch the tender groin. Duffy let loose with a low growl and then leaped to her feet. Playfully, she

[199]

pranced around Sanders, circling him Indian fashion. "Son-of-a-bitch!" Sanders exclaimed as he scooped up the little dog. "The bastard who was camped here is the one that hit you. Kicked you, probably. Is he the one who has Davey? Show me, Duffy. Davey, where's Davey? What happened to Davey?" Duffy turned and started to circle a small grove of trees, the trees that held the electrical unit. She sniffed and pawed at the ground as she made her circling pattern. "Okay, I got it. Good girl, Duffy. Good girl." The lantern circled the trees with a wide sweep and then centered on the ground. He squatted down and was able to make out tire tracks in the hard-packed, sandy ground. The truck with the pop-up had camped in this spot. It wasn't a startling discovery—any of the police officers could have told him. What was startling was the way Duffy kept circling only the back end of the campsite, where the pop-up had rested. To his mind it meant that Davey was in the pop-up. He squinted in the yellowish light at the panting dog. "Davey was in the pop-up. You got hurt here and made it back to the Ryans. He wasn't that lucky, was he?" Sanders kept walking around the back end of the campsite, trying to envision what had happened to Davey Taylor. "You got hurt and probably ran off to lick your wounds. I'm not saying I blame you. The question is, did Davey hide in the pop-up or did the couple grab him and keep him in the truck with them? I think he hid; what do you think, Duffy old girl?" The terrier whined in answer, nuzzling Sanders's leg. Satisfied that the agent was watching her, Duffy lay down, her head on her paws. Sanders frowned. "Are you tired, Duffy?" The dog lay quietly, staring at him with wet brown eyes. "I see, you're sticking with your story. That's good enough for me. C'mon, you deserve a ride back." He held out his arms to the little dog, allowing her to squirm and wiggle and finally nestle her head on his chest.

Sanders walked back to the Ryan's RV. Gently, he lifted the dog out of her warm nest. "When this is all over, I'm buying you the biggest steak of your life. Just me, you, and Davey." Duffy was still, her head cocked to the side. She woofed softly and then scratched on the RV door. Sanders brought up his hand to wave to the terrier. He lowered it. *That* would have been foolish. The dog's back was turned to him.

He felt better, but he was still worried. The wind buffeted him as he went back to the camp store. He tried unsuccessfully to light a cigarette in the wind and finally gave up.

Mac Feeley was waiting for him, an evil-smelling cigar clamped between his teeth. Sanders wondered what the agent looked like without the cigar. Jesus, he would probably look naked.

"Everything's taken care of; the kid's picture will be in all the morning papers. Nothing's going on here. What say we get some shut-eye?" His tone was hopeful but he was resigned to what he knew would be Sanders's answer.

"I have to call headquarters. But first I want to talk to Robert Redford over there."

Feeley grinned. "The guy's a piss, Sanders; he's combed his hair four times in the half hour I've been standing here."

"Officer Ordway, isn't it?" he asked the young blond policeman. "I'm Stu Sanders, with the FBI. Were you around when they dug up Lombardi's body?"

"Yeah, and I'm still around. Pulling double duty is no way to spend your life, if you know what I mean," the young man told him.

"Did you see the body? Was there anything unusual about it?"

"Yeah, if you consider that bodies don't grow in the ground around these parts," came the flip reply.

Forcing himself to keep cool, Sanders persisted. "Were you at the scene? Man, that must have been rough duty. I understand it wasn't a pretty sight."

"I wasn't the one who dug him up, but it made the ones who did pretty sick. We don't have much crime down here. Drunks, petty thefts—this is a small town. Ever since Wild Adventure was built, things have picked up a little. Hired two new policemen last year, and there's room in the budget for another one this year. My brother's got a bid in for the job."

Sanders listened with pretended interest. "Sharp guy like you, you could go far. You look the type who keeps on his toes. Bet you've got it all over these locals. You should set your sights higher; maybe I can do something for you with the bureau."

"No, thanks. If this is the kind of case you guys deal in every day of the week, I'll just sit back and collect a salary for traffic control. A few weekend family squabbles, a couple of buzzed-out teenagers, an occasional robbery—that's my speed. Don't get dirty that way." He picked an imaginary speck of lint off his uniform jacket.

"Dirty. I heard digging up that body was real dirty work," Sanders tried again.

"The worst. The stink was awful. Don't think I'll ever forget it. I'll never be able to smell that stuff again without remembering."

"Stink? I thought Lombardi was dead only twenty hours or so. Bodies don't usually start to stink that soon."

Ordway's face stiffened and his demeanor changed. "Yeah, well that son-of-a-bitch stunk to me." Ordway turned back to the magazine he was reading, apparently determined not to say any more on the subject.

Sanders grinned wryly. So there was something the local police were holding back. Some bit of information. It was always the same story —the search for glory. They wanted to be the ones to come up with the answers, and the only way to do that was to withhold information. It was a fact of life Sanders understood, and he'd come up against it before. Now what he had to do was make a definite connection between Balog and the dead man. He needed to find something concrete so he could be certain he wasn't chasing shadows. Davey's life depended on it. As of now, Balog was a suspect wanted for questioning. Or so they said. If they wouldn't willingly part with the information, he'd discover it for himself. Moving closer to Feeley, Sanders said in a low tone. "Talk to him, Feeley, I want to call in and I don't want him listening to my end of the conversation. Two can play this game."

"We got nothing in common," Feeley grumbled.

"Then asphyxiate him with your damn cigar. Keep him occupied."

The bureau chief picked up the phone on the first ring. "Carmichael," he barked into the phone.

"Sanders here. Buzz, I want the okay to send Feeley into Newark. I've got a ninety-nine percent pure-gold lead I want him to check for me. We're just holding up the walls here, and the locals are withholding information. Feeley can be back by morning. I want him to go to the apartment that belonged to Balog."

The chief agreed immediately. "You got it. No new leads on the kid, or is this part of it? You've only been there for a few hours and already you've come up with a snitch. How reliable is he?"

Sanders' face was pained. "L.A. and N.Y.P.D. are the only ones who have snitches. We at the bureau have sources. Sources, Buzz. The lady in question is operating on full power. In my opinion she's one hundred percent."

"Stu, I don't mind telling you this entire case is a pain in the ass. If I never see or hear from another local cop again, I'll die happy. Feeley tells me that Chief of Police Allen and his squad have been dubbed Allen's Assholes. True or false?"

Sanders strained to see Officer Ordway through the thick smoke coming from Feeley's cigar. He was combing his hair into a high pompadour. Robert Redford, my ass, he thought. A pale Travolta, maybe. "Sounds fairly accurate to me. I'll let you know my opinion tomorrow."

"You holding anything back on the kid, Stu?"

"Only theories and personal opinions. You know they count for zilch as far as the bureau goes."

"Tell me about it."

"I don't think the kid was snatched by any syndicate. It doesn't fit. What I've got to do is make a definite connection between this Balog character and the dead man, then follow up on that. I say if I find Lombardi's killer I'll find the Taylor boy. I think the kid saw something, got scared, and ended up in the guy's pop-up."

"Your snitch drop that in your lap?"

The pained look crossed Sanders' features again. "In a manner of speaking. You could say she pointed it out to me. I promised her the biggest steak dinner of her life if it pays off."

"Is that on or off the expense account? You sly dog, I always knew you had it in you. A word of caution from one who has been burned. That young stuff out there is hard to handle. They don't mind givin' if you don't mind gettin'. You know what I'm talking about, don't you?"

Sanders grinned. "This little lady, I can handle. I'll check in mid-morning. Have a good night, Buzz."

"You too, Stu."

A harsh violet-colored light was coming through the plastic drapes when Cudge opened his eyes. For the briefest instant he couldn't remember where he was or why. It was the security light in the parking lot behind Snookie's, giving off its vaporous violet rays designed to eliminate shadows.

In bed beside him, Candy Striper, turned on her side to face him. She wasn't pretty, with her makeup streaked and her mouth partially open. Why did he always have to end up with the dogs? Each time she exhaled the odor of stale wine and cigarettes assaulted him. She was a pig, he decided. He'd known it last night, but he thought she had something to offer. He only hoped what she was offering wasn't a roaring case of VD. Lie down with dogs, get up with fleas, as the old saying went.

His head felt heavy and he could hardly lift his arm to read his watch dial. Four-forty. In the morning? It had to be. Yesterday afternoon he'd brought the tire to the gas station next door to Snookie's.

He sat up quickly, holding onto the wall for support. Shit! That mechanic said he'd throw the tire into the back of the truck when he'd finished with it. What if someone stole it? All those niggers coming out of Snookie's—what if they stole his truck?

"Hey, what's the matter?" Candy groaned. "What time is it?"

"I gotta get outa here," he rolled over her to get out of bed. The mattress sank beneath his weight, and the bedsprings screeched in protest. Candy's body was lush and soft beneath him and he remembered flashes of what it had been like with her last night. Soft, warm, like he'd been plowing into a featherbed.

"You got an old lady some place that's looking for you?" she asked sleepily.

Elva. How could he have forgotten about Elva? What if she decided to skip out on him? Go to the cops herself? Pin the whole rap about Lenny on him. Then it wouldn't be just that little kid to worry about, there would be Elva too. Cursing under his breath that he'd ever gone into Snookie's and got entangled with Candy, he searched for his clothing. Never should have gotten sidetracked. He should have stayed to watch the mechanic fix the tire and then gone right back to the camper, just the way he'd planned.

"Hey, babe, any more wine left in that bottle? My mouth's dry." Candy's voice was husky with sleep and hangover.

"Get it yourself," he snapped. "I gotta get going. Where the hell're my boots?"

"Find 'em yourself."

He bristled. "Watch your mouth. Where's my boots?"

"How should I know? They're your boots. What did you do with them?"

"I don't even remember taking them off."

"You didn't. I did," Candy smiled with satisfaction. "Hey, babe, why don't you crawl back in bed here? I got something to show you."

"Save it," he answered uncomfortably, not liking women to take the initiative. "Didn't you get enough last night?" He found his boots and something soft and rotten came off the bottom onto his hands. "Shit!"

"What's that?"

"Dog shit," he moaned, looking for something to wipe his hand on, finally deciding on the bedcovers.

"Hey! Don't do that!" Candy sat up suddenly to inspect the damage. "Christ, ain't you got no sense? Don't wipe that stuff on the covers. One thing at least," she said, turning on the lamp for a closer examination, "it's not dog do, it's apples. Even so, watch where you put it."

"Apples!" Sure, all those rotting apples on the road where he'd pulled in the pop-up, he must have stepped on them and bits of the pulp wedged between the ridges of his soles. Apples. Elva. He had to get back!

Candy settled back against the pillows in a languorous pose. "What's your hurry, babe? It's not even morning. Come on back to bed. This time it's for free."

"It's always free," Cudge growled, tying one of the laces. "Your kind always are."

"Like hell! That little parlor game we played is going to cost you exactly thirty bucks."

"Don't bug me, Candy, I ain't in the mood. Right now you're treading on thin ice. You think I'd pay to screw an old whore like you?"

"Old whore! Listen, you'd have to pay anybody to jump in the sack with you. And double if they'd been there once already. You ain't exactly Casanova," she mocked. "Tell me, you always have that much trouble gettin' it up or was it just the wine?"

Cudge loomed over her, standing close to the bed, hands curling into fists. "One more word and you're askin' for it. One more word. I don't want no more trouble, so just shut up!" He seemed to be fighting himself as he stood over her, forcing himself to back down, to quell his sudden rage. "Where's my shirt?" Not waiting for an answer, he looked around the shabby room.

When he moved away from her, Candy propped herself up on her elbow. "You don't really have any connections in Vegas, do you?"

"What do you think?"

"I think no. So the deal's off. I told you I've got expenses and that wine we drank together last night really knocked me on my ass. Far as I'm concerned, last night was a lost cause, and I ain't got nothing to show for it. So, how's about that thirty dollars I helped you win from that guy."

"You gotta be kiddin'. That's my thirty bucks. I won it. You already got all you're gonna get."

Candy sat up in bed, the blankets falling away, revealing her full, round breasts. "The way I see it, you parked your ass in my bed, and that'll cost you thirty dollars."

He faced her in the yellow lamplight, his eyes cold and hard. The air between them seemed to become dense and still, as Balog's menacing presence seemed to emanate hostility. His square, cropped head burrowed into his powerfully wide shoulders; his barrel-staved chest expanded with each deep intake of air. Thick, muscular legs were planted firmly apart, lending him balance, preparing him for the attack. Thin, mean lips curled downward, heavy pugnacious jaw jutted forward. Candy heard a high, frightened whine and realized with horror it was her own.

When his fist crashed down on her, she managed to fall sideways, taking the blow to her shoulder rather than her face. His hands were in her hair, dragging her off the bed, her knees scraping the floor. He lifted her to her feet, then knocked her backward.

The corral gate in his brain had swung open with nerve-cracking velocity. The beast within lunged forward to freedom, sharp-edged hooves cutting into his brain tissue. Blackness obscured his vision. Rage ripped through him; he was almost senseless. Razor-tipped horns gored his sanity and attacked again and again. He was no longer a man; he had become the beast.

The floor came up under her with a spine-jarring suddenness that robbed her breath. A booted foot kicked her thighs, her breasts, her ribs. The world turned red when a fist found her face, breaking her nose, knocking teeth loose. She was helpless, defenseless as a rag doll in the jaws of a mad dog. She struggled against unconsciousness, fighting to stay alert, knowing it to be her only chance to survive. But when oblivion came she surrendered gratefully, praying for death.

She was still, no longer crawling across the floor to escape his onslaught. How long had she been like that? Still as death. Cudge backed away, stumbling over an overturned chair. He saw the room—the overturned lamp, covers pulled off the bed, the blood splattered on the faded wallpaper. There was a smear of blood across the floor where she had pulled herself to find shelter under the iron bed.

Incredulous, he looked down at his hands, just beginning to feel the tingle that preceded pain. He'd probably broken his little finger when he was hitting her. It was sticking out at a crazy angle. Gritting his teeth, he straightened it and heard a sharp crack before it settled into place.

Thinking he should wrap it to keep it in place, he searched the room, seeing one of the long, black stockings Candy had worn during her dance on Snookie's bar. It was thin and long, suitable. Winding the nylon around his knuckles, he looked around for anything he might have left behind. Now he had to pick up his truck and make tracks. He didn't want to think about what he'd done to Candy. He didn't want to think about anything. He'd have to keep his head, keep his temper under control. From now on, he promised himself, every move he made would be planned. He wouldn't let the corral gate swing open again.

Davey woke slowly. He knew at once where he was and why he was there. He examined the four corners of the pop-up. Balog wasn't there. Brenda was sleeping soundly, her arms wrapped tightly around him. He had to go to the bathroom; it must be morning. He shouldn't have fallen asleep, but Brenda had been so scared, he had felt her heart pounding when she held him. He didn't know what he feared more: going off alone in the dark or what the man would do if he found him. He strained to see the fingers on his watch. Trying not to disturb Brenda he brought his wrist up to his ear. He sighed, Mickey was still breathing. The big hand was on the seven and the little hand between the five and six. He felt confused, but knew he must leave the safety of the pop-up and try to find Aunt Lorrie and Uncle Tom. Through the mesh windows he could see daylight between the trees, streaking the sky a gunmetal gray. First, he had to go to the bathroom. He needed some food to take with him in case he got lost again. He had to be prepared. Should he wake Brenda and say good-bye? He should thank her for helping him. Carefully and quietly, he inched from Elva's lap to the floor. He held his breath when his foot touched his discarded leg brace alongside the small refrigerator. Should he put it on? Maybe Aunt Lorrie would feel better if he wore it. He struggled with the familiar straps, trying to be quiet. Wincing in discomfort when the padded straps touched his ankle, chafed from his walk through the zoo with Aunt Lorrie and Uncle Tom, he remembered to pull his sock up the way his aunt had shown him.

Hurry, hurry, he told himself, recognizing the onset of panic. No time, no time, Mickey's fingers told him. He decided not to awaken Brenda, she might want to keep him with her the way she had done the night before. Uncle Tom told him once that sometimes the right thing to do was often the hardest. It was going to be hard to go through the woods, and he might become lost. So it must be the right thing! To get away from here—away before he came back.

Too late! He was back! "Brenda, Brenda, wake up. He's here. Wake up, please wake up." Davey coaxed. Elva sat up. "He's here, Brenda. I heard the truck."

"Oh, my God! You have to hide, B.J. It's too late," she echoed Davey's words. Fear filled her and then suddenly she wasn't afraid of the monster looming in the doorway. "Come here, B.J. Stand here by me. I won't let him hurt you, not this time. You do what I say, you hear?"

Davey swallowed hard. How could she protect him? But he did as she instructed. Maybe he could help her. He was little; maybe he could scoot between the man's legs or something the way Duffy did when she was playing. He knew he wasn't playing a game, but if he pretended it was all for fun, he might be able to get away. He also knew his chances were better than Brenda's. She looked more scared than he was. He was going to hit her. Davey knew it and Brenda knew it. She took the blow on the side of her head, and at the same time shoved Davey toward the door. "Now, run, B.J., run!"

Davey didn't hesitate. He was past the man and out the door and running as fast as his legs would go. This was no game. This was real. He wanted to cover his ears so he wouldn't hear Brenda's screams and the man's hateful shouts.

On and on he ran, the patchpockets of the apple red windbreaker ballooning alarmingly. He fought for air as he staggered through the sodden leaves and twigs. It was good that they were wet and didn't make noise. He had to take off the brace; it was slowing him down. Could he stop? Did he have time? He had to stop; he had to take the time or the man would catch him. If he caught him, he'd never be able to tell Aunt Lorrie about Brenda and how she helped him. He sat down on a matted pile of leaves. The straps were tight and still damp from yesterday when he wet himself. It was always easier to put on than to take off. He flushed. It was an accident, he told himself. There, it was off. He couldn't take the time to appreciate how good it felt to have his leg free. His sneakers were filthy and drenched. They were beginning to look more and more like Uncle Tom's sneakers. Did the man hurt Brenda? Was Brenda dead? He hated that word. He hated the man. He didn't know how he knew, but he knew that the man hit Brenda. Hit her again and again and again, till she didn't breathe anymore, and he would do the same thing to Davey if he caught him. *Run.* He had to run. He had to run fast.

His bulk filled the pop-up's narrow doorway. His hands were flexing as though working an invisible pair of hand grips, the long tendons in his forearms were hard and prominent under his skin. The meager light of early morning was behind him, throwing his silhouette into relief and hiding the brain-exploding rage on his blunt-featured face.

Elva backed away, shaking. For an instant she imagined he hadn't really seen B.J. escape past his legs and out the door. But she knew she was wrong. His posture was threatening and lethal. But B. J. was safe.

"What were you doing here with that kid? How long have you been hiding him?" His voice boomed and thundered, cracking in her ears, bounding off her fear. She'd always been afraid of him, ever since she was a little girl. She'd never understood why Mama had ever married him or had children with him. There was no kindness in the man, only a love for the cheap hooch he bought in town and for the nights when she could hear Mama's whimpering from the other side of the bedroom wall. He was mean, and he was feared.

"Papa, don't. I didn't do nothing wrong. Honest, I didn't." She could smell the familiar liquor, sweet yet rancid, each time he exhaled. He'd been drinking again. There wasn't food on the table, but the welfare check could buy hooch the same as it could buy food. Poor B.J. He was just a little boy and he needed milk, butter, and eggs. Instead, all he got was thin potato soup made with dry skim milk. Poor B.J. All eyes, scared eyes, that watched the doorway waiting for Papa to come home. Praying he wouldn't. And Mama. Grim mouth, hunched shoulders, red hands from too much laundry and trying to keep the place clean.

Papa advanced on her, striking her in the thigh with his heavy boot. "How long have you been hiding that little bastard? You tell me or I'll give it to you; I'll finish you for good!"

The words were different, but they meant the same. Just like that night when Papa came home and heard B.J. crying because he was hungry and afraid because he heard Mama crying from the other side of the bedroom wall. After that night B.J. had never cried again. And she had never stopped crying. And it was all happening again, only this time it would be different. She wouldn't let Papa touch B.J., wouldn't let those hands harm her little brother. This time, she told herself, she would save him, protect him the way she should have done the first time.

To Elva, the camper had become the poverty-ridden shack in the Pennsylvania foothills. The smell was the same. Liquor, dirt, fear. And the smell of dry urine from where little B.J. slept.

This was the second chance she had always prayed for. It was the same as all those other times, but it was different too. B.J. would be all right; she would see to it.

Desperation widened her eyes, panic slammed into her ribs, nearly taking her breath away. He was big and powerful, and he could snap her in two if he wanted. She could hear the low intake of his breath, and it sounded like the growl of a beast. He moved toward her with sure, slow steps. She could sense his lust for the kill, she could almost reach out and touch it. An icy finger seemed to touch her shoulder, but she was too paralyzed to move, trapped in his gaze like a rabbit in the beam of a headlight. Somewhere in the back of her brain she heard her mother screaming, "Don't touch my baby; don't touch him. Brenda, help! Brenda, help!"

B.J.'s bright blue eyes materialized before her; he watched her, pleading, wincing with the blows, but always watching her, needing her, wanting her to do something, anything, to save him.

His hands were in her hair, yanking her to her feet. She yielded to his strength; she could feel her scalp pulling away from her skull. "No! Leave him alone! He's just a baby!" She was screaming, searching for his eyes with her bony, nail-less fingers, smacking, punching, her struggles ineffectual against him. This time she would stop him. This time she wouldn't hide under the bed while he beat her little brother. B.J.'s accusing eyes wouldn't look at her after it was all over. She wouldn't have to see that last tear that hadn't had a chance to drop from his unseeing eye onto his baby's cheek. This time it would be different.

With all the force she could muster she kicked, aiming between his legs. She felt him flinch and heard his sudden gasp. He flung her from him; she felt herself sailing through the air until she crashed down amid the cartons that littered the floor. The pop-up rocked wildly on its moorings as the world tilted before her.

Pop-up? This wasn't Papa. Mama wasn't screaming; those were her own screams. B.J. was dead, long dead. Cowering in a corner beside the refrigerator, Elva shielded her head with her arms. This was Cudge, and he was just like Papa. Nasty, mean—a killer. Before the cast-iron frying pan came crashing down on her, Elva-Brenda had an insight that she'd never been quite able to put together before. She didn't have to wonder anymore why she stayed with Cudge—she knew. He was her punishment. She'd always known it would end like this. He was Papa all over again, and because he was, he gave her a certain security. Violence had been her birthright. And violence was Cudge. Through him, she would be able to pay for her sin of not saving B.J. She would die, just the way her little brother had died, and then her soul would be saved.

Her arms came away from her head. She allowed his weapon to fall, allowed herself to succumb to the blows. And always there was little B.J.'s face, eyes watching, waiting for her.

The round, plastic disc on the zipper of his jacket bounced against his neck as the little boy ran through the woods, his breathing harsh and ragged. Faster, his mind screamed, don't let him get you. You have to find Uncle Tom. Uncle Tom can stop him; Uncle Tom can do anything. He was getting tired. And then he heard the words, and his sneakers picked up speed. "I'll get you, you little bastard. You ain't getting away from me. I can see that jacket you're wearing all the way over here."

He was lying. If the man could see his jacket, he must be almost next to him, Davey thought. Still, maybe he should take it off and carry it. No, that would mean pulling down the zipper, and sometimes it stuck. He didn't have time; he had to keep running till he couldn't run any more. The man was lying; he was trying to scare him. Looking neither to the right nor to the left, Davey ran furiously straight ahead.

The trees were thinning, and it was easier to run between them. Perspiration ran down Davey's forehead as he staggered ahead. It was so hard to breathe. Maybe he could hide somewhere and wait till he felt better, just a little while. He couldn't stop. If he did, the man would find him and kill him. If only Duffy were here. If only Uncle Tom were here. But they weren't—he was alone, and he had to find Duffy and Uncle Tom all by himself.

Saliva formed in the corner of his mouth when he heard curses coming from his left. His gasping breaths were making too much noise. His hand over his mouth to seal in the harsh sounds, Davey floundered ahead. He was slowing down, and tears of frustration gathered in his eyes. He stopped and listened to the early morning silence. He was at the end of the woods with only young trees growing on the edge of an open field. Davey looked ahead and then behind him. If he went across the field, he would be out in the open. If he stayed behind, the man would put his hands around his neck and make him stop breathing. He had to hide for a little while and think. Uncle Tom always went off by himself to think when he had a problem. Davey looked around. There was no hiding place among the young saplings. If the voice came from his left shoulder, maybe he should go in the direction of his right shoulder.

Quickly he veered off his straight path, almost backtracking, but to the right. Hardly daring to breathe, he crouched down behind a wide tree and clamped one hand over his mouth to still his harsh breathing. His other hand fumbled with the zipper on his windbreaker. His eyes closed as he anticipated the sound the zipper would make as he pulled it down. It moved down but got stuck in the metal at the end. He needed two hands to make the jacket open. A minute was all he needed, but he had to decide which was more important—keeping his hand over his mouth or getting rid of the red jacket. He crouched lower against the tree trunk. Being quiet was the most important thing; the zipper would have to wait. It took three numbers on the Mickey Mouse watch before he felt it was safe to remove his hand from his mouth. He would wait one more number, he told himself, before he tried the zipper. His fingers felt stiff and sore. Sometimes if he just jerked the plastic circle, the zipper would open. Other times he had to have someone help him. He crossed his fingers and then yanked at the plastic disc. Davey grinned. He struggled out of the jacket, careful to make no sound. What to do with the jacket? Mom would be mad if he left it behind. She always said you had to value your things and take care of them. He looked at his sneakers. He might get away with the ruined sneakers, but not two things. He had to take the jacket with him. If only it wasn't red. From now on the only red thing he was ever going to like was Santa Claus. The windbreaker was two colors, brown on the inside. He pulled the sleeves inside out and proudly put his arms back into the jacket. Cautiously he stood up and realized he had to go to the bathroom. He grinned again. He fumbled with the zipper on his jeans and groped for a few seconds. He was still grinning when he zipped his pants and looked around. He nodded to himself. Just like Uncle Tom.

Davey looked around, pleased that he blended so well with the forest colors. The man would have to have real good eyes to find him now. He felt confident as he started out, but a sharp noise directly ahead made him drop to the ground.

"I know you're here somewhere, you little twerp. I been following your footprints. You ain't gonna get away from me this time. I took care of Elva, and I'm gonna kill you too."

Davey flinched. The voice was so close, almost at his head. Play dead. He didn't like the sound of the words. Dead was dead. If you played dead, you might get dead. He would pretend he wasn't here, that he was back at the zoo. Poor Brenda. He wondered if the man put her in the hole or if she was still in the pop-up. He wished he knew. She had helped him.

"You know I'm gonna catch you, so you might as well come out from wherever you're hiding. I was only kidding. I ain't gonna kill you. People don't kill little kids. You come out now, and I'll take you to your folks. I'm gonna count to three, and you come out, okay?" Davey remained still. That was a lie. What he said the first time was the truth. He was trying to trick him, make him come out, and then . . .

"One, two, three. Okay, you had your chance, you little bastard."

Sounds of crashing and swearing fell on Davey's ears. How close the sounds were. He was shaking with fear, and he wished he could see where the man was. He didn't dare lift his head or make any movement at all. He was safe because of the jacket; wait till Uncle Tom found out how clever he was. The sounds were lessening as if the man were moving further away, but his curses and threats could still be heard. The noise didn't frighten Davey as much, and he lifted his head and risked a look. There was no one staring back at him; a long sigh escaped him.

Davey Taylor struggled to his feet. He looked at his watch. The little hand was on the seven and the big hand on the twelve. That was the hour, seven o'clock, he told himself. Seven o'clock in the morning. If he were home, Mom and Dad would just be getting out of bed. It was breakfast time. He wished he had had time to take one of the cupcakes out of the bag on the refrigerator before he left the pop-up. He couldn't think about food now. He had to find a way to get out of the woods and find a road where there were cars.

Davey felt safe as he trudged through the woods. The man had gone in the other direction, so he felt he could take his time. Of course he couldn't do anything that would put him into the man's hands, but he wanted to rest. His legs ached furiously, and the knee that needed the brace kept bending when he put his weight on it. His hands were scratched and scraped and bleeding, and he could feel where the side of his face had scraped into a tree. Touching it lightly, he brought droplets of blood away on his fingertips. He was scared. When had he had his last shot? Was it still working? Would the bleeding stop? His ankles and knees felt tender. Was it from running or was it like before he started the shots, when his joints would swell from spontaneous bleeding?

Painfully tired and frightened, Davey hid in the brush under the trees. He would sit there and listen, watchful for the bad man. Lying on his belly, head cradled in his arms, he tried to stay awake. Two thoughts crossed his mind as he dozed off: He wished he was still a baby, so he could put his thumb in his mouth, and Brenda had called the bad man Cudge.

12

WHEN SARA TAYLOR stepped out of the bathroom after her morning shower, she was dry, powdered, cologned, and naked. Slipping her toiletries into an Yves St. Laurent cosmetic case, she placed it at the top of her suitcase. Andrew would bring both their suitcases home on his late afternoon flight. She hoped no unexpected problems would arise and that Andrew's appearance in court would be completed by the afternoon. She could count on it, she thought, remembering how well she had drilled him on his testimony.

She must see about breakfast. For Andrew, hot cakes, sausages, one scrambled egg, and toast. Melon for both of them and a large pot of hot coffee. She had to eat something to get her thoughts in order, and that would take stamina. If she lived to be a hundred, she would never again think of what had happened in the shower. She would put it out of her mind and never let it surface.

"Would you please tell room service that Mr. Taylor and I would appreciate our breakfast now. We have to be in court by nine.

"Time to get up, darling. All you have to do is shower. Everything is laid out for you. Breakfast will be up shortly. I don't want to rush you, Andrew, but sometimes you have a tendency to dawdle. Today you have to hurry; it's already seven o'clock." She wouldn't think about it when Andrew was in the shower, and there was nothing for her to do. If she turned on the television, she would be distracted and not think about it.

The television set came to life with a light-hearted comedy show. Sara frowned, everything had sexual connotations of one sort or another. She changed the channel to an early-morning talk show. An author was describing her latest book about men's sexual fantasies. Damn. Again, she flipped the channel selector. Cartoons. That was certainly safe. She heard the water being turned off. Andrew would be in the sitting room in another minute, and she could question him again, give him a short run-through to be sure he hadn't forgotten his lines. What was she going to do on the plane for two and one-half hours? She would have all that time to remember. Davey—she would think about Davey. And Lorrie and Tom and what she was going to say to them. How could they lose her son? How dare they allow him out of their sight! Safe ground. Davey and Lorrie were safe ground for now.

Andrew was tieing his tie when a knock sounded at the door. Two waiters carried in the breakfast plates and silverware. After they left, Sara lifted the stainless-steel covers. She shook out Andrew's napkin and handed it to him.

"Looks good. Aren't you eating, darling?"

"Just some melon. You know I don't like to eat before a plane trip. This is more than enough. The round scoop of butter makes the hot cakes appealing, don't you think, Andrew?"

Andrew nodded as he chewed industriously. "This breakfast is a surprise, all my favorites!"

Sara Taylor's smile didn't reach her eyes. "You deserve only the best, Andrew, and that's what I want for you."

"Are we taking the bags to the courtroom or do you think I should come back for them?" Andrew asked as he pushed his empty plate aside.

"You might want to freshen up before you leave for your plane. Leave them here or they'll just be a hindrance. The limo will be waiting, so there shouldn't be any problem. You might even want to shower; I heard just a short while ago that it's going to be eighty-nine degrees today."

"I'm glad we don't live here anymore, I can tell you that," Andrew volunteered as he pushed back his chair. "Are you finished with your coffee? I like the change of seasons at home. What about you, Sara? Do you ever miss Florida."

"No, darling, I don't. Perhaps though, we should start thinking about moving out of New Jersey. It's so . . . so crime-ridden. Connecticut would be nice; let's consider it in the spring. I'm ready when you are."

"Then let's go and get this over with, so I can be home with you and Davey for dinner this evening."

"We don't know for certain that Davey has been found. As of last evening, he was still lost, but I'm sure he's been found by now. Our son is a resilient little boy, but he did miss his shot, and that's what worries me."

"I feel just as you do; Davey will be waiting for both of us. Sara, instead of punishing Davey for wandering off, why don't you make a wonderful dinner with all his favorites. We'll make a party of it, and afterward have a serious talk with him. We don't want him to think we're angry with him, but he has got to realize what he's done. My father used to do that with me. The real punishment came from having to stand there with no defense for what I'd done, and my father understanding perfectly. My mother too. They were never divided when it came to me. Whatever one said, the other agreed. Like we do with Davey."

"It sounds like a tremendous idea." That was something she could do on the plane ride. She could plan the menu and think about the talk she and Andrew would have with Davey.

"I, for one, won't be sorry to see the last of this hotel," Andrew said closing the door behind him. "You'd better give me the key, Sara."

"Darling, I really don't want to go and leave you here. I feel that my place is with you, but our son . . ."

"Sara," Andrew said putting his arm around her shoulder. "I don't want to hear another word. We agreed and the matter is settled; I'll be fine. I'm just sorry that I made such a botch of things yesterday. Today, I'll do much better. The state will have no problems. Mr. DeLuca will be more than satisfied."

"I rather doubt that," Sara said sotto voce.

"What did you say, darling?"

"Nothing. Just woolgathering aloud. It wasn't important. We're fortunate that we left when we did. Traffic is building up. You're going to be the first witness, so it is imperative that you be on time."

Thirty-five minutes later the limousine pulled to the curb of the courthouse. Sara hated the pushing and shoving crowd of reporters shouting questions. As she walked beside Andrew up the stairs, she kept her gaze straight ahead, her step firm and sure. It wasn't till one of the security guards opened the door for Sara that she saw Roman DeLuca. She felt a flush creep up her neck.

"Good morning, Andrew. Mrs. Taylor," he said, greeting them. Sara wondered why Andrew was Andrew and she had been Mrs. Taylor, ever since they first met DeLuca. Andrew was whisked off by two court bailiffs, and Sara was left standing next to Roman DeLuca and one of the men from Sanders's unit, Michael Jonas. Stu Sanders had introduced Jonas to Sara and Andrew, identifying him as an assistant supplied by the state of Florida. Sara was shaken. She wondered if he, too, was part of the syndicate.

"You don't strike me as the type to make foolish mistakes, Mrs. Taylor," DeLuca's eyes narrowed. "Why didn't you take my advice? You'll have no one to blame but yourself."

Sara felt herself grow rigid. "I don't make mistakes. I always take full responsibility for my actions. As for your advice . . ."

"Spare me, my dear. You had your chance last night and you ignored it. We don't play games." DeLuca turned to his associate. Sara felt mesmerized as she watched him. His lips barely moved. "Take care of the lady, Jonas."

"Yes, sir," came the clipped reply.

It happened so fast, Sara didn't know how it came about. One minute the three of them were standing alone, the next minute there was a swarm of reporters. She stepped aside, clearing the way for DeLuca to take center stage. The agency man named Jonas moved at the same time, jostling against Sara. She knew, without seeing the gun, that the man was wearing a shoulder holster, and she felt the hardness of the leather as she was thrown against him. The color drained from her face, as she understood what DeLuca meant with the words "take care of her." He must have thought she wasn't leaving. It was her own fault for allowing him to think she wasn't giving in to his threats. The fact that she was on the verge of telling him meant nothing. She couldn't tell him now, while he was holding court on center stage. She would leave now while all the commotion was going on. DeLuca would find out sooner or later that she was on the flight. She turned, ready to leave, when she felt a touch on her arm.

"We'll leave together. Don't say anything; just move casually."

"Take your hand off me," Sara hissed.

The grip became more secure. "Smile, pretty lady, so all the reporters can snap your picture. I mean it."

He did; she could feel it. "You wouldn't dare do anything here in full view of all these people. You aren't an associate of Stuart Sanders. You're one of DeLuca's thugs, not a government agent. I also know what you're wearing under that custom-tailored suit."

"Then you know I mean business. Keep smiling and walk slowly straight out to the car."

"Why? Where are we going; that's assuming I go with you."

"For a little ride. You talk too much."

"I was just going to the airport." Sara didn't like the man's looks or the cold, controlled way he spoke, knowing that he had no intention of taking her to the airport. The shoulder holster said all there was to be said. Where was that seedy-looking reporter from the slick tabloid? He had offered five hundred dollars for her exclusive interview late yesterday afternoon. Her mind raced. What was his name? She had to think and think fast. Peter? Percy. Percy Strang, that was it.

"Let's get on with it, Mrs. Taylor. You're wasting both our times. I'm not going to tell you again."

"I can see that," Sara smiled up at him. "One moment and then I'll be glad to join you for coffee." She made her voice purposely high and shrill, knowing one or more of the reporters would look her way. She gave them all a dazzling smile and then asked for Percy Strang. The reporter from the Miami *Herald* looked disgusted. Sara could almost read his mind: The gossip tabloids always got the dirt because they *paid* for it. It always came down to the buck. An honest reporter had to hustle, and he was lucky if he got two inches of printable news.

"Yo! Here I am, Mrs. Taylor. Changed your mind, I see."

"Why not, I can spend five hundred dollars just as easily as the next person. Why don't we go for coffee?" Sara asked.

"You got it. I'll even buy."

"How generous of you." She felt panic rise in her chest as the clamor around Roman DeLuca quieted, and everyone could overhear the exchange between the wife of the state's star witness and the reporter from the *Tatler*. "When will you pay me?" Sara demanded as an afterthought.

"As soon as these nimble fingers get everything down in black and white."

"A lady could hardly ask for more." Sara felt all eyes on her as she shook Jonas's hand off her arm. "I'm so sorry, Mr. Jonas to renege on our breakfast date. However, five hundred dollars is five hundred dollars. I'll see all of you later. Gentlemen," she said nodding her head and walked quickly to Percy Strang's side.

Sara linked her arm through Percy Strang's as she led him down the hall, outside the door, and then down the steps. The limousine was standing at the curb; the driver inside was reading the paper and smoking a cigarette. She dragged the reporter with her as she leaped into the back seat of the luxurious car, "Take me to the airport, driver, and please hurry. You don't mind, do you, Mr. Strang? I mean about going to the airport. If we have time, we can have coffee. I thought it would be best if we talked on the way. This way you won't feel I'm trying to put you off. I don't have much time, and when it's time to board, we'll have to stop the interview." At the reporter's disappointed look she went on, hastily adding, "Of course, you can always come to New Jersey or call me long distance. My son disappeared yesterday, and that's why I'm going home now. No one knows. It's your exclusive, Mr. Strang. However, I don't want to talk about that just yet. Later, we'll get to my son. For now, why don't you and I get to know each other? You tell me what it is you want to know, and I'll answer to the best of my ability."

"Are you saying your son was kidnapped? Jesus, Mrs. Taylor, I don't know what to say!"

"I knew you would feel like that. That's the reason I said we would talk about it later. I do have one rather small favor to ask of you though."

"For an exclusive like that, Mrs. Taylor, I would try to walk on water for you."

"Yes, well, that won't be necessary. I want you to stay next to me every minute till I board the plane. Don't leave my side. If you see, what I mean is, if you suspect—don't leave my side. Is it a deal, Mr. Strang?"

"Of course it's a deal. This is the kind of stuff reporters only dream about. How am I ever going to thank you?"

"By staying next to me and not letting me out of your sight."

"Is there a microphone in this limo? How do you give the driver instructions?"

Sara felt faint. God! "I don't know; I'm not sure."

Percy Strang fiddled with the small grill above the ashtray. "Is this a rented limo or did the district attorney provide it for you and your husband?"

"The district attorney? Oh, God. Mr. Strang, look outside. Is this the way to the airport?"

"Beats me, Mrs. Taylor. I'm based out of Chicago, and I was sent here to cover the trial. We could be going to Cuba for all I know."

"Press that gadget and ask the driver how much further it is. Do it now!" Her voice was shrill, and Percy did as he was instructed.

"Another five minutes, ma'am," came the reply. "The turnoff is just ahead. You can see the sign from here."

"Thank God," Sara sighed.

"Mrs. Taylor, I don't know if you're nervous or not, but I do think there's something you should know. When we pulled away from the curb back at the courthouse, a car pulled out right behind us. It's been following us ever since. Being a reporter, I'm trained to notice such things," he said importantly, hoping the elegant Mrs. Taylor would be impressed.

"Oh, God," Sara moaned. Whoever it was in the car wasn't following her to the airport to see if she got on the plane. If she knew nothing else, she knew that for a fact. She was going to be killed. She could taste her own death; it was bitter, laced with bile.

"Do you read the *Tatler*, Mrs. Taylor?"

"All the time. My housekeeper buys it and leaves it in the kitchen," Sara said feverishly. She should have told Andrew. Left a message, something. What lies would Roman DeLuca tell her husband? Poor Andrew, he thought he was going home to a wife who was going to cook a wonderful celebration dinner, and everyone would live happily ever after. "Shit!" she said succinctly.

Percy Strang frowned. He pursed his narrow lips in disapproval. Mrs. Taylor slipped a notch in his esteem. Back at the courthouse she had seemed so elegant, so regal, like a princess, and she would certainly look smashing on the inside of page one, right next to the story he had done on the woman who had grown another kidney—a genuine medical miracle. Sara Taylor would definitely give the page a touch of class.

The chauffeur leaned his head back and spoke. "Which airline, ma'am?"

"Airline?" Sara repeated.

"Yes, ma'am, where do you want to be dropped off?"

Sara's mind raced. Eastern? Delta? Pan Am? She couldn't remember. They had come down on Eastern, but that was no reason to assume DeLuca had made her return reservation on Eastern. "Eastern," she said firmly. The check-ins couldn't be that far apart.

Sara's mind raced as the limousine came up to the curb. Perhaps the driver would deliver a message to Andrew, or should she have the reporter deliver it? She couldn't make up her mind. If she did write a note to Andrew, she might place him in danger, and Andrew couldn't function in a crisis. Andrew needed her and she was failing him. Should she write the note or not? The decision was taken out of her hands the moment she stepped to the curb. A dark face asked if she had any luggage just as DeLuca's man, Jonas, leaped from his car.

"Mrs. Taylor, Mrs. Taylor, wait for me," Jonas shouted with a smile on his face.

"Mrs. Taylor, didn't you hear the man? He's calling you, he wants you to wait for him," Percy Strang called as he ran through the open doorway behind Sara.

She ignored him as she headed for the Eastern check-in counter. A policeman, a security guard. God, where were they? Miami had enough crime to warrant an officer every twenty feet. Jonas could hardly accost her here in a public airport; the syndicate didn't gun down women in public, or did they?

It had been so long since she prayed that Sara felt the words catch in her throat. She couldn't remember the simple little prayers she had learned as a child. She had never been one to rely on the Almighty to help her, preferring to handle her own affairs in her own way. If she didn't see a uniform soon, she would have to go to the check-in and tell the reservation clerk. Tell him what? her mind shrieked.

"Mrs. Taylor, where are you going? Why are you so upset? Didn't you hear me? There's a man running after us who wants to talk to you. Perhaps it's news of your son. I hear you, but I can't understand what you're saying. Can't we stop for coffee now so I can start the interview. You really are making me work for this story."

Sara half turned. "I'm praying, Mr. Strang. That man who you are so concerned about is trying to kill me. He may even kill you. That's why I'm trying to get away from him. Coffee is out, I'm sure you can see that now. Where is he, Mr. Strang?" Sara asked in a strangled voice.

Intrigue, kidnapping, killing—all the ingredients for a first-class story. Some journalist in the sky must be looking out for him, Percy thought happily. He almost tripped over his own feet as he tried to keep up with Sara. "He's right behind us, and I think you should know he's gaining rapidly. Look, Mrs. Taylor, I'm no he-man type. Why don't you find a cop?"

Sara picked up speed. "I would if I could. Do you see one anywhere?" Sara shot back.

"You could scream," Strang said.

"And then what? The man following us is connected with the syndicate. He works for the district attorney who is also connected with the syndicate. Where do you think that leaves me, Mr. Strang?"

Sara wanted to scream with frustration. Where was she going anyway? Who was she fooling? If she did find a policeman, what was she going to say? Jonas would whip out his credentials and tell the officer that she was distraught. The officer would gladly hand her over to the district attorney's right-hand man; she didn't have a chance, and she knew it. She wasn't going to be allowed to get on any plane. Jonas could even say she was mentally unstable. Who was going to believe her against someone with his credentials? He was a combination of Madison Avenue, Ivy League, the military, and law enforcement. And what was she? Right now, she was a high-strung, perspiring, middle-aged woman being trailed by the star reporter from the *Tattler*. Somehow she had to get away from him in this gigantic airport. Once she was in Jonas's custody, it was the end. The local police would probably give him an escort out of the terminal.

"Andrew, Andrew, I'm so sorry," she murmured. Frantically she looked around, trying to see some way of escaping the man trailing her. Maybe she would be better off on the outside; she could walk around the airport endlessly and still not get away. An exit. A diversion. Percy Strang. It was difficult to breathe.

"I don't understand any of this," Percy bleated. "We really have to stop and catch our breaths. Mrs. Taylor, are you listening to me? If you sit down calmly to talk and think, we might come up with a solution to this . . . this predicament. What I'm saying is, this is a busy, well-populated airport. The man behind us isn't going to . . . and isn't he one of the men assigned to guard you and Mr. Taylor? Mrs. Taylor, you aren't listening to a word I'm saying. You're overwrought; you must be mistaken."

"You're right, Mr. Strang, I'm not listening, and that's because you don't know what you're talking about. Back in the courthouse I purposely singled you out to get me away from the man following us. He is wearing a gun in a shoulder holster. As long as you walk directly behind me, as you're doing now, he won't dare shoot me. I'm frightened, and I don't mind if you know. You should be frightened too, Mr. Strang. These people are evil and will stop at nothing; they're the ones who kidnapped my son. Now do you see why I have to get away from that man? He has no intention of letting me board any plane. I did something foolish this morning, and I'm going to pay for it with my life. I think I've accepted that, but I'm not giving up without a fight, I can tell you that." Her voice was barely a whisper, hoarse and frightened.

"Come now, Mrs. Taylor, aren't you being melodramatic? Somehow I can't accept all of this. You're upset about your son, and the fact that your husband is a key witness in a murder case. It's understandable that you're building mountains out of molehills. What do you say to a cup of coffee?"

Oh, God, he wanted coffee and she was going to die. She felt like throwing up. They she saw the diversion she needed. A group of chattering South American soccer players was advancing down the concourse with much good-natured back-slapping and hilarity. If she quickened her stride, she could reach the Exit sign at about the same time the players did. If Strang could manage to join the crowd of players, he could conceivably stall for time. At least she could get outside where she could run.

The words came in controlled gasps. "Do you understand what I'm telling you? If you do this, I promise you the story of your life. Ten minutes, that's all I need."

The story of his life! The big scoop! The words every journalist dreams of. The big by-line. He would do it; it would spread across page one and page two. The woman with three kidneys would have to wait for another issue. This was the big one; the one he had dreamed about all this past year, ever since he walked into the *Tattler* offices and applied for a job. They had only asked him two questions: Do you type? Are you gay or straight? His answers yes, he could type, and he could go either AC or DC were the right ones, and he was hired on the spot. Now was his big chance! Even if Sara Taylor *was* crazy, it was a story.

Sara felt the color drain from her face as she closed the distance between the soccer players and herself. How lightheaded she felt. Maybe she could get out of this after all. The Exit sign blurred. "Now," she whispered hoarsely.

Strang almost didn't hear her. Suddenly, he threw up his arms and then walked smack into one of the approaching players. "My God, you're a sight for sore eyes," he shouted as he wrapped his skinny arms around the player's neck. "I want you to endorse some new soccer balls for me. You and your friends move right over here," he babbled as he pushed the players together into a huddle under the Exit sign.

Sara gasped, she had made it! She was through the door. The question was, what was on the other side of the door?

She was out! Dear God, she was out! Where was she? A sign said, Authorized Personnel Only. She paid it no heed as she raced along a concrete corridor and then down a short flight of stairs. Another red sign said, No Admittance. She didn't stop; she didn't think. She pushed open the door, hearing the pounding of rushing footsteps behind her.

She felt a rush of cold air. He knew what she had done, and he was following her again. There wasn't much time left. Still, she had to try. Oh, Andrew, I'm so sorry, so very sorry. Maybe she should have taken her chances with the airport police. Maybe, maybe, maybe. The end would be the same, of that she was convinced. Only the location would have been different—a lonely road with a bullet through her head, or worse yet, a blow to her head and the car set on fire. The end would be the same. She was going to die; she had to die. She had disobeyed Roman DeLuca, tried to outsmart him, and now it was too late! He'd never let her get away with it, especially if Andrew helped the state's case on the witness stand. She should have obeyed DeLuca's rules.

Sara ran wildly, legs pumping furiously, breath labored and painful. She was heedless of her path, aware only of open spaces and concrete.

Then she was aware of a voice on the public address system. "Unauthorized persons on the runway! I repeat: Unauthorized persons on the runway! Clear the runway! I repeat: Clear the runway!"

Over and over the message was repeated, and each time the volume was raised. They were referring to her and Jonas. She saw running figures converging on her path, and her heels beat into the concrete as she ran for the open. Help was on the way. She was within a hair's breadth of winning!

"Clear the runway! Clear the runway!" and then: "Will somebody clear the goddamn runway? A man and a woman are on runway six. Clear the runway! Moving aircraft! Moving aircraft!"

Sara kept running, knowing her life depended on it. Heading toward her from scattered outbuildings were shouting, waving men, some dressed in overalls, others in shirts and ties. She risked a glance behind her. Jonas was still there, grim and determined.

The address system roared to life again: "Moving aircraft! Moving aircraft! Aircraft alerted; I repeat: aircraft alerted! Clear the runway! Goddamn it, can't somebody catch those fools? Clear the runway!"

Safety was only yards away. There was a buzzing near her head, loud and whining. She mustn't stop, mustn't think! She was almost home, a winner again.

The aircraft appeared out of nowhere. One moment there had been nothing but open space and then she was faced with a monstrous moving object separating her from safety, leaving her within Jonas's grasp. She had to get to the other side; she would.

Her hair was being pulled, by a steady stream. She felt like carpet lint being sucked up into a vacuum cleaner. The whining in her ears became louder; there was a squeal she recognized as the screech of brakes. Unable to comprehend, Sara screamed. Her last conscious thought was of being fed into a lion's jaws, she was being sucked into the powerful cavern of its mouth.

Michael Jonas skidded to a stop. His chest heaved with exertion, and his eyes wide with the horror he had witnessed. But he'd seen worse. He had known exactly what he was doing when he chased her onto the runway. DeLuca might protest, but he would be pleased. If there was one way to climb to the top, it was by obeying orders. DeLuca had said to "take care of her," and he had. Aside from being windblown and out of breath, he was none the worse for wear. It was over.

Feeley took his new assignment good-naturedly. It was better than tramping through the woods with Sanders and his lantern. "Just remember, you're buying breakfast," he called over his shoulder. He slammed the car door and slipped into gear. What was he supposed to do with a mothball? Dead bodies, little kids, mothballs, camping in the woods in October.

Sanders trudged into the campground just as dawn broke. He felt more certain than ever that Davey Taylor was close by. Feeley wasn't back and he wondered who was going to replace the blond policeman behind the desk. A quick catnap was what he needed for a fresh start when Feeley returned. He should have been back by now. He nodded curtly to the young officer who was slipping a long-handled comb back into his shirt pocket.

Feeley shook him awake at 8:45. "You know something, Stu. I can't drink coffee out of a cup anymore. If it doesn't come out of a container and have a lid, I can't get it down. These are terrible, aren't they?" he asked wolfing down the fast-food breakfast.

"Never mind the food. What did you find out?"

"The same thing the cops found—traces of blood. It was a hell hole; you wouldn't let your dog live there. I rousted the landlady, and let me tell you, she was a piece of work. She was nipping on a bottle of beer at 5:45 in the morning. Said it beat coffee for a pick-me-up. She heard sounds of a fight and a lot of banging around, same thing she told the cops. I did find a couple of mates to this," he said holding out six mothballs in his hand. "I found them on the steps. I figured it must mean something, so I brought them along. I looked all over the apartment but couldn't find any more. There was an empty box in a paper bag by the sink. No other trash. I hung around till the work force crawled out of the woodwork. If there isn't someone to hold up the corners at 7:00 A.M., Newark would fall apart. No one saw a thing," he said disgustedly.

At Sanders's bleak look, he added hastily, "I don't know if this means anything, but as I was getting into my car, thanking God it was still there, a little kid came up. He wanted a quarter, probably to play the numbers. The long and the short of it is, he was playing stickball outside the building when Balog and a girl carried an ironing board into the truck. The kid said Elva, that's her name, always carried the dirty clothes in a paper bag to the laundromat around the corner. He said he saw her do it lots of times. The kid was a regular little wiseass, said you don't take ironing boards to the laundromat, because you can't iron there. He also said the clothes looked heavy, and the guy was sweating. I gave him a buck." He was pleased with himself, knowing Sanders was pleased.

He was. "Heavy, huh? This kid say anything about talking to the cops?"

"You gotta be putting me on. He's a street kid. Street kids don't talk to the cops unless it's to tell them to fuck off or drop dead. Nah, he thought I was a relative—it was the cigar. I guess I looked like a big butter-and-egg man."

Sanders put two Rolaids into his mouth. "That was the worst breakfast I ever ate." He'd give his right arm for one of Nancy's four-star weekend breakfasts of French toast, pancakes, and scrambled eggs with lots of bacon on the side. He had to call her soon, before she went out for the morning to do her shopping.

"It could have been a body. You have to admit it was clever, if that's the way they got him out. This Balog is our man, no doubt about it. The locals must know it too, only they think they've got the jump on us. And who are we, anyway? Just some tired men looking for a lost kid."

"It's adding up. The mothballs sort of frost it, if you know what I mean."

"Yeah," Feeley said, mangling the soggy end of his cigar. "While you were playing Rip van Winkle, I was watching the bird with the phone. He kept looking at me while he was carrying on this conversation. Call came in a little after eight. I asked him point blank if it was something we should know, and he told me it was a personal call. You want to check it out?"

Sanders rubbed the stubble on his chin. "Do you think it was a personal call?"

Feeley shrugged his shoulders.

"Then let's check it out."

Sanders got right to the point. "This is a bureau office. Any calls that come in pertain to our case. My partner said you received a call a short while ago. Let me see the log sheet."

The officer's face drained of all color. "It was a personal call. A pal of mine was going off duty and they put him through here to me. It was personal."

"Let me be the judge. We can call your pal, but that would take time. Make it easy for all of us."

The pale face flushed. "Well, you see, what I mean . . . my buddy and me know this hooker. She's okay, if you know what I mean," he added hastily, noticing the look on Sanders's face. "Anyway, she got busted up during the night. Some dude from out of town fed her a line about making her a showgirl in Vegas, and she fell for it. Somebody found her and called the hospital in Point Pleasant. She's being operated on right now. My buddy went over after he finished his shift to see if he could get a line on how it happened."

"And?"

"And all he came up with was it was some guy driving a pick-up he parked behind the garage. Gus, the guy who runs the garage, said this dude came in late yesterday afternoon to have a tire fixed. He steered him into the saloon where Candy dances. That's it," the cop sighed, relieved that they weren't going to bust his ass. What the hell, his personal life was his own. So what if he and his buddies knew a few hookers. You didn't log personal calls.

"Did the guy from the garage say anything about the truck; what color it was?"

"No, but my buddy said it was one of those hippie rigs, all painted up and . . . oh, Jesus. That was the guy, right? Oh, Jesus!"

"What was the name of the hospital again?" Sanders barked.

"Point Pleasant General. Candy is being operated on now for a busted spleen, fractured collar bone, and two cracked ribs, and my buddy says her face will never be the same."

Sanders's stomach turned sour. He chewed up two more Rolaids. He turned to Feeley. "Sack out for an hour or so. I'll check the police report. No point in hanging around the hospital. We'll get to her doctor later on this morning."

"Go away, I'm asleep already." It was true, Sanders thought in amazement. Loud, gusty snores rippled around the room. The cigar never moved.

Outside the office, Sanders stopped to gather his thoughts. Balog was still in the area. Everything pointed to it. The beaten woman, the flat tire, the description of the pick-up by the service-station owner. But where was Davey? He would have staked his life on it that Davey was with Balog and his traveling companion. He snapped his fingers. Right, there were two of them. One could have stayed with the boy while the other went to town. No, it didn't fit. A man on the run with a kid in tow just didn't take the time to visit a hooker. It didn't fit.

Unless, he didn't even want to think about it, but the only way to get his thoughts past it, was to take it out and look at it. Unless Davey was already dead. Unless he'd seen too much, and Balog knew it and had disposed of him.

Still, it didn't fit. It wasn't right. What about the woman with Balog? Elva, Feeley said her name was. Would a man leave a woman behind to guard a kid while he took himself off for a little relaxation? Nah, no woman would stand for that. Okay, so this Elva didn't know Balog was paying a house call. He left her alone somewhere with the camper and Davey—where did Davey fit?

Start again. Davey sees something. Probably Balog burying Lombardi, if Lombardi was killed inside Balog's apartment. That's who they were carrying out on the ironing board. Davey is spotted. He runs. He couldn't have been caught or Balog would have settled it right there in camp and dumped the body with Lombardi's. He snapped his fingers. *That* was why the grave was open and left. They had to make a run for it. Someone *had* seen them. Davey! Davey runs. Hides. Maybe in the back of the camper. They close it, not noticing the kid, and Balog makes his trip to town never knowing the kid was in the camper!

And the woman? Elva? Sanders breathed a sigh of relief. Women didn't usually hurt children. He had to count on that. The rain last night. Elva must have opened the camper. Davey *could* have made his escape.

The forest outside the Wild Adventure Amusement Park was shaped like a horseshoe with an open field between the ends. Widespread farms dotted the perimeters of the open field, and it was in this direction the boy headed. The roof of a large barn caught his eye, along with the silver silo standing beside it. He almost laughed aloud at his discovery, but some inner voice warned that he couldn't count on victory just yet. There was still the open field to cross, and then he had to find someone to call his aunt and uncle. Whoever lived near the barn might take him to the police, and they would let him wear a police cap and give him an ice cream. They always did that on television.

Cautiously on tiptoe, Davey walked to the edge of the forest, where he could survey the open field, judging the distance. He must cross it. There was no other way. If he walked or ran, the man named Cudge might spot him. He was afraid, feeling vulnerable and anxious to find safety.

A squirrel in the tree overhead scurried out onto a low-lying branch and then dropped to one beneath it. Petrified by the sound, Davey dropped to his belly and dug his head into his folded arms. He waited, lying motionless, barely breathing, until the squirrel was a foot in front of him. Davey opened one eye and stared into the shiny brown buttons that were the squirrel's eyes.

Crawling on his belly, he inched his way out to the field. He wiggled and squirmed his way across the muddy terrain. Mom sure was going to be mad when she got a look at his clothes. Aunt Lorrie would never be able to get them clean. He was part of the earth, and for a few brief seconds he revelled in the feeling as his fingers clawed through the muddy ground, pulling him closer and closer to the red barn. By the time he reached the back of the red barn he was exhausted but ex- hilarated. He had done it. He had gotten away from the man. Now if he could find someone to call his Uncle Tom, he would be home by —he looked at his watch. He was dismayed to see that Mickey's shiny face was obliterated by mud that had seeped through the crystal. Davey felt like crying. First, he ruined his sneakers and then his jacket and now his watch. He got to his knees and wiped off his hands. Mud splattered every which way. He laughed delightedly. If Mom could only see him now. She would take a fit. Aunt Lorrie would laugh. Uncle Tom would shake his head and turn a hose on him. Dad would inch closer to Mom; there would be no smile on his face. As Uncle Tom would say, he couldn't worry about that now. He had to find someone to help him. He looked over his shoulder to see if the man who breathed like an animal was anywhere near. But the open field was empty.

The rolled cuffs of his new jeans flapped at his ankles as Davey trudged around the side of the barn. Turkeys daintily picked at corn that littered the barnyard. Everything smelled sweet and clean. He wished he had a drink; even toothpaste would taste good in his mouth now. As he walked toward the turkeys, they started to gobble and disperse. A white-haired woman walked out of the barn, holding a pitchfork. "Well, well, what have we here?"

"Lady, I need someone to help me call my aunt and uncle. Will you call them for me?"

The pitchfork fell to the ground at the woman's feet. "You're lost, is that it? Bet you wandered off from the amusement park. I thought it was closed for the winter."

"It is. I was camping there with my aunt and uncle, and I don't know how to get back. Are you a grandmother?" he asked inquisitively.

"Well, bless my soul, funny you should ask that. I am, seven times over." At Davey's frown the woman smiled. "That means I have seven grandchildren, the last one about your size. How old are you?"

"I'll be six after Christmas," Davey said proudly. "I would 'preciate it if you called my aunt and uncle. I have to get a shot at noontime. Do you know what time it is?"

The old woman looked at the sun. "Pretty near one o'clock, little fella."

Davey pondered the answer. He wished he had paid more attention when Mom was teaching him how to tell time. "Is that before or after noontime?"

" 'Bout an hour after. You come along with me and I'll try to dust you off a little, but I don't think it's going to help. You need hosing down in the trough, but it's a mite too chilly for that. Wait on the back porch while I make the call. Would you like cookies and milk? I make the best ginger cookies in these parts."

"I'd like that," Davey said agreeably.

"Come along then and you can tell me where your folks are staying. Do you know the campsite number?"

"It's close to the pond; I don't know the number. We have an RV. Do you like being a grandmother?" he asked, feeling safe from the man and anticipating being with the Ryans again.

"I suppose I would, if I got to see my grandchildren, but I don't. My young'uns can't be bothered coming out here to the farm. They like city life. I still have one boy here that helps me when he isn't—what I mean is, he still lives here. You sound like you don't know too much about grandmothers. Don't you have one?"

"No. Do you make apple pies and a big turkey on Thanksgiving and Christmas? I always see grandmothers do that on television."

"No, I don't, son. More like chicken parts, a leg and a thigh and canned cranberry sauce. It doesn't bother me too much anymore. It used to though. Well, here we are. You sit here on the steps and I'll fetch you the cookies and milk. How did you get so muddy?"

"I crawled on my belly across the field," Davey replied truthfully.

"You ask a dumb question and you get a dumb answer," the old woman laughed. "I'll be back in two shakes."

Davey sat down; his leg was aching, and he was tired. The cookies and milk were going to taste good. It was the first time he had ever seen a grandmother up close, and she looked like grandmothers were supposed to look. He wished he had one—he wished a lot of things. He wished Duffy was here. He wished Uncle Tom would drive up to this house and hug him.

"Here you go. What's your name, little fella, so I know what I'm talking about when I call the campground?"

"My name is Davey Taylor, but my aunt and uncle's name is Ryan. Uncle Tom and Aunt Lorrie. Uncle Tom signed in when we camped. Uncle Tom is the only one at the campground who has an RV."

"Mercy me, what's that noise? Looks like we have another visitor. Land sakes, weeks and months go by, and nary a soul stops by, and today we have two visitors."

Davey laid the cookie he was about to eat back on the plate.

"There you are, you little rascal," Cudge Balog accused playfully as he climbed from the pickup. "Thought you would give me a little scare, running off like that, did you? Excuse me, ma'am, this is my son, and he ran off on me this morning. You see, he didn't want to do his chores around the campground. I have a rule that each child does his share. This rascal likes to play. I'm sorry if he gave you any trouble, ma'am."

Fear gave Davey the impetus to get to his feet. He moved over to the woman and hung onto her dress. "He's not my father; he's a mean, bad man, and he's telling you a lie. Please, call my aunt and uncle and tell them to come and get me. He's not my father."

"Now, why are you upsetting this nice lady with your little stories? Someday, this boy's going to write books. I just know it," Cudge said airily. "He does have some imagination."

"You killed Brenda! He killed Brenda. I heard her scream, and I ran away." Davey looked with imploring eyes at the old lady. She didn't believe him; he could tell. Desperately, he tried again. "Grandmothers are supposed to believe little kids. I'm telling you the truth. It's not nice to tell lies. My mother says it's wicked to tell lies."

"Well, I'm glad you remember something your mother said," Cudge replied as he advanced a step. "Come along now, Davey, and give this nice woman some peace and quiet."

"Now, just a minute," Elsie Parsons said sharply. "This little tyke don't look like no liar to me. What's it gonna hurt if I call the campground to see if his aunt and uncle are there? It's only going to take a few minutes."

"What's going to take a few minutes?" a nasally voice inquired. "What's going on here?"

"Sid, this here boy is Davey Taylor. This man claims to be the boy's father. The boy says he ain't. I found him by the barn this morning looking like this. He wants me to call the campgrounds for his aunt and uncle. I think we should call the police and let them straighten it all out."

"Now, Ma, you don't want to go sticking your nose in someone else's business and get yourself in trouble. If the man says he's the kid's father, he is. Who you gonna believe, the guy or the kid? Kids lie all the time. He probably done something wrong and lit out." No police.

First thing they'd be tramping all over and find his patch in the cornfield. Smoking pot was one thing, but growing it was something else. No police.

Cudge grinned and slapped the youth on the shoulder. "You're absolutely right. Davey wasn't in the mood to clean up the campsite this morning and just took off. He's a mighty big source of worry to his mother, I can tell you. Now, you get your tail in that truck before I take a switch to you. Apologize to these nice people for the trouble you caused them, and we'll be on our way. Ma'am, I do want to thank you for taking care of my boy here." He held out his hand to the old lady. She backed off a step and then another. What could she do? She had seen the look in Sid's eyes at the mention of police. Good Lord, what had he done this time? Your own came first, and then you worried about someone else's kids. He seemed like such a nice little boy, well mannered and polite. The father, if he was the father, left something to be desired.

"You mean you aren't going to help me?" Davey asked incredulously. This nice grandmother couldn't mean what she said.

"No, she ain't gonna help you," Sid told him. "You go on with your old man and stop bothering people and telling lies, or you're going to wake up some morning with a nose a mile long."

Davey backed off a step and found himself against the old woman's legs. "He's not my father! He's not! He kills people! He kicked my dog." He could feel the old lady tense as he tried to hold on to her. He was glad he didn't have a grandmother if this was what they were like. Just as Cudge reached for him, Davey dropped to his knees and raced around Cudge and down the steps of the back porch. Sid raced after him and caught him by the collar of the windbreaker. He literally lifted the little boy off the ground. "Where's your respect for your old man, kid? Now you get in that truck and act the way you're supposed to. I'll personally tan your hide if I hear another peep out of you."

Before Davey knew what was happening, he was thrown into the pick-up. Sid's leering face staring at him through the windshield made him want to cry. Only babies cried. He wiped at his eyes with his muddy sleeve, leaving streaks of dirt on his cheeks. He was never going to get away now. He was going to be dead. His eyes went to the CB unit on the dashboard and then to Cudge, who was backing off the front porch. Quickly Davey locked both doors. He had the CB speaker to his mouth before Cudge was down the steps. The emergency channel. "Breaker, do you read? This is Panda Bear. Breaker! Breaker!"

Cudge could feel the heat of his anger the minute he saw Davey with the CB. It was all over if the kid knew what he was doing. His rage intensified as he raced to the pick-up. Out of the corner of his eye, he saw Sid walk to the back of the house. The old woman had entered the house as soon as Cudge was off the rickety steps. He was alone with Davey.

Davey looked around wildly. "Help, help me. This is Panda Bear. Breaker, Breaker, do you read? This is Panda Bear!" He too had seen Sid walk to the back of the house. The grandmother wasn't on the porch anymore. It was just him and the man.

"Help!" he screamed. "This is Panda Bear. He's coming! Breaker, Breaker, he's coming. Somebody answer me. Do you read?" Frustration gripped him when he saw Cudge dig in his pocket for the keys. He had to get out before Cudge got in. He didn't know what to do. If he stayed in the truck, the man would kill him. Sid wouldn't help; the grandmother was afraid. Whatever he would do, he must do alone, like before. There was no one to help him. He had to think and, above all, he couldn't cry. If he cried, he wouldn't be able to see. Swallowing hard, Davey tossed the speaker onto the cracked leather of the driver's seat, and he pulled at the lock on the cab door. The moment Cudge opened the door to climb into the truck, Davey had his door open. He jumped down and took off at a dead run down the road and out to the front of the farmhouse, then back across the open field into the woods. He knew that if he had the farm at his back, the amusement park would be ahead of him. That meant Aunt Lorrie and Uncle Tom would be close by. He had to run straight, and he couldn't stop for anything. Run, run, run.

Tattered shoelaces slapped the wet ground as his short legs pumped away. Danger was behind him, he could feel it, smell it. On and on he ran, his arms flailing the air as he fought for breath. Once he fell sprawling in the muddy field. He picked himself up and raced on, not looking behind him to see if Cudge was gaining on him. He knew Cudge was close, but he couldn't run any faster. Aunt Lorrie would be waiting for him, arms outstretched to hug him, mud and all. She would laugh and tell him a story about making mudpies, and then he would laugh. He wanted to hear the story; he wanted her to hug him. He wanted to look at Uncle Tom and see him grin. If Cudge caught him, he would never see Uncle Tom and Aunt Lorrie. The red sneakers picked up speed. Curses sailed through the air, but he ignored them. Careening wildly from right to left, Davey headed into the welcome darkness of the forest. He didn't stop. Faster. Run. Aunt Lorrie. A sob caught in his throat.

A thicket of low underbrush caught his eye as he raced ahead. Without thinking, he dived low. Brambles and stickers scratched at his face as he burrowed deep into the undergrowth. Cudge was close. He could hear him now, feel the cold stream of danger getting closer and closer. He waited, his eyes squeezed shut. He didn't want to see. He had to be quiet and still.

At first he couldn't comprehend the sound. It was a roar, a deep, hard rumble that came from the belly; like when Uncle Tom threw back his head and had a good laugh. He wanted to lift his head to look around to see where the sound came from, if he could identify it. The man chasing him didn't make the sound. This was different. He tilted his head and listened as the rumbling was repeated. It was from the wild life preserve. He must be close to the animals and on the other side was safety and love and Duffy.

Davey's breathing eased when he realized the sounds weren't coming from the man. He wasn't afraid of the animals in their cages.

Davey cautiously inched his way out of his nest. Everything looked so big to him as he lay on his stomach; even the scrubby bushes looked immense. He waited a moment, hoping the animals would roar again so he could tell which direction he should go. He tried to remember; if only he hadn't been so afraid. When he heard the sound again, he positioned his foot carefully. He would go the way the toe of his sneaker pointed. For the thousandth time he wished Duffy was with him.

He crawled backward on his belly from his hiding place and again looked around. Satisfied that the man wasn't anywhere around, he stood up. A wave of dizziness overcame him and he swayed, feeling sick to his stomach. Both hands grappled for the bushes, and with all his willpower he steadied himself. He couldn't get sick now. He shook his head several times and felt better. He was hungry and he really didn't feel well. How much further did he have to go? If only his watch worked, he might feel better. He was going to have a lot of explaining to do when he got home. Mud on his sneakers, jacket, and watch and he had missed his shots!

The old woman was at the screen door looking out at him. Her son Sid watched too, waiting to see if Cudge would run after the boy or jump into the truck and try to overtake him before he ran across the open field into the woods.

"Whatcha lookin' at, old lady?" he bellowed. "If you two had minded your own business, I would've had him!"

The woman looked at him a moment longer and then retreated into the house, closing the door firmly. Sid was belligerent. "Ma don't think that's really your kid."

Cudge turned on the teenager. "Oh, yeah? And what do you think, punk? You should've kept out of it, and I would've had him."

Sid gathered his courage. He really didn't want any trouble with this man, but he felt compelled to stand his ground. "I don't think that's your kid, either. I never saw a kid run away from his own father that way, not even me when I was bad."

"That's because you never had me for your old man. What's on the other side of the woods?" he demanded, stepping closer to Sid.

"The amusement park. Only it's closed now."

"Where's the campground from here?"

"Due north . . ."

"I didn't ask you that, did I?" Cudge bellowed in rage, reaching out and grasping Sid's shirt front. "I asked you where."

Sid pointed across the field to the right, opposite to the direction the boy had taken. Cudge grinned, he knew Sid was afraid, and it gave him a sense of power. It was almost like being with Elva when she was scared.

"Stay out of my way, punk." He shoved Sid aside. "I eat punks like you for breakfast and spit them out before lunch. I knew a punk like you, once. He was Eye-talian. I took care of him, and I could do the same for you." He was reading a defiance in Sid's eyes he didn't like. "Don't think about calling anybody. A man has a right to his own kid, don't he? Besides, you may not like it if I tell anybody that you've got a patch of marijuana out behind the house."

Sid was amazed. "How did you know?"

"I always know, punk. You reek of it, and you just told me all I need to know. Even if you weren't growing the stuff, you'd be real unhappy when the cops came beating your door down to find your little stash."

Cudge jumped into the truck and fired the ignition. It wasn't going to be easy to find that kid, but he'd do it, just the way he'd traced him here to the farmhouse. He'd drive back to the park and leave the truck in the cover of trees, where it couldn't be spotted. Then he'd grab the kid and shut his mouth for good.

Bouncing down the road, Cudge took his time. He didn't need a broken axle now, not when the kid was within his reach. "It's either him or me. And it ain't gonna be me!"

The turns in the road took his full concentration. The weather was blowing up and storm clouds were gathering. For a fleeting moment he thought about Elva lying in his pop-up. He was glad she was dead, and he didn't have to listen to her squawking that he should leave the kid alone. Elva was never a survivor, not like him.

If he could just get his hands on that kid! His problems would be over. "It's always the little things that trip a guy up," he muttered aloud, "little boy, little dog. Elva with her little bit of brains. Candy Striper for a little piece of ass; Lenny, for a little bit of money." He groaned. How did this all happen? This wasn't the way things were supposed to work out! When he was a kid, he had believed he could overcome his poverty, the filth, the ignorance. And all he'd done was carry it all with him.

As he drove he kept his eyes trained to the edge of the woods, expecting at any moment a mud-smeared figure to emerge. Christ, that kid was smart, smarter than he'd ever been, that was for sure. In a lot of ways, that kid was like he'd been—Short, pale, blonde, and trusting. He'd trusted that bastard Norman to take care of old Peggy, yet he ended up having to do it himself. That was probably the first lesson he learned, when Norman went back to Grandma and got a dollar for the job his little brother had had to do.

Well, he wasn't a little boy anymore; he was grown up, a man. And when he got his hands on that little boy's neck, he was going to finish him for good.

The CB in the truck squawked. "Breaker, Breaker. Do you read me, Panda Bear? Come in, Panda Bear!"

Panda Bear. Where had he heard that before? Then he remembered. When he was cruising through in north Jersey, looking for a place to dump Lenny, Panda Bear had come on the CB channel and told them about the campground. So that's your name, eh, kid? Panda Bear.

"Breaker, Breaker, do you read? Come in, Panda Bear."

Cudge reached over and flicked the radio off. The sharp click was the way Panda Bear's neck was going to sound when he caught him.

13

SANDERS CHECKED IN with his chief and then set out in Feeley's motor-pool car. He couldn't explain why, but he knew Davey Taylor was close, close enough to touch if he could just reach out in the right direction.

Up and down the dirt roads the car roared, nearly going out of control. He braked, almost going through the windshield. No goddamn seat belts. He would register a complaint with Buzz as soon as this case was wrapped up. He sat pondering his next move. Instinctively he wanted to keep going to the park and wildlife preserve, the same route he had followed on foot last night. There was something out there, something he might have missed.

Well after one o'clock he returned to the camp office. It was time to clean up and get on with the day. He had to call Nancy; she would be back from marketing by now, but he wanted to shave and shower first. He always put forth his best effort for Nancy, even if she couldn't see him.

Sanders went to the camp showers, where he cleaned up quickly. Out-of-season campgrounds offered no hot water to make anyone want to linger on a brisk autumn day.

A loud knock startled him. "Come in," he shouted as he put away his shaving gear. "Yeah, what is it?" Sanders demanded of the reflection that met his in the mirror over the sink.

"Your man thought you would want to hear about this." It was Officer Delaney, and Sanders liked him on sight, from the top of his neat haircut to the tip of his polished shoes that were buffed to a high sheen.

"Feeley? I thought he was asleep. Something come in that sounds important?" Calling Nancy would have to wait. He liked the alert look in the young officer's eyes.

"Yes, sir. And he was asleep, but he sleeps like me, with an eye open. You have to do that when you're in law enforcement."

"Tell me about it," Sanders mumbled as they walked through the sodden leaves. "That was some storm we had last evening."

"Good thing it was over early. As it was, the power company was out all night working. We get storms like that around here this time of year. I hear there's another blowing up." His tone was easy but his respect for Sanders was evident. "The call is from a shut-in who monitors police calls, Citizen Band, short-wave, you name it. He said he didn't know if it was important or not, but he heard a child calling for help on the emergency channel a little while ago. I have to be honest with you; this turkey calls in on a regular basis. He sees UFOs once a week, hears calls for help, and once he said he heard a gang rape going on in back of an eighteen-wheeler."

"The kid have a handle, the one on the emergency channel?" Sanders waited, hardly daring to breathe, for Delaney's answer.

"Yes, sir. The handle was Panda Bear."

"Jesus Christ!" Sanders exploded as he broke into a run.

"Your man has the caller on hold," Delaney shouted. For a big man, Sanders moved fast as he raced ahead to the offices. Delaney looked after him, wondering if he could ever join the state police. That was the big-time. He'd wear a snappy uniform, a snap-brim hat and, of course, those polished sunglasses. If he stuck to his decision to live alone, he could save up and buy a yellow sportscar.

Delaney took his work seriously; he was willing to forego marriage so he could give devote his life to law enforcement. That was the supreme sacrifice. A talk with Sanders could be helpful. He hoped the caller had his marbles all in one bag this time around. Delaney hoped the child on the emergency channel was the Taylor kid, and that he was okay. Mrs. Ryan was a nice person, she deserved good news. There was a chance that he would be the one to tell Mrs. Ryan. He would get pleasure out of telling her and seeing her eyes light up. Childishly he crossed his fingers. He nodded briefly to Feeley as he took his position behind the desk. Sanders was just hanging up the phone. He waited, not sure if he liked the look on Sanders' face. It was Sanders' case, and Sanders didn't have to confide in Delaney. Delaney crossed his fingers again.

"Feeley, you stick around and work the phone. Find out if anyone else heard the call. Let's see if we can't pinpoint it a little more accurately." Sanders looked at the scrawled note in his hand. "The guy's name is Rob Benton, and I'll take him. He lives right here in Jackson. Delaney, find out how many turkey farms there are around here. This Rob is certain there were turkeys he heard in the background." Sanders grimaced. "He said he hates turkeys, actually what he said was he was afraid of them." He looked directly at Delaney, defying him to say the caller was a crackpot.

Delaney's gaze was unblinking. "You ever have a bunch of turkeys gang up on you? It's hairy, I know what he's talking about. And yes, there are three or four turkey farms around here. As a matter of fact, there's one right next to the amusement park. The end of the farm runs parallel with the wildlife preserve. The old lady who owns the farm has a son who's on every cop's list from here to Forked River."

"Check it out, Delaney. I'll see you in a little while." Damn, the call to Nancy would have to wait, Davey Taylor came first. He wished he had a lucky horseshoe or a rabbit's tail.

As he steered the high-powered car down the dirt road, he tried to calculate Davey's minus hours, but he gave up. While he waited for the light to change at the main road, he saw newspapers in a vending machine on the corner. Leaving the door open and the engine running, he picked up a paper: Davey's picture was on the front page. The traffic light changed and several horns beeped. He ran back to the car, tossing the paper on the seat beside him.

He could imagine Nancy's reaction to the picture. Nancy would say he was adorable. "I know you're on the loose, kid. You can find your way back, I know you can. I got a steak dinner going on your getting back okay. You just hang tight. I'm going to find you."

Ninety minutes later Stuart Sanders was back at the same light, waiting for it to change. Rob Benton's story was unshakable. The guy had heard only what he had repeated. He also said he had monitored the channel from that moment on, and there were no more calls. Sanders believed him.

Davey started off, looking over his shoulder every few minutes. He didn't feel well, but it was not as bad as it had been a few minutes ago.

He jammed his grubby hands in his jeans and trudged through the woods. His face lit up as he withdrew a handful of crumbs—from the grandmother's cookies. He ate up the crumbs and then licked the last bits from between his fingers. As he walked along he kept licking at his fingers, savoring the spicy ginger. The grandmother was right, she did make good cookies.

Something jingled in his pocket. The three quarters clicked companionably together. The flashlight was still in the zipper pocket on the sleeve of his windbreaker. He felt for it; it was still there. If he could just keep away from that Cudge, he would be okay. He cocked his head and listened. The woods were silent, except for the rustling of the leaves overhead. From time to time a squirrel raced through the treetops. Davey grinned. The squirrels were getting ready for winter. Just like he was getting ready for whatever was going to happen to him next. So far he had missed two lunches, one dinner, and one breakfast. He ticked the meals off on his fingers. Four! He would tell Digger he had missed four meals and was still alive. When you didn't eat, you turned into skin and bones and died. Digger knew what he was talking about. He said it almost happened to him on one of his trips to the hospital. They fed him with a tube and he was almost skin and bones. Davey's face puckered up as he tried to figure it all out. There must be two kinds of dead. The kind the man made happen and the kind Digger was talking about. He wondered what happened to the skin and bones. He would have to remember to ask Digger the next time he talked to him.

Davey walked slowly on through the woods for another half hour. His leg ached and he wished he had someone to talk to. It would feel so good to have Duffy scampering around his feet, even if he was too tired to play with the dog. Duffy would be able to smell Cudge if he got too close. Duffy would bark to warn him in time to find a hiding place. He would tell Digger how good he was at finding hiding places. Digger would appreciate his low-flying dives into the brambles. Poor Digger, he hoped the doctors fixed his legs right this time. Davey stopped, every sense alert. It was quiet. There were no squirrels, no rabbits running through the brush. He was still safe.

Then Davey noticed two things: a loud banging noise and the way the woods were thinning out. He strained to identify the banging sound. He had heard it before back home, or was it at Uncle Tom's house? He grinned, how could he have forgotten? He himself had helped make the sounds. Last year, Uncle Tom had let him bang the nails for the tree house he built in the backyard. Banging nails. Aunt Lorrie had hurt her thumb and then quit to go make lemonade. Uncle Tom said banging nails was men's work, and lemonade was women's work. They drank the whole pitcher. He must be close to people who would help him. He walked slowly to the very edge of the trees, careful to shield himself by not stepping into the bright sunshine. He dropped to his knees and then to his belly and crawled to the side. It looked like the muddy field by the grandmother's house, but different. He propped his elbows on the ground, letting his chin rest in the hollow of his cupped hands. What made this place different? The posts that were sticking out? The pebbles and stuff they used to make cement? The driveway. It was a parking lot, he thought jubilantly, a parking lot without cars. Now he knew where he was—the amusement park. If he were really smart, he might be able to find his way back to Uncle Tom without anyone's help. He didn't know directions. If he made a wrong turn, he could get lost again or it could find him. In his mind, he had begun to think of the danger Cudge presented as "it." There was something about *him* that was less than a man, something inhuman. Davey instinctively recognized the force of the man's brutality as bestial, closer to animal than human. When he'd seen the man and Brenda putting the dead body in the ground, he had run from danger. "It" had chased him then too. He remembered the sound of it tearing through the woods, pounding the ground. He had heard its heavy panting and he'd pictured a huge wild animal, one with evil red eyes, and horns that cut the earth. It was a huge, black bulk that hid the sun and cast a giant shadow, and it wanted to kill him.

A hard knot in his stomach seemed to squeeze out his breath, making him feel he was going to be sick. He was sweating, and he could smell his own fear. He'd smelled it before, in the hospital getting new blood. Then, he'd tried to think of something else and that's what he would do now. He wouldn't think about it.

He wanted to find the man who was banging nails. He had been successful by crawling on his belly; he would do it again. If he stood up he would be a target for . . . He would crawl on his belly. It was muddy, and a shard of broken glass winked at him from the left. He would have to be careful. When he reached the other side, where would he be? Shielding his eyes from the sun, he peered across the parking lot, seeing the tip of a roof, trees, bushes, and a very high fence, the kind that had little holes in it. Dad called it chain-link. Fences had gates, he knew, like back at home where the gate was always closed, so Duffy couldn't get out of the yard. Sometimes Dad locked the gate when they went on vacation. No cars in the parking lot meant the park was closed. But if it was closed, where was the man banging the nails? He had to find the gate and get inside to the man with the hammer.

Davey was fifty feet from the end of the parking lot when he heard it. His heart pounded in his chest when he lifted his head to look around. Cudge was at the far end of the parking lot, and he was starting to run. Davey got to his feet and ran to the fence. There was nothing —no gate, no hole in the fence. He turned left and ran.

Where was the gate? He should have found it by now. He must be at the back of the park; he had to find the gate. He was almost free now. He couldn't let it get him. He tripped and sprawled in the coarse gravel, and then he saw a small hole under the fence, but it wasn't big enough. Frantically, he dug at the wet earth. He could feel it, smell it coming closer. The hole was big enough for Duffy, but not for him. He dug faster, scooping the earth this way and that. He could feel it now—the hot breath of the animal chasing him. No more time, but he had to try. Lying flat, he put his head through the opening. Then he wiggled first one shoulder and then the other. He was stuck. Duffy always got on her belly, her paws straight in front of her. He did the same but it was too close. The smell was almost overpowering. He felt the points of the fence dig into his jacket and his back. He didn't care how badly it hurt; he was almost through. His rump was stuck. Again he wiggled, the small spikes of the fence digging into his jeans. He wasn't going to make it. He could hear a laugh.

"Got ya, ya little bastard. You ain't getting away this time." But he wasn't caught yet. Just because he was stuck didn't mean Cudge had him. Only his backside and legs were on parking-lot side of the fence. With all the strength in his body Davey strained forward. Just as Cudge Balog reached down to grab Davey's foot, the little boy strained again. Steel bits ripped down his left haunch and on down the back of his leg. He was through! Cudge only had his sneaker. Davey struggled to his feet and turned around. He was aghast at the rage-filled face staring at him through the fence. "What did you do to Brenda?" he cried. "You hurt her! I know you hurt her!" Davey backed away from the fence. "I'm gonna tell everyone you hurt her. You'll be punished."

A bellow of pure venom shot from Cudge: "I'll kill you! I'll get you yet! You ain't getting away from me this time, you stupid kid. This place is all closed up. You won't be able to get out, and there's no one in there to help you. I'll get you. I'll come over the top of this fence, and that's the end of you."

Davey stared at the fence top and then at Cudge. He could climb over it, and he would. Davey knew he had to run fast and find the man with the nails. Screaming for help, Davey took off. Why wasn't the man with the nails answering him? Where was he? Why couldn't he hear the banging now? Maybe the man had finished his work and gone home. The thought was so terrible, he shouted again and again.

Cudge dropped the red sneaker as though it were burning his fingers. He'd been close, so close he'd almost had him.

It was impossible to think over the roaring noise in his head, or was it the thunder. Panting with rage, blind with frustration, he was unable to think what his next move should be.

An eight-foot fence separated him from Panda Bear, and by the time he climbed it the kid would be long gone.

He twisted the sneaker in his hands, and it became the fragile neck of Panda Bear. Panda Bear—stupid name for a kid. Only the kid wasn't so stupid; Cudge would give him that.

Cudge had been smart when he was a kid, and he had been mean. It didn't seem strange that he, a grown man, was chasing a little boy, when he should have been planning his own escape. Something about the boy reminded Cudge of himself. That made Panda Bear his equal, as dangerous as he was, as cunning and ruthless.

Cudge hadn't been much older when he had to put old Peggy down. There wasn't a doubt in his mind that the boy would put him down if he could.

As Cudge ran along the perimeter of the fence, looking for a way in easier than climbing the fence, he thought about the little boy. Each step was closing the distance between them, and sooner or later he would come face to face again with his defiance. As the the distance between them closed he was approaching someone with the same potential for killing that he had. Cudge, the man, was chasing Cudge, the boy.

Stuart Sanders tapped his fingers on the steering wheel while he waited for the light to change. He'd been riding around for what seemed like hours, thinking, reviewing, but always on the look-out for Davey.

A car full of teenagers passed him just as the amber light flicked to green. Surprised, he checked his watch; it was two-thirty already, and the high school was letting out. That was when he noticed a billboard and an eye-stretching arrow pointing to Wild Adventure Park. Maybe he could spot the turkey farm on the way.

He allowed a van and a sports car to pass him before he inched into the moving traffic.

Within minutes the main gates to the park were in sight, but the appearance of a secondary road, probably for employees, caught his interest. After a circuitous route of several miles, the road ended in a gravel-topped parking area. The gates were chained shut.

Sanders turned off the engine and surveyed his surroundings, attempting to pinpoint his location. Last night he hadn't come this far through the woods. On the map the distance between the park and the campground hadn't seemed so close.

He knew he wouldn't have any difficulty in gaining admittance to the park; all he had to do was flash his credentials. He could even climb the fence, if he had a mind to.

Back at the car he retrieved the binoculars he'd borrowed from Feeley. Training the sights on the horizon, he scanned the treetops, seeing the tall girders of the ferris wheel. Rides, thrills, and adventure waiting till spring, when flocks of children would swarm over them laughing and shrieking. He wondered if Davey Taylor had ever ridden on a ferris wheel or carousel.

Lighting a cigarette, he turned to his left, and walked along the fence. He took a drag on the cigarette as he retraced his steps past the gate, along the perimeter of the parking lot. He would have missed it if he hadn't dropped the cigarette. He was grinding it out with the heel of his shoe, when he noticed the hole under the fence.

[249]

A mud-caked red sneaker was lying near a mound of earth. Sanders dropped to his heels. He hadn't realized he had been holding his breath until it exploded from his lungs, making him light-headed. Both hands held the bedraggled sneaker. The hole under the fence was just about big enough for the kid to belly through. It was freshly dug.

"Good boy. You're almost there. Just a little longer and I'll find you, Davey."

The pain that had been gnawing at his stomach quieted. Davey was free, loose, not in Balog's hands. At least not for the moment. He gripped the sneaker as though trying to squeeze information out of it. Looking at the little shoe, thinking about Davey, the chewing in his stomach began again. Davey wasn't the kind of kid who was careless with his things. He never would have left his sneaker behind, unless something prevented him from retrieving it. Or someone—Balog, a known killer—chasing a little boy who had seen too much to stay alive.

Davey Taylor was on the run. His path took him across a parklike area that was littered with outbuildings that looked like the quonset huts that came with his army and soldier set. All the buildings had wide doors like garages, and there were stacks and stacks of trash cans nestled inside one another. There was no safety to be found here, nowhere to hide. He ran forward blindly, not stopping for his bearings or taking notice of his surroundings.

Past the utility buildings, along the storehouses and equipment garages, he ran. His sneakerless foot hurt from the pebbles and irregularities in the walks. And it was cold and wet from the puddles left by last night's rain.

Ahead of him was the visitors' area of the amusement park. The rides were like abandoned erector sets, stark and alien against the vibrant golds and reds of the autumn leaves. To his right was a tall, semicircular amphitheater with an eye-filling blue dolphin poised in flight pictured on the stark white concrete. The brick path widened into an expanse of cement surrounding the desolate rides. Between two towers hung a huge pirate ship painted bright red and suspended over a now empty pool of water. Aunt Jemima, which he recognized from the pancake box in Sara's kitchen, was displayed on a low, octagonal building against which little white tables and chairs were stacked.

Glancing up at the sky when a dark rain cloud hid the sun, Davey saw the tall pylons which supported the guide wires for the Sky Ride. Many buildings dotted the area between the trees. The distance he had covered on his short, aching legs was vast to the little boy. Once, for an instant, he drew up short, staring at a candy-land structure that sported peppermint sticks for columns supporting a sugar-frosting roof and ice-cream-cone façade. He was reminded of how long it had been since he'd eaten, and how good a cupcake would taste right now. Chocolate browns, vanilla whites, shiny red balls that looked like cherries fascinated him. It was the stuff dreams were made of, the kind of house the Sugar Plum Fairy lived in, a palace of confectionery delights.

Then he remembered his predicament, and with great effort he forced his weary legs on. The knee that usually had the support of his brace was sore and throbbing. Mustering his courage yet again, he ran onward, heading for a small building where he hoped he could hide.

The building had two doors, and by stretching back, Davey could see pictures on the doors. He could tell by the triangle of the skirt that the ladies' room was on his right and the men's room to his left. He reached for the knob to the men's room and then hastily withdrew his hand. The man would look for him there. Without a second's hesitation he opened the door to the women's bathroom. Heavy hinges held the door, preventing it from closing immediately. He leaned against it pushing it closed; he felt almost safe. Unlike the bathroom door at home, there was no lock on the doorknob. If he got in, the man could get in. Frantically he looked around for a telephone.

Sinks, toilets with doors, and a garbage can—everything looked clean and forgotten, as though no one was coming back. There was nothing here, not even a sliver of soap on the sink. He decided not to wash his hands and dirty the sink, but he had to go to the bathroom. Six doors had silver coin slots, and were locked shut, but one door at the end stood open. He had only Mr. Sanders's three quarters; he didn't want to spend them going to the bathroom. He looked in the open door as he unzipped his jeans. Carefully, he held up the seat while he urinated. He liked watching the steady stream as it hit the water. As he zipped up his pants a door slammed. Arrow swift, he had the door closed and locked. He hopped on the seat and braced his hands against the door. He sucked in his breath.

He could tell the man was mad by the way the door banged against the tiled wall. Davey waited while footsteps sounded. Looking down from his perch he could see heavy, yellow boots that were caked with mud appear and disappear as the man stalked back and forth. With a cursing growl, he moved toward the door. Davey waited for the sound of the closing door, but he didn't hear it. Did that mean the man didn't pull it closed, or was he still there waiting to catch him? He wished he could hear the sound of the workman banging the nails. He was tired, and his arms ached. He would wait a little while longer; he couldn't get caught now—not when he was so close to Aunt Lorrie and Uncle Tom. He had to be more careful than ever, and when he thought he couldn't stand another second of waiting, he heard the snick of the closing door. There were no footsteps, no muttered curses. He was gone.

Davey gingerly pulled back one arm and then the other. He dropped to the floor. He turned around as he massaged his arms. He reached out a quivering arm to flush the toilet, but he quickly withdrew it. The frothy bubbles would have to stay—toilets made a lot of noise in places like this. This place wasn't safe; he had to leave. If the man came back, he would see the open door, and then he would know Davey had tricked him. The thought pleased Davey; he had really tricked him. When he left the bathroom he would go to his left, because if he went right he would end up back at the hole in the fence. He had to keep going in the opposite direction; he had to stay behind the man.

As Davey started out, he listened for sounds of hammering; his entire body was alert to any movement within his line of vision. He shivered, it was getting cold. Now that he wasn't hiding and as worried as he was back in the bathroom he realized he still didn't feel good. If only he could lie down and take a nap, but he couldn't. It was important to keep going, to find Aunt Lorrie and Uncle Tom. If he lay down and fell asleep, the man would find him.

Davey slowed as he trudged around the park, bewildered by the shadows the giant rides created. He knew he had to be quick at the first sound that fell on his ears. He wished he could read, so he would know what all the signs meant; he certainly was doing a lot of wishing. When he got back home, he would try to remember how many wishes he had made since he got lost. He would make Digger laugh with all of his wishes.

Where was the man with the hammer? Why hadn't he seen anyone to ask for help. Then he saw Cudge, just ahead. He was stalking the area in front of a place that sold hamburgers, according to the picture on the sign. The little round tables and chairs were supposed to be polka dotted mushrooms and toadstools, and Cudge was bending low, peering under the benches. Davey crouched low. Sometimes, like now, he was glad he was small. When you were little, there wasn't so much of you to see. He maneuvered his way behind a big red trashcan, and he watched Cudge work his way around the perimeter of the restaurant. His heart hammered in his chest and he felt as though the ocean was slapping at his ears.

Davey was getting colder and he was so tired. He stifled a yawn, never taking his eyes from Cudge's slouched form. He drew back suddenly. Cudge was standing upright now and looking around, deciding which way to go. Davey risked a quick look. He was walking to a low, white building with a red and black sign that said, Maintenance, Authorized Personnel Only. Davey watched as he opened the door and looked inside, but he didn't go in. He risked another peek. Cudge seemed to debate a moment and then opened the door again. Just as quickly, he closed it. That was good. As soon as Cudge moved on, Davey would run into the building, now that he knew the door wasn't locked. Maybe someone in there could help him—the man with the hammer. If it wasn't safe for Cudge to go in, it would be safe for Davey. He hadn't done anything wrong; he needed someone to help him.

Crossing his fingers that the man with the hammer was inside the building, Davey was still bothered why Cudge hadn't gone inside. He might come back later and go inside; it was so hard to to think what he would do.

Cudge veered off to the left toward the fun house. Davey knew it was the fun house with all the characters painted on the outside. Someday he could go in and see if it was really funny. Cudge walked up the steps and disappeared from view. Davey went up to the low building. He yanked open the door and pushed it closed. The second before it was about to lock into place, he grabbed the handle to try to muffle the sound. Fearfully he looked around.

Lockers lined one wall, and open-stall showers lined the other. To the left, in a room littered with cartons and boxes, he saw a desk with a pushbutton telephone. Davey's heart sank—he didn't know how to work the buttons, but he had to try. Maybe the phone didn't work if the office was closed. Frantically, he jabbed at the numbered buttons, only to have the phone squeal in his ear. He tried again and again with the same results. He sat down in disgust on the swivel chair; he must be dumb. Digger would laugh at him. He had been trying to call his own house, when he should have been trying to call the operator or the police. O for operator.

Again he pressed the button. He waited patiently, his legs swinging from his perch on the swivel chair. "I need you to help me," he said to the nasal voice that answered. "There's a man after me, and he kills people, and he's chasing me. My Aunt Lorrie is worried about me; I know she is. Can you tell her where I am so she can come and get me?"

"Does your mother know you're playing with the phone, little boy?"

"My mother is in Florida with my father," Davey replied.

"So you sneaked away from your aunt, and you're playing with the phone. Little boy, that's a serious thing you're doing. Somebody right now might need my services and you're taking up my time with your pranks. Hang up the phone and don't play any more tricks on me or the other operators."

"It's not a prank. This man is trying to catch me, and I'm hiding in an office. He kills people. He killed Brenda and he kicked Duffy. Please help, and call my Aunt Lorrie for me."

The impersonal voice on the other end of the phone relented. "What's your aunt's telephone number? Where are you calling from?" Maybe the kid was telling the truth. Weirdos called in every day. She was overdue, as a matter of fact, for some kook to bust her.

"She's at the campground at Wild Adventure. I'm in a white building that has a red and black sign. It's next to the pony ride and the railroad track."

The voice froze. "Is it now? Listen, you little twerp, I happen to know that Wild Adventure is closed for the winter. Now you stop all of this foolishness and hang up that phone. This minute, do you hear me? If you call again, I'll report you to my supervisor. That's big trouble for your folks, kid. Now hang up and go play with your friends."

Davey obeyed the authoritative tone in the operator's voice and replaced the phone. He looked at the black telephone. He hated it. Why wasn't there someone who could help him? If only he had a CB; telephones, he decided, were for grown-ups. His face puckered in thought. Stuart Sanders had given him three quarters and told him he might want to make a phone call. That must be why he was having so much trouble—he had to pay for the call. He was up and off the chair. Outside in the locker room he noticed the phone on the wall; it was the kind you put money in. As he anxiously felt in his pocket for the quarter, he vowed that this time he wouldn't make a mistake. He would call Mr. Sanders's house and talk to him. The agent had told him to call any time, no matter if it were day or night. Davey wondered if he would need the operator again.

For almost a full minute Davey stared at the phone. He couldn't reach it. Maybe if he dragged the bench over and stood on it. He had to try. Pulling and tugging, he managed to drag the heavy wooden bench directly underneath the phone. Standing on his tiptoes, he managed to jiggle the receiver loose. He listened to the dial tone and waited. Nothing happened. Maybe he had to put the money in first, but he couldn't reach the slot. Panic was making him clumsy, and the slippery phone fell from his grasp. There had to be a way to use the phone; there just had to be. Mr. Sanders would help him. Mr. Sanders would know what to do.

A cardboard carton with the words Supreme Motor Oil on the side was stacked against the wall. Davey jumped down and tried to push one of the cartons over to the bench. It wouldn't budge, and he wanted to bawl with frustration. Only babies cried, he admonished himself. Maybe there was something inside that he could lift out. Quickly, he pulled the tape off the box. Two-inch staples closed the opening. Fingers wedged between the staples, he pulled and tugged until he managed to rip the box open. Davey lifted out two tall cans of motor oil and then carefully stepped on both cans. It might make him big enough. It was worth a try.

"Digger, you aren't going to believe this either," he muttered to himself as he climbed back on the bench. He positioned the cans close together. Holding onto the dangling receiver and the short, taut wire, he steadied himself. Now he could reach the coin slot. With shaking hands he dropped the money in and waited for the dial tone. Mr. Sanders' card was in his hip pocket. He punched out the numbers and waited.

"What number are you calling please?"

"I'm calling 549–8877. I want to talk to Mr. Sanders, please."

"Hang up and dial your party again. What area code are you dialing?"

"What's an area code?" Davey asked.

"You're calling from area code 201. Do you wish the same area or further south? The area code is 609 for the Trenton area."

"Is that the area code for Montclair, New Jersey?"

"No, you're calling from the correct area code. Hang up and dial again."

"Thank you, lady." He liked the smile in her voice, just like Aunt Lorrie's voice. "Do I have to use another quarter? I put one in when I called you. I only have three quarters."

"When you hang up, the money will be refunded."

"Okay," Davey said replacing the receiver. The ping of the quarter in the slot made him smile. This time Davey paid careful attention to the pushbuttons, not wanting to make a mistake. He had been here for a long time, and he was beginning to wonder if the man might come back.

"Deposit forty-five cents please," a voice said in his ear.

"How much is that? I just have two quarters," Davey said.

"Forty-five cents. Your nickel will be refunded," the voice said quietly.

"You have to wait a minute till I get it out of my pocket." Davey deposited the two quarters and waited. The phone on the other end rang. Davey counted the rings: four, five, six. "Hello, this is Michael Sanders speaking."

Davey listened to the almost grown-up voice. "This is David Taylor, and I'd like to speak to Mr. Sanders, please."

"My dad isn't here. I'll call my mother. Just a minute."

"What do you mean your dad isn't there?" Davey shouted into the phone. "Mr. Sanders said I could call him any time during the day or night. I have to talk to him and I don't have any more quarters."

"Gee, that's tough. Hold on, I'll get my mom."

While Davey waited for Mrs. Sanders to come on the phone, he heard shouting voices outside the building. The man was looking for him! Not now when Mrs. Sanders was going to come on the phone! He listened to the ensuing argument.

"The park is closed, mister. How did you get in here?" a gruff voice demanded.

"I climbed the fence, that's how!" Cudge snarled. "My kid got in here by digging under the fence out by the parking lot. I had to climb over, because the hole he dug wasn't big enough for me. Are you sure you ain't seen him? He's about this high, has blonde hair? I gotta find him before his mother takes a fit!"

Davey quelled his initial instinct to run outside to the man Cudge was talking to and ask for help. He remembered the grandmother and how she had refused him.

"Mister," the other man's voice continued, "I haven't seen any kids around here. I've been working all day over by the roller coaster, dismantling the cars and getting them ready for next spring. There's no kid around here. You'd better be on your way before I call the police."

There was a sudden change in the man's voice, as though something had suddenly choked off his words. "Now look, mister. If you want, I'll go around and ask the shut-down crew if they've seen anything." He spoke faster, higher pitched, as though he were scared. Davey knew— the man was afraid of Cudge too.

"I want to find my kid. I'm not leaving till I do!"

"I know, I know. I've got kids of my own. Come on with me, we'll go around and ask the other guys. We'll be punching out for the day pretty soon. Maybe somebody's seen him."

Panic stricken, Davey dropped the phone and jumped down from his perch atop the oil cans. He had to get away. If the man was afraid of Cudge, too, he'd just hand him over the way the grandmother had done.

He looked around; there was no door! Maybe at the other end of the locker room. Saliva dribbled down his chin; he was too frightened to swallow. Into the small storage area behind the locker room he ran. A large red sign that said Exit was over the wide doors, wider than the one he'd come in through. Hand trucks loaded with cartons lined both sides of the corridor. Silently, he inched open the door and peered out.

The sun was gone now and the sky looked dark. A strong breeze that smelled of rain was sending fallen leaves and paper spiraling upward. He could hear voices outside. His heart pounding, he inched the door back into place. Without thought or direction, he ran. Faster and faster. Up the incline past the miniature golf course, around the bend to the haunted house and down the rise to the old-fashioned carousel. Sobbing, gasping for breath, he ran blindly, not caring where he went as long as he was putting distance between Cudge and himself.

Would Cudge go into the building? Would he see the cans on the bench? The phone, he'd see the phone. He'll catch me!

Faster, always faster, he staggered, pushing himself onward, he had to keep running away. He had to get away and be safe. Safe so Aunt Lorrie and Uncle Tom could find him.

14

SANDERS WENT to the police station behind city hall, where he found a distracted Chief Allen. The ensuing confrontation added further fuel to the fire in Sanders's digestive tract.

"What's this bullshit you're giving me, that you don't have any available men? You have a fifteen-man force here, or is that just for the taxpayers' benefit?"

"We do. I have fifteen men. Two out with the flu, one on vacation, one who has a death in the family. That leaves me eleven, count 'em, eleven." Allen glowered at Sanders.

"Call in for help if you need it," Sanders suggested.

"Don't need it, this is our baby, and we'll handle it. Eleven men and two murders."

Sanders thought of the prostitute they had found beaten. "When did she die?"

"Who?"

"Who else, the hooker your boys are so fond of." He restrained his rising temper. Discipline, he told himself. Discipline.

"No, Candy is holding her own. We're not stupid here, Sanders. We found traces of rotting apples on the floor and bedcovers in Candy's cottage. All her shoes were clean, so we knew it had to be tracked in by whoever beat her up. Turns out we were right. A few of these dirt roads leading out from the orchards are littered with dropped apples that bounce off the trucks."

"Another little tidbit that didn't appear in the police report. Just like the mothballs," Sanders went on, to Allen's surprise. "So, what did you find?"

"A camper. The same one that Balog was pulling, according to the plates. And a woman. Beaten the same way Candy was. Only it's too late for this one."

Sanders clenched his teeth. "Balog—the same man is responsible for beating of two women and the death of one, and for the murder of the man whose body you dug up in the campground. He's involved with the Taylor boy. Where Davey is you'll find Balog. Now, are you going to move, or do I move you myself?"

"Forget it, Sanders. This doesn't involve you. What you do about the kid is fine with me, but stay out of my business. We'll handle it." Allen reached for his hat with the polished gold braid.

"Where are you going now?"

"Out to the camper. The body hasn't been removed yet, and I want to see for myself. Another thing, there's a storm brewing, due to hit here in the next hour or so. A good rain will obliterate any leads, so we've got to work fast."

"I'm coming with you," Sanders said. "I'll follow in my own car."

Bouncing down the road behind Chief Allen, Sanders hit a pothole that he thought would swallow the front end of the car. Less than a mile from the main highway was the parked camper. Allen's men were already crawling all over it. "He doesn't need a rain storm to 'obliterate his leads.'" Sanders swore under his breath. "His men are doing it for him."

Hopping out of the car, he moved toward the camper, elbowing through the uniformed men. The camper was rocking on its moorings from the men's shifting weight. The interior was dark and filthy, littered with cartons and discarded cupcake wrappers and empty soft drink cups. The clear vinyl windows were in place, keeping the air within stale and close.

Sanders noticed an odor he couldn't immediately identify. Whatever it was, it was hours old, and smoking had weakened his sense of smell. He turned to one of the other men. "What's that smell?"

"Smell? Oh, yeah, it must be the mothballs. We found a few of them rolling around in here."

"No, it's something else. Ammonia?"

The young policeman shrugged his shoulders. "Urine maybe. Now that you mention it, it sort of reminds me of my kid brother's bedroom when he used to wet the bed."

That was it—dry urine. He'd changed enough diapers to know that smell. Poor Davey, trapped in the camper, no bathroom . . . Sanders could imagine the little boy's discomfort.

"There she is, Mr. Sanders." Chief Allen drew his attention to a form beneath the blanket he was lifting. "Not a pretty sight, is it?"

"Seen worse," Sanders told him, meaning it.

The girl perhaps was little more than sixteen or seventeen—perhaps because she was small and scrawny. The coroner would soon find out her age. One side of her face was battered, and an arm was twisted into an unnatural angle. From the way she was curled on the floor she might have been trying to defend herself from being kicked. Sanders's eyes followed the line of her body, coming again and again to the girl's hand, relaxed now and open. Her nails were bitten down to the quick.

The man who had done this was an animal, worse, a killer. And every instinct told him that Davey was marked as his next victim. Sanders left the camper and went back to the campground to call in for additional men.

When Mac Feeley saw Sanders stride into the camp office, he knew better than to utter a word. Sanders only looked like that when he was at the end of his rope. Sanders grabbed the phone and punched out the section chief's number.

"Buzz, there are some new developments here, and I need help." Quickly, he reviewed the situation.

"Can do, Stu, but they won't get there till around 5 P.M. It's the best I can do. Take it easy. We'll get him before it gets dark. If he is in the park and he's there under his own power, we're okay. Sounds like your theory was right. I want to meet that kid when this is all over."

"You and a lot of other people. Talk to you later."

Sanders turned to Feeley. "A second body turned up. Have Delaney . . . forget it, he's being recalled. Where is he?"

"He left just before you arrived. The body you're talking about was found on the other side of the highway in a pop-up that was jacked up and minus a tire. According to Delaney, there was no positive identification, but it seems likely that she was traveling with Balog. I don't

[261]

understand where this guy is, or what happened to his pickup. Beats the hell out of me why we haven't come up with something on that rig. From the description I've heard, it should be easy to spot."

"I need someone to stay here at the phone." Sanders chewed his lip. "Hey, wait a minute, we're forgetting the Ryans! Go get them, Feeley, and bring them here. They can take the phones. You camp out in Allen's office, in case something comes in and he's not generous in passing it on. I'll go to the park myself. It's the best we can do till five, when Buzz's troops arrive. Doesn't this remind you of the time we were in Birmingham and only had three men, working around the clock for four days?"

Feeley's eyes were dreamy. "There was this waitress that made the best damn goulash I ever ate. She had other talents, too, but the goulash was her specialty. I'll call and see if I can get the park opened. If it comes down to Allen as the only one who has the authority, I suggest you storm the gates. Let Buzz take the heat."

Sanders looked at the phone; he had a few minutes to call Nancy now, while Feeley was calling the Ryans. Talking to Nancy would give him the lift he needed. He dialed and waited. Busy. He waited another few seconds and dialed again. Still busy, damn it. She was probably talking to her mother. He liked the old lady, but she sure could talk, for hours.

Lorrie Ryan was breathless when she burst through the door. Sanders noticed that her hand was still in her sweater pocket holding fast to the cold pack and the vial of antigen. The minus hours were gaining on them. He looked down at Duffy, nibbling at his shoelaces.

Quickly, he briefed the Ryans, ending with the sneaker. Lorrie Ryan sat down on the swivel chair and let the tears flow, as she held the muddy sneaker. Still, she didn't relinquish the hold she had on the cold pack. "Is it a positive or a negative sign?" she asked quietly.

"I think it's safe to say it's positive. I'm taking the dog with me." He avoided looking at Tom Ryan. "I could use some help, if you think Mrs. Ryan wouldn't mind being left behind at the phone."

"I'm fine, Mr. Sanders. I know what to do. Tom has a battery-operated CB with him. I'll keep one set here in case . . . when you find Davey. It's got a strong frequency and can pick up in a range of four miles."

Sanders looked at his watch. He'd try one more call to Nancy; this time he got through. Lorrie and Tom walked to the side of the office to allow the agent some privacy. How different he looked, Lorrie thought, gentle and so relaxed; yet just seconds before he had been a professional in a grim hunt for a killer.

"I miss you, too. We're about ready to wind down here, I should be home by tomorrow. Anything good in the mail? Did Elizabeth Taylor call?" he joked.

The voice on the other end of the phone was warm and soft. "A bill from the water company. A seed catalog, an invitation to join the Y.M.C.A. Your brother called twice to invite us to a dinner party two weeks from Saturday. Your broker called this morning and, yes, we had a funny call just a little while ago. I didn't take it myself, Michael did. When I got to the phone there wasn't anyone on the line."

"What kind of call?" Sanders asked.

"Michael said it was a kid. Said his name was David Taylor, and he wanted to talk to you. He only had one quarter left or something. Michael said he sounded a little confused, and then he said you told him he could call any time of the day or night. Is something wrong, Stu? How old is David Taylor?" she asked anxiously.

"Davey Taylor is five years old. He's a hemophiliac and he's in a hell of a lot of trouble. If he calls again, Nancy, try to find out where he is. Call me here at this number. Where's Michael now?"

"He went to soccer practice. Stu, he told me everything there was to tell. You know how conscientious he is. Is there anything I can do? Five, did you say?" she asked.

"Nancy, when I tell you about this kid . . ." something caught in his throat. "That quarter he said he had. I gave him three of them and told him to call me if he ever needed me. I said to call any time, and you would know where to get in touch with me."

"Stu, where are you?"

"At the campground near Wild Adventure."

"Then he doesn't have any more quarters to call! Oh, Stu. Will you be able to find him?"

"I'm sure as hell gonna try. I have to go now, Nancy."

"I love you, Stu, hurry home. Bring the little boy with you, if you can."

"There's nothing I would like better. Take care of yourself. I have big plans for you when I see you."

"Promises, promises." Sanders could hear the smile in her voice when she replaced the receiver in the cradle. He couldn't dwell on Nancy now.

Sanders motioned for the Ryans to join him. "Okay, we know he's alive and able to make a phone call." He explained about the three quarters. "What we do know for sure is this Balog doesn't have him in his clutches. Mr. Ryan, you coming?"

"Damn right I'm coming, and call me Tom," and they set off.

He was tired of running. What if he just let the man get him? How much did it hurt to die? But being dead meant going into a hole in the ground and not seeing anybody any more. He wanted to play with Duffy and hug Aunt Lorrie and fool around with Uncle Tom. It would be nice to see Dad again, and Mom too.

Davey Taylor leaned back against the rough bark of a tree in a sheltered little grove which overlooked the entrance to a giant flume ride. He wasn't safe here, he knew; he'd have to run again, but if only his legs could rest a little while, if only his knee didn't hurt.

He was too tired to move. He wanted to cry and fall asleep. Thinking about Aunt Lorrie and Uncle Tom wasn't helping him forget he was hungry. Spaghetti would taste good now. He would suck the long strands through his teeth and not care if little drops of the sauce splattered all over his cheeks and shirt. Mom was always showing him how to roll it on the fork. His mouth started to water when a sound behind him made him whirl around. What little color there was in his face paled. It was a fat gray squirrel searching near the trash cans. He couldn't go any farther; he just couldn't. His legs weren't working very well, and he had to take a nap. When he woke up he might feel better. He should have his orange pills with a glass of water and then take a nap. He felt better after he took the pills. He shivered—it was getting colder. His eyelids were drooping, and he didn't like the feeling. It made him vulnerable out here in the open, where the man could see him and catch him.

Painfully, he struggled to his feet, cautiously looking around. Everything looked okay, but the sky was getting black and he wondered if it was suppertime. How hungry he was. Peanut butter and jelly would be good too. He liked to lick the dribbling jelly off his chin with his tongue. "Very poor manners, David," his mother always said. He knew he shouldn't be thinking about food because it made him hungrier. He crouched over and rubbed his knees, noticing his shoeless foot. He shrugged. A fellow had to do the best he could. He had to find some-place to hide before he fell asleep, but everything was locked up or out in the open. If he curled up on the bench on the carousel, the man could see him easily. A good hiding place should be enclosed. The sky was getting blacker by the second. A streak of lightning tore across the sky, making Davey's heart pound in his chest. A rumble of thunder echoed around him, frightening him still more.

It was bedtime dark when he decided to crawl beneath the carousel's platform. He dropped to his belly and crawled beneath the circular structure. There was more room than he thought. Torrents of rain beat against the colorful carousel, and the heavy thunder and lightning made a Fourth of July display.

Davey Taylor burrowed into a ball, as though he were back in his cradle. Embraced by the darkness, he was shielded from the warring elements overhead.

The storm was threatening when Sanders and Ryan entered the parking lot area just outside the gates of Wild Adventure. Duffy sat between them, her nose keen for Davey's scent.

Leaving the car, Tom matched Sanders's athletic stride. They glanced at the ominous gathering of thunderheads, each dreading the rain that must delay their search for Davey.

"We don't have time to wait for someone to open the gates, Tom, so the best thing we can do is climb the fence. I'll give you a hand up and you go over first. Find a garbage can and toss it over the fence, and I'll follow you."

"Okay," Tom said as he placed his foot into Sanders's cupped hands. He grasped the fine links of fencing, feeling them cut into his fingers. He was going to feel this tomorrow, he thought, as he dropped to the ground. The first roll of thunder sounded. He tried to ignore it—to acknowledge it was to accept that Davey might be in the storm, unsheltered and afraid. He vowed that somebody would pay for this, by God, or his name wasn't Thomas Joseph Ryan. He ran back to the fence with two cans. Sanders was a big man and might need some help when he got to the top of the cyclone fence.

"I think you better come back to this side for now. Take my word for it, this is one place neither one of us needs to be in with a storm like this. That lightning is vicious. We can sit in the car until it blows over, *if* it blows over. That storm last night was a piece of work—lasted six hours."

"Yeah, I know," Tom said gasping for breath as he dropped to the ground. A look of dismay crossed his handsome face. "I forgot to toss over the can. I'm sorry, Sanders."

"C'mon, here she comes," Sanders bellowed as he made a dive for the car door. A river of rain beat against the car as the battle raged overhead. "I guess you know we're stuck here. I can't see to drive in this. Jesus, I haven't seen rain like this since I left the farm thirty years ago, and then I only saw it once. Later on they called it a hurricane."

"You know something, Sanders, I'd give everything I own, everything I hope to own for the rest of my life, if I could see Davey safe and sound." Sanders nodded, knowing it wasn't a half statement, but a full statement of truth.

A brilliant flash of light ricocheted in front of the windshield. Sanders swallowed hard when he saw the look on Tom's face. "Sanders, tell me that Duffy is in the back seat."

He would deserve the whiplash he got from the quick swivel he did. "Oh, Jesus. She went under the hole in the fence where I found the sneaker. She must have picked up Davey's scent. When you got the trash cans, did you see her?"

"No, but I wasn't looking. I thought she stayed with you."

"If I were a crying man, I would bawl my head off about now," Sanders said.

"There must be something we can do. We can't just sit here. That dog weighs all of six pounds, and the wind will kill her if she doesn't find a safe spot to take shelter. She's not an outside dog, Sanders. She's a house dog; she won't even go outside when it rains. The cook spreads a paper by the back door for her. She's frightened to death of thunder and lightning."

Sanders hated negatives of any kind. "I know. I also know that you are a reasonably intelligent man. No one with reasonable intelligence would think about opening this car door. Believe me when I tell you I know what you're going through. Let me tell you what happened last night and the little dance she did at Balog's campsite."

When Sanders voice droned to a stop, Tom's head fell back against the headrest. "We wait, is that it?"

"That's half the life of a cop."

It was shortly after eight when Sanders and Tom sloshed their way into the camp offices. It was still raining but showed signs of slowing. There was no sense in staying in the parking lot waiting for a break in the weather.

How like Tom to look like he'd been betrayed: by the storm, by the police, and by circumstances in general, Lorrie thought. "Guys, I have good news, excellent news as a matter of fact." Maybe it was the lilt in her voice or the sparkle in her eyes that made Tom grin. Her comments were directed to the wet, shaggy man standing next to her husband. "Your man Feeley called in around four-fifteen, just a few minutes after you left. He said," she could barely contain her excitement, "that an elderly lady stopped by the police station shortly after he arrived, carrying a copy of the Asbury Park Press. She said Davey was at her farmhouse around noon. And, yes, she's the one with the turkey farm." Without waiting for comments from either man, she rushed on. "She's simply beside herself, poor soul. I gave her time to get home and then I called her. She assured me that when she saw Davey last he was all right. Oh, Tom, he's all right! The little guy was and is making it on his own. I can't believe it. Where's Duffy?" she asked suddenly.

"She got away from us. Hopefully, she's with Davey wherever Davey is," Tom said happily.

Lorrie's hand clutched at the cold pack. "Mr. Feeley says all the roads are flooded, especially the causeway. Your men might be delayed even longer, Mr. Sanders. They closed off the parkway an hour ago. He's been most kind, calling in every twenty minutes or so to keep me alerted. Lordy, I almost forgot. The woman from the farm said after she went into the house, she watched Davey in the truck and saw him talking into the CB. That clinches your shut-in call." She deflated suddenly. "It's such a vicious storm out there. Where could he have sought shelter? Mr. Feeley says trees, giant trees are down all over the place. God, Tom, what if he was in the woods?"

"Mrs. Ryan, so far he's been fine. There's no reason to think he isn't all right now." He hated to ask but he had to, for his own peace of mind. "Did the farm woman say if he was showing any ill effects from missing his shots?"

"I asked her, and she said the boy seemed right as rain to her. She did say he was hungry, and that he looked like he had been wallowing in the pig trough." She laughed, but sobered at once. "We won't know his blood condition until he takes his next shot, and even then it might be a while. Look, we're on borrowed time and have been since noon yesterday. I don't want to go over it again. No matter what we say or do, our little Panda Bear is critical."

"I know that kid is in the park. Logically, everything points to his being there. He may be disoriented. Instead of trying for the main roads, he ran off to a place he recognized, and that's the park. He's trying to find the two of you; he knows the campground is near the park. Davey is trying to find his way home." There was that lump in his throat again. "And you know what? He's going to make it."

"What about that maniac that's on the loose, the one with the truck? How long do you think Davey can elude him? The kid's got to be tired and hungry. We can't hide our heads. What happened to him during the storm?"

"Tom, I don't have any answers. I'm like you right now, just feelings and instincts. Balog is a murderer. I know you don't like that word, but so far Davey has given him a run for his money. He's running in panic. Those CB nuts can smell a cop a mile away. They chatter away all day and night. If Balog had his set on, he's got the drift of the way things are going. Guys like him don't have the smarts to run. Instead, he's going to concentrate all his efforts to find Davey. He's not thinking clearly. Davey is, thinking clearly that is. As bad as Balog wants him, Davey wants you two twice as bad."

"If Balog does find Davey, will he kill him?" Lorrie asked in a shaking voice.

Sanders' answer was succinct. "Yes."

"I'm glad you didn't lie to us," Tom said rubbing at the stubble on his chin. "If you'd given me some cockamamey dissertation, I would have decked you on the spot."

"I know that too," Sanders said striving for a grin. It didn't come off.

"Are we going back out?" Tom demanded.

"I don't know about you, but I am, as soon as I can locate some kind of protection. Maybe we can find some boots and slickers." Sanders's gaze shifted to Lorrie. "It's still coming down in torrents. When our back-up men arrive, you'll have to direct them to the park. You can do that, can't you, Mrs. Ryan?"

"I can. I'll stay here by the phone. We left the RV open. You know, just in case," her voice dwindled off.

"Good thinking on your part, Mrs. Ryan. You two do whatever catching up you have to do, and I'll see about getting us some kind of raingear. My wife didn't call, did she?"

"No. I'm sorry, Mr. Sanders, she didn't."

"Any word from Sara?" Tom asked carefully. He kept his eyes on the rain that trickled across the storeroom floor. It was a cold rain, and it was still coming down hard. Sanders would be drenched by the time he got to the main office.

Lorrie shook her head. "Perhaps we should call her and give her the latest developments. What do you think?"

"I hate to tell you what I think. Why don't we leave well enough alone for now. Like Sanders said, we're going on hunches, instinct, and gut feelings. Those words are not something Sara can deal with."

"The power went off twice while you guys were out," Lorrie said.

"What did you do, just sit here in the dark?" Tom asked.

"I didn't have much choice. It wasn't so bad. I noticed a box of candles over there in the corner, but I don't have any matches. I'm sure there must be some of those some place, but . . ."

"Let me get them for you. The storm isn't over yet." Quickly, Tom ripped open a carton and fished out a fat yellow candle. "You keep this lighter here with you." He dug in his pocket, coming up with a length of fishing line, a sinker, and two hooks. The other pocket yielded a half pack of Lifesavers, thirty-seven cents, two marbles, and half a shoe lace that he had intended to tie on to his sneaker. There was no lighter.

"Try your shirt pocket. Weren't you smoking a cigar this afternoon?" Lorrie giggled. He was the oldest kid she knew.

"Right again," Tom said in his best W. C. Field voice.

"Here we go. Best I could do," Sanders said, handing Tom a pair of knee-high green boots and a bright orange hooded slicker. "I think I should warn you that if we fall into a pond or lake we'll both go straight to the bottom. This stuff must weigh eighteen pounds."

Tom bent to kiss Lorrie on the cheek. She wrinkled her nose. He smelled like mildew and detergent. "Find him, Tom. Please find him," she whispered. Tom nodded as he stretched his neck so the stiff rubber didn't chafe at his neck.

Sanders drove carefully as the heavy rain beat down on the car. There was no way he was going back to the camp offices. He knew Davey Taylor was out there somewhere and he was going to find him—Tonight. Not tomorrow, tonight.

"We aren't going over that fence again, are we?" Tom asked.

"Hell, no. We're going to do it the way they do in the movies. We're going to shoot off the locks and walk through. Just out of curiosity, how would we make it over the fence in these Dior originals?"

"That's what I like about you, Sanders. Your keen wit and utter logic." Tom laughed. He felt more confident, sure that they would find Davey soon. He wouldn't think about the cold rain and the dark.

"I feel like an asshole," Sanders said harshly.

Tom frowned. "Why?"

"Because, according to the book, we should be back at the offices waiting for the others. Having you along with me is a no-no, right off the bat. We never involve civilians in anything that might be dangerous. I'm not going by the book, is what I'm saying."

"Fuck the damn book," Tom said briskly.

"That's what I say," Sanders said glumly.

"The only way I can get hurt is if the collar on this slicker slices off my neck."

"Okay, we're here. If Balog is in the park, he's going to hear the shot. I don't think the rain is going to muffle it all that much. If it was still thundering, I'd feel better."

Tom stood back while Sanders aimed the gun, holding the lantern high.

Tom blinked the rain from his lashes. Two shots and the lock was still intact. "Just how the hell rusty are you?" he demanded.

"Would you believe astigmatism? No, huh? How about the damn rain keeps beating down the sight? This should do it." He was right. Tom heard the clink of the double-lock against the chain link. "Okay, we go!" Tom swung the wide gate backward. He waited till Sanders approached him and handed over one of the camp lanterns.

"Okay, Ryan, you know that this park is laid out like a horseshoe. We're standing in the middle. You take the right tip and I'll go left. Shoot this flare if you need me, or if you find Davey. I'll fire off a shot if I find him. There was only one flare, and I can't let you have a gun. As it is, I'm going to go on report for this."

"I'll deny it," Tom said forcefully.

"Deny what?"

"That you let me come with you. I'll say I followed you on my own. I would have, you know."

Sanders nodded. "Good luck, Ryan."

"Same to you."

Sanders held the camp lantern in front of him as he waded through six-inch puddles. When was this rain going to let up? He shouted for Davey and Duffy till he was hoarse. The wind and rain carried his cries back to him. It was eerie and he didn't like it. Over and over he shouted, though he knew it was useless. Maybe, just maybe, the dog would hear his shouts and bark. And if she did, would he be able to hear the dog?

"I know you're out there, kid. Give me a break, Davey. Do something; anything would be a help at this point. Help me to help you." Sanders pleaded. The rain was running down his arm, and he switched the lantern from one hand to the other to shake the water off his sleeve. It was cold; the boy must be freezing.

The agent stopped to check on his surroundings. To his immediate left was the roller-coaster and the children's rides. To his right was the Lehigh Valley Express train for little kids. Beyond the tracks a small section of the park was devoted to the children's rides. Neither area offered shelter of any kind. He saw only steel skeletons of framework. Should he go to the left or the right?

An hour later he was almost ready to give up. The rain slackened suddenly and then stopped completely. In the dim, yellow light that the lantern cast along the miniature train tracks, he could at least see where he was going. Just ahead were the carousel and the end of the children's area. He was at the end of his tip of the horseshoe. The space between the two tips was the Wild Life Preserve. The boy wouldn't go there, not if he knew about the wild animals. Surely, the Ryans must have explained the layout of the park when they camped. He tried to remember what kind of fencing—more cyclone. His own children had wondered if it was strong enough to keep the animals in and the people out. Something teased at him, some tidbit of information that his son had commented on last spring. One of the animals—Delilah, the lioness—had given birth to six cubs. That was it. Her mate, Sampson, was extremely protective of Delilah and the cubs. God help anyone who strayed into the prowling lions' den.

Everywhere Sanders looked there were fallen branches and uprooted trees; anything that hadn't been nailed down was scattered before the wind. Swinging the lantern wide to get a better view, he was startled to see a monstrous oak lying across the Lehigh Valley Railroad. It would take a team of ten men to move it. He didn't like the destruction he saw. "Where are you, Davey?" Maybe he was crazy after all; maybe Davey had never come back to the park.

15

UPON AWAKENING, his movements were slow, sluggish. At first he was unaware of the softness nestled close to his chest. When he came fully awake, he wanted to howl in glee at the comforting feel of his little dog. "Duffy!" Davey cried, "how did you find me? Where did you come from? Where's Uncle Tom and Aunt Lorrie? Good girl, you can lick my face all you want," he laughed happily. "I'm so glad to see you!"

He put his arms around his dog and hugged her. "We have to be quiet, Duff. You can't bark and don't run away this time. You're all wet," he said suddenly, "and so am I."

Almost instantly, he remembered where he was and why he was hiding under the carousel. "It's good you're here, Duff. I don't know my way back to camp and you can show me the way. Boy, is everybody going to be surprised when we come back together. Just you and me, Duff. We're a team, just like Mom and Dad. I only wish Mr. Sanders was with you; he'd know what to do, only he's in Florida with Mom and Dad." It was good talking to the dog; Davey felt reassured that soon he would be safe at home.

Duffy's companionship relieved some of his hunger and weariness. As long as he had Duffy, he could talk to her and it would make the hike back to camp easier.

Brows puckered, he decided it must be very late. At least newstime on television. Duffy always was let out when the news came on. Then the doors were locked and everyone went to bed. "We'll just wake them up, right, Duff?" He smiled to himself in the darkness, visualizing the expression on Lorrie's face when she answered the door of the RV. Duffy whined low in her throat and then continued with her furious licking.

"You're tickling me, Duff! We've got to get out of here. Do you think you can find your way in the dark?" He grunted the question from the effort of inching out from under the carousel. He shivered in his wet clothes. Now that he was on the pavement and exposed to the wind, he could feel the cold all the way down to his shoeless foot.

"Be quiet, Duff, real quiet. I don't know where that man is now. I know he's here, somewhere, waiting to catch me. I'm going to be right behind you. If he catches us this time, he's going to kill us both. I don't want to be dead, and I don't want you to be dead. Don't bark," he cautioned in a firm voice. Duffy trotted off with Davey following close behind.

The rain was coming down steadily and Davey was cold. Duffy must be cold too.

The pavement dipped. Duffy growled, menacing as her small body hit the pond of water. Davey's sneakered foot slipped, and he found himself in water up to his chin. He thrashed about wildly as he struggled to reach higher ground. The rain continued to beat down in steady driving torrents. Carefully, not allowing himself to panic, he tread water till he was at the edge of the little pond. He groped for a handhold, only to find himself slipping back into the brackish water. Duffy stood sentinel, barking loudly to offer encouragement. Her stubby tail swished furiously against her haunches as she crept up to the edge and then backed off. "It's no use, Duff, I can't get out of here. There's nothing to hold on to, I need someone to pull me out. Quiet, Duff, stop barking and go get Uncle Tom. Go on, girl, go get Uncle Tom. I'm not going to drown. I know how to float on my back. Go on, girl. Go!" Purposely, with all his might, he forced his voice to be like his mother's when she spoke. "It's the best thing for me, Duff, go get Uncle Tom."

The terrier cocked her head to the side and whined, her little paws restless on the coping surrounding the pond.

"Go on, Duff! Get Uncle Tom!"

The urgency in her master's voice alarmed Duffy, releasing in her a torrent of high-pitched barks of protest.

"Be quiet, Duff!" Davey ordered, the iron command bringing instant obedience.

Davey rolled over in the water. It was better lying on his back than playing dead-man's float. He never wanted to play that game again. Not ever again now that he knew what dead was. Blackness engulfed him, closing off the world, leaving only the sensation that he was floating inside a watery womb. He could feel fear closing in, choking off his air. He stiffened, feeling himself going under, the weight of his clothing dragging him down. Tentatively, he dropped his legs, the one shoeless little foot stabbing out a speculative toe to touch bottom. There it was, not very far down, but it felt slick and slimy, unpleasant. Yet, by standing on tiptoe, his head and face were out of the water.

He wished for a light so he could see how big the pond was and find a way out. He had a light! Mr. Sanders had given him a flashlight before he left home. It had been in the zippered pocket of his sleeve, but was that before or after he turned the jacket inside out? He could feel the tears pricking at his eyelids. He could feel his neck stiffen at what he thought his mother would say at a time like this. "David, crying solves nothing. You must use your brain and think. Tears are a sign of immaturity. You must reserve your tears for important things, such as grieving and weddings." He wasn't exactly sure what grieving was, and he only had a vague idea about weddings. What he did know was that the position he was in did not call for tears, according to his mother. He swallowed hard. The flashlight was in the pocket of the arm on the same side as his foot with the shoe. Now that he knew where it was, he imagined he could feel it. He had to unzip his jacket and take it off, or he had to get his arm free of the clingy, nylon windbreaker. Experimentally, he shifted his arm, trying to take it out of the sleeve, working at the zipper and sleeve under water. He had to balance himself on his toes so he didn't go under. He yanked at the zipper and managed to get it down halfway, and then it stuck. His toes gave out, and he slipped beneath the water. Gagging and sputtering, he rose to the surface and flailed out with his arms. His teeth began to chatter and he had to control them, because the more noise his teeth made, the colder he felt. Flopping over on his back the way he'd been taught, he let the rain drizzle down on him. It reminded him of a waterfall he had seen in one of his picturebooks. He wasn't afraid of the rain or the water. He only had to think of a safe way to get out of the pond. Duffy was making low, growling noises that would rise to a high pitch. She was afraid for him, Davey knew, but he needed all his energy to think of himself.

He was concentrating on testing the bottom with his foot to find a shallow place to get a foothold, when he heard a muffled curse. The raindrops were pelting his body, and a dim circle of light played near him. The man! If he went under the water, he could only stay under until he counted to four. He would make noise coming to the top and then he would have to take deep breaths. And Duffy! He would get Duffy! He was caught. They both were.

When the light reached the edge of the little pond, Davey could make out the big man's work boots and wet trouser legs. He knew who was holding the lantern. It wasn't Uncle Tom and it wasn't Mr. Sanders.

"You're really a pain in the ass, kid. You made me tramp this goddamn place in the rain for hours. I thought you might have gotten away while I went back to the truck to get the lantern. Guess I was wrong. Get over here and I'll pull you out. Right, over to the edge. Move it!" he commanded.

Davey hesitated. To put himself into the hands of the man was unthinkable.

"Better do what I say, kid. I see that little bitch of yours; I'll hold her under the water and finish her off real fast. Move it!"

Bitch! Duffy? Was he talking about Duffy?

"You hear me, kid? Get your ass over here so's I can grab you. You want to see your dog drown?"

He did mean Duffy! Davey obeyed unwillingly. Maybe it was better to be out of the water. Maybe he could get away from him again or yell for his aunt and uncle. As long as he didn't hurt Duffy. Please don't let him hurt Duffy!

The little dog was snapping and snarling when Cudge reached down to lift Davey out of the pond. He hauled him out effortlessly.

"I thought I heard that mutt of yours barking. Even the rain couldn't muffle that sound. Dogs are one thing I know something about, kid."

Duffy was in a frenzy, remembering the scent of the man who was touching her master, his voice low and menacing. She kept her distance from his feet, having learned her lesson once. But she threatened with barks and snarls, snapping, attacking, and feinting.

"You better call her off, kid. Looks like she's forgot what I gave her once before. Dog ain't got no brains, and if she don't stop, I'll kick whatever brains she does have all over the pavement." It wasn't his words that made Davey cringe but the cruel laugh that followed.

"Duffy! Duffy, down girl. Down girl!" The dog sat back on her haunches, tilting her head curiously, deep sounds rolling in her throat.

"Pick her up!" the man ordered. "Pick her up and carry her! I got someone I want you to meet. As a matter of fact, he's dying to meet the both of you."

"My uncle is going to find me," Davey said, feeling his lower lip quiver. "He's going to come and get me and take me away from you. And Duffy, too!"

"Well, ain't your uncle gonna be surprised when he gets here and you're not. C'mon, walk! My friend is waiting."

Davey knew he didn't want to meet anyone this man knew. Still, he couldn't resist asking, "Who?" hoping it was going to be Brenda. Maybe he was wrong, and Brenda was okay, and the man hadn't hurt her.

"The sign says his name is Sampson. A real live lion, like in the jungle. The kind that eats kids like you and doesn't even burp. Now shut up and walk!"

Tom Ryan and Stu Sanders met in front of the Space Port where kids would come to plunk their quarters into electronic machines and play computer games like Space Invaders and Indy 500. To their left, in the darkness, they could read the marine blue and white sign that read "Remote Control Yacht Races."

"No luck, eh, Ryan?"

"Same as you, from the sound of it." Tom answered, disgust in his voice.

"He's here," Sanders said bitterly, "I know it! I couldn't be wrong; all my instincts feel it!"

"What now?"

"We go back to the car and call in to your wife at the office. Maybe she's heard something. And if those back-up men from the department arrived, I'll have them come down here. Also, I want my section chief to get in touch with somebody and have the goddamned lights in this place turned on. Even if Davey's not in the park, but somewhere nearby, the lights should attract him."

"Great idea, Sanders. But I'm pretty certain the storm will have knocked the power out. You wouldn't believe the size of the trees I've seen tonight pulled up by their roots."

Sanders' face fell. He hadn't thought about the power. "Yeah, well, it's worth a try. Anyway, it's time to call in. And didn't your wife pack a Thermos of coffee in the car for us? I sure could use some."

Shoulders hunched against the autumn cold and the drizzle of rain that sent icy rivulets down his spine, Tom turned toward the parking lot. He had been so sure that they'd find Davey. And now even the dog was gone.

"Did you make a search down the main concourse, Ryan? There are restaurants, the big ferris wheel at the far end, and the carousel. I never made it over there myself."

"I thought you covered that area. Let's take a look. I can wait a little longer for that coffee. How about you?"

"Right," Sanders said grimly, feeling that Davey wouldn't be found on the main concourse. But he'd never rest unless he covered it.

They walked side by side, searchlights fanning the ground, looking for a clue that might lead them to Davey. Both men kept their thoughts to themselves. It was beginning to look as though they were on the wrong track. Every lead was cold.

"Hey, watch out." Sanders cautioned. "What's that?" His light was on the pavement, seeking the shiny object that had reflected the beam back at him. "There!"

Tom's eyes followed the beam of light. The disc was silver, shining and new. A quarter. He picked it up, holding it for Sanders to see, his manner almost reverent.

"Hot damn!" Sanders slapped his thigh. "That's one of the quarters I gave Davey. I know it is. I won't let myself believe otherwise!"

Their steps were imperceptibly lighter, their gloom lifted. "Duffy!" Tom called, loud and clear, the rain drizzling into his mouth unnoticed. "Davey! Where are you son, it's me, Uncle Tom!"

Fingers reached out and yanked his collar, pulling him backward so violently that he almost lost his hold on Duffy. He hadn't realized how heavy the little dog could be until he had to carry her so long.

They had left the main amusement park behind, circling the far side of the parking lot until they came into the trees again. The rain had almost stopped now and the wind had died down. The air was cold and Davey was colder. His remaining sneaker squished with each step he took, and he could feel a blister growing on the bottom of his foot. The foot that had lost its shoe was tender and sore. But it was so cold that he almost couldn't feel it any more.

They came up to another cyclone fence, like the one at the parking lot, only this one was higher and had pointy wire strung along the top. Cudge's lantern cast its gloomy light, and Davey could hardly see the top of the fence, even when the man held the light high.

Duffy was nosing into his neck and sometimes he could feel her shiver. She was cold too. He wrapped his arms protectively around her, warming her, trying to keep her from Cudge's notice. Somehow the responsibility of his dog gave Davey the courage to go on. He wanted to cry; he was miserable, he decided, remembering it was the word Sara used to describe her headaches.

The man was looking for something. He kept lifting the lantern, scanning the fence, and then looking off into the distance.

Again, Cudge prodded him forward, leading him across the field toward the next stand of trees. The grass was short and the ground was soft and muddy. Several times, while climbing up an incline, Davey almost fell, his knee refusing to support him. But he thought of Duffy and what the man might do to her, and he kept pushing forward.

A little while later the man reached out and yanked on his shoulder. "This is as far as we go. We're gonna sit down over here. That's where you can see the lion and he can see you. Bet you thought lions slept at night. They don't, especially not this one. He's got his old lady in there and some cubs. He stays up all night to watch and protect them. He don't want no wise-ass kid coming near that fence to upset things. Know what I mean, kid?" Cudge snorted. "You ain't even gonna make a good bite for that big guy. He's gonna chew you to pieces in one gulp."

"Are you going to kill me?" Davey asked fearfully.

"Yeah. No. It's gonna be my fault, but that there lion is the one what's gonna do it. All day long all I thought about was wringing your neck, but then I came across Sampson here and decided he should do it for me. Besides, why should I hang for killing you? You ain't nothin' but a little brat. I don't like brats, you especially. I wouldn't be out here

[279]

if it wasn't for you. Elva would still be alive, and we'd be on our way to Florida. You spoiled everything. Wringing your neck is too good for you. When that lion sinks his teeth into you, you're gonna get what you deserve, and more."

Davey was frightened, sitting on the cold, wet ground, watching Cudge pace back and forth.

Duffy curled into his lap, making herself into a little ball to keep warm. When Cudge's pacing brought him too close to her master, she lifted her head, baring teeth and growling.

"Shut that bitch up," Cudge warned. Then he stopped to think a minute and lifted up the bottom of his army-colored jacket, pulling off his belt. He leaned down to reach for Duffy and was rewarded with the threat of snapping, tearing jaws.

"Here," he threw the belt at Davey. "Make a leash out of this and hook it to the fence there, now!"

Davey's fingers fumbled with the belt. He wasn't sure how to put it on Duffy. It was wide, thick leather, like his good Sunday shoes, and it wouldn't fit around Duffy's neck without choking her. The next best thing was to put it around her middle, sliding the strap through the buckle and sticking the strap end through one of the holes in the fence. The man seemed satisfied now that he could stay just beyond the reach of the belt, and Duffy couldn't get him.

"You know what kind of fence that is, kid? It's called horse fencing. I noticed this afternoon that they use it to section one kind of animal off from another. It keeps them from eating each other." The man seemed to find that funny, because he threw back his head and laughed. Davey didn't like the way he laughed. It wasn't a nice laugh like Uncle Tom's, or even Dad's.

In the dim halo of lantern light Davey could make out the curving stretch of horse fencing. The high wire was halfway down, a giant tree leaning across it. The tree seemed to be ripped out by its roots, falling against the wire, pushing it almost flat.

"Don't like it, hey, kid? Neither did I, when I come across it earlier today, when I was looking for you. Old Sampson there gave me a scare when he charged the wire. Only he don't seem too interested in getting over. Guess it's because his wife and kiddies are there."

Davey was silent, looking through the darkness to where Cudge was pointing. Duffy was restless, straining to the full length of the belt, trying to stay near her master.

"You don't believe me, I can tell. You're just as stupid as Elva ever was. Look, kid. I'm gonna show you something that's gonna make you wet your pants."

How did the man know he'd wet his pants? It was so long ago, when he was locked in the camper. Davey saw the man pick up the lantern and step closer to the fence. There was a fallen branch lying on the ground, and the man picked it up. Immediately, Davey's eyes flew to Duffy.

"Worried about your little doggy? I'll tell you when it's time to worry. Look! Look over here!"

Davey did as he was told, watching as Cudge ran the end of the branch against the fence, making a harsh grating noise that seemed to break the still night air.

Immediately, like a yellow streak, something came bounding forward, charging. The very earth seemed to shake! His belly felt the way it did when the big bass drum came marching behind the parade. Boom! Boom! Sampson's roar was the loudest noise Davey had ever heard. Even at the zoo he hadn't thought the lions sounded like this. Like all the thunder put together in one big sound that made your ears pop and the bone in your back melt like ice cream on a hot day.

Duffy yelped with fright, rolling over onto her back in instinctive submission. Again and again she tried to crawl away from the fence, held back by the short length of leather that held her.

Davey's eyes nearly popped. He clapped his hands over his ears, squeezing his eyes shut, wanting it to go away. Before he had been scared, but now he was terrified. Again Sampson roared, a rumbling beginning in his deep maned chest and exploding through his fanged, cavernous mouth. Yellow eyes reflected the light of the lantern, watching, daring, defying.

"How do you like him, kid? Pretty big, huh?" He laughed again, the sound smothered by another of Sampson's warnings. "Let me tell you how I'm gonna kill you. Want to hear? Course you do." Cudge was talking fast, he was scared of Sampson too. But he seemed excited too.

Cudge rushed on, his words slurred, almost unintelligible to Davey. "I'm gonna toss you right over that fence. And that old lion only has to lift his leg and *bam!*" he smacked one fist into the other hand, "you've had it! Just like that! Only I'm gonna rile him up a little first. Sorta whet his appetite, if you know what I mean. Then he'll be in fine form when you hit the ground."

"My uncle will get you, he's looking for me. Me and Duffy!" The instant Davey uttered the words he was sorry. Cudge lashed out with the back of his hand and cuffed him on the side of the head. Dizzily, he shook his head to try to clear it. He should have kept quiet. Tears brimmed in his eyes. No one had ever hit him before. No one. Ever. He didn't like it one bit. He was helpless and scared.

"If that uncle of yours does show, kid, I'll throw him over to the lion right after you. Then that damn dog. What do you think of that?" Cudge bellowed. When he saw the dread on the little boy's face, he smirked. "Didn't I tell you I knew a lot about dogs? Well, I do. And I know how to kill them. I'm a real expert!"

All the wind seemed to go out of Cudge, and he wanted to sit down some place dry—and warm. He was exhausted, physically and mentally. Thoughts of Elva kept popping into his head, and he would push them away. It couldn't be that he missed her, that stupid, scrawny broad. Why had he ever gotten mixed up with her anyway?

Davey focused on the fence, watching the lion pace back and forth, his feline eyes reflecting the light from the lantern and adding a light of their own. Duffy was quiet, stretched out as far as the belt would allow.

The man sat down opposite him, leaning back against a tree. A match flared as he lit his cigarette, and Davey saw Sampson walking away from the fence. "He's going back to his family," Davey thought. "Just like I wish I could go back to mine."

"Did I tell you I used to have a dog?" Cudge repeated himself. "Well, she wasn't exactly mine. She belonged to my grandmother."

Davey glanced at Cudge and then back toward the fence again.

"What's the matter? Don't believe me, do you? It's true. I wasn't any different from you when I was a kid. Matter of fact, I was just like you. Trouble, always trouble. Least, that's what my mother used to say. She'd say, 'Edmund Balog, I don't know what's come over you; you used to be such a good little boy. What made you change?'

"I used to pretend I didn't know what she was talking about. Nagging at me all the time. Only I did know, and I knew when I changed too. I wasn't any older than you when I found out what lives inside me. Only I never told anybody. Couldn't. And when I look at you, kid, I know the same devil that lives inside me is inside you too. All I gotta do is look at you. Think about what you did to mess me up with the law, with Elva, with everybody, and I know it's there inside you too."

His voice droned on. Davey was only half listening. The man wasn't his biggest fear right now. It was there, behind the fence, tearing jaws and thunder voice. Sampson.

"There were times when I didn't know why I'd ever been born. I ain't never had a friend. You know that, kid? Never, except for Elva. And she wasn't a friend as it turned out. *You* made her turn against me! She was all right till *you* came along. So maybe I did think she was stupid. Maybe I did think about getting rid of her, but I never would've done it. Never! But then you had to mess everything up."

Davey lifted his head and looked directly at Cudge.

"Don't get me wrong. Maybe you couldn't help yourself. I never could when I was a kid. This thing inside my head would always mess me up. What's yours like?" Cudge lowered his voice, whispering conspiratorially. "Mine is like a bull, black and tough, with hooves that seem to cut into my brain, and long, sharp horns that fill my head inside till I can't even think! And heavy, real heavy. Pounding around in there till I think I can't stand it. And then it takes over. Making me do things I'd never, ever do on my own. It was what made me kill Lenny. And Elva too. And the other night I beat up this girl, for no reason, except maybe she was breathing. It ain't my fault," he said.

Davey listened as the man talked about a dog he had when he was little. He'd been "good" then, he said. Davey couldn't imagine anything good about someone who could hurt Brenda or kick a dog like Duffy. If you killed someone, you weren't good, you couldn't be.

Cudge's voice droned on and on, having a strangely soothing effect on the little boy whose eyes never left the fence. By reaching out with his fingers, he could touch the fur on Duffy's neck, and it was reassuring.

Out of the corner of his eye, he noticed movement by the fence. Duffy lifted her head, staring straight ahead. The lantern light and the man's voice must have disturbed the lion again.

No, it was too small for Sampson. It was one of the babies. Just a cub, bigger than Duffy, but a baby nevertheless. He knew he had to sit still and watch and pretend to listen to the man.

Davey felt sorry for the little cub as it sat lopsided on its haunches looking out at him. He wanted to get out. It must be terrible to live with a fence around you all the time. Cudge's voice was almost hypnotic. Beyond the circle of light the boy could discern a larger form, or was it two shapes? The mother and father lion, he decided. A smile touched his lips. More cubs were nursing from the mother. The thought delighted him; the mother must be sleeping, and the father was watching, so nothing happened to his family.

Lion families were different from his mother and father. If Aunt Lorrie and Uncle Tom had children, Uncle Tom would be like Sampson—watching, protective. His family was different. Mom was the one who watched and took care of them. She was the one who said what was good to eat and where it was nice to play and work and how things should be done. Dad was almost like one of the children, except he went to work and earned money. But Sara worked too, accomplishing her work with fewer problems than Andrew.

Mom likes things perfect, Davey thought, whether it's the dinner or the house. I have to be perfect too, but I'm not. Maybe if I didn't need to get a shot every day or have to wear a brace sometimes, I *could* be perfect.

The loud, belly-rumbling roar startled him. Cudge was still talking, unaware of the lion's threats. The cub was still near the fence and he wanted to go over to the cub and bend down and whisper, "I can't take you out. You'll have to get out by yourself. There's a way. Use your brain, and be smart, and find it by yourself. Just like me."

His thoughts made his stomach tighten. Sampson was near the fence, standing over his cub, anxious and uneasy at the human intruders. Davey held his breath against the expected roar. Instead Sampson picked his baby up by the scruff of the neck and arrogantly marched back to the lioness, dropping his bundle.

That's what fathers are supposed to do, Davey thought, comparing Sampson to Andrew. They're not supposed to let the mothers do all the important things. Daddies were supposed to make their babies feel safe. Mommies couldn't really make babies feel safe when the daddies were afraid all the time.

Cudge was in a world of his own as he rambled through his memories, telling Davey things he had never revealed before. And as he talked, the difference between the little boy and himself became less clear. He seemed to be a child again, Davey's age, talking about the night-walking monsters that haunted him, recognizing the monster that inhabited his body, compelling him to destroy and even to kill. In the dim, flickering lantern light, Cudge came to believe that Davey was the young Edmund Balog, capable of all things evil. The future of little Edmund Balog became the destiny of Davey Taylor. Every pain, every weakness, was inevitable, and there was only one way to stop it from ever happening again.

All the potential for evil was there—in that innocent-looking child. And this time Cudge was going to stop it before it was too late. The evil had already taken hold. The boy was as much to blame for Elva and Candy as he was. And now, because of the boy, he was going to have to kill again.

The roar, when it came, made Davey clap his hands over his ears. The movement made Cudge stop talking. "I thought I told you to sit there and not move. I ain't ready to dump you over that fence yet. The only reason that lion is bellowing like that is because he wants me to toss you over there. He probably ain't had anything to eat for a week. You're gonna be real sweet meat to him, kid."

Davey drew his knees up to his chest. He was so cold he couldn't feel anything any more. I didn't do anything to that lion, he told himself over and over. Again, he saw movement by the fence. A smile tugged at his lips. The little cub was back, sitting on its haunches. "You're too little yet to get out. When you get bigger you can dig a hole and crawl out by yourself," Davey whispered.

Lightning swift, Cudge was on his feet. He sprinted up the slippery tree trunk that straddled the fence, ignoring the soggy leaves and branches that stuck out in every direction. Mesmerized Davey watched the sure-footed Cudge as he broke off a branch and then proceeded to pound at the top of the wire fence. Davey watched in horror as sparks flew in every direction. He wouldn't hurt the little lion. Or would he? Bellows of rage ripped through the night as Cudge pounded again and again, the sound echoing in the night. The little lion sat quietly, oblivious to what was going on about him. Davey thought how much the cub must want out of the fenced-in area, to sit there while Cudge tormented his father. Duffy barked and showed her teeth in anger, straining at the belt, wanting to protect herself and Davey. Another rumble roared through the night. Cudge turned and almost lost his footing on the slippery tree trunk. "Don't even think about moving, kid."

Davey was stunned. Why hadn't he thought of running the minute Cudge started up the tree trunk? He could be off somewhere trying to hide from him. He was angry with himself, angry that the little lion was occupying his thoughts, and that the father lion was not taking his baby back to its mother. He could still run if he wanted to. Cudge was halfway up the big tree. He would have a small headstart if he got up now and ran, but the cub held him rooted to his spot beneath the tree. It wasn't afraid of the pounding noise, and it wasn't afraid of its father's authority. How bravely it was sitting there. All the cub wanted was to get by the fence.

Sampson backed off and then advanced. Without lowering his eyes, he used one monstrous paw to push the little cub to the side. His two front paws pushed the fence out against the fallen tree. A storm of sound erupted from the lion's cavernous mouth. Davey shuddered but was pleased to see that Cudge, afraid, quickly backed off down the tree trunk. The cub was safely back sitting on its haunches between the big lion's back paws. Davey sighed with relief.

"That was for starters," Cudge said, wiping his hands on his sodden jeans. "I wanted to show you that that lion means business, and so do I. You getting my messages, kid?" Davey nodded.

Cudge sat back against a tree trunk. To Davey his eyes looked like shiny marbles. He wondered why his cheeks kept twitching. He decided that Cudge was as cold as he was. He was still talking and that was good; he didn't seem so mean when he talked. He kept saying the same things over and over. Davey wished he knew why. He didn't want to think about Cudge or why he did anything, but he needed to think what he would do if Cudge dragged him up the tree trunk and tossed him into the lion's mouth. What would the little lion think if he saw his father chew Davey to pieces?

The lion pawed the ground as he prowled the close confines allowed him by the fallen tree.

An overwhelming urge to cry came over Davey. Not for himself, but for the little cub sitting by the fence. It wasn't fair; it just wasn't fair.

It wasn't going to be fair if his mother punished him for losing his sneaker either. He would explain to her what happened.

Cudge's voice was making him sleepy. He was repeating the same stories that Davey could barely comprehend, but Davey couldn't fall asleep now. He had to stay awake and plan how to get away. Maybe Cudge would fall asleep and wait for morning to push him over the fence. Davey looked at the camp lantern, hissing and sputtering from the rain. Maybe it was running out of kerosene. He had watched Uncle Tom pour kerosene into a lantern. Lanterns didn't hold very much, only enough for one night; you had to put more in the next day. He wondered if Cudge knew you had to add more every day. The lions were quiet. Cudge wasn't talking any more.

Davey's heart started to pound and his ears hurt with the silence that surrounded him. The heels of his feet dug into the loamy earth. "Come here," Cudge said hoarsely as he crooked his finger for Davey to get up and go to him. Davey dug his heels deeper into the soggy ground. "Making me come and get you ain't gonna help now."

Davey didn't waste a minute. He ran between the trees, away from danger, away from the man. He had the sensation that an animal was close behind him. The man had changed into a beast with horns again, just as he had told Davey a little while ago, when he was talking about the devil inside him. It crashed through the trees, grunting and panting —and then there was silence. Davey was running, down the hill, onto a level ground where the earth was muddier and softer, making it harder to run.

A sound pierced through him. Again. Duffy! He ran away and left Duffy!

"Hey, kid! Guess what I got that's yours!" A bellowing laugh and an angry yipping followed by Duffy's cry of pain.

There was nothing to think about. There was nothing else to do. He had to go back; he couldn't let it hurt his dog. Not Duffy!

Sampson roared, the sound splitting the night. Duffy! Davey ran as he had never run to save himself, with vigor renewed by his panic. Heedless of branches scratching his face and neck, stumbling across hidden roots and slippery leaves, gasping to climb the incline, he ran. He could see the light through the trees. He was getting closer. Save Duffy! Don't hurt Duffy!

At first he thought Cudge was gone, and Duffy with him. Sampson grumbled, mouth opening to precede his earth-shattering bellows.

"Up here, kid. I thought you'd come back. Look what I've got and won't have for long!"

Davey looked along the fallen tree straddling the fence. Cudge was laughing, lying on his belly with his arm hanging down. Duffy swung from the belt looped around her middle, just feet away from Sampson's reaching claws. The lion snarled in protest, jaws snapping, saliva stringing from its mouth.

Duffy struggled, short legs twitching, head arching backward. Davey's heart nearly burst with terror. "No! No!"

No thought for his own safety. Only for Duffy! His feet found a hold on the split tree trunk. It was slippery and wet, and he had to dig into the bark with his fingers to hold on. It was high, higher than he'd ever been before.

Duffy swung out again, lower this time. At the last second Cudge yanked on the belt, pulling her out of Sampson's reach.

Sampson stood on hind legs, clawing at the furry object swinging over his head. Growling, frothing, Sampson attacked again, falling short of his prey.

Davey climbed higher, faster, reaching out. Slipping on the central trunk that was too wide around for him to hold on, he fell into the lower branches, nearly going over the fence himself, right down into Sampson's mouth.

Cudge didn't seem to notice that Davey was just underneath him. Again, he swung Duffy out, the belt within inches of Davey's grasp. Again, that breathless moment before he hauled Duffy out of Sampson's reach.

"Hey, kid, come and see. Where are you! Don't you want to feed the lion?" he laughed again, a wicked, nasty sound. "Hey, kid, where are you? You better answer before your dog is this cat's breakfast!"

The dog swung outward again. Davey stretched out, feeling the limb bend under his weight. He held his breath. He had to be ready and strong; his hands had to be strong.

Duffy arched again, coming full circle. Squeezing his eyes shut, Davey reached out, feeling the fear-rigid body come into his grasp. One instant Duffy was swinging out over Sampson's head and the next she was in Davey's arms. He couldn't hold her. He was losing his balance. He must save her!

The decision was made. A quick eye judged distances. Grasping the end of the belt, Davey swung his pup outward, back toward the fence. It wasn't too high, he prayed. Only Sampson couldn't get out because the tree had curved the top half inward. At the last second, he released the belt, waiting for an endless moment to see that Duffy had cleared the fence and dropped to safety on the other side.

"Hey! What the . . ."

Cudge was reaching downward, through the branches, through the last of the autumn leaves, to get him. Davey ducked, avoiding the hand by a narrow margin.

Again, a rustling of branches as the hand groped for him. Cowering backward, Davey was afraid to move for fear he would fall into Sampson's mouth. The little cub, frightened by its father's rage, pressed against the fence. The lantern, on the ground where they had been sitting, sputtered and flared before going out. Then he realized that night was almost over. Each second was an eternity as Davey sat frozen in a paralysis of terror.

The arm was reaching for him again. Muttered curses sounded above him. He couldn't see Cudge, but he knew where he was by the arm searching through the branches.

The cub pushed against the fence again. Sampson roared, his yellow eyes staring at a point above Davey's head. The cub was pushing against the fence, wanting to get out. It was crying because it was afraid, but it would never get out unless it was smart and brave.

Strength flowed back into Davey's limbs. His brain started to send signals to his body. Wait, he told himself, wait. He wanted to be safe and free again. He would never be safe as long as Cudge could get him.

The arm pushed through the branches again. Courageously, Davey allowed the fingers to just brush against his jacket before he leaned as far out of Cudge's reach as he could and still hold onto the tree limb. He had to be smart. He had to wait.

He watched Sampson's eyes. Every time Cudge reached down between the branches from the tree trunk above, Sampson's eyes shifted to follow the movement as the leaves rustled. Again, Davey allowed the fingers to just graze against him.

[289]

He heard the shifting of weight, and Cudge's change of position was noted in the lion's yellow eyes. The arm came reaching out.

Safe. He wanted to be safe! There was no other way.

Davey gripped the limb with his knees, locking his ankles one to the other. Then he saw the arm; he felt it and heard Cudge's grunts above his head. He saw the shifting of Sampson's eyes, and swiftly, with all the strength he possessed, Davey seized the arm, and pulled.

The sudden action caught Cudge off his guard. He'd had to crawl so far out on the tree that he couldn't keep his balance. He felt himself falling through the branches, and he tried to grab hold of something to stop the momentum of his fall.

He was falling. Inches and then feet. The yawning jaws of fate waited for him. The ground bit into his back as he hit, knocking the wind out of his lungs. He felt the weight on his chest, heavy, hard, and frightening. He could smell its breath, hot and hungry.

Terror, in the face of death, brought its own kind of oblivion.

The sounds were terrible, both from the man and the lion. I won't look, he told himself, burying his face in his arms, waiting for endless gut-crushing moments for the man's screams to stop.

He had used his brain and he was safe. Safe as the little lion sitting at the bottom of the fence.

Safe.

Davey slid down the tree limb, feeling a sense of his own power. The minute his cold, numb feet touched the wet ground, his legs gave out on him.

Safe.

He needed to rest a minute. Just rest. A minute.

A soft sound near him. Duffy. He wanted to see her. See if she was all right. But it was still too dark—the flashlight.

A sigh escaped him as he forced his fingers to work. Off came the jacket and down came the pocket zipper. Plump fingers worked at the switch. Again. Again. He banged it against his knee. It was too wet. Again, he flicked the tiny button. This time he was rewarded with a feeble light. Quickly, before it went out, Davey shone it on Duffy.

His fingers felt all over her dark fur, feeling for bloody gashes and wounds. He touched her all over, the way he'd seen the vet do when they brought Duffy in for her shots. Only once did the pup yelp with pain, when Davey touched her middle while he was removing the leather belt.

"You're gonna be fine, girl. Your tummy's just sore. Let's see you walk, Duff. Can you walk?"

The optimistic tone of her master's voice revitalized Duffy. She could be her old self again if Davey could.

There were sounds coming from the other side of the fence that he didn't want to think about. But a high mewling sound caught his ear. The cub. His eyes scanned the bottom of the fence. The little lion stared back at him in the wan light. "It's okay now. You're almost big enough—like me. You belong with your mother. Go on now, go back there and get warm. Maybe some day I'll come and see you again," Davey whispered. The cub's eyes were unblinking. Clumsily, he placed his two paws against the fence. *"Almost* isn't good enough," Davey said in a firm, hard voice. Without another look or glance, Davey called Duffy to his side.

He was going home.

When Davey walked up the gravel road to the camp, the first thing he saw was the RV parked outside the offices. A little farther on he came to the storeroom entrance. The lantern hanging on the tree was all the beacon he needed. He wiped his muddy hand on his jeans before he opened the door.

He stood framed in the lantern's light. Lorrie Ryan lifted her head from the desk, and sleepily she rubbed at her eyes. "Oh, my God!"

"I'm hungry, Aunt Lorrie."

Lorrie swallowed hard. "My God, I bet you are. Come here. I want to touch you."

"I need my shot," Davey said rolling up his sleeve.

"I got it right here, Tiger," Lorrie said, taking her hand out of her pocket. Quickly, she swabbed off a clean spot and drove the needle home. "I hope this works, sport," she said clutching him to her. "Oh, God, I've been praying that you would get back all right. Everyone is out looking for you. I'm hugging you too tight, aren't I, Davey?"

"Uh-huh. Gee, you smell good. When will we know if I'm okay?"

Lorrie gently pushed him from her. "I don't know, Davey," she said honestly. "In time, is the best I can do for right now."

Davey grimaced. "Like *almost*, right?"

"Yeah," Lorrie smiled. "Like almost."

"I lost my sneakers, Aunt Lorrie."

"Who cares," Lorrie grinned.

"I ruined my new jacket."

"No big deal," she continued to grin.

"I wet my pants twice, maybe three times."

"I used to do that on a regular basis when I was a kid. Your mom used to call me 'Stinky Pants Lorrie.' God, am I glad to see you! Wait till your Uncle Tom sees you. How did you do it? Where have you been? Oh, God, we were so worried about you," she said drawing him to her again. "Mr. Sanders is out looking for you. The FBI is looking. We've all been so worried about you."

"Where's Mom and Dad?"

"Yeah, well, they're still in Florida. They're coming home though. You'll see them soon."

Davey's features closed. "Did you call Mom and Dad and tell them I was lost?"

"You bet, right away. They'll be here soon, really they will."

Davey nodded.

"Right now, we have something more important to do. I'm going to let you get in the RV and blow the horn. Three long, hard blasts and then three more. That means good news. Your Uncle Tom and Mr. Sanders will come back here if they hear that. I'll try to get them on the CB. Go to it, sport."

"I'm kind of tired, Aunt Lorrie. Would you do it for me. I want to sit down for a while."

Concern filled Lorrie's face. She recovered quickly. "You bet. You sit right down there and wait for me. I'll bring back a blanket and something to eat for you."

She was back in minutes. Davey was curled up in the swivel chair, sound asleep. Tenderly, she wrapped the fleecy yellow blanket around him. "Thank you, God," she said silently.

They sat like four mother hens outside the RV waiting for Davey to wake up.

Tom handed out beer to Feeley and Sanders and then opened a bottle for himself. Lorrie sipped a Coke, her eyes never leaving the RV door.

"When are you going to tell him about his mother?" Sanders asked in what he hoped was a neutral voice.

"Soon," Tom said just as neutrally.

Feeley sucked at the rim of his beer can. "Knowing what I know about that kid now, I think he can handle it."

"He's right, Ryan," Sanders said briskly. "We can't hang around here any longer. Our job is done, for all the good we were. I would like to take a look at him before I leave, if it's okay with you."

"Sure," Lorrie said, "go on in."

Sanders set his beer on the camp table and entered the RV. He tiptoed over to Davey's bunk. Davey lay with his eyes wide open, staring at the roof of the RV. Duffy, freshly bathed, snuggled against him. "How's it going, kid?" Sanders asked as he sat down on the edge of the bunk.

"Okay, Mr. Sanders. I did what you said. I remembered everything you told me. Your quarters and the card with your phone number."

"I know you did, Davey, and I'm proud of you. You can join my team any time. I've got to be going now. I just wanted to make sure you were all right."

Davey sat up on one elbow. "I'm all right, Mr. Sanders. I'll *always* be all right." His round eyes were serious, his voice confident, faintly reminiscent of his mother's voice. And then the sparkle was back and the lopsided grin. "Boy, Mr. Sanders, you should have seen me floating in that pond, and there was this little lion. Boy, did he ever want to get out of that fence! He's not ready to be by himself yet. Some day he will be. I guess everyone has an 'almost' time. Don't you think so?"

"You bet I do. Listen, I made a date with Duffy to buy her the biggest steak in town. I have a date with you too. I'll call your aunt and uncle and set up a time. I'd like it if you could meet my wife and kids."

"Gee, that sounds great. But you better call my mom and dad instead. Bye, Mr. Sanders. Thanks for looking for me, but you didn't have to. I got home all by myself."

"What's a guy to do?" Sanders grinned. "I figured as long as they were paying me, I might as well give it my best shot. Seems like yours was better than mine." He held out his hand. Davey held out his and they shook. Davey grinned. "Almost, Mr. Sanders, I'm almost grown up."

"You take it easy now. We'll get together soon."

There was that lump in his throat again; he should have had the beer. What the hell, he could drink it on the way.

Roman DeLuca was hurriedly escorted down the studio corridor by an assistant director. The jury had reached its verdict during the early morning hours, and now he was going to be interviewed on a television news program.

They had found the accused guilty, and that made DeLuca a winner in the public's eye. It would probably help to put him in the governor's seat. He trained himself to smile grimly, professing that justice was served—only it wasn't supposed to be this way. He had miscalculated the determination of one person, Sara Taylor. At least he had achieved his goal. The killer of Jason Forbes hadn't been linked to the syndicate, and he would see that it wouldn't be, ever. But it would have been easier if Sara Taylor had been more cooperative.

After the verdict was announced, the reporters had gathered outside the courtroom, waiting for him. The moment he had stepped from the elevator they converged, demanding answers to their questions. Yet their manner was respectful when they dealt with State's Attorney Roman DeLuca. They liked him, the press did, and they knew he was climbing the ladder to success. He even looked the part, with just the right shade of bronze to his skin, set off by his immaculate white shirts and custom-made suits.

Flashing his brilliant smile, he listened attentively to the first question. He sobered at once as he replied. "I'm shocked. There are simply no words at a time like this. My sympathy goes out to Mr. Taylor who made such a brave and admirable contribution to justice."

"Mr. DeLuca, do you know of any reason why Mrs. Taylor would ignore the warning shouts and cries to get off the runway? Did something happen the press isn't aware of?"

DeLuca put on what he called his "sincere, humble smile." "Haven't I always been open with the press?" Not waiting for a reply, he continued somberly. "I understand there was some personal problem at home concerning the Taylor's son. It would seem Mrs. Taylor was distraught. I knew this and told Federal Agent Jonas to take care of her. It's very unfortunate, and I'm truly sorry. Mrs. Taylor was a remarkable woman in many ways."

Another reporter asked: "What kind of personal problem, Mr. DeLuca?"

"Now, if I told you, it wouldn't be personal any longer, would it?"

"The Taylors have a hemophiliac child, don't they?" a chunky man in a sweat-stained blue shirt shouted to be heard over the chattering throng of reporters.

"Yes, they do. If that's all, gentlemen, I have a hard day ahead of me and I'm expected at WKBA's television studio."

"Mr. DeLuca, do you still have 'no comment' on your plans to run for governor?"

DeLuca grinned; he was on solid ground now. "I think, ladies and gentlemen, that . . ."

Agent Michael Jonas listened to the suave, controlled voice. The bastard. He hadn't lied; he hadn't fabricated a thing. Up front all the way with the media. What right did the attorney have to use him like that? Saying he, Jonas, had overplayed his hand and used a thug's tactics. When DeLuca had said "take care of her," how could he know the prosecutor meant to keep her out of the courtroom. Christ! Even Sara Taylor had *misunderstood!*

16

DAVEY'S MIND wandered as he sat quietly in the small chapel. He didn't understand the meaning of the words, and he didn't like the way the minister looked at the people. He wished he could be outside with Duffy, running through the leaves or talking to Digger on the CB. But most of all he didn't like the words "Memorial Service."

He fidgeted.

Lorrie watched Davey out of the corner of her eye. He didn't understand; he was too little. He should be outside in the wind running with Duffy. Instantly, she was contrite. What an awful thought. He should be here! After all, the service was for his mother.

How sad, she thought, as she let her gaze circle the small chapel. Aside from her and Tom, and Davey, of course, the only others present were Stuart Sanders and his wife. A slim, freckled, clear-eyed woman, who was obviously very much in love with her husband. Private memorial services were very lonely, but Andrew had wanted it that way. It was Tom who said the words aloud, and Lorrie had to agree that he was probably right no matter how much it hurt—they had no real friends. Who would Andrew ask to come to Sara's service? By choice, they had excluded everyone from their lives. How sad that only she and Andrew were grieving. And as long as she was being honest, she was also relieved in a way.

The service was over. It had been short.

Outside in the brisk, autumn air Andrew didn't seem to comprehend where he was. In the car parked at the curb was his luggage. He was going away. He should be saying something to Lorrie and Tom, but he didn't know the words. If the service had been for him, Sara would have had just the right words to say. Now that he was on his own and had to think for himself, he was lost. Davey. He had to say something to Davey before he left. God, what could he say? Where were the words? Where?

Davey stood awkwardly beside Stuart Sanders and his Uncle Tom. His round gaze was speculative. Tom Ryan watched to see which one was going to make the first move. Stuart Sanders didn't realize he was holding his breath until Davey squared his shoulders and walked over to his father.

"Dad?"

"Yes, son."

"It's okay that you're going away. I think it's a good idea for you to go off by yourself. You don't have to worry about me. I'm going to be okay. Aunt Lorrie says it's still too early to tell if the antigen is going to work, but she's going to take care of me. I have Duffy. Aunt Lorrie is going to bring all my things and my CB over to her house this afternoon. I'm okay, Dad."

Something pricked at Andrew's eyes. "I know that, Davey. That you're going to be all right. I was worried that you wouldn't understand."

"I understand, Dad. Here," he said digging in his pocket for a slip of folded paper. "Aunt Lorrie wrote down her address and phone number for you. I put Mom's picture in your suitcase and one of me and Duffy that Uncle Tom took at the Philadelphia Zoo." Manfully, he extended his hand.

Andrew felt pinpoints behind his eyes smart. He took his son's hand in his own. "Thanks, Davey. I'll call you when I get settled." For an instant Andrew felt as though Sara were with him. Arranging last minute details and offering her approval.

"Okay, Dad. Drive carefully and don't forget to stop for gas."

"I won't, Davey. You take care now."

Davey nodded.

Tom Ryan nudged Stuart Sanders. "Is it my imagination or did Davey get taller in the past several days?"

Sanders's penetrating gaze shifted to the small boy in the gray flannel suit and cap. His lips narrowed to a grim, white line. "Wrong word, Ryan. The key word here is control. Davey Taylor is in control now."

Tom moved a fraction of a step closer to his wife. He didn't like the sound of the word, much less its meaning. He wouldn't mention it to Lorrie.

Davey Taylor watched his father climb into the blue sedan. His eyes never left the road till the car was long out of sight. He turned slightly to face the Sanderses and the Ryans. His eyes glinted momentarily in the chill October light. He had something better now. He had a family. Just like the little lion.